Mangrove Squeeze

Mangrove Squeeze

LAURENCE SHAMES

HYPERION

NEW YORK

Library of Congress Cataloging-in-Publication Data
    Shames, Laurence.
        Mangrove squeeze : a novel / by Laurence Shames. — 1st ed.
            p.   cm.
        ISBN 0-7868-6301-3
        1. Title.
        PS3569.H328M36   1998
        813'.54—dc21   97–35880
                                                                           CIP

                            Designed by Nicholas A. Bernini
                                    First Edition
                            10 9 8 7 6 5 4 3 2 1

DEDICATION

for my mother, Helen Ruth Shames,
with love and gratitude

A man who has been the indisputable favorite
of his mother keeps for life the feeling of a
conqueror, that confidence of success that often induces
real success.

—SIGMUND FREUD

ACKNOWLEDGMENTS

While creating the character of Suki, I was repeatedly visited by images of two beautiful Key West women. M. F. and N. McC., you know who you are.

On all matters of nuclear physics and homemade explosives, my valued adviser was Dean Athanis. All technical mistakes are his fault.

Four books into a wonderful relationship, I am almost running out of ways to thank my editor, Brian DeFiore—except to say that my respect and affection for him have deepened with each project. As for Stuart Krichevsky, staunch ally for a mere fifteen years and counting, let me say that our conversations have been at least as enriching as the contracts. Well, almost. Mollie Doyle—you have been splendid.

Finally, for her endless patience, kindness, and capacity for joy, I thank my wife, Marilyn. You are, not to put too fine a point on it, the world's greatest human.

Part
One

ONE

"Reservation?" said Sam Katz. "Whaddya mean, you have a reservation? This is my house."

The tourists looked unhappy and confused. It had been a long day and full of disappointments. Up north the roads were icy; they'd had to get up before dawn to make the first flight out of Lansing. Miami was not as warm as they'd hoped; they'd lied to themselves, pretending it was warmer than it was. The traffic on Key Largo was as annoying as the traffic anywhere else, and the sun had set before they reached the pretty part of the drive, south of Seven Mile Bridge. A fatiguing and deflating start to a vacation; and now the husband leaned across the counter with its registration book, its heavy silver bell. "You're telling me," he said, "this isn't a hotel?"

"Hotel?" said Sam Katz.

He was tall for an old man, with dark and soupy eyes that turned down at the outside corners, making him look sad sometimes, other times amused. His fluffy white hair, translucent at the edges, burgeoned out and back like Einstein's, and his shoulders sloped down at a steep angle from his neck. He wore a hearing aid except when he was listening to Mozart or Glenn Miller on his yellow Walkman. "Don't be ridiculous, young fella. I grew up in this house."

The wife glanced furtively around the office. There was a black metal rack stuffed with promotional brochures for snorkel trips, sunset sails. There was a cardboard stand that held applications for credit cards. Meekly she said, "But the sign outside—"

"Sign?" the old man said. "Who puts a sign? My parents built this house. They came from Russia."

The husband had a book with him, a guidebook. He put it on the counter and started riffling through it.

Sam Katz paused a moment, then continued. "Okay, Poland. The boundaries back then, who knows? A mishmosh, Europe. They came in a wagon. I was seven, eight years old. I had no coat, they had me wrapped up in a tablecloth."

The tourist had found his page. But then he sneezed. He was wearing shorts. He'd changed into them in a men's room at Miami airport. His leg hair had been on end the whole way down the Keys.

Sam Katz said, "Gesundheit. Whaddya think, it's summer?"

The tourist turned the book around and pointed it at Sam. "Look, it says right here. Mangrove Arms, 726 Whitehead Street, corner of Rebecca. Charming Victorian, recently refurbished . . . "

Now Sam looked unsure, abashed, unsettled by hard evidence. He blinked at the guidebook and his skinny shoulders sagged, his shrunken neck shifted in the neatly buttoned collar of his yellowing white shirt. He bit his lip, cleared his throat.

He was greatly relieved to hear his son's voice through the open doorway near his back. "Dad? Dad, I hear someone?"

The tourists were even more relieved. They exhaled and fell silent.

In a moment, Aaron Katz appeared.

He had his father's soft brown eyes, downturned at the corners. He was smallish, wiry, and it seemed at first that he had bluish hair and some appalling skin condition that made him look like a cheap garden statue come to life. On closer examination, he proved to be totally covered in fine gray dust, a residue of plastering or of sanding or of grout. Renovation; physical labor—he was getting to love it because it wasn't what he was used to and it wasn't what he was good at. A loose staple had ripped the elbow of his shirt. He had

Band-Aids on four fingers, and he wore them proudly—emblems of the awkward joy of change.

Until just a few months before, he'd been a very well-paid desk guy, a rising star in the arcane Manhattan world of mergers and acquisitions. Then a few things happened. These things did not seem obviously connected, yet in Aaron's mind they were joined by mysterious ligaments such as held together the stanzas of an Oriental poem.

At work, his department shrank, and Aaron, himself secure, was told to do the firing of his junior colleagues. At home—over take-out Thai, as he vividly remembered—he came one evening to the simple and sickening realization that he and his wife were not working toward the same life, after all. And his father—a widower for six years and a man with one son only—started running stop signs, losing the keys to the house in Merrick, confusing one decade with another. Either Aaron took him in or he would soon end up in a pale green room playing Colorforms among demented strangers.

Somehow these strands wound together in a noose, and quite suddenly it had seemed to Aaron that his only choice—not the decent choice or the honorable choice but the only choice—was to fire himself as others had been fired, to leave his marriage and bundle up his father and try to build a different life from the soggy boards and salt-rusted nails of an old compound in the tropics.

This wild and abrupt upheaval—Did it make any sense at all? Any less than staying where he was? Aaron had always been a rather sober fellow; by temperament and education, he was a man who thought things through. So he analyzed; he agonized; he bolted.

And now he was smiling at practically the only guests in his tumble-down guest house. He sneaked a look at the brief reservation list beneath the counter. "Ah," he said, "you must be the Karrs. From Michigan."

The tourists nodded eagerly, extravagantly grateful at being recognized, confirmed.

Aaron started reaching out a hand, then pulled it back when he remembered it was filthy. He was forty-one years old and the clean-hands, clean-shirt part of his working life was over. He was doing something on his own. He said, "Welcome to the Mangrove Arms. I'll show you to your room."

Six miles north, in the big glassed-in dining room of a modern water-front house on Key Haven, Gennady Petrovich Markov crammed a hunk of rare roast beef into his broad and floppy mouth, bit down with enough gusto to shake the arc of blubber beneath his chin, and said with appreciation, "Keppitalism. Is werry good seestem."

His friend and business partner, Ivan Fyodorovich Cherkassky, vis-iting from a somewhat less grand dwelling on the next canal, sipped his Clos de Vougeot and agreed enthusiastically. "With brain," he said, "with nerve, you can improve your seetooation."

Markov put down his knife and fork just long enough to empha-size a point with the raising of a fat and dimpled finger. "Not improve it only, but control it. To control it—is key to everything."

He turned to a young man sitting on his right, a handsome fellow in blue jeans and with a hairdo from the fifties, a little bit Elvis, a lit-tle bit James Dean. He stroked the young man's wrist and said, "Remember this, Lazslo. Control. Is key."

Lazslo Kalynin stared briefly out the window at moonlight on the waters of the Gulf, then gave a bored and noncommittal nod. He was Markov's nephew and his ward; he owed his uncle his very existence in America. He owed him his job; all his jobs. He owed him his classic Cadillac convertible, Fleetwood '59, red with white interior. He owed him his Old Town bachelor pad, decorated with posters of gangster movies and Harley-Davidsons; the half-dozen Gibson guitars that he could barely play; the large amounts of folding cash he always car-ried in his cowboy-style wallet.

But gratitude was not in his nature—he'd never learned it, didn't see the point—and he hated giving up an evening of his downtown life for the shut-in, suburban dullness of Key Haven. He had even less patience for the endless and obsessive political musings of these old men with their embarrassing accents, their stretched-out vowels and phlegmy *h*s and *r*s with too much tongue.

Communism. Capitalism. Who cared? Why couldn't they just forget about Russia? Why couldn't they just grab and squeeze the promise of America like *he* had—without looking back, without comparing it to something else?

Markov had paused in his eating, expecting a reply; Lazslo had to say something. He glanced at his uncle's monumental stomach, which had been stuffed and prosperous for as long as anyone could remember. He said, "You controlled things pretty well in the old days."

His uncle, flattered, smiled but disagreed. "Enjoyed, yes," he said, as the housekeeper silently refilled their glasses. "Controlled, no. For scientist in Soviet Union, life was comfortable, true. Caviar. Trips to Asia, trips to Cuba. Women. Good. But problem? Any time they can take away. Why? Because never is it really yours, never you really own it. In America, you own. You pay money and you own."

Happy in his certainty, he went back to his red and bleeding roast beef. Juice glistened on his chin.

Lazslo, drawn despite himself into the discussion, said, "But even here, plenty of people, the money runs out, they lose everything, just as easy."

Ivan Cherkassky, the family friend, leaned forward in his chair, propped himself on sharp skinny elbows. He had a doleful scooped-out face, pockmarked and lumpy, like what was left when a wedge of melon had been spooned, with scrunched-together features arrayed between a pointy chin and a high but narrow forehead. He wagged a finger and said, "Is not the same. Here, when people they are losing things, is because they have been stupid."

"Exectly," Markov concurred. "Stupid. Which is why," he added gravely, "we must always plen."

Lazslo could not quite stifle a cockeyed smile nor keep a needling tone out of his voice. "Plan?" he said. "That's a tactful way of putting it."

The comment worried Ivan Cherkassky. Everything did. His slippery eyes flashed left and right, he glanced behind himself. He chided in a whisper, "Lazslo, please, be careful how you say."

"The KGB is listening? The commissars, the generals? They come with Geiger counters maybe? Still looking for certain missing state property when there isn't even a state?"

"This is funny?" said Cherkassky. "No."

"Luzhka," said Gennady Petrovich, using his favorite diminutive. "Soviet Union—you make jokes but you really don't remember, do you?"

Lazslo pecked at the French wine that he did not enjoy. He liked American beer. He liked American cars and American music, American cigarettes and American cheese, and he wanted to be down on Duval Street, chasing some American tail. He was twenty-six. He'd been seventeen when he got out of Moscow. With the facility of the young, he'd shed his accent and his beginnings almost perfectly. He said, "I *can* remember. But why bother?"

"Why bother," said Ivan Fyodorovich wistfully. The eyes went distant in his hollow face. "The cupolas, the snow on fur hats, so fresh you can see each flake—these you never miss?"

"Cut me a break," said Lazslo.

"And your parents?" said his uncle. "You think about your mother, your father?"

Lazslo thought it over, not for long. His parents, still troweling potatoes and knocking worms off cabbage on the other side of the world, were frightened round-faced peasants wearing coarse wool scarves. He said, "Only when you ask me if I do."

Markov put down his knife and fork, and patted his nephew's hand. He turned with pride toward Ivan Fyodorovich. "You see, Ivan," he said, "is solid, this boy. No reason to worry about this boy."

Softly but immovably, Cherkassky said, "I wish he is more careful—"

The doorbell rang, and Cherkassky fell silent before a single indiscreet syllable might perhaps be uttered. A moment later the housekeeper approached the table. "It is the mayor," she announced.

Markov frowned, produced a napkin, wiped his greasy chin. "Barbarian," he muttered, pushing back with effort from the table. "A man cannot enjoy his dinner?"

The handsome Lazslo could not hold back a smirk. "Be nice, Uncle," he whispered. "Smile at the dog turd."

The fat man rose, motioned to the others to keep on eating. "I come back," he said, "as little time it takes to reach into my pocket."

TWO

They weren't bums, exactly, and they weren't exactly homeless. Their names were Pineapple and Fred, and they lived inside a giant hot dog.

They didn't own or rent the hot dog, but for all practical purposes it was theirs. It used to be a vending wagon, a novelty item that plied the trade on Smathers Beach. When the former owner got sick of selling wieners, he unhitched the wagon from his truck and abandoned it in the no-man's-land just east of the airport, in an expanse of mangroves that had been closely guarded military property back when Key West was a more important, more strategic place. Now they were simply unimportant mangroves, and in the mangroves the rule was finders-keepers.

Fred and Piney had lived in the fiberglass frank for three years now, and had made it rather homey. Below the curving sausage, the bulbous yellow roll was roomier than it looked, with a big window that had been the service counter, and an unlikely little door between the twin swellings of the bun. Fred could lay his sleeping mat full-length along the side of the roll that held the sink and the sauerkraut steamer. Pineapple's bedding fit neatly against the little propane fridge and underneath the rotisserie where the pronged wieners had gone round and round, getting redder, sweating as they went. Lying on their backs, the two men, by candlelight, could trace out squiggles of mustard molded in the ceiling. It was not a bad place to live.

On this particular January evening, they were lying there, when Pineapple broke a long silence. "Ya know what I sometimes wonder about?" he said.

Fred sucked his beer. Then, in a here-we-go-again sort of tone, he said, "No, Piney, what do you sometimes wonder about?"

Pineapple scratched at the sparse and scraggly beard that made a ragged frame for his long thin face. It was an archaic face, medieval, with an ascetic slot for a mouth, and nervous simmering eyes sunk deep in bony sockets. "I sometimes wonder," he announced, "if I was invited to the White House, would I go?"

Fred guffawed so that he sprayed a little beer and had to wipe his nicotine-stained walrus moustache on the back of his hand. "Piney," he said, "why would you be invited to the White House? You're a fuckin' dirtbag."

Pineapple squirmed against the scratched chrome door of the little fridge. He said, "Let's leave that on the side for now. My question is this. I'm invited, do I go?"

Fred stared up at the ceiling. The ceiling was rough from the mold of the fiberglass, he could see fabric on the inside of the frank. "And whaddya wear?" he asked. "Shorts with the ass out and no shoes on your stinking feet?"

Piney said, "What's the difference what I wear? Besides, don't call me a dirtbag. I got a job."

His job, which he went to fairly often, was holding a sign downtown, on the corner of Whitehead and Rebecca.

There was an ordinance against billboards for parking lots, but there was no law saying a person couldn't sit on the curb, holding a sign on a stick. The sign said PARKING, painted inside an arrow. The only hard part of the job was making sure the arrow pointed in the right direction. Piney sat in the shifting shade and looked around. Sometimes, if people gave him paperbacks, he read. Mostly he watched the town go by and framed questions to consider.

Fred said, "Plenty a dirtbags got jobs. And if you're talking White House, it does matter what you wear. Fancy place, it matters."

"Okay, okay," said Piney. "But what I wear, that comes after. First question is, I'm invited, do I go?"

"And the answer is," said Fred, "of course you go." He crunched his beer can, tossed it into a sagging paper bag propped up in the corner, popped another. "Everybody invited goes. Astronauts, football teams."

Pineapple raked his scraggly beard, said with satisfaction, "Me, I wouldn't go."

"The president would be all broke up," said Fred.

"Ya go, it's like sayin' y'approve."

"Piney," said Fred, "have a beer." He knew that Piney hadn't had a drink in years. Have a beer—this was just something he said when his friend was launched on a flight of screwball tangents and strong opinions, some inquiring ramble that, in other men, would probably be powered by alcohol. But then he added, "Approve a what?"

"You're on TV," said Piney, "the whole world looks at you, says, there's one more smiling idiot that approves . . . But not me, nuh-uh, no way. Me, I don't approve."

Fred said, "Approve a what, is what I'm asking?"

Pineapple didn't answer right away. A plane came storming up the runway, which ended about 150 yards from where the hot dog sat in the mangroves. The noise got louder every second as the engines revved and the propellers whined, until the craft became airborne and the clatter changed over to a screaming whoosh. When the plane passed overhead—so close that, in daylight, you could count the rivets in its belly—the clamor seemed less a sound than a pressure, a downward crush of air that flattened the candle flames and seemed to squash the fiberglass wiener deeper into its roll.

As the racket was subsiding, Pineapple said, "Just, ya know, approve. In general. Like everything is hunky-dory."

Fred thought it over. Something had shifted when the plane went by, his sodden bag of beer cans and stew cans and soup cans tipped over in the corner and spilled some nameless residue on the floor. "Ya mean," he said, "it isn't?"

"I know what you're thinking," Aaron said, as, with a suitcase in each hand, he led the tourists across the lighted courtyard to their room. A light breeze rattled the palm fronds, a hint of chlorine wafted from the pool. "You're thinking, the man's delusional, he shouldn't work front desk."

In fact the couple from Michigan weren't thinking that at all. They were thinking, mostly, about how tired they were. They watched their feet as they took cautious steps along the unfinished brick path, and they wondered vaguely about the piles of dirt and stacks of lumber scattered here and there, the bound-up shrubs whose roots were balled in burlap, waiting to be planted.

"He's perfectly with-it a lot of the time," Aaron went on. "Comes and goes. You know. Besides, he wasn't supposed to be working the desk, just sitting. So he could call me. With the power tools, I guess I didn't hear."

The tourists nodded. The husband, a weekend putterer himself, said, "Must be a lot of work, this place."

Aaron blew air past dusty lips. "If I'd only known how much."

The wife said, "The older gentleman. He's your father?"

"Brilliant man," said Aaron. "Inventor, engineer. Self-taught. Still holds a couple patents. But let's face facts, seventy-six, he's slipping pretty bad."

The wife said, "How nice you've kept him with you."

"We've always been close," said Aaron. "Usually he worked at home. Had lots of time for me. Made lunch together. Omelets. Taught me baseball in the driveway. Grounders on hot asphalt. Other kids were jealous, fathers working in the city all the time."

The husband said, "Plumbing. Electric. Landscaping. Lot of aspects to a place like this."

"Tell me about it," Aaron said.

"It's nice when families stay together," said the wife.

"Most days," Aaron said.

"Contractors down here, workers," said the husband. "Can you get good help?"

Aaron tried to smile. He said, "You're on vacation. Why talk about depressing things?"

"Age doesn't have to be depressing," said the wife.

Aaron tried to smile once again. It wasn't easy. He'd been up since five that morning, because the woman who was supposed to do the breakfast called to say her tattoo had started bleeding underneath her skin and she couldn't work that day. So Aaron made the muffins and then he toiled with the gardener till noon, but then the gardener had to meet his parole officer to have a new transmitter fitted to his ankle. Aaron wolfed down some lunch then mixed up a batch of mortar for the bricklayer who was supposed to be finishing the path, but by the time the bricklayer appeared, drunk and bellicose, the mortar had hardened in the bucket, become geology.

The husband, looking off toward the half-painted clapboard building he was being led to, now stubbed his toe against that very pail. Catching his balance he said, "Guidebook says recently refurbished."

Aaron said, "Probably means the *last* refurbishing. Climate eats buildings. Sun. Termites. Mildew. Old owners went broke."

"How sad," said the wife.

"They got happy again at the closing," Aaron said.

They'd reached the porch steps of the back building of the Mangrove Arms. Moonlight rained down on gingerbread trim that had been scraped but not yet refinished, on louvered shutters stacked up in a crisscross pattern on the veranda, waiting to be rehung. In the clearing, Aaron's coated hair and skin gleamed morbidly. He said, "Be careful, the banister isn't bolted down."

"Our room," said the wife. "It's finished?"

The suitcases were heavy, Aaron strained to lift them high enough so that they wouldn't bump the stairs. "Your room," he huffed, "is beautiful. Everything brand new. Sconces, headboard. Carpenter just hung the door today."

They entered the building, which had a wonderful and complicated smell, a smell of many layers: of oldness and newness, of work and hospitality. Toasted sawdust cut through potpourri, lavender soap overlay the tang of drying varnish. Aaron motioned his guests to precede him to the second floor, then steered them down a hallway to the right. He stopped just shy of the door to their room, put down the luggage, and fished in his pocket for the key.

But as he moved to unlock the door, it struck him, very distantly at first, that something wasn't right. He knew how to open a door. It didn't take thinking about. But in his exhaustion nothing came easy, nothing flowed, even automatic gestures had to be conceived anew. So he stared at the door as he brought the key closer, and finally, squinting, he puzzled out, still disbelieving, what was wrong. The lock was where it should have been but there wasn't any keyhole. Instead, there was a lever you worked with your thumb.

Aaron froze, the futile key suspended in midair.

After a moment the husband said, "Asylum-style. Lock 'em in 'stead of out."

"Asshole locksmith," Aaron hissed, then caught himself. "Excuse me. Let's try a different room."

THREE

Suki Sperakis hated making sales calls.

But it was a weekday morning; and making sales calls was her job; and it was no worse, she told herself, than other jobs she'd had in the course of twelve years in Key West.

It was no worse than waitressing. No worse than being a line cook, shuttling in a sweat between the griddle and the deep-fat fryer. No worse than driving a taxi in a town where lost tourists in pastel convertibles were always careening the wrong way onto one-way streets.

Sometimes—not often—Suki thought about those jobs, the grimy work for scrape-by pay, and wondered if she should have finished college. Three more semesters, she could have had a psych degree from Rutgers. But then what? Marry the dull, reliable college boyfriend and start a career that would require thirty years of pantyhose. Save up for a little house in a development so new that there'd be no grass to hold the mud in place. Scratch ice off windshields while waiting to deal with the equal terrors of fertility or the lack thereof . . . The snare would build up season by season, and for better or worse, Suki was one of those people who could see the whole completed trap before the first piece of it had been nailed down; who understood, moreover, that the first piece *was* the trap.

So, precociously, at the age of twenty-one, she'd headed south. What made it harder was that she hadn't known what to call herself for doing so. She wasn't a hippie—born too late, and too much of a loner. She was not rebelling against anything in particular, nor fleeing anything more than typically gloomy. She didn't think of herself as especially artsy or original. She was just determined, simply and implacably, to live a pleasant life. She'd given back the scholarship, ditched the boyfriend.

Regrets? Sometimes, sure. Strangely, though, the heaviest regrets could be outweighed by light and airy clothes. Open shoes. Warm breeze on her face. Besides, her current job—selling space for the *Island Frigate*—wasn't really so bad. It was nowhere near as obviously dead-end as most Key West employment; it might conceivably lead to something that could actually be interesting.

So she wrapped a skirt around herself. She did her eyes. They were wide-spaced, big, and blue—surprising against the blackness of her thick, unruly hair. There weren't many blue-eyed Greeks around, and her eyes made people notice and remember; they were an asset she'd learned to live with. She grabbed her satchel with its rate card and ad samples, and she rode her bike downtown.

Today she was making cold calls on potential new accounts. There were new ones all the time, because the turnover in Key West businesses was phenomenal. Duval Street rents were extortionate, pushed way up by the boom in T-shirt shops, mostly owned by Russians who didn't seem to care about the cost. The tourist market was notoriously fickle, rattled by everything from last year's hurricane to this week's murder in Miami. And many Key West proprietors were flaky as well as undercapitalized, had a mantra in place of a business plan. Sunglass shops, towel stores, cafes—no wonder so many of them went belly-up before a single season had run its rocky course.

Then there were the guest houses. Havens of heartbreak. Bankruptcies waiting to happen. How many of them had come and gone during the years Suki had lived here? Fifty? A hundred? All those fantasies exploded, all those nest eggs squandered. Gay guys too in love with wallpaper to notice that their cash flow was from hunger. Marriages stressed to the breaking point by stuffed toilets, bounced checks; sex preempted by a dread of the jingle of the front-desk bell. Why would anyone want to run a guest house?

She didn't think it was the money. More, maybe, just to have a place—a place to go, a piece of the town. An address where life could find you.

But other people's reasons—that was not her problem. The rent on her apartment was problem enough. So she hustled through the morning, sold a one-eighth page to a cappuccino joint that might or might not survive long enough to pay the bill, a sixteenth to a dim shop that offered custom goods in leather.

At around eleven-thirty she hopped back on her bike and rode from Duval Street down to Whitehead. It was shadier there, and quieter. Enormous banyan trees and strangler figs tunneled the street; their canopies had been hollowed out to make way for telephone and electric wires, and still the waxy leaves were dense enough to baffle sound. Homes mingled with businesses; black people from Bahama Village rode their bikes amid the pinkened tourists. After the relentless contrivance of Duval Street, Whitehead seemed like a real place in a real town. Besides, there was a promising account down there. The forlorn old Mangrove Arms had recently changed ownership yet again.

So she pedaled to the corner of Rebecca Street, where she saw a ragged man with a scraggly beard, holding a sign on a stick. Longtime locals in Key West all knew each other's faces if not their names. Suki vaguely smiled at the man; he vaguely nodded back from his perch atop the curb.

She stepped off her bike and took a moment to contemplate the troubled guest house. It was never going to be a showplace, yet it was clear that this most recent owner was no mere passive dreamer but a thrashing and ambitious one.

Emblems of work and hope were everywhere. Boards had been unsnaggled in the weathered picket fence. Rotten planks had been replaced; the new ones were a slightly different color, like the skin around a healing wound. The runaway hibiscus had been pruned into some semblance of a hedge; sun-shy impatiens, the dirt around them fresh as birth, had been tucked in among the stems. A hand-routed sign, tastefully funky, hung nearly straight from a beam on the porch. Suki saw the changes, felt the urge behind them— theurge to salvage, to restore—and, in spite of all she'd seen, she thought, who knew, maybe this time the old dump would make it.

She climbed the stairs, followed the wraparound veranda to the office door at the side, and, stepping in, she saw an old man with fluffly white hair sitting behind the desk. She hugged her satchel against her side and said her spunkiest good morning.

The old man said, "What?"

Suki said it again. Then she saw that the old man's hearing aid was in pieces on the desk blotter in front of him, next to a tiny screwdriver. She pointed at it.

He said, "Great gizmo. Voice activated. Picks out certain frequencies. Clever."

Suki nodded. "I was wondering if I could see the owner or the manager."

"I can hear okay without it," said Sam Katz. "What?"

Suki, louder, repeated her request.

"Manager?" the old man said. "What manager? You're standing in my workshop."

Key Westers not infrequently made loopy jokes that other people failed to see the humor in. Suki decided the old guy must be kidding. She smiled and said nothing.

The pause forced him to reconsider. He blinked, glanced around at the potted palms, the cubbyholes for mail and keys. "Wait a second," he said at last. "I'm not in my shop. This is Aaron's place. My boy. Florida."

"Yes, Florida," Suki said, not quite shouting.

Sam Katz shook his head, pointed to his brain. "Worse it's getting. Mornings usually I'm good. So you want to see my Aaron?"

"If he's the owner, yes."

"A real mensch, that kid," said Sam. "His mother and me, I don't know what we did, but something we did right. He was a big deal on Wall Street, ya know. Did great. Picture in the *Journal*, the whole schmear. The way, ya know, they trace it. Then just gave it up. Walked away. Got tired of the pressure, the bullshit. Pardon my French."

"No problem," Suki said. "I'm from Jersey."

"I'm from the Bronx, whaddya know . . . Sometimes I think . . . ah, never mind."

"What?" said Suki. "What do you think?"

Sam looked down at the tiny pieces of his hearing aid. "Sometimes I think maybe he gave it up, partly anyway, to have more time for me. I shouldn't 've let him do it."

There was nothing Suki could say to that.

Sam drummed his fingers lightly on the desk blotter so that tiny screws and washers danced. "You'll wait a minute, I'll find my son."

The old man was gone a long time, long enough for Suki to wonder if maybe he'd forgotten what errand he'd set out on. Outside, bees buzzed, warblers cheeped.

Finally Aaron Katz appeared, alone, in the doorway behind the counter. Today he'd been wiring telephones, crawling under beds and nightstands to chase elusive dial tones in and out of walls. It was frustrating work but relatively clean; without the plaster dust, his hair was curly brown, his face the ruddy color that comes not from lying on the beach but working in the sun. He wore a shirt from a past life—a business shirt of rich fine cotton, but now wrinkled along the placket and fraying at the collar, the French cuffs rolled up past the elbows. Reaching a hand across the counter, he said, "Hi, I'm Aaron."

"Suki," she said as she clasped. "With the *Island Frigate*."

"That's a paper?" Aaron asked.

It was not a great start, and Suki searched for a way to save face for her employer without offending a potential customer. She said, "You're new in town."

She said it gently but it made Aaron look down at his shoes. Tenure was everything in Key West, and everybody came to realize that without needing to be told. "Couple of months," he said, gesturing around him. "But I don't seem to manage to bust out of here very often."

"You're doing a great job with the place," said Suki, maybe a shade too glibly.

Aaron rallied. "Wrestling with my own incompetence," he said. "And the truly impressive incompetence of others."

There was a brief pause. They were looking at each other. Brown eyes, blue eyes. Necks and mouths and shoulders. Looking without talking was more intimate than was quite polite.

Suki said, "The *Frigate*'s a weekly. News, reviews, opinions, politics. It's really the locals' paper."

Aaron said, "Okay, I'll subscribe."

"It's free," said Suki. "I'm selling ads."

Aaron pursed his lips. "I'm in the tourist business. If it's a paper for the locals—"

"That's why the tourists read it," Suki cut in quickly. "So they can feel like locals."

Aaron's right eyebrow shot up. He was glad to be out of New York and away from the daily yank and whine of business, but he still appreciated quickness, moxie, salesmanship. He smiled, said, "Good save."

Suki smiled back. Smiling, her whole face opened. Aaron couldn't tell if he was looking more intently now or if it was just that she was showing him more, allowing him to see. She had a disconcerting upper lip that was fuller, lusher than the bottom one. There was a slight gap between her two front teeth. She was a little fleshier than was fashionable, with the sort of fullness that put appealing creases where the shoulder met the arm. Bantering with her, Aaron had begun to feel like they were dancing—no matter that the registration

counter with its silver bell loomed chastely between them—and he
didn't want to stop.

He said, "What's the circulation?"

She said, "Forty thousand."

"Paper's free," he said. "How do you know?"

She bit her lip—the upper one. "The truth?" she said. "We have no
idea how many get read. Forty's what we print."

"And distribution?" Aaron said. He'd never before thought of it as
a sexy word.

"They get dropped off at groceries, bookstores," Suki said. "How
many end up as rain hats, bike-basket liners? No one has a clue."

"You shouldn't admit that to advertisers," Aaron said.

"Hey," said Suki, "I'm from Jersey. Someone asks me a question,
they almost always get an answer."

Aaron hesitated, wished he hadn't. Without momentum he was
lost. Fact was, he wasn't very suave, and what nerve he'd ever had
with women had in recent times dried up from disuse. Flow was
everything; rhythm bypassed fears, made things that were excruciat-
ingly difficult seem in that instant easy, inevitable even. In the last
heartbeat that he could possibly have said it, Aaron said, "Then I'll ask
you something else. Any chance you can stay for lunch?"

He'd barely finished speaking when he understood that something had gone inscrutably and entirely wrong. Suki's face slammed
shut, she hugged her satchel tight against her side. With a hardness
that surprised them both, she said, "It's a little early in the day to get
hit on."

Wounded, baffled, Aaron said, "Was I hitting on you? I thought I
was offering you a bowl of pasta."

Suki looked down, seemed equally confused. She said, "I'm sorry. I
don't know why I said that. Except there are so many jerks in this
town—"

"And I'm probably just one more of them."

She raised her eyes. "I didn't say that. I don't think it. Look, I have
a date for lunch."

"Oh," said Aaron, and for an absurd instant his face clouded with jealousy, was taken over by an impulse from a part of the brain too ancient to learn manners or even common sense.

Suki saw the look, surprised herself by feeling that she wanted to explain. "I don't mean a date date. I'm having lunch with Lazslo."

She said it like it was a name that everyone in town would know. Aaron didn't. Now he couldn't tell if he was jealous because Suki was having lunch with this guy or because apparently he mattered in Key West, and Aaron didn't, and maybe never would. He said, "Who's Lazslo?"

"You'll know when I know," Suki answered.

"And what's that supposed to mean?"

She looked down at her watch. "I have to go. Listen, what I said, it was just a reflex thing. Don't hold it against me."

Aaron nodded but he felt a sorrow in his stomach, the pointless sorrow that comes from losing something before you ever had it. "And what about the ad?"

"Another time," she said. "Next time."

She turned and headed for the door. Aaron watched her go and listened to her footsteps on the porch. They made a syncopated, shuffling sound, the rhythm of a happy kid skipping.

FOUR

That evening, sitting on his deck and watching the early winter dusk go from pink to purple to slate above the flat water of the Gulf, Gennady Markov sipped his frozen vodka and casually announced: "The mayor is a feelthy peeg."

He said it without rancor, without indignation or even mild censure; in fact the mayor's puny venality amused him.

"Feelthy peeg is good," said Ivan Fyodorovich Cherkassky. He said it without pleasure, even though he was dipping a cracker into a mound of caviar whose grains softly twinkled in the failing light. "With feelthy peeg, nobody looks too close, you know what you must do."

Markov turned to his nephew. Lazslo, dressed in denim, and with a big silver belt buckle between his navel and his groin, was also holding a glass of liquor, but he found it rank and sour, he touched it to his lips but didn't drink.

"He came again today, Luzhka," the older man said. "Always I am surprise. Never I remember how short he is, how his pants fall on his shoes. I always think maybe he is paperboy or something."

Markov laughed. Cherkassky did not. Lazslo made a show of joining in but his thoughts were somewhere else.

His uncle continued. "He say 'Hello, Meester Markov.' I say 'Hello,

Meester Mayor.' Then he start in with some crazy nonsense with the stores—how you say, the backsets?—"

"Setbacks," Lazslo put in absently, though he wasn't really listening. He was thinking about his lunch with Suki Sperakis and wondering if there would come a time when she would go to bed with him. Usually, yes or no, he could tell right away, he didn't waste time. A woman liked his car, his clothes, was aroused when he was recognized in places, fawned on. Or not. He could tell. But with this one it was different.

"Setbacks, yes," said Markov. "So many feet from street, so many feet from next guy. Mayor say, 'Is wiolation.' I say, 'Meester Mayor, just tell me what you want.' He say, 'racks on sidewalk, block people walking. Is other wiolation.' I say, 'Meester Mayor, we are not children here. Please, say what you are asking.'"

"Coward," said Ivan Cherkassky, wiping a cracker crumb from the corner of his mouth. "Peeg and coward."

Lazslo nodded in bland agreement. But he was picturing Suki, not the mayor. The blue eyes framed in black and wild hair, generous breasts squeezed and rocked by arms that gestured lavishly. She was a little older than he, and Lazslo found this very flattering, intriguing. She was funny, sharp, interested in what he did, how he thought; she made him feel smart, substantial. This excited him. And older women, people said—they knew their own minds better; rumor had it they were bold, might take the lead and grab you by the leg, might suggest nasty and nonstandard acts in risky and forbidden places. So why was Suki so hesitant, so coy?

"So finally," continued Markov, "I say, 'Excuse me one moment, Meester Mayor.' I go away. I come back with t'ousand dollars. I give it to him. I say, 'Does this take care of wiolation?' The money he puts in his pocket. Front pocket, like cowboy. He smiles. He say, 'Meester Markov, you sure must sell a lot of T-shirts.'"

"Idiot!" Cherkassky said.

"So you know what?" Markov rolled along, grabbing his nephew behind the neck, pulling their faces close, their foreheads almost touching. "You know what, Luzhka? I give you all credit. 'My nephew,' I say, 'my nephew is marketing genius.'"

At this Lazslo Kalynin could not help snorting as he backed away from his uncle's grasp. Too loud, he said, "Marketing genius as long as the idea is losing money."

The words seemed to break into small particles that persisted in the salty air. The two old Soviets dropped their chins and looked around themselves, but they saw no spies, no informers, only palms and shrubs whose colors were leaching out into the deepening twilight.

Ivan Cherkassky frowned, did not try to mask his disapproval. "Lazslo," he said, "you say these things, I wonder where else you say them. I feel them in the bottom of my stomach. Reckless. Careless."

The young man was feeling feisty, probably a side effect of stifled lust. He said, "Not careless, Ivan. Just not constantly afraid like you."

The family friend sipped vodka, slowly ran a hand over his fretful concave face, then said very softly but with unexpected vehemence, "I am afraid, yes. Always. I was afraid under Brezhnev, afraid under Gorbachev. I was afraid when all the changes came—afraid to stay and afraid to leave. And still, today, I am afraid every time a canister must cross a border, every time we send a shipment. But I am sixty-three, and I am here, and I have money, and I am not in prison. Why? Because fear has made me very careful. Think about this, Lazslo."

There was a silence and it soon turned rancid.

Scolded by Cherkassky, Lazslo felt suddenly that he'd been insulted, belittled, taken lightly, all day long. Suki, with her teasing, her deflections—she enticed him but she treated him like a boy. These old men—they gave him no respect, no real power of his own. Sullenly, he stared off at the horizon, where the seam between the sea and sky was closing for the night.

Gennady Petrovich Markov blinked off toward the dimness that had all at once turned grumpy, tried to figure the precise moment when things had gotten somber. With the geniality of the fat, he attempted to leaven the mood, to restore good cheer in time to salvage appetite for dinner.

"Gentlemen," he said. "Gentlemen, why so serious? Is just another visit from the mayor. Is only one small bribe."

There was only one good thing about the kind of work Fred did: It was the kind of work where every day was payday.

He did casual labor. On the mornings when he felt like working, he'd grab his shovel and his rusty old bike from where they leaned against the hot dog. He'd walk out of the mangroves, then ride past Houseboat Row and a mile north on U.S. 1 to the seven-thirty shape-up on Stock Island. He'd stand there yawning in the early light among the other hopefuls—black guys with big shoulders, stringy white guys with stringy hair—and a foreman would assign the jobs.

Mostly it was digging holes. Amazing when you thought about it, how many different kinds of holes there were, how many perforations even in a little town. Holes for fence posts, holes for pools. Holes for water pipes and holes that trees got planted in. Square holes for the studs that held up carports; round holes for the tubes of parking meters. Kidney-shaped holes for the sandtraps on the golf course; box-shaped holes for the graves of pets. Holes for flower beds, holes for hot tubs, holes that Fred spent hours digging without ever being told the use of.

At the end of the workday, the laborers were brought back to Stock Island, and their pay—minimum wage minus this and minus that—was figured to the penny and delivered as cash into their toughened hands. For Fred this was the prelude to an evening out.

When he had money, he went to bars.

He liked bars—the noise of them, the randomness. He liked the way the click of billiard balls sometimes fell into a rhythm with the songs on the jukebox. He liked the smoke, the sound of people laughing. He liked to eavesdrop on the fishing stories, the travel tales. He liked it that, in Key West bars at least, anyone could talk to anyone, and that, as long as you didn't get too loaded or too shrill in your opinions, you were always allowed to come back.

So on this particular January evening, Fred pocketed his pay, dropped his shovel at the hot dog, and rode his bike downtown. He stopped for an outdoor shower at County Beach—stripping to his boxer shorts between the parking area and the gazebo, holding the chain that started the flow of tepid water, then changing into fresh clothes in the men's room. He double-checked that he hadn't lost his money or his little piece of soap, and continued on his way.

He rode to the Eclipse Saloon, an old favorite. It had a U-shaped bar whose edge was thickly padded and covered in black vinyl. It was good for resting your elbows and occasionally your head. Beer was cheap and cheeseburgers came automatically with fries and slaw, no hidden extra costs. Off Duval, it was mostly a place for locals, but a sprinkling of sunburned tourists provided some amusement. Rich people went there, poor people went there, and most folks dressed about the same.

Fred grabbed a stool on the side that faced the door. He drank, he smoked, he ate. He watched a little basketball. Once or twice he joined in conversations, and didn't seem to notice that his joining in wasn't really all that welcome.

Dinner hour passed and the place gradually started thinning out. There weren't that many empty stools, but there was one on either side of Fred.

That's when Lazslo Kalynin came walking in.

Fred was looking toward the door when Lazslo pushed through it. He didn't know who Lazslo was, but he instantly recognized a pissed-off, brooding guy, a guy who needed distraction and a drink. Even in the young face, there was a tightness at the corners of the eyes; the posture was clenched and the lips seemed thinned out, cramped, from too much held inside.

Lazslo walked around to Fred's side of the bar, blindly grabbed a stool on Fred's right. Before he'd even sat, Fred said, "Lemme buy you a beer."

Lazslo blinked at him, his face skeptical and no softer. His hand-tooled wallet was stuffed with twenties and with fifties. His running shoes were up in triple-figures. His belt buckle was real silver and he had real gold chains around his neck. His haircut cost more than everything Fred was wearing. "You're buying *me* a beer?" he said.

Fred either didn't hear the sarcasm or elected to ignore it. He said, "I have money and I see a guy needs a drink, I'm buying that person a drink. That's me, okay?"

Lazslo said, "I need a drink?"

Fred said, "You need somethin', man. You look like a scorpion crawled up your ass and died."

Lazslo gestured at the few damp bills sticking to the bar in front of Fred. "Your money's almost gone, sport."

"And when it is," he said, "that's how I know when to go home. You'll have a beer?"

Lazslo looked away. His face was in the midst of a gradual process that seemed more an easing of gears and cables than of skin and flesh. His forehead slowly smoothed, his eyebrows dropped, blood flowed back to his cheeks. He exhaled deeply, blew away his evening with the old Russians, an evening of whispers, paranoia, endless reminders that the world was full of enemies. Now here was a stranger, a bum, sensing his funk and his anger and fearlessly approaching, reaching out to him for no good reason in the world, offering a pointless kindness. This was what he loved about America.

The bartender came over, said, "Evening, Lazslo. What'll it be?"

The young man in denim touched Fred on the shoulder. "This gentleman," he said, "is buying me a Bud."

FIVE

"Nice job on the T-shirt shops," said Donald Egan, publisher and editor of the *Island Frigate*.

"Whaddya mean?" asked Suki, looking up without much interest from her cramped and cluttered metal desk.

"They doubled all their advertising. You didn't know?"

Suki went back to her paperwork. She used the computer when she had to, but she preferred the concreteness of the old way, the paper clips and tape and staples. It felt like childhood, a project for a rainy day in Trenton. She had a pencil between her teeth. She didn't answer.

"Lazslo called," Egan went on. "Himself. Doubled everything. All eight stores."

Suki snapped some carbons out of credit card receipts, said nothing.

Egan said, "That's a hefty commission. I thought you'd be more pleased."

Suki looked up. She wasn't smiling. She said, "He wants to get into my pants."

Egan shuffled his feet. He was fifty-eight, and southern. He knew the world had changed and he knew that Key West wasn't western Tennessee, but he didn't think he'd ever get used to young women being quite that frank. Where was the fibbing, the pretense? He mumbled, "Your business, how you sell."

"Thank you, Donald," Suki said. "I knew that."

Her boss started to walk away. There wasn't far to walk. The *Frigate*'s offices consisted of a room and a half of what once had been a grade school on Southard Street. One wall remained covered with a scratched old blackboard, eraser ledge and all. A broad wrought iron fire escape was bolted to the frame of a full-length window. And the place, in spite of the passage of years and the illicit smoke of Donald Egan's cheap cigars, still smelled faintly of the powdered disinfectant used to mask the stench of young children throwing up.

Egan, perplexed, now doubled back, and with his hands on his ample hips he stood once more above Suki's desk. "You're doing very nicely for us," he said. "I don't understand why you're not more—"

"I hate the T-shirt shops," she said.

"They're half your income," Egan said.

"That means I have to like them?"

Egan lifted a yellow thumbnail to his teeth. "Look, none of us is thrilled—"

"None of us is thrilled," she interrupted, "that the old locals are being all squeezed out. That none of the quirky little stores can possibly survive. That the whole downtown is just a tacky ugly strip for the cheap bastards who come off the cruise ships, buy a frozen yogurt and a T-shirt with a jerky slogan, and that's their whole impression of Key West."

"Suki. Things change. That's the marketplace. Commercial real estate. Supply and demand."

"Bullshit," Suki said. "There's something cockeyed there and you know it."

"There's no hard evidence," Egan said.

"They can't be making money. Those stores are fronts for something."

"Oh, yeah?" said Egan. "What?"

"How the hell should I know?"

"You see? Speculation. Nothing more . . . Besides, the jealousy thing, the prejudice thing—you sure that isn't creeping in? These people are foreigners, immigrants."

"Who cares?" said Suki. "*Sperakis*, Donald. Wretched refuse of the Aegean. Sardine fishermen. Bee farmers. Do I have anything against immigrants? Do I have anything against Russia? Put a well-chilled Stoli in front of me, you'll see what I have against Russia."

"Well then—"

"What I'm against is people laundering money and fucking up my town."

"Libel, Suki. You don't just accuse people of laundering money."

"Especially if they're advertisers," she said.

The publisher said nothing.

Suki put her hands flat on the desk, craned her neck and cocked her chin. "Look, I realize I'm only the cupcake who bats her eyes to sell the space, but I can do arithmetic. Twelve thousand a month for rent—per store. Five, six employees on every shift. A measly eight, ten bucks a shirt . . . "

"No one knows the details of their business," Egan said. "This is all just speculation."

"Speculation," Suki said. "Exactly. So why don't you assign one of your crack reporters to get past the speculation and find out what the story really is?"

Suki paused for breath, and Don Egan reflected ruefully on his staff. Crack reporters? There was Peter Haas, restaurant reviewer, known to while away an entire afternoon searching for an adjective to describe the texture of a salmon mousse. Chrissie Kline, drama critic who thought everything was smashing. Casper Montero, literary editor, whose flights of metaphor tended to fly right past the limits of human comprehension. These were crack reporters?

Egan got depressed. But Suki wasn't finished. "I mean," she hammered on, "isn't that what newspapers do? Get the story? I mean, is this rag a paper or isn't it?"

The question hit Egan squarely where he lived, and he wished in that moment that Suki wasn't such a damn good seller, that he could afford to fire her.

He carried a notebook, Egan did. He smoked cigars—not the fashionable expensive ones, but the stubby stinkers more proper to the city room. He'd been a real newspaperman once, covered fires and murders as a young man back in Chattanooga; he wanted badly to believe he was a bona fide journalist still. That certainly was his public stance. Over cocktails he spewed forth strong, informed opinions. He wrote editorials graced with slyly damning southern wit, commentaries that seemed courageous until you realized that his targets were always the obvious and safe ones—the buffoonish politicians who never changed, and couldn't sue, and didn't advertise. Where was his nerve when it came to opponents who might fight back?

Cornered, the publisher pulled rank. He leaned in close to Suki. "Listen," he said. "I give you credit for what you do. But you don't run this paper. I do. And this paper isn't taking on the T-shirt shops. Understood?"

Suki bit her lip, the upper one. She looked around the office. There was no one there but the two of them. It was late afternoon and a soft gold light, conspiratorial, was filtering past the trees outside and through the big school window. The dusty chalkboard called up youth, with its desperate passion for fair play, its rambunctious conviction that headlong crusades were not only possible but necessary, the very crux of what a person should do.

"Okay, Donald," Suki said. "I get it. This paper can't afford to piss off the Russians. But give me the satisfaction of admitting one thing, just between the two of us. If you didn't have a mortgage, if you still had the balls, wouldn't you like to? Wouldn't it be satisfying?"

"Excuse me," said Sam Katz, softly and politely, to the person on his left. "Could you please tell me where I am?"

The person on his left was also old, and also had white hair, but of a very different sort. This other man's white hair was neatly parted, slicked down with old-fashioned tonic. It glinted with hints of pink and bronze, and topped a tan thin face with bright black eyes above a long but narrow nose. This man looked at Sam a little strangely, but tapped the padded vinyl in front of him and gently said, "A bar. You're in a bar."

Somewhat impatiently, Sam said, "A bar, yes. I see my drink, I see the bottles. A bar. But where?"

The other man tugged lightly on the placket of his shirt, which was made of peacock-blue silk, the seams topstitched with navy. It appeared he was trying to hold on to his own tenuous certainty. "A bar," he said, "in Key West, Florida."

"Exactly!" said Sam Katz, sounding not only reassured, but vindicated. "Key West, Florida. With my son. Aaron. He left me here to run some errands. That's exactly where I thought I was!"

The other man said, "Good."

"But then," Sam resumed, "just for a second, I thought I was back in Europe. Odessa. Poland. Somewhere."

The other man sipped his orange juice and gin, calmly said, "Poland, no. Not even close to Poland."

Sam said, "I only thought it for a second. Ukraine, maybe."

"Not Ukraine. No. Hm. I wonder why you thought that."

Sam fiddled with his hearing aid, said, "It was like I was hearing a conversation." He splayed his elbows across the upholstered edge of the bar and leaned in closer. "A nasty conversation, I have to tell you, about a woman with large breasts."

The other man said, "Large breasts. Hm. And you were hearing this in Polish?"

"Polish. Russian. Yiddish. Who can tell? I was a kid when I learned it. A lot of the words, they're all mishmoshed together."

"Breasts," mused the other man. "Polish." He sipped his drink. Then he dropped his chin and whispered. "Don't turn around, okay?"

"Okay," said Sam, and promptly turned around. Behind him, maybe twelve feet away, two young fellows were shooting pool. One of them had hair like Elvis, a big silver belt buckle, and gold chains around his neck. The other had an enormous jaw and chunky sculpted muscles; he wore no shirt, just a thick pair of suspenders that crossed between his bulging hairy pecs and rested snugly on the ropy strands that ran from his neck onto his shoulders.

"Russians," whispered the other man. "I couldn't tell ya if they're talking titty, but I'll bet that's what you heard."

Sam kept looking at them. The hairy fellow in suspenders shot. The ball hung but didn't fall. He called the ball a *brozhni vykovskyi*.

"Russian, right?" whispered the man next to Sam.

Sam nodded, relieved. "Means farting masturbater."

"Those guys," the other man said, "they're from the T-shirt stores. The handsome one, that's Lazslo, runs the enterprise, though people say his uncle really heads it. The bruiser who don't bother wit' a shirt, I don't know his name, I think he manages a store."

Sam said, "How you know all this?"

The other man shrugged, pulled lightly at the extravagant wings of his collar. "I hang around. I look around. I talk to people. Hell else I got to do?" He reached out a gnarled and spotted hand. "Bert's the name. Bert d'Ambrosia."

"Sam. Sam Katz."

They shook. There was a pause. Bert said, "You remember Polish, Russian, all these years. That's quite a memory."

Sam blew air past resonating lips. "First things you learn, last things you forget. I remember songs, rhymes, smells. Other than that, my memory's shot."

Bert reached a hand below the edge of the bar. Disconcertingly, he seemed to be stroking his groin. "Funny what goes," he said. "Me, ticker's spastic, pecker's finished. But the feet still move and brain's about as good as ever, which probably isn't all that very. How long's your wife been dead?"

"How you know my wife is dead?"

Bert said, "All old men sitting in a bar at four o'clock, unless

they're drunks their wife is dead. Mine's been dead twelve years."
He continued stroking his crotch. "Company," he went on. "Company
is what you need. Company and conversation, keep your mind alert."

"Alert," Sam echoed. He said it wistfully.

"Tell ya what," said Bert. He reached into his topstitched and
monogrammed chest pocket, produced a silver pen, wrote a phone
number on a cocktail napkin. "Call me if ya like. We'll have a conversation, play gin rummy. For now I gotta go."

Slowly, stiffly, he began to rise, and Sam saw that he had a tiny
ancient chihuahua in his lap. He couldn't help pointing at the creature and saying, "You know, I saw you stroking, I was thinking—"

Bert said, "I saw what you were thinking, and I really didn't give a
shit. One good thing about getting old. Ya rub your crotch, who cares?
Your crotch don't even care." Still not entirely free of his chair, he
held forth the little dog. "This is Don Giovanni. Shake Sam's hand,
Giovanni."

The geriatric animal made a monumental effort to lift a scrawny
paw. Wanting to save it the trouble, Sam reached down and gently
grasped its foreleg. The bones felt more like a bird than a dog. The
creature's fur was sparse and faded, its drooping and enormous
whiskers insecurely anchored at the scaly edges of a dry and twitching nose. Cataracts whitened both its eyes, milky film cascading over
the bulbous and weirdly gleaming irises.

Sam said, "That's the oldest dog I ever saw."

Bert said, "And what are we, spring chickens?"

Erect now, finally, he hugged the dog against his tummy and
strolled leisurely away.

SIX

The couple from Michigan, as happened not infrequently, cut short their stay at Mangrove Arms.

Maybe it was the pecan shells that the woman who did the breakfast had neglected to remove from the muffins. Maybe it was the tiny pellets of black rubber that shot inexplicably from the jets of the hot tub. Maybe it was a superstitious fleeing from the broken mirror of the medicine cabinet that had come unstuck from the wall and shattered in their bathroom sink. In any case, the Karrs had booked for six nights but left after three, signing off on their credit card and saying a somewhat embarrassed goodbye before moving on to spend the rest of their vacation at a real hotel.

Their early departure put Aaron in a sulk, and he sat for a while at the front desk, brooding. The sulk was not about money. Aaron had done his projections; he was losing money not much faster than he'd planned for; he could afford to lose considerably more. But it galled and baffled him to be working day in and day out at something that very possibly might fail.

He'd never failed at anything before. School had come easily. Sports had not, but still, with his father's help he'd turned his very mediocre talents into pitching records that still stood at Merrick Junior High. Quick and eager, he'd shined at summer jobs. Wall Street he'd figured out in half a dozen years—the phrases, the logical illogic, the perfect ties. In each arena, he'd defined the challenge, made something of a game of it, and psyched it out. Satisfying.

But what about now? Here was a simple machine—two small wood houses on a shady street in a town that millions of people paid money to visit. Why was he having such a damned tough time getting this machine to fly?

Brooding, turning the problem this way and that, he did not hear skipping footsteps coming up the porch stairs, and he was taken by surprise when Suki Sperakis walked into the office. She took advantage of his inattention, studied him a moment before he raised his eyes. She said, "You're not having your best day." It was not a question.

Aaron looked at her—the rich black hair, the wide violet eyes— and tried to smile. "It shows that much?"

She said, "Jews, Greeks, Italians. All those Mediterraneans, they can't hide their moods worth a damn."

He said, "You're here about the ad?"

"I'm here," she said, "to say I was unfair to you the other day."

"Hey," he said, "forget it. I guess I came on like a pushy jerk."

"No," she said. "You were being very nice. Civilized. A bowl of pasta—civilized. And I just didn't get it. It isn't what I'm used to."

Aaron looked at her. Her hair had been swept back by the momentum of her bike ride, the strands of her throat were tanned and mobile where they vanished under the thin cloth of her blouse. He said, "What are you used to, Suki?"

She gave a brief and mirthless laugh. "This town? Imbeciles passing through. Drunks trying to be clever. Losers wanting to keep you down."

"That's too bad," said Aaron.

"What's too bad," said Suki, "is that it makes you tough, leathery. Sun does it to your skin, the jerks do it to your heart."

Aaron wasn't sure if he should answer that. He was new here, didn't know the rules. But he heard himself saying, "Maybe not as tough as you think you have to be."

Suki looked down, hid her unlikely blue eyes behind their faintly dusted lids, as though by not seeing she could take a break from being seen. "Maybe not," she admitted. "Unless I really work at it. And sometimes I work at it too hard. Like when a nice guy offers me a plate of macaroni and I jump right down his throat."

Aaron had to laugh. "Plate of macaroni?"

"Hey," said Suki, "I'm from Jersey. Bowl of pasta—that's New York. Jersey they say plate of macaroni."

There was a pause. They looked at each other across the front desk counter. The look went on just long enough to be a little dangerous. Aaron remembered to inhale and the breath caught in his throat. He said, "I have a klutzy question, Suki. This Lazslo you had lunch with, you involved with him or not?"

The mention of the name brought a hardness back to Suki's face; her lips, which had been slightly parted, pressed together like the shells of a threatened oyster. "Involved?" she said. She seemed to think it over. "Funny word. Discreet. But vague."

Aaron said, "Look, you don't have to answer. I don't have any right to ask."

Suki said, "You might say I'm involved. You might say I'm getting more involved. It's anything but a romance, though."

Aaron ran his hand along the varnished surface of the counter, said, "Okay, I guess I deserve a riddle for an answer."

Suki bit her upper lip. "Aaron," she said, "I'm not playing games with you. It's just not something I can talk about. Not yet."

He pursed his lips and nodded. Jealousy pinched down again. It was idiotic but there it was. She saw his eyes receding.

She moved closer to the counter then. The move was sudden, headlong, like the dash of a scared kid on a diving board who wants to fly and fall and get it over with. Quick as a jab, her hand swung up above the polished wood. There was a piece of paper in it, warm and crinkled. "My numbers," she whispered. "Call me if you want to share a plate of macaroni."

She pushed the paper toward him and she smiled with relief. There; she'd done it. She'd opened herself and didn't feel wounded, softened herself and it hadn't hurt at all. In fact she felt tickled and playful and new. Her boldness doubled back and made her braver, and she amazed herself by leaning across the counter and kissing Aaron on the cheek.

It happened so fast that he wasn't sure it had happened at all; the feel of her lips was so light that he couldn't quite tell if they had touched his skin or only charged some air between them.

In an instant she had pulled away. Her eyes slid off his and found respite in the silver bell between them on the counter. It was polished like an apple, attached like a trophy to a base of fine dark wood. Pleased with herself, she smartly rapped the little top hat of its ringer.

Long after she'd spun away and skipped along the porch, after she'd climbed onto her bike and ridden past the ragged man who held the PARKING sign, Aaron was still hearing the fugitive echoes of its high bright tone.

"You ask a lot of questions," said Lazslo Kalynin.

"I'm interested," said Suki. "I want to know you better."

It was well into the evening. They'd had a fancy dinner and now they were sitting in his Caddy. The car was parked on the promenade up near the airport, its front grille almost touching the seawall, facing out toward the flat, moonstruck waters of the Florida Straits. The weather was cool, too cool to put the top down, but Lazslo had the top down anyway. Wasn't that the whole point of an American convertible?

He gestured extravagantly so that the open collar of his shirt splayed wide, revealing wisps of chest hair. "You want to know me," he said, "you should know how I make love."

Suki let that pass. "The stores," she said. "You're so young to be in charge of all those stores."

Lazslo shrugged. It was something he'd seen people do when they wanted to look modest. On him it didn't work.

"And the rents," she said. "Eight locations in a five-block area. The volume has to be phenomenal."

Lazslo's arm was draped now over the white leather seat in back of Suki. He let it fall against her shoulder. Laconically, he said, "Everyone likes T-shirts."

She wriggled out from under his hand. "Some people think it's impossible. Some people think it can't be what it seems."

Miffed at her retreat, he said, "Some people are assholes."

"Envy," Suki said. "Maybe they just envy your success. But they say all kinds of crazy things. Money laundering. Russian Mafia."

Lazslo gave a harsh, clipped laugh that flew up from the topless car and was quickly blotted by the night. "Russian Mafia!" he scoffed. "There's no such thing as the Russian Mafia."

Suki swiveled in her seat, showed Lazslo her eyes, whose blue was thinned to an indistinct but compelling pallor in the moonlight. "That's what the Sicilians said for decades," she purred. "Even got the FBI to believe them for a long, long time."

Lazslo swiveled too, so that his knee was pressing hers, lightly prying her thighs apart. "But the Sicilians," he said, "the Russians. Completely different cultures."

Suki, with an effort, let her leg stay where it was. "Really?" she said. "How so?"

Lazslo felt the warmth of her knee through his jeans, let himself imagine there was no clothing between them. "The Sicilian mob," he said, "they started off as a defense against outsiders, conquerors. Sicilians trusted other Sicilians and hated everybody else."

"And the Russians?" Suki said.

Lazslo leaned forward, gestured as if her breasts were in his hands. "For Russians, the enemy was always other Russians. The state. Over here the goody-goodies, over there the crooks, the liars, the power-crazy. Insiders, outsiders, there was no one you could trust. Old Soviets, they carry suspiciousness inside them like a virus. So how could the Russians ever organize like the Sicilians?"

Suki said, "So they must've found some other way to organize."

Lazslo leaned back, his groin pushed forward underneath the steering wheel. "They organized—" he said. And then he stopped.

The stop was as jarring and abrupt as interrupted sex, and carried in its wake the same gamy confusion. Lazslo noticed all at once the chilliness of the evening, felt the heat and avidity coursing off him. Desire was making him stupid. He was showing off, being just as careless as Ivan Cherkassky said he was.

"How should I know how they organized, if they organized?" he said. He tried to smile, it came out a grimace. He tried to look sexy, it came out both carnivorous and pleading. He said, "And that's the bedtime story for tonight. Now, are you coming home with me?"

Slowly, she moved her knee away and shook her head. "I'm not that fast, Lazslo. I told you that."

Lazslo said, "I'm not that patient. I told you that."

Suki shrugged, using nothing but her eyebrows. She said, "Your basic standoff."

His gaze hardened. He looked at her breasts, he looked at her lap. It was rude and he knew it was rude. He started the car, took a bleak solace in the angry rasp of the engine turning over. He backed hard off the promenade, prideful of the Caddy's elephantine leaning. Without looking at Suki, he said, "Maybe I won't call you anymore." He threw it into drive, burned rubber as he careened onto A-1A.

Suki said nothing. If he didn't call, didn't continue to chase her, she was off the hook. Her lunatic crusade, which she'd never exactly decided to pursue, but which somehow seemed to have called her, recruited her, would go away, dissolve, before any damage had been done, before anyone but her knew that it had ever been conceived.

But they both knew he would call again.

He wanted her. He wanted to break down her resistance and then to arch above her, sweaty and triumphant, and have her damp compliant face admit to him that she'd been crazy to resist. And there was something else as well, something that tugged and plucked at Lazslo, though he couldn't name it, something that transfigured ordinary lust and made its object an obsession. He knew, deep down, that she was trouble.

SEVEN

"Fred," said Pineapple, "ya know what I sometimes wonder about?"

They were strolling through the mangroves that stretched back from the hot dog, looking at the sky. Winter nights there in the marsh could be quite wonderful. No mosquitoes in the winter. Egrets stayed so still that it was sometimes many minutes before you noticed they were there. In winter the mangrove leaves gave off a clean and wholesome smell, a smell of salt and wax.

"No, Piney," said the patient Fred, wiggling his can of beer. "What do you sometimes wonder about?"

Winter stars were wonderful too. The stars seemed closer then, they had a roundness, like they were shiny indentations punched in tin. Satellites etched their courses among the whirling constellations, and if you watched long enough, you saw them return in the exact same places.

"I sometimes wonder," Pineapple said, "if you were in a spaceship, say out there by Orion, and you started going faster and faster, till you were going as fast as the light, and you turned your headlights on, would anything happen?"

Fred sipped some brew, wiped his walrus moustache on his hand. "Fast as the light," he said, "you'd be squooshed."

"Okay, but leave that on the side for now. The headlights come on? Yes or no?"

Fred thought it over. "Middle a space, whaddya need headlights for?"

Piney gave up on that one, fell briefly silent. They strolled. Off to one side, slabs of ancient rusted military fence tugged against their stanchions; up ahead, the unnatural shapes of flat-topped earthwork pyramids poked bluntly toward the sky. Piney started in again. "Fred, you think life is interesting?"

"Interesting," said Fred. He scratched his ear. "I dig holes. I drink beer. Interesting is not the first word springs to mind."

"I do," Piney said. "I think life is interesting."

Fred guffawed. "Nothing happens to you, Piney. You sit on your ass and hold a fucking sign."

"What happens, that's not what makes it interesting. What happens, that's really, like, beside the point."

Fred didn't follow up on that, and Pineapple kept strolling, looked up past the fringe of mangroves. Way high up, so high that you could barely see the flashing of its wing lights, a plane was moving south to north; Piney decided it was coming from Peru and going, maybe, to Chicago.

"Fred," he said, "d'you think people's faces change, d'you think they look different, when they're in love or something?"

"Jesus Christ," said Fred.

"Today I saw a woman go into a hotel down on Whitehead Street. She came out a few minutes later and she looked completely different."

"Prob'ly got laid."

"Coupla minutes, Fred. Don't make it crude. She came out, she had a glow."

"Who gives a rat's ass?"

"I thought that was interesting. This is what I'm trying to explain. Not what happens. Things like that. That's what makes life interesting."

Fred polished off his beer, crushed the can and dropped it. "Piney," he said. "Being you, even for a minute—it must be a really odd experience."

*   *   *

The Ukrainian busboy had a pale and doughy face, and he was still wearing the smock he'd worn at work. Originally crisp, almost medical, it was stained now with lobster juice and butter sauce and splotches of wine and smears of vinaigrette. The busboy smelled of detergent and grease, and he couldn't decide on a posture. One moment he was stiff, skinny shoulders back as if trying to look military, and the next he was scrunched and furtive, quailing.

Finally, Ivan Fyodorovich Cherkassky said to him, "Stay still, Pavel. Are you a Ukrainian or a cockroach?"

The busboy stalled in his squirming. It seemed to take a monumental effort, as if his skin was holding back a platoon of snakes and worms. He cleared his throat, said to the two old Russians who sat while he stood, "I come because I think you like to know. Twice already they are there together. One time lunch, now dinner. Hexpensive, I tell you. And always they are talking, talking, talking."

Cherkassky turned his scooped-out doleful face toward his colleague. They were sitting across from each other on leather settees in Markov's living room. A fire was blazing in the fireplace and they were drinking cognac. It might have been Moscow except it was nearly the tropics. Markov waved his snifter casually, indulgently. He even smiled. "They are young," he said. "They like each other. Of course they talk, talk, talk."

Cherkassky frowned, turned back to the busboy. "And all this talking, talking, talking. They talk of love? Of politics? Of business?"

The busboy flicked up his unspeakable sleeves, interlaced his fingers. "Yes," he said.

Cherkassky spanked the arm of the settee. "Which of these, fool?"

The busboy hitched back his skinny butt, executed an appalling shallow bow. "Always I am clearing, running," he explained. "Salad plates. Butter. Cleaning, someone spills. I only hear a little now, a little later." He stood there fidgeting.

Markov raised a fat hand, gestured over him. He reached into the pocket of his brocade smoking jacket, produced a hundred dollar bill. He gave it to the busboy, then motioned him away with a gesture like pushing crumbs.

When he was gone, Cherkassky said, "This worries me, Gennady."

Markov swirled his brandy. "Like everything, Ivan." He paused, then claimed an old friend's prerogative to tease. "Still you are the fretting bureaucrat. Straight from Gogol you are."

The thin man didn't smile. "For a newspaper she works. This I do not like."

Markov snorted. "Newspaper? Business propaganda only. Selling restaurants, selling T-shirts, selling shnorkels."

"Ink on pages," Cherkassky insisted. "Is a paper."

"She is not journalist," protested Markov. "Only she sells adwertisements."

Ivan Cherkassky put down his glass, slowly ran a hand over the lumpy hollow of his face. "Gennady," he said. "To you this boy he walks on water. You laugh, you pat his hand, you do not see. But I am telling you, this talking, talking, talking, it is bad."

Markov waved his snifter. Fat in his maturity, goatish in his youth, he was no believer in disciplining appetite, arguing away desire. He said, "He wants to fuck her, Vanya. Can I tell him not to talk?"

Cherkassky stared into the unlikely fireplace, watched yellow flames lick against the bricks. "Yes," he said with certainty. "You can."

EIGHT

Aaron Katz swung slowly onto A-1A and tried to get his mind around the notion that he was bringing his old and slipping father on a play-date.

A couple of evenings before, Sam had found a cocktail napkin in his pants pocket. Written on the napkin was a name and number, but Sam couldn't quite remember whose they were, or how the piece of paper had gotten in his pants. He'd put the napkin on his nightstand, hoping that it would catch his eye at some receptive moment and everything would click.

And sure enough, he finally remembered Bert—the shiny hair, the ancient dog, the offer of companionship. He said to Aaron, "Can we call him up? D'ya think it would be okay to call him up? Would you bring me for a visit?"

So they were driving now along the beach, toward the Paradiso condo. Palms leaned backward against a fresh east wind. Beachgoers danced over the thin imported sand that hid the native lacerating coral. Enormous freighters looked like bathtub toys as they rode the Gulf Stream, out beyond the reef. Sam and Aaron didn't talk because the only things they thought of were things they didn't want to say.

Aaron was thinking: *I wonder if he'll be all right, if he'll get confused and panic. What if he goes wandering off?* He thought how nice it would be if his father had a friend, and he caught himself day-dreaming guiltily about the things he could do if he had more time to himself.

Sam was thinking: *This having to be driven everywhere, accompanied—it was a nuisance.* For all the many things that he forgot, he seldom forgot that he was in the way. A burden. His son worked too hard. Was lonely. Needed friends, a woman. Needed time to find those things. Maybe Sam could still discover something of his own, a place to go, a way to keep his dignity and his distance. It would be better for everybody.

They reached the Paradiso complex—three long squat buildings cradling a pool and a putting green and tennis courts and a gazebo—a perfect little swath of Florida across the road from the Atlantic Ocean. Aaron parked. Father and son walked up to an iron gate and punched in Bert d'Ambrosia's number on the intercom. A buzzer buzzed and the gate swung open.

Bert met them at the pool. He was wearing a mustard-colored linen shirt with big rough buttons made of bone, and he was holding his dog like the dog was a football. Everybody said a nice hello, but Aaron felt awkward, shy; felt, absurdly, like a parent at a prom. Eager to go, he said to his father, "So you'll call me later? The number's in your wallet."

Bert said, "Don't expect him soon. What if we find a couple broads or something?"

Sam said of his new friend, "A regular comedian."

Aaron patted his father's shoulder then turned his back on the two gray men and the moribund chihuahua. But crazily, as soon as he began to move away, he found his steps were weighted down with grief. It was a brilliant sunny morning. Nothing was wrong, everyone was fine. But as he walked back toward the iron gate he just felt torn apart. Loss. A strange word. It seemed to mean an absence, something missing; but loss was also a presence all its own, a fanged and snarling monster ready at any moment to break its chain and snatch someone away.

The condo gate swung open at Aaron's approach, started swinging closed again as soon as he had passed. It clicked shut with a terrible finality, like the school door on the first day of kindergarten.
Aaron grabbed a deep breath to open up his throat. He thanked God
he had no children of his own. He didn't know how anyone could
stand the love and sorrow of doors clicking shut on both sides all
at once.

"Peter," Suki said, "how do you get into the database?"

Peter Haas, the restaurant reviewer, looked up from his computer
screen. He had lank sandy hair and owlish horn-rim glasses, and he'd
been trying to decide whether a certain chocolate terrine was better
described as ambrosial or celestial. He tried to look a little bit
annoyed though he was relieved to be interrupted. "What do you
want to look up?" he asked.

Suki bit her lip, the upper one. She said, "Just, you know, in general. How to use it."

"There's no category just-in-general." Peter said. "You've got to
plug something in."

Suki said, "Okay. Pick something."

"You pick," Peter said.

"Okay," said Suki. "How about . . . how about, um . . . Russian
Mafia?"

"Russian Mafia?" said Peter, and he looked at her over the tops of
his glasses. "Hm. Would we look that up under Mafia or Russian?"

"This is what I'm asking you," said Suki.

"Maybe just crime," said the restaurant reviewer. "Or organized
crime."

"Look, how do you get started?" Suki asked. "I mean, just get into
the system?"

"Might still be under Soviet Union," Peter said. "Breakup of. Or
even Cold War, aftermath of."

"Maybe we should start with something simpler," Suki said.

"Could be cross-referenced," Peter said, "with individual crimes—extortion, murder."

Suki leaned lower over Peter Haas's chair. "All I really want to know—" she began. Then she straightened up and said, "Oh shit. I smell Donald."

The restaurant reviewer sniffed the air, which second by second was becoming fouled with the approach of a cheap cigar. The publisher's heavy step could now be heard on the metal grid work of the outside stairs.

Suki said, "Can we talk about this later?"

Peter said, "But—"

"Later, Peter, please? You'll take me through it step-by-step?"

The restaurant reviewer shrugged agreement.

Suki sniffed. "That stink," she said. "Do you think it would be more exact to call it rank, or putrid?"

"Uncle, I am not a child," Lazslo said.

He'd been summoned to Key Haven for lunch, but Key Haven generally took away his appetite. He poked at his *blini* and looked across the seawall to the Gulf.

"Put more sour cream," Gennady Petrovich Markov advised. "You hardly have any sour cream."

"I have enough," said Lazslo.

Markov frowned, took another hefty dollop for himself. He watched it slide fatly off the silver spoon, then returned to the business at hand.

"No," he agreed. "You are not a child. You are a fine young man, and like every fine young man you are following your *schwantz*, and your *schwantz* sees only half the picture because it only has one eye."

"What picture?" Lazslo said. "I'm dating this woman. That's the only picture."

"For a newspaper she works," said Markov.

"And I run a chain of T-shirt shops. What's the problem?"

Markov put down his fork. An instant later it was in his hand again, like fork and hand were magnetized. Pondering, he yet managed neatly to fold another buckwheat crepe. "Lazslo. You don't want to admit you understand, but I know you understand. Of all the women you could have. Ivan Fyodorovich is very concerned."

"Ivan Fyodorovich!" Lazslo said, and he launched into a manic pantomime of the scoop-faced Russian's tireless paranoia. He pulled his brows together, dropped his neck, vulturelike, between his shoulders. Eyes darting, he glanced nervously behind himself, then underneath the table. "Ivan Fyodorovich! Are you hiding? Are you listening?"

Markov smiled even as he shook his head in disapproval. "Luzhka," he said, "a real American you have become. You think everything is joke."

"Uncle, most things are."

"And some few things are not," countered Markov. "For your own good, Luzhka, please stop seeing this—"

Lazslo was pushing some food around his plate. "You're just a little bit too late," he interrupted.

"Late?"

Lazslo tried to stifle a triumphant grin. He was several years too young to manage it, and a hint of a lubricious smile broke through his irritated look. "I called her up this morning. She's coming to my place for dinner."

"Your place?" said Markov. A thrum of vicarious lust pulsed through him, he reached across the table and lightly squeezed the muscles of Lazslo's forearm. Then he took another *blini* from the platter and shoveled up another wad of sour cream. "So tonight's the night you—"

"Don't jinx it, Uncle," Lazslo said.

Markov chewed some pancake, wiped his fat lips on a napkin. "Okay, Luzhka, so you fuck her once—"

"How about twice?" said Lazslo.

"Then have more *blini*," Markov said. "As many times you like. But please, after tonight you call it off. Promise me."

Lazslo looked toward the green water, the distant mangrove islets floating on their silver nests. He didn't promise. Instead, he said, "Don't I always, Uncle? Right afterwards, I almost always call it off."

NINE

Aaron Katz had a million things to do, but the relief of having his father taken care of for a while somehow broke his focus, and he gave himself over to the rare delicious pleasure of goofing off. There were shrubs to be planted, but he didn't want to plant them. There were red and black and yellow wires poking out of walls, needing to be sorted, but he didn't want to sort them, didn't want to jump at unexpected sparks. He sat down on the porch swing meant for guests, and for some few minutes tried to imagine he was a guest himself, enjoying the blessing of an uncluttered mind.

Thoughts of contractors and invoices and canceled reservations fell away, and what was left when the annoyances receded was a vivid but ambiguous recollection of Suki Sperakis kissing his cheek.

A mystery, that kiss. So sudden it might almost have been an accident, a spasm rather than a choice. Was it sexy or just sisterly? An offer of more and slower kisses or just part of her apology, a conciliation between new friends? If it was nothing more than friendly, why would she have rung the bell?

But how available was she, really? There was that cultivated toughness to contend with. Then too—Aaron recalled in spite of himself—there was that other involvement. Not romantic but getting deeper. Whatever that meant. This Lazslo person, this bigshot in a dinky little town. He probably had a fancy spotless car. Pastel silk shirts, perfect for the climate, casual but pricey. Got sucked up to in restaurants, was given the best tables. Had all the things, in short, that Aaron used to have, and now told himself, maturely, he could do without. He told himself they were jerky things, trivial, he didn't need them anymore; and he hoped like hell he really meant it.

He rocked on the porch swing, tried to claw his way free of the slime of jealousy. He steered his mind back to Suki herself. Her eyes. Things she said. Plate of macaroni.

He found himself on his feet and heading into the office. The piece of paper with her number on it was in a cubbyhole behind the desk. Stiff-legged, his chest a little tight, he was moving toward it, but not directly. He arced, he dodged, he was circling the phone number like it was something dangerous—a ticking suitcase, a big dog sleeping. Finally he slipped behind the desk and seized it.

There were two phone numbers on the little piece of paper. Aaron tried the home phone, got an answering machine, didn't leave a message. At the second number a bored male voice answered, said, "*Island Frigate.*" Aaron asked for Suki and she soon picked up the line.

"Suki? Aaron Katz."

For a second she was flustered. She'd been reading on a computer screen about the Russian Mafia. *Criminal chaos in a society come unmoored. The violent disorder that had all along underlay the veneer of Soviet authority.* The switch to peaceable, mild Aaron Katz was a little befuddling, and she said a somewhat distracted, weak hello.

Aaron didn't know what to make of it. Was this the same bold woman who had rung his bell? Tentative in turn, he said, "I was wondering if I could take up your offer on my offer."

Suki said, "Excuse me?" *No one knew how or if the Russian Mob was organized. If there was a mastermind, he was very, very brilliant. More likely there were a thousand separate cells grabbing shreds of wealth and force ...*

Aaron said, "Will you share a meal with me sometime?"

In Russia it was *looting on a national scale. As if the entire country was blacked-out and the police had gone away. There was nothing too big, too small, too sacred, too egregious to be stolen.* Suki said, "Yes. I'd like that."

There was a pause. She hoped he wouldn't ask her for tonight; she didn't want to have to tell him she was busy. Nor did Aaron want her schedule, clearly fuller than his own, thrown up in his face. He played it safe and gracious. "When's good for you?"

Suki bit her lip and thought. Tonight at Lazslo's place would be a war. She would have to smile through her distaste, probe while trying not to be pawed. She deserved an antidote to all of that. "How's tomorrow?"

"Tomorrow's great," said Aaron. "How about Lucia's?"

"Lucia's," Suki said. "We're not talking macaroni now. Lucia's, that's pasta."

"Eight o'clock?" said Aaron.

"I'll be there," Suki said.

"I do not like it," said Ivan Fyodorovich Cherkassky.

He was sitting in his living room, which was modern and beige and spare, its paintings empty of figures, its furniture undented by humanity. The room lacked a fireplace and a cart of liquor and was altogether less grand than his old friend Markov's. His windows looked out at a less expansive view of patio and sky and dredged canal. Sourly he said, "The mouth opens when one tries to open other things."

Markov's voice sounded wet and wheedling through the telephone. "Ivan," he said, "it is the last time he will see her. He gave his word."

"The word of a boy whose pants are out of shape," Cherkassky said. "You trust this word?"

"He is infatooated," Markov said. "He will have her, and then his *schwantz* will droop, and the world will not be changed, and she will seem less beautiful, and it will all be over."

Cherkassky fretted. He looked across the narrow, still canal to the garish mint-green house on the other side. So stupidly cheerful, these Americans, with their houses of peach and turquoise, archways and walkways of bright tile, their obnoxious optimism and cars the colors of candy. Finally he said, "Would have been much better if you tell him simply no."

"Ivan," said Markov, "do you remember, long ago, what happened when your *schwantz* would stand?"

The scoop-faced man hung up.

He sat there in his unlived-in living room and he thought a while. He didn't pace, he didn't fidget. He just looked out the window and wondered why it was that the more wretched his life became—the more devoid of joy, the more totally inhabited by mistrust and disapproval—the more determined he was to safeguard it at any cost. He once again picked up the phone.

He called the Belorussian woman who cleaned Lazslo's apartment. He told her to get on her scooter and come to Key Haven right away.

"So Sam," said Bert, "when you worked, what kind of work did you do?"

Sam scratched his head through the tangles of extravagant Einstein hair, said modestly, "I invented things. I was, ya know, a tinkerer."

"Invented things?" said Bert. He was impressed but also distracted. His chihuahua needed attention.

They were sitting poolside at the Paradiso, in the shade of a metal umbrella painted like a daisy. But the sun had shifted and now Bert had to reach across the table to slide his dog back into the retreating shadow.

"Gets dehydrated," he explained. "Eyeballs dry up. Lids stick. He goes ta blink, his ears wiggle but nothing happens wit' the eyes. Looks confused. And his little asshole too. Dries up. Looks like chapped lips. Crinkly. Vet said rub a little Chap Stick on it. Can ya believe it, Chap Stick. I gotta remember which pocket his is in, which pocket mine. So wha'd y'invent?"

Sam didn't answer right away. He watched the pale chihuahua, sublime in its passivity, being slid across the surface of the table, its tiny toenails screeching softly against the paint. When it was safely in the shade again, it seemed to smile; its mouth twitched open, showing mottled gums. Finally Sam said, "I invented very simple things. Useful little gizmos. Like, you know that kind of can opener, it has a wheel, you squeeze the handle and the wheel bites through the top? I invented that."

"You invented that?" said Bert. "You musta made a fortune."

Sam said, "Before that wheel, you opened a can, you got dents in your fingers, that's how hard you had to squeeze. But a fortune? Ach! I sold the patent, flat-rate, to a company. Moved my family to the suburbs. Spent a lot more time at home."

"Retired right away?"

"Nah," said Sam. "Kept working. Built myself a bigger workshop. Fiddled with crystal radios, phonograph needles, wireless intercoms. But I liked being home. Seeing my boy grow up. Helping with homework. Going to the bakery together, now and then a day game at the Stadium. Simple things . . . And what did you do, Bert?"

The table they were sitting at was right next to the pool. The breeze was fresh and it was too cool for swimming, but that didn't stop the short-term guests from swimming anyway. They kicked, they splashed, the liquid noises obscured the words when Bert said softly, "I was in the Mafia."

Sam wasn't sure he'd heard right. He double-checked that his hearing aid was in. He looked dubiously at his new friend, the skinny face, the banana nose. He said, "You were in modeling?"

Bert leaned in a little closer, spoke no louder but bit the words off cleanly. "Not modeling. Mafia."

Sam said, "Now you're making fun of me."

"An old man," said Bert, "does not make fun of another old man. God doesn't like that shit."

There was a pause. Tourists splashed; a red biplane dragged an ad across the sky above the beach.

Finally Sam said, "So you're in the Mafia now?"

"Retired."

Sam pursed his lips. "Things I've read, movies—I didn't think you could retire."

Bert said, "Special case. I died."

Sam wagged a finger in his face. "God doesn't like that shit," he warned.

So Bert told him the story. The dread subpoena; the murderous stress of being called to testify. The heart attack on the courthouse steps. Ambulances, sirens, the mask thrust over his bluing face. And finally, the deliverance of a dead-flat EKG. Twenty-seven seconds of eternity, before they shocked him back to life. Enough for Bert to persuade his bosses that he'd fulfilled his solemn pledge: He'd come in living, and gone out dead, and this second go-round should be his own.

"What it all comes down to," he concluded, petting the head of his comatose dog, "is that it don't mean diddle what we did before. Now is now, what's left of it. Ya get old, things level out."

"Yeah," said Sam, "I think that's true."

"Prime a life," said Bert, "things are all uneven. This guy's rich, this guy's poor. This guy's a bigshot, this guy's a pissant. Old, it gets equal again, like wit' little kids. Ya need other kids ta play with, that's all. We're just a coupla kids in Florida."

Sam thought that over, made a futile attempt to smooth his fluffy hair. "Except," he said, "in my mind I'm not a kid. In my mind I'm not retired even now. I still think. Try to. I try to think of something useful. Nothing comes, but in my heart I'm still inventing."

Bert toyed with the mustard-colored placket of his shirt. "Okay, ya put it that way, I guess I'm not retired either."

Sam looked at him a little funny.

"I mean," Bert explained, "ya retire from work but ya don't retire from habits. A certain way of looking at the world, a way of reading people, situations. Comes in handy sometimes."

"That's what I want," said Sam Katz.

"What's what you want?"

"Still to come in handy. Be of use."

"That's a luxury," said Bert.

"Dream up some idea, put together some gizmo that still might come in handy."

"Ya never know," said Bert.

"That's right," said Sam. "I never do."

Bert reached across the table, tapped Sam's wrist with his gnarled and spotted fingers. "A great idea, a useful gizmo, it could pop into your head at any second."

"*Oy*," said Sam. "Things pop out. They don't pop in."

"Stay with it, Sam. Ya never know. Besides, what choice ya got?"

TEN

I t was twenty after seven, and Lazslo Kalynin was inspecting himself in the full-length mirror on the inside of his bathroom door.

He hooked his fingers in the corners of his mouth and stretched his cheeks out wide to look for specks between his teeth. He tilted back his head to search out errant nose hairs. He leaned in close to examine his pores, to root out clogs, and preempt the occasional pimple.

When he had dealt with minor flaws, he turned sideways to appraise the bigger picture, trying to imagine how a casually passing stranger might perceive him. He came away pleased with his stylish haircut, manly but hip; with the rich sheen of his blue silk shirt, the understated chains beneath it; with the hug of his jeans, whose fly was cinched together not with a zipper but a rank of cool steel buttons. When Suki undid them, she would be greeted, titillated, by a swath of flame red briefs.

Content with his person, he strolled through the apartment, whose every primped pillow and dimmered light switch said seduction. Ludmila, the Belorussian housekeeper, had not only done the dinner preparations, but had left big vases of fresh flowers on the dining table and next to the sofa. The Gibson guitars, acoustic and electric, were strewn here and there with a studied carelessness. The Harley posters were straight on the walls. A six-pack of CDs had been loaded up with music designed to showcase Lazslo's sensitivity, his many moods.

At 7:35 the doorbell rang.

Lazslo patted his hair and checked the tuck of his shirt before sweeping open the door—and then he tried not to show his disappointment when he saw how Suki looked. He'd imagined she'd be all made up, her full mouth red and beckoning, wearing something slinky, showing hints, at least, of perfumed cleavage. In fact she'd left her blue eyes unadorned, her lips unpainted; she wore no scent, and her loose concealing blouse was buttoned resolutely to the neck. If Lazslo's brain registered the message, his glands negated it at once. She was teasing, he decided, continuing her strategy of being hard to get.

He was standing in the doorway, leaning at an angle he thought was very sexy, blocking passage with his arm against the jamb. He said hello and gave a meaty smile. Unyielding, he stayed there in the portal, and they both knew he was trying to exact a toll of contact before she could pass into the apartment. She managed a weak greeting, thinking *What an asshole.*

Not for the first time but nearly for the last, she wondered how far she could push her luck with this preening brat, and just what the hell she was trying to accomplish, as she arched like a gymnast to slip past him without their bodies touching.

"Fred," said Pineapple, "ya know what I sometimes wonder about?"

They were sitting on the seawall just south of Houseboat Row. The sun had been down an hour or more but there were still faint gradations in the sky, hints of pink rays being smoked out into negatives. Fred didn't take the bait and Pineapple went on:"Luck."

The word brought forth a snort from Fred. "Luck? What about it?"

"Like for starters, whether it exists."

Fred thought about the people he dug holes for—people with big houses, swimming pools. He thought about people he met in bars—fat bankrolls, nicely dressed. Some of these people, he admitted, seemed a lot smarter than himself. Others really didn't. He said, "Damn straight, it exists."

Pineapple looked across the shallows where unlikely shoots of mangrove were colonizing the sea, buying back land for North America one sand grain at a time. "Ya think it changes? Luck, I mean?"

"Ours hasn't," said Fred. He sucked his beer.

"Finding the hot dog, that was lucky."

It was true but Fred had staked out the bitter position and now he didn't want to change. He said, "Piney, is there some point you're aiming at?"

"Not really," acknowledged the man with the medieval face. "It's just that, well, ya hear different things."

Fred left that alone, rested his beer on the seawall and lit a cigarette.

"Like ya hear people say," Pineapple went on, "don't push your luck, like you only have a limited supply, and once it's gone, that's it."

Fred said, "And you're shit outa luck from there."

"But then," said Piney, "other people, they make it sound the opposite, like exercise, like the more you push your luck the more you have."

"I don't see the point of exercise," said Fred.

"Like, in battles," said Pineapple, "the guy that leads the charge hardly ever gets shot. Not in movies at least."

"Exercise," said Fred, "I get enough fuckin' exercise digging holes and riding my bike for beer. What kinda bullshit is more exercise?"

Pineapple looked down at his long thin legs as they dangled over the seawall, his bare feet just a few inches above the flat water that held the dying colors of the sky. "Fred," he said, "we weren't talking about exercise."

"Ya think I don't know that? We were talking about war movies."

Piney gave up on conversation and looked down at the ocean.

Lazslo wished that she would drink more.

He kept topping up her Chardonnay. He topped it up when

they were sitting at table, eating steak; he topped it up now that they had moved onto the sofa. Every time he drank some beer, he went to replenish her wine, finding each time that the level of her glass had barely budged. As if to compensate, he drank more beer himself.

He couldn't decide how the evening was going. Suki was keeping her distance—that was bad. But conversation was very lively—that was good. Except there was a tension in the talk, a constant tugging—and he couldn't tell if that was playful or just difficult. Lazslo spoke of Caribbean islands, exotic travel—sensuous things that cost money, that Suki was supposed to believe they might do together if she became his lover. But she followed up on none of that. She talked about rents and business and politics and crime.

"The diving off Cozumel," Lazslo was saying now. "Fantastic. And Yucatecan food—great fish with lime and orange sauces, none of that rice and beans garbage."

Suki had an ankle folded under her against the velvet of the couch. She leaned back just outside of Lazslo's reach. She said, "And how about the food in Russia?"

Lazslo made a gesture of distaste. He didn't want to speak of Russia. He was an American now, with flame red underpants and Bruce Springsteen on the stereo. He said, "Russia, no big fat juicy steaks. No asparagus in January."

Suki said, "Amazing, what's happened to that country."

"Forget that country," Lazslo said. "Dreary, cold. When, so close, we have the Grenadines, the Cayman Islands . . . "

He moved to touch her hair, her ear. He had to slink, almost grovel to reach her. She had time to seize his wrist and fend it off. She said, "Caribbean, that's just vacation. Russia, that's history. Fascinating."

She released his wrist, and Lazslo found himself lying at an uncomfortable and undignified diagonal. His lunge had sent a throb up to his head, and he very vaguely realized he'd gotten one Budweiser ahead of himself. He said, "Fascinating?"

"The way authority just collapsed," said Suki. "The way a Mafia seemed to spring up practically overnight, good Soviets suddenly becoming master criminals."

Lazslo straightened up, regrouped. He put his hands on the cool glass coffee table and studied her a moment. Her eyes were bright and wide, her throat a little flushed. Her fingers were splayed out on her knees and for the first time all evening she was leaning toward him. A shrewd, sophisticated thought occurred to him. He didn't recognize it as a desperate stratagem whispered by his gonads. He topped up her Chardonnay, and said with a worldly lift of his eyebrows, "This Mafia stuff—I think it excites you."

Suki held his gaze a moment then looked down as if caught at something naughty. "Maybe it does," she said. She sipped a little wine.

"Why?"

"Oh I don't know. Maybe just the boldness of it. The daring."

The word echoed in Lazslo's loins. Ill-advisedly he swigged some beer. He said, "Daring, yes. Especially when you consider the constant fear that Russians lived with."

"Turning to crime," said Suki, a little breathlessly—"it's like a crazy but perfect facing down of that fear, the final rebellion against the control—"

"The control," said Lazslo, "that was giving even ordinary people a million daydreams of revenge, of breaking loose." He'd swiveled toward her now, his knees far apart, a hand on one ankle.

"And," said Suki, "the sheer scale of what they're doing over there—"

"Ha!" said Lazslo. "Americans can't even begin to understand the scale."

Suki said nothing, just reached for her glass next to the vase of extravagant flowers, and sipped some Chardonnay.

"What Americans don't get . . . " said Lazslo. "Look, American criminals—even your big bad Mafia—all they do is nibble around the edges. Skim a little here, break a little piece off there. In Russia, we . . . What they've done in Russia is go to the very heart of the wealth. You understand?"

Suki only looked at him. Her lips were slightly parted, her shoulders rounded toward him.

"You say daring?" he went on. "Your tough Americans, they rob a drivethru teller in a shopping mall. Russian Mafia, they cruise right into the treasury. They steal history. Old Church ikons. Jewels left over from the tsars. Famous paintings. Even military hardware."

"Military?" Suki said.

"You forget your own propaganda?" Lazslo said. "The Soviets put guns before butter—isn't that what you were taught? The masses starving while the generals get fat? So where else is more wealth?"

Suki reached toward her wine then stopped her hand. Lazslo widened the angle of his legs and savored her discomfiture.

"Military, yes," he went on. "Why not? Renegade scientists and highly placed bureaucrats—why couldn't they steal guns? Missiles? Nuclear material? Daring enough for you, Suki?"

Suki licked her lips. Her hands were bundled in her lap. She couldn't speak.

Lazslo was titillated by victory; he gloated. "So now you are shocked. Crime excites you and now you are shocked."

Suki sipped some wine, took a moment to collect herself. "Well yeah," she admitted. "Sort of. But all that wealth—where does it go? What good does it do you in Russia?"

Lazslo swigged some beer. "In Russia? No good at all," he said. "It has to travel. Say you have church art—you open up a shop in Moscow? No, you go where the collectors are. Paris, New York, Hong Kong. Say you have something for which there is a great demand in Libya, Iraq—"

"Iraq?" said Suki. "Libya?"

He wiped his mouth on the back of his hand, slid toward her on the sofa. With difficulty she held her ground.

She murmured, "What would they want in Libya, Iraq?"

Weirdly, Lazslo laughed. It was a barking laugh with lust and reck-lessness and maybe a hint of secret fear in it. "What," he said, "would feed their pathetic fantasies of destroying the West someday? Yes, the wealth has to travel. And you know what? That kind of travel is very, very tiring. So after that, the money needs vacation. Someplace sunny. Relaxing."

"Weapons, Lazslo? Are you saying bombs?"

"Someplace easygoing. Full of beautiful women who don't ask so many questions."

"Lazslo, do they smuggle bombs?"

He snorted. "Bombs? No one's *that* crazy . . . Spare parts, maybe. Useful ingredients perhaps."

"Ingredients? . . . Ingredients?"

He studied her. Her eyes were wide, her chest was heaving. He chose to see arousal rather than horror. "Enough ingredients to make Chernobyl look like a weenie roast, okay? You have a strange idea of foreplay, Suki."

"So your uncle," she said. "The shops—"

Lazslo hushed her with a hand raised like a traffic cop. He leaned very close, arched over her. Heat pulsed off him and his breath was sour with hops and barley. "Mafia excites you," he whispered, "you must be very ready."

Ready to throw up, she thought.

"No . . . I'm not," she said. At a measured pace intended to reveal no panic, she began to slide away from him along the sofa.

He groveled after her, put a damp hand on her breast.

She brushed away his fingers and got her legs unfolded. She smoothed her blouse and started standing up. "I've had a lovely evening, thank you, but now I'm going home."

Lazslo was watching her rise, enjoying the flex of her butt as she straightened her knees, measuring the weight of her chest as she lifted her shoulders. "You're what?" he said.

She rounded the coffee table, got the big piece of glass safely between them. "You've been a gracious host," she said. "Delicious dinner."

Lazslo sat there, tipsy, blinking, watching her recede across the living room, past the kitchen with its undone dishes, moving inexorably toward the door. He felt suddenly foolish with his thighs so far apart, and he was almost too baffled to be angry. His titillation had followed every zig and zag of hers—except that his had been real, and had left him unsatisfied but drained. He rubbed his jaw and, with the thwarted certainty of the foreigner who thought he knew the rules, he said, "An American woman, she comes to your place, she spends the night with you."

Suki's hand was on the doorknob. She looked back across her shoulder. "Call me un-American," she said. "I hope we'll talk again soon."

ELEVEN

Next morning at the Mangrove Arms, Aaron Katz was in such a buoyant mood that not even finding a drowned and bloated fruit rat in the pool skimmer could put a damper on his spirits.

He vacuumed the pool, scrubbed the line of scum around the edges of the hot tub. He watered the impatiens; plucked a troubling number of yellow leaves from the hibiscus plants.

He looked in on his father, who was sitting at the front desk with his eyes closed, his yellow Walkman cradled in his hands, his headphones threaded through his silver hair and an expression of untethered ecstacy on his thin-skinned face.

He checked on the tattooed woman who did the breakfast, who seemed this morning to be trying some odd experiment with giant pancakes.

The Mangrove Arms was still the Mangrove Arms—badly installed runners still puckered on the stairs, crooked sconces still flicked off and on in accordance with the inscrutable whim of distant switches—but today Aaron was seduced again by the charm, the promise of the place, the very idea of it. It continued eating money, guests were few and happy guests were fewer, and yet it seemed in spite of everything that things were working out. He had a date that evening. His father had a new friend, someone to visit. Life was opening up. Key West, this transient place whose heart was hidden under mounds of promotional brochures and tacky T-shirts and empty bottles, was embracing him.

Standing in the kitchen amid the sweet carbon smell of sticking pancakes, he poured himself a cup of coffee. He'd had one sip when the house phone rang. He picked it up, said, "Front desk."

An unhappy and abashed male voice said, "Uh, well, yeah, it's about the toilet."

Aaron put the coffee down. Undaunted, or daunted only slightly, he started rolling up his sleeves and tried to remember where he'd put the plunger. "I'll be right there," he said.

On Key Haven the mood was altogether darker.

The Belorussian housekeeper had unscrewed the false bottoms from the vases, had gotten on her scooter and brought the tapes to Ivan Fyodorovich Cherkassky. Grim-faced, expressionless, perched with a disembodied lightness on one end of his undented sofa, Cherkassky had reviewed them, had listened to the incriminating passages a second time, a third. He'd summoned Gennady Markov to his home and, together, they listened to them yet again.

"You see?" the thin man said. "You see what comes from being too easy with this boy?"

Lazslo's uncle said nothing, just looked out the window at the still canal, the silly mint-green house across the way.

"Reckless," Ivan Fyodorovich hammered on. "Careless. I told you, Gennady. And now this."

Markov laced together his fat fingers, worked them nervously. "Maybe you make too much of it, Ivan. It was idle boasting, talk to get her clothes—"

"Stop being stupid," said the scoop-faced man. "Stop making excuses. It does not matter why he said these things. He said them. To this woman. You know what has to happen."

Markov chewed his knuckles. He tried to think of some other way but he knew there was no other way. Absurdly, it grieved him that Lazslo didn't get to sleep with her before she had to die.

As if tracking his old comrade's thoughts, Cherkassky took them one step farther. "He must do it himself," he said.

Markov gripped the arms of his chair as if bracing for a car crash. "No!" he said. "There are others who could—"

"He made the mess," Cherkassky implacably replied. "He must clean the mess. A lesson every child should learn."

"Child, yes," said his uncle. "Child, Ivan. This boy is not a killer. To make him do this is big mistake. It will change him. It will coarsen him."

There was a silence. It was broken by a sudden metallic laugh that didn't quite sound human, a single syllable of mirthless release that carried all the disgust and censure that Ivan Fyodorovich had been keeping mostly to himself for a long time now.

"Coarsen him?" he said. "The boy could be no coarser! With his beer, his blue jeans, his ignorant erections that he follows sniffing like a barnyard dog. He has no dignity. No responsibility."

"But Ivan—" protested Markov.

"He is an animal!" Cherkassky pressed. "Nothing but tubes and appetite. Now he follows the tube between his legs. Older, he'll be a slave to the tube of his gullet. Like you, Gennady. Given time, he'll end up fat and sloppy. Congratoolations, Gennady! You wanted a son, you found one."

Markov burrowed deep into his chair. He looked like he might start to cry. "Ivan," he said, "I do not see why you attack—"

"Attack?" said Cherkassky. He hadn't budged from his unrumpled place at the corner of the sofa. Except for that one swift cackle, he'd barely raised his voice and his expression hadn't changed. "I do not attack. I am making clear. Your nephew is worthless."

"But the stores," said Markov. "The work he—"

The scoop-faced man ignored him. "And you," he went on. "I cannot call you worthless because for one thing you are very good. Very good to hide behind. Wide. Fat. A fat soft pillow. At home in your big impressing house where the mayor comes for bribes. In this way you are valuable. But only in this way. Remember that, Gennady. And now you will call your nephew and you will tell him he must do this thing today. You understand?"

Markov stared out the window. The sky was flawless blue. Water twinkled, flowers sprouted everywhere, but he saw only desolation. Control. He'd never had it in the old country, and he didn't have it here. Strong at science, weak at life, he'd always surrendered to being used and fed. His eyes watered with self-pity, smearing the view. Breeze was lifting palm fronds and pressing them back, they looked like panicked arms raised up to protect a face. "I understand," he said.

"But I have dinner plans tonight," said Suki, cradling the phone between her shoulder and her ear. She was sitting at her desk at the *Island Frigate*, confronting invoices and receipts and paper clips, catching up on the boring things she'd been neglecting and that paid her rent.

"I really want to see you," Lazslo said.

"That's nice," said Suki. "But it doesn't change my plans."

He paused, sought to convey great effort, a baring of the soul. "I really liked talking with you last night."

"Really? I didn't think you did. In fact getting you started was like pulling teeth."

"Talking about Russia," Lazslo said, "it isn't easy for me. But . . . But I woke up this morning and felt relieved, cleaned out."

Suki slapped the stapler, said, "I'm glad the therapy is going well."

"There's much more I want to tell you."

"How about tomorrow?"

"How about a drink this evening?"

Suki rolled her eyes and sighed. "Lazslo," she said, "you're always trying to hurry things. Haven't you gotten it by now? That doesn't work with me."

"A drink," he said. "A chat. An hour of your time. I'll pick you up at six."

Suki bit a pencil, looked at the old school clock on the wall. "Six-thirty. And I absolutely have to be free by eight."

"Free by eight," repeated Lazslo. "I promise."

TWELVE

Suki locked the door of her apartment, dropped the key into the small bag she carried on her shoulder, and stepped down from her porch. Six-thirty; the early part of dusk.

The light was soft and shimmering, it seemed to fall in grains of different brightnesses, and the first thing Lazslo noticed as she moved toward his car was that she was trying much harder to look good for whomever she was having dinner with than she had for him last night. Her eyelids were discreetly lined and shadowed faintly blue. She wore pale lipstick whose main effect was to trace out the tantalizing crinkles of her upper lip. Her dress had a funny pattern of apples and pears, and its cloth was of a kind you could almost imagine you were seeing through. When she closed the Caddy's door behind her, the faint draft carried her scent of citrus and vanilla.

She said a blithe hello that Lazslo found it beyond his strength to answer. Resentment of her dress, its thinness and its ungrudging neckline, clamped his throat. The weight of his mission locked his jaw. Silently he put the car in gear and started driving.

Suki said, "Jeez. For a guy that wanted to talk . . ."

Lazslo turned his head to look at her. His neck didn't seem to pivot easily and ropy veins were standing out below the skin. "It's hard for me," he said. "I told you that."

Suki swiveled in the cracked white leather seat. "Why?" she said. "It's all so far away, remote. Or is it, Lazslo?"

He didn't answer. He drove. They came to Petronia Street. He should have turned right, to head downtown. He went straight instead.

Suki said, "Where are we going?"

Without looking at her Lazslo said, "I thought we'd go to Egret Key."

"There isn't time for Egret Key," she said.

"Fifteen minutes up," he said. "An hour for a drink or two. Fifteen minutes back."

"Cutting it too close," said Suki.

Lazslo glanced over at her then. He tried to make his eyes and voice facetious, but what came through was hate. "Very important, this dinner."

Suki let that pass, said, "Look, let's just go to Raul's."

But Lazslo had the steering wheel. "Free by eight," he said. "No problem."

He took a left on Truman and headed out of town. Bayview Park slipped by; they passed the statue of Marti. At Garrison Bight the charter boats were tied up in their slips, the ripples in the water were reflected on their transoms. It was a mild evening but Suki realized suddenly that she was much too warm. It registered for the first time that the Caddy's top was up.

"Lazslo," she said, "you never put the top up."

His only answer was to drive a little faster.

She'd started feeling wrong by now. It wasn't fear, not yet; just the clammy and featureless unease from which fear sometimes bubbled up, a jumpiness such as steals the grace from birds when a storm is on the way. She said, "Lazslo, if all you're gonna do is sulk, maybe you should take me home."

Lazslo just kept driving.

* * *

"How's the omelet, Pop?" said Aaron Katz. "You like it?"

His father's mouth was full of egg and cheese, he couldn't answer right away. Finally he said, "Perfect. Loose inside. Just the way I like."

"Great," said Aaron, toweling his hair. He was mostly dry and halfway dressed, bustling around the kitchen in boxer shorts and ancient slippers and just now buttoning his shirt. "So Pop, you'll be okay tonight? You'll be okay?"

"I'll be okay," said Sam. "It breaks my heart you worry. Stop worrying." He went back to his eggs.

Aaron said, "Who taught me how to worry, Pop? I learned from a master."

Sam chewed. "Who? Me? You think I worry? I don't worry. I care. That's different." He swallowed then looked around, a quizzical expression scrunching up his soupy eyes. Something wasn't right, he couldn't put his finger on it. He appraised his glass of juice, his stack of toast. Finally he said, "Aaron, you forgot my tea."

"Tea," said Aaron. Still drying himself, he moved to the stove where a pot was gently steaming.

"The whistling kind," said Sam, "it wouldn't happen you forget. A brilliant invention, the whistling teapot."

Aaron dunked a tea bag in the boiling water. "So you'll watch TV, you'll read a magazine. Okay?"

Sam Katz smeared butter on his toast. "It's nice to see you nervous. I think you really like this girl."

Aaron said, "You always think you know."

A little smugly, Sam ate toast.

"Besides, who said I'm nervous? I'm just making sure you're set."

"Making sure I'm set," said Sam, "for that you don't miss buttons on your shirt."

His son looked down, abashed, at his misaligned shirttails, the sure sign of a *shlump*.

"And Aaron," Sam went on—then twisted up his face and pointed inscrutably to the corner of his mouth.

"What, Dad? What?"

"Go shave again," his father said. "You missed a spot."

On the silent drive up U.S. 1, Suki watched the pelicans, the way their coasting flight sometimes paralleled the sagging arcs of the power lines. She watched tide streaming under bridges, foam-topped chevrons stretching back from every piling. She watched the first bold stars burn through the darkening sky ahead of them.

She watched those things to calm herself. It almost worked. By the time they reached their turnoff, eight, ten miles above Key West, she almost believed that nothing was amiss, not really; Lazslo was just a moody guy, a macho kid whose pride was hurt. His sulk would pass, he'd get talkative again. Probably he'd say intriguing things, useful things, maybe even things that would be worth the milky ache that Suki was feeling in her stomach.

He turned right off the highway. The road that led toward Egret Key was badly paved and narrow. Grasping mangroves blotted out the fading light and the deeper darkness was not soothing. The Caddy's headlamps glared back from waxy leaves, from scarred and ulcered trunks. Frogs and lizards scurried off, their bulbous eyes flashed red.

Suki swallowed back a sour taste, sought to guide her thoughts to the bar at Egret Key Marina. She'd always liked the place. Funky, friendly, a locals' retreat the tourists hadn't found. She thought about the thatched roof, the mismatched glasses. A drink, an hour, and then she really had to call this whole thing off. She was pushing her luck. It wasn't worth the way she felt.

Lazslo drove. Egret Key was just a speck of land across a stubby causeway, and she tried hard to keep believing they were really going there. The brutish set of Lazslo's jaw, the hard clench of his hands around the steering wheel, made her fear they weren't. Two hundred yards ahead, a hand-hewn sign, propped crookedly in limestone gravel, pointed out the turn. Suki shut her eyes a moment, prayed that she would feel the car begin to slow and veer. She didn't feel it.

Halfway through the dark and tiny intersection, she said, "You're missing it."

Lazslo didn't turn and didn't touch the brake. His eyes straight forward, he said, "I don't feel like a drink. Let's just go somewhere and talk."

Suki struggled with her voice, tried to keep it normal. She told herself she was from Jersey, she could handle this. "I feel like a drink," she said.

He moved his head just slightly on a neck that seemed mechanical, unoiled. He said, "It's always your way, Suki. Not tonight."

He drove. The road got bumpier and narrower. The mangroves leaned in closer, squeezed down like a funnel. Suki said, "I don't like this, Lazslo."

He didn't answer.

She firmed her voice like she was training a dog. "Take me home."

His lips pulled back for just an instant in a travesty of a smile. "And not talk about Russia?" he said. "About the Russian Mafia that interests you so much?"

"I don't care about that anymore. Let's turn around."

"Don't care?" he said. "After all your hard work pumping me? All your flirting? All your teasing?"

The paved road ended, gave onto a tunneled byway of coral powder and honeycombed gray rocks that crunched beneath the Caddy's tires and clattered against its groaning undercarriage. Looking back, Suki saw rising swirls of dust infernally shot through with a red gleam from the taillights. She was wearing sandals. She worked her toes against their insoles, straining for a solid grip. She wondered if she would have to run away, if she would have a chance to.

"Don't care?" Lazslo hammered on. "After all your questions, all your stringing me along? . . . Crime excites you, Suki. Are you excited now?"

He drove. The car rocked crazily, nauseously, through holes and over rocks. Suki's mind, cradling its sanity, dosed out fear in increments but still stopped short of believing he would murder her. His object, she imagined, was hideous unwilling sex; his desire had sickened over into monstrous rage, his intention was to force himself on her. She willed her body far away. She thought with pity of her clothes, the soft thin dress with the pattern of apples and pears. Her voice let go at last, became a pinched despairing moan. She said, "For God's sake, Lazslo, turn the car around."

He continued straight ahead. Mangrove leaves threw light back at his distorted face. His eyes flashed a vacant silver, the corners of his mouth were flecked with dried saliva. The car rocked so violently that his foot lurched off the accelerator. At a sudden curve he slowed still more. Suki flicked her door handle and rolled out of the car.

The ground was sharp and hard but she didn't feel the impact, only tasted coral and noticed grit against her cheek.

She clambered to her feet and started running through the dark, back along the dusty road. At the second step she lost a sandal, jagged nubs of limestone bit into her arch. She heard the Caddy crunch to a stop, the clicking open of Lazslo's door. She ran. Crickets were rasping and tiny panes of sky, triangles and diamonds, showed between the mangrove leaves. Her ribs were bruised, her breath came short and cramped.

She heard the steps behind her, pounding, crunching. If the mangroves opened up for her, perhaps there'd be a place to wriggle into, to hide; but they didn't open up, just loomed ragged and impenetrable, scabby trunks clustered close as strands of hair. She ran. She heard his breathing, the wheeze and catch of it. She heard a grunt as he lunged and grabbed her shoulder, his dreaded weight dragging her to the ground.

She pivoted as she fell, went down kicking and clawing. Coral rubble slammed against her back, hammered air out of her lungs, but still she bucked and flailed. Her knee found Lazslo's groin; her fingernails bit into the skin of his cheek, raked down deep and hard. She pummeled his sides and kicked at his ankles, but his thick torso and thighs crushed down, exhausted her.

He leaned and fended until her arms grew rubbery, her legs went numb. Then her body understood that it was over, and she was visited by the mercy that descends on doomed animals when pain and panic are no longer of use, and sad peace rolls back the eyes and stops the flanks from quivering. Her arms came up around her face like palm fronds blown back by the wind, but they offered only faint resistance as Lazslo's hands locked down around her throat.

Vaguely she felt the grit of the road against her scalp, saw a narrow swath of stars between the ranks of mangrove. The last time she smelled air it was scented with salt and seashells.

Part Two

THIRTEEN

Aaron Katz arrived at Lucia's at ten of eight and was shown to a so-so table in the middle of the room.

He took the seat that faced the door, ordered a bottle of Barolo, and did the things that people do when they are waiting in a restaurant, alone. He took more time than was necessary to unfold his napkin. He fiddled with his silverware and read the menu several times. He fended off the feeling that people were looking at him, and when he'd finished his first glass of wine and his date hadn't yet arrived, he tried to check his watch without anybody seeing.

At 8:25 he got up to use the men's room and the phone. There was no answer at Suki's house and he didn't leave a message. He expected she would be sitting at the table, harried and apologetic, when he returned to it. She wasn't.

He reclaimed his napkin, nibbled bread. He sipped more Barolo. He had no reason to be worried for Suki, and in the absence of worry, annoyance and self-mockery set in. It had been a long time since he'd been stood up; then again, it had been a while since he'd had a date. But why would Suki fail to show? She'd offered him her number, kissed him on the cheek—was this all some screwed-up game she invented as she went along? Was she, like a lot of people in this town, just plain nuts?

Aaron lived with that theory for half a glass of wine, took a hollow solace from it. Stood up by a crazy woman, just as well. But finally he rejected the notion. He'd seen just enough of Suki to understand that if she was crazy, her craziness wouldn't take the form of failing to appear, but of appearing too wholeheartedly. A hell-bent candor, an in-your-face thereness—if the woman was nuts, that's what her nuttiness was made of.

So why hadn't she arrived? Aaron began to worry after all, but only faintly. Key West was a safe place, a loony but a gentle place, a place where people survived their errors. Not a place where awful things happened.

At a quarter of nine the waiter came over, stood at Aaron's side. He tried to be kind, offered a smile he hoped didn't come across as patronizing. He said, "Perhaps you'd like to go ahead and order."

Aaron tried to smile back. He'd read the menu half a dozen times but now remembered nothing on it. "Just bring me," he said, "a plate of macaroni."

At the Eclipse Saloon around that time, Fred had eaten his burger and his fries and slaw, had washed them down with quite a few beers, and was at that stage in his race to bankruptcy when he had to pay close attention to just how many damp dollars he still had on the bar. It was better for his fragile standing in the place if he cut himself off as the last of the money was going, rather than making the barkeep do it for him.

So he was looking down, counting, concentrating, lifting the bent edges of soggy singles to make sure they weren't stuck together, when a voice above him said, "Hello there, sport."

Fred looked up, saw a guy who looked familiar, in the way that people in bars often looked like other people one had met in bars. Except that this guy's eyes looked like they'd been stained with some image of catastrophe, and he had thin lines of dried blood on one cheek. His shirt was torn on the side and his tight jeans were abraded at the knees and mottled with fine gray dust. He said to Fred, "You once bought me a beer, remember?"

Slowly it was coming back to Fred. Some evening a week, ten days ago. Pissed-off guy with a funny name. Drank a Bud and hardly talked. Fred said, "Looks like you need one even worse tonight." He gestured toward the soggy bills. "But you're outa luck, my money's about gone."

The seat next to Fred was vacant, but Lazslo didn't sit, just leaned in a little closer. "Tonight," he said, "I'm here to do something for you. Come to the john with me a minute."

Fred narrowed his eyes. The guy didn't look like a queer but not all queers did. He said, "No offense, pal, but go fuck yourself."

Lazslo fell back then leaned in again, his catastrophic eyes were pulsing. "Hey," he said, "it's nothing like that. You crazy? It's business. Wanna make a thousand dollars?"

The amount, heady and all but inconceivable, captured Fred's imagination. His reaction had less to do with greed than awe. He'd never had a thousand dollars in his life. He glanced quickly around the Eclipse's U-shaped bar, wondered if a thousand dollar bills would be enough to pave the whole entire thing.

Lazslo let the thought settle in a moment, then, limping slightly, moved off toward the men's room.

Fred sucked down some beer, allowed a discreet interval to pass, and followed.

He found Lazslo at the sink, washing his hands. He washed them a long time then lathered them again with pink soap from a dirty dispenser hanging crooked in its bracket. Still washing, he told Fred to lock the door. The lock was only a flimsy hook and eye, wood splintering where the bent screw was half pulled out.

Lazslo said, "I need someone to lose my car."

Fred leaned against the partition between the sink and the urinal, looked at Lazslo in the mirror. "Lose your car?" he said.

"Take it to the Everglades and lose it. Sink it. Ya know, in a swamp."

"Lose your car," Fred said again.

Lazslo flicked water from his fingers, reached up for a paper towel. There were no paper towels and he dried his hands on his jeans. The jeans gave back some fine gray dust and he cursed and washed his hands all over again. "Five hundred dollars now," he said. "The other five when the car is sunk and you make it back to town. I'll pay you here tomorrow night."

"Why you wanna sink this car?" asked Fred.

"Questions," Lazslo said, "that's not part of the arrangement."

Fred rubbed his walrus moustache. He'd lived in Key West a lot of years, he didn't want this guy to think he didn't know what was what. "Drugs."

It was not a question and Lazslo didn't answer, just tried to coax his clawed face and stained eyes into an expression that suggested, Yeah, it's drugs, some residue of some shit in the glove compartment.

Fred said, "This car, what kind of car is it?"

Lazslo frowned. His voice caught. He loved that car. "Cadillac. Fleetwood 1959. Mint condition."

Fred's nose tickled, he rubbed the tip of it. "Shame to sink a car like that."

Lazslo held his hands up like a surgeon, letting them dry in the air. He'd been outrunning exhaustion and disgust and an insanity of guilt, but with every moment they were catching up with him. He was no longer the least bit confident that he was thinking straight or that he'd settled on the right sucker for the job. Once again he felt the heat of Suki's throat against his thumbs.

Wearily, his eyes receding, he said, "Yeah, it fucking is a shame. So thousand dollars. Yes or no?"

Fred thought about it a moment more, then said, "Sure, why not?"

Lazslo told him where the car was parked, handed him the keys and ten exotic fifty dollar bills. "Everglades," he said. "Make sure it fucking disappears."

Fred pocketed the money and then just stood there, his elbow on the dented metal partition.

"So what're you waiting for?" said Lazslo.

Shyly, Fred nodded toward the urinal. "Ya don't mind," he said, "I gotta take a leak."

FOURTEEN

"Fred," said Pineapple, "I'm not so sure this is a good idea." They were cruising past the incongruities of Houseboat Row—the gangways festooned with flower boxes, gingerbread trim carved in the shapes of anchors and compass roses. Fred had stopped off at the hot dog to pick up his roommate; he couldn't resist showing off the doomed car. Together, they'd figured out how to put the top down; Lazslo's Fleetwood was now open to the stars.

Fred drummed lightly on the steering wheel. "Not a good idea?" he said. "Why not?"

Piney didn't answer.

Fred said, "Piney, how many times in your life you get to ride in a Caddy? Lotta people, they get to do it once. They get a bigass Caddy hearse with that chrome thing like a baby carriage. Guys like us, would we even get that one fancy ride? In a pig's eye, we would."

They reached the intersection of South Roosevelt and the highway. Fred was having a splendid time savoring the car. He snuggled his butt against the cushy, low-slung seat, squinted with pleasure at the softly glowing numbers on the speedometer. He steered with one hand while the other absently fondled the curves and knobs and swellings of the dashboard.

Pineapple said, "Fred, you got a license?"

He didn't answer. He was having some second thoughts about picking Piney up. If he was only gonna be a killjoy . . .

"What if a cop stops us? What then, Fred?"

"Fuck 'em if 'ey can't take a joke," said the driver.

But Pineapple was not impressed and Fred tempered his bravado.

"Look, I'm not even going the speed limit," he said. He turned north, the same way he turned on his rusty bike to get to the seven-thirty shape-up on Stock Island. He wished it was morning now and the whole crew could see him roll in behind the wheel.

"The guy whose car it is," Piney chipped away. "What if he reports it stolen?"

"Why would he report it stolen?" answered Fred. "He wants it lost, not found."

"What if he changes his mind?"

Fred kept driving but his enjoyment of it was already starting to erode. After a moment he said, "Why would he tell me lose it if he wasn't pretty fucking sure?"

"This guy says sink his car and I'm supposed to follow his logic?" Piney said. "All I'm saying, I'm saying it's a little strange a guy pays you money to sink his car. I'm not sure it's such a good idea is all I'm saying."

Fred pushed in the cigarette lighter, told himself he was having a better time than in fact he was by now. It was just a car, after all; all he was doing was pressing on the gas pedal and holding the wheel, and no one but Piney was there to see him do it. Besides, his sober friend's worry was infecting him, he was beginning to feel a little spooked himself. He said, "I guess I shouldn't 've taken you along."

Piney didn't respond to that. He'd found the button that made his seat recline; he was leaning way back and looking at the constellations. After a moment, he said, "What if this guy did something really bad, I mean really, really bad, and we're helping him get away with it?"

It was Fred's turn not to answer. He crossed from Stock Island onto Boca Chica; the ugly riot of down-market commerce yielded to the fenced-off bleakness of military property. Up ahead, driving in the opposite direction and weaving lane to lane, was a cop car with its blue lights flashing. Fred held his breath until he was good and sure the cop was after some other jerk. But now he was hardly enjoying the drive at all.

"Long ways off," he said, "the fucking Everglades."

"A deal's a deal," said Piney.

"Ya just said," Fred reminded him, "we shouldn't help this guy get away with something bad."

Pineapple kept looking at the stars. "Just as possible, I guess, he's a good guy that's in trouble."

"Piney," said Fred, "fuck we gonna get home from the Everglades?"

"Bus or something," said his friend. He didn't sound concerned. "Not like we're in a hurry."

"Look," said Fred. "I said I'd lose the car. Sink it. In a swamp." They were leaving Boca Chica and entering Big Coppitt; cinder-block taverns hunkered lower than the roadway between convenience stores and signs for RV hookups. Fred gestured broadly through the windshield. "Plenny a fucking swamps right here."

Pineapple said nothing.

"Lose it here as good as anywhere," Fred said.

"Better swamps up north," said Piney.

But Fred's mind was made up. His eyes were tired. His beer buzz had faded and left him paranoid about police. "What's good about a swamp?" he said, and he started looking for a turnoff that seemed promising.

He found one barely a mile farther on than Lazslo had driven with Suki, earlier that evening, and he steered the Caddy toward the mangroves.

"How's this look to you?" asked Fred.

They'd gotten out of the car at a spot that was like a thousand others in the Keys. A narrow dusty road, utterly flat, had petered out at a vague frontier between land and sea. On either side, mangroves grew so thick that it was impossible to see if their roots were sunk in dirt or water. Ahead, though, scattered shoots were pegged in what was clearly a last gasp, a lonely stranding of the overreaching ocean. Moonlight gleamed unwholesomely on that stagnant water, and with the car's engine finally switched off, the place was busy with tiny furtive sounds: scratching, lapping, dripping.

Pineapple said, "Looks a lot like where we live."

Fred gestured toward the liquid part. "Bet it's good and mucky under there."

"Hard to know," said Piney.

Fred stepped back, eyeballed the moonlit Fleetwood like an artist sizing up a painting. Suddenly the car looked huge and very tall, its tires like something off a tractor, its tail fins high as masts. Hopefully he said, "Just need a couple feet of water and then some good soft muck."

The thing about a swamp is that you could only see the top of it, but something was telling Pineapple that this place wasn't deep enough. "We could go a little farther north," he said.

Fred ignored him. He didn't want to get on the highway again. He said, "Trick's gonna be we gotta build up some momentum. Back up down the road, floor that sonofabitch, skate it in there good and hard."

Pineapple said, "We?"

Fred rubbed his walrus moustache, tossed his cigarettes and matches on the ground. "Chickenshit," he said.

He got back in the car, started up the engine once again. Absurdly, he turned the headlights on. He put it in reverse, slowly backed up maybe fifty yards. He shifted into neutral then paused a moment to stoke his courage. Pineapple had moved off to the side, giving his friend plenty of leeway. Above the idling motor, Fred called over to him, "Here goes nothin'."

Gradually he pushed the accelerator to the floor. The big V-8 rumbled, then whined, then bellowed in a clattering roar that seemed composed of shredding fan belts and sundering rotors and pistons slamming home like the devil's own dildos. At the height of the din Fred threw the Caddy into drive.

For an instant nothing happened, it was like the heartbeat's delay as a whipped horse connects the pain with something being demanded of it. Startled gears and rods engaged; the huge tires bit into the coral dust, spitting stones and screeching. With the slow momentousness of a rocket lifting off, the Caddy leaned back then started humping forward.

Inertia overcome, it took off fast. Dust billowed; rocks flew. Pineapple saw his friend streak past, terrified, saw that his elbows were locked as he squeezed the wheel, his lips pasted back against his teeth.

The roaring auto barreled through the contested boundary of earth and sea, mowed down some baby mangroves and squashed a frog or two. Tepid water splashed against its grille, the enormous tires grabbed for purchase in the muck, spun like eggbeaters in batter.

For a time the car became a fat unwieldy boat, confused wakes spreading from its bulky hull as it churned and labored onward, the exhaust pipes shooting forth twin geysers. Then water shorted out the lights and turned the fuel to poison, and with a deflating suddenness the engine died, the ripples calmed, and the wild ride was over.

The car had traveled maybe fifty feet from shore and was immersed not much deeper than the bottom of its doors.

Even so, Fred's knees were shaky when he climbed out and stepped cautiously into the mild water. Sure enough, the muck was soft and swirly beneath his feet; his leg spiked through to midthigh and he trudged ashore with the dazed gait of the sole survivor of some dreadful wreck.

Pineapple met him at the water's edge and, together, they gazed out at the car. Moonlight played on its windshield and on the pleats of its folded-down top.

After a moment's contemplation Piney said, "Not exactly what I'd call sunk."

Fred said, "It'll settle. Give it time to settle."

They gave it time.

Fred wanted to believe he saw the car subsiding. He thought the top of the back fender had been exposed at first, and now it wasn't. The water made a short horizon that was just at the seam where the trunk opened.

Piney was strolling back and forth around the clearing. After a while he said, "Fred, people who live in houses, you think they do things half-ass?"

Fred reclaimed his smokes and lit one up. Match light played off his cupped hand. "You saying I did this half-ass?"

"I didn't say that. I was just wondering."

They watched the car some more. Crickets rasped. The mangroves gave off a waxy smell.

Pineapple said, "Better swamps up north."

"You keep saying that," said Fred. "What the fuck's a better swamp?"

"Deeper."

"Deeper," said Fred. "Now you say deeper. You could've said that before."

Piney shrugged. "Deeper's better. Kind of obvious I thought."

They watched the car. Sometimes it seemed to be settling lower and other times it didn't. Then it started making noises.

"D'ya hear that?" asked Fred.

It was a faint scratching sound, but then it stopped. Soon it started in again.

"Chassis rubbing through the muck," Fred theorized. "Wait and see, once it breaks that crust on top, it's gonna settle good and quick."

But the Caddy didn't settle noticeably faster, and after a time the scratching changed to a weak but rhythmic thump that carried with it just a hint of metallic ring. Pineapple looked at Fred. "That sound is dry," he said. "That's not an underwater sound."

Fred said nothing, listened hard. The car seemed finally to be diving slowly downward. The thumping got just slightly louder, took on the insistence of a pleading knock. Then there was a sound that could only have come from a human throat, a whimper.

The hair stood up on the back of Piney's neck and he was wading out before he'd stopped to think.

"The trunk," Fred hollered at his back, "I think it opens underneath the dash."

Piney plodded on. He sank knee-deep, thigh-deep, crotch-deep in the muck. His puny and heroic steps seemed to break some stalemate between gravity and friction, and the Caddy started sinking faster. Water gurgled as the bottom bubbled under it like cooking oatmeal. By the time he reached the car, the door was sealed by marl. He propped his hands against the bottom of the window frame and, straining with his skinny arms, he lifted and wriggled free of the mud and managed to flop over the door, landing face-first in the driver's seat. He found the lever, yanked it.

The trunk latch opened, the lid popped up.

Fred saw water cascading over the lip of the trunk as if it were a failing dam. The weight of the intruding sea made the Caddy's stern tilt downward, it groaned with the shift in its balance. Water flooded in, little eddies twisted around the tail fins.

Fred sensed a different kind of movement too, sensed it before he saw it. A human being was struggling toward the air; he knew it. A moment passed; breath stalled but the water didn't rest.

Then, ghostly white as they emerged into the moonlight, a pair of hands came groping forward, waved at nothing then found a flange of metal to hold on to. The fragile fingers clenched down hard and, with the stunning purity of effort that brings a baby bird to the high edge of its nest, Suki Sperakis, her hair wild, her eyes wide-open but unseeing, raised her bruised and ashen face.

FIFTEEN

Pineapple half-dragged, half-carried her ashore. His knees finally buckled at the last couple of gummy sloshing steps, and he deposited her, wet and tattered, as gently as he could at the vague edge of the land.

Fred leaned down, clutched her underneath the arms, and pulled her farther up the clearing. He looked down at her as he moved her. Her eyes had closed though the lids were twitching in the moonlight. Her dress had a pattern of apples and pears. It was torn here and there, and streaked with an oily dust that the water couldn't wash away. Bruises were beginning to ripen on her arms; one cheek was red with shallow nicks, pitted like a strawberry. Her neck was stamped with the handprints of her failed murderer, the smeared outlines of fingers and thumbs could be read in a ghastly pink just starting to take on tinges of sickly green and purple. "Jesus Christ," he muttered.

He became aware of the obscene wet lump of fifties in his pocket. He moved off to light a cigarette.

Piney shook water off his clothes, caught his breath, knelt down near her swollen face. He brushed wet and tangled hair back from her forehead, and murmured nervously, "You're gonna be okay, you're gonna be okay."

Her eyes opened. They didn't open very wide this time, but there was sense in them, they tracked. Very softly, through a ravaged voice box that felt like it had been pummeled with a bat, she said, "Tried to kill me."

Pineapple shushed her, stroked her hair.

"Lazslo." She swallowed. Swallowing burned and ached like she was choking down a jagged piece of gravel. "Tried to strangle me."

Piney nodded, kept his hand against her forehead. "He muffed it."

Fred had moved close again, was standing over them. "We'll put that sonofabitch in jail," he said.

"Rest now," Piney said.

She let her eyes fall closed. What came was not exactly sleep but some blessed suspension of fear and pain. Her body weighed nothing. The air was no temperature. She heard the crickets and frogs and the two men talking nervously, but the sounds came from some other world. Time passed, was measured not in minutes but in tiny increments of healing, of remembering how to be alive.

At some point she heard somebody say, "Doesn't matter if it gets us in trouble. We have to get her to the hospital."

Through her stupor she understood that there was danger in the words. She moaned. When she remembered how to open her eyes, Piney was crouching next to her again, his face was close. She turned toward him, said, "No."

"But—"

She reached out weakly, seized his wrist. "There's more of them," she rasped.

"More of who?" asked Fred.

Suki moved a little. She whispered: "Russians." Sensation was slowly coming back to her. She realized that the ground was hard and that her clothes were wet. She said, "I'm cold."

Fred and Piney looked at one another. They had no food or water; there were no blankets. It was late at night; they were miles from the highway or a phone. They'd been hired by a killer to lose a corpse, and now the intended victim was talking crazy and didn't want to go to the hospital.

"Cold," Suki said again, and closed her eyes.

Piney stroked her head and looked at the friend who'd thought this was a good idea, a lot of fun. Fred threw down his cigarette and started gathering driftwood for a fire.

Aaron Katz did not sleep well that night.

He'd strolled home from his humiliating evening at Lucia's doubting that this dinky little town would suit him, after all. Too few choices. One straight, attractive woman turned out to be a liar or a flake, and your chances of ever finding romance were significantly reduced. Made a fool of in one good restaurant, your options for a decent meal shrank radically. For some brief moments he almost missed New York, where you could fall out with three-quarters of your friends, end your marriage, write off entire neighborhoods and whole sectors of the economy, and still have plenty to do. That was the glory of the city, and for several moments on that glum walk home he almost missed it—until he remembered it was January, and he was strolling in shirtsleeves, and not looking over his shoulder as he strolled, and that he hadn't had a headache or a bellyache in months.

He sucked in some mild salty air, listened to the rustling of the fronds, and reminded himself this was simply one bad evening, and you didn't go sour on a whole new life because of one bad evening.

He reached the Mangrove Arms, walked through the dark office and the kitchen to his father's back apartment. He found the old man asleep in a chair with his Walkman on. Aaron eased off his headphones, reedy Big Band clarinets still singing through the tiny speakers. Sam didn't wake up so Aaron tossed a blanket over him, kissed him on the forehead, and let him be.

In his own room he undressed and washed, and propped up his pillows to read in bed. Even as his eyes grew heavy he understood that sleep was going to elude him, but after half an hour he put down his book and switched off the light.

Soon he gave in to twisting the sheet, tormenting the pillow. But, though his body was restless and twitchy, his ego, at least, was gradually going to sleep. His embarrassment at Lucia's shrank down to its rightful size as something trivial, his disappointment revealed itself as off the mark. And as those things receded, concern for Suki came forward and grew.

That was what mattered; of course it was. This concern for her, stunning in its plainness, came to him unbidden and surprised him by its potency. Why hadn't she appeared? He removed himself from the question, and discovered an unselfish interest that perhaps was no more than common decency, but could stand equally well as the start of real affection. Like his father said: I don't worry; I care. There's a difference.

He rolled over and looked at the clock. It was 12:51, much too late to call. But caring had prerogatives that went far beyond issues of pique and jealousy and proper form. He switched on the bedside lamp, found the scrap of paper with her number on it, dialed.

The phone rang four times, five, then Suki's answering machine picked up. The sound of her voice made Aaron swallow now. He left a message. He just wanted to know she was okay. She didn't owe him any explanations or apologies. He just needed to hear she was all right.

Fred and Piney slept a little bit but by first light they were wide awake.

The black sky turned lavender and seemed to take on roundness, billowed like a vast balloon and floated off the ocean. Detail came back into the world, and Fred saw to his surprise that Lazslo's Caddy had continued settling after all. By now it was sunk entirely except for the gleaming chrome peaks of its tail fins and the very last pleat of its folded-down top. "Whaddya know," he said by way of eulogy: "It died like a convertible."

Piney said nothing, just glanced over at the sleeping woman who was supposed to have been buried with the car.

After a while the sun rose. The sky exploded yellow and heat uncoiled like a snapped rug across the surface of the water. Suki squirmed against the ground, blinked herself more or less awake, struggled up onto her elbows. Piney, vigilant, crouched down to reassure her.

"How are you today?" he asked.

By way of answer she reached up carefully to touch her discolored neck, then nodded. "Who are you?" she said.

"No one special," he admitted. "Name's Pineapple."

"Pineapple," rasped Suki. She was hurt and she was lying on the ground. She was helpless. Helplessness bred either blind trust or utter terror; trust used up less strength. But she wanted more convincing. She looked harder at Pineapple, the ascetic face, the scraggly no-color beard. "I've seen you," she said, "where?"

"Whitehead Street," he said. "I hold a sign."

She closed her eyes. Pieces of the world were re-forming for her. She saw Whitehead Street behind her eyelids, the banyan trees and Bahama shutters. "Whitehead and Rebecca. You sit there on the curb."

"I've seen you too," said Piney. "Usually you're on your bike."

Suki half-smiled at that. On her bike. The idea reminded her that there were such things as simple joy and safety. On her bike in sunshine with a whole universe of air to breathe.

Fred was standing a little ways away, pacing and smoking. Now he moved closer. "We just happened to end up with the car," he said. "Shouldn't have done it but I did it. Didn't mean no harm. No hard feelings, right?"

It was a pretty feeble explanation, but Suki said, "I guess."

Piney said, "Do you remember what happened, how you got here?"

Suki looked away. She bit her lip, the upper one. She nodded.

Piney said, "You should really see a doctor, go to the police."

Suki wriggled on the ground. Her violet eyes got wild. "Maybe," she said. "Might be too big for the police."

Fred threw down his cigarette. "Too big?"

"A Mafia. They're everywhere. Hong Kong. Libya. Stolen jewels. Plutonium."

Fred looked at Piney. Piney looked at Fred.

"You think I'm crazy," Suki said. It was not a question.

There was a silence. The tide was coming in. Their clearing was shrinking at the edges and Lazslo's Caddy was totally submerged.

"Think it if you want," Suki went on. "I don't blame you. But look, I'm supposed to be dead. I'm safer if they think I am. That much makes sense, right?"

The two men looked at one another. They weren't betting if it made sense or it didn't.

"Can you hide me for a day or two?" said Suki.

"Hide you?" Piney said.

"Till I think things through a little."

Piney looked over at his roommate. Fred had the guilty lump of fifties in his pocket and they both knew that they owed her.

"Well, sure," said Piney. "But we don't exactly have a home."

"We have a home," corrected Fred. "But it's a hot dog."

"A hot dog," Suki said. She reached up and gently touched her ravaged throat. She laughed weakly and it felt like a fist was pushing up her gullet. "They'd never think of looking for me there."

SIXTEEN

A round ten o'clock that morning, when Ludmila the Belorussian housekeeper let herself into Lazslo's apartment to clean, the first thing she noticed was a meaty smell. It was somewhat strong and gamy, but not at all unpleasant. It smelled like salt and iron, like a butcher shop in the old country, where the refrigeration wasn't very good, and streaks of blood and smears of fat would collect at the low edges of dented pans. She thought, with vague surprise, that Lazslo had been cooking without her help, feeding some pointy-breasted American tramp to get her into bed. But when she went into the kitchen she found no pots on the stove, no dirty dishes on the counter, except for one tall glass with a stain of bourbon at the bottom.

Curious, she looked around the living room. No rumples in the sofa, no pillows on the floor; no lipstick-covered filters in the ashtrays.

She moved into the hallway that led to the bedroom. The meaty smell got more insinuating as she went, though the corridor was as it always was, save for the crookedness of the sports prints and Harley posters on the walls.

The bedroom, on the other hand, was a housekeeper's hell.

Bureau drawers had been yanked open, they gushed out sleeves and cuffs and collars. The dresser top had been swept clean of change and papers and souvenirs, all of which were strewn along the carpet. In the master bathroom, the medicine chest mirror hung askew on flaccid hinges, jars and bottles had been smashed against the tiled floor. Through the open closet door, Ludmila saw anarchic twisted piles of silk and linen clothes, tormented hangers poking through them.

And on the bed, wearing tight jeans and a mostly open shirt, lay Lazslo, his throat cut ear to ear.

The blood had all drained out of him. Some of it was matted in his chest hair but most had spilled onto the sheet, giving its folds the engorged and spongy look of springtime moss. His eyes were open, the irises rolled up toward the brows. It was an expression that in old church paintings suggested ecstasy, but Lazslo didn't look ecstatic. He looked confused, affronted, his shattered arrogance still unbelieving that things were turning out so badly. The two sections of his neck were stretched into a ghastly smile by the weight of his head; his gold chain had found its way into the appalling slot and was lodged against a notch in his windpipe.

Ludmila looked at him a while. She didn't scream, her stomach didn't turn. She was neither glad nor sorry he was dead. His dying, probably, had something to do with the false-bottom vases with the little tape machines inside, but that was not Ludmila's problem. She did what she was told, she didn't have to understand what happened.

She went to the telephone and called Ivan Fyodorovich Cherkassky. She told him what she'd found.

Cherkassky expressed his shock and sorrow. A violent country, barbaric, he complained. A terrible crime, a tragedy. Lazslo's uncle would be devastated. But in the meantime, Ludmila, as a good citizen, must call the police, and only the police. Did she understand?

She understood. She called the cops. And by the time the lady officer arrived with her clipboard and her walkie-talkie, Ludmila had forgotten most of the little English she could speak. She was sent home, having been told she might be asked more questions later. She got back on her scooter and she gave the dead man no more thought.

* * *

The taxi driver took one look at the three of them and demanded payment in advance.

Two dirtbags, one with shoes, and a beat-up barefoot woman in a torn and filthy dress, calling from a pay phone on the highway late on a weekday morning. God knew what the story was. Coke-whore, maybe. Some wacko triangle with sex rights in dispute. No concern of his. This was the Keys, where lost souls were free to travel their chosen route to hell, as long as they could pay the fare. The driver looked surprised when Fred handed him a new if somewhat soggy fifty.

They drove from Big Coppitt past the Navy base at Boca Chica, past the rancid clutter of Stock Island, retracing the path that Fred had driven, barely twelve hours before, in Lazslo's Cadillac. At the top of Key West they turned left, toward the ocean side, and when they'd passed the houseboats but before they'd reached the airport, at a stretch where there was nothing but mangroves on one side and Cow Key Channel on the other, Fred leaned over the backseat and said, "Here's good."

"Here?" the driver said. He looked around as he applied the brake and he saw no reason in the world why anyone would stop there. No houses, no motels; no liquor store, no welfare office. Inwardly he shook his head. Just three dirtbags going from nowhere to another nowhere.

They got out of the cab and walked into the mangroves. The air smelled of iodine and the limestone rocks were warm beneath their feet. Not much more than twenty yards in, with the road noise already swallowed up in foliage and the light sliced into jungle patterns by overhanging boughs, Suki caught her first glimpse of the hot dog. She saw the service window cut into the swelling roll, the squiggles of mustard embossed on the frank. "It's adorable," she said.

Pineapple and Fred just looked at one another.

With Piney leading, they climbed the cinder blocks that led to the ripped screen door on the side. Suki entered, saw the sauerkraut steamer and the pronged rotisserie, her hosts' bedrolls and their eating kits. Then, in a broken mirror hanging from a peg above the sink, she saw herself.

She wished she hadn't. Her spirit had found its own mood, independent of her body, and except for the raw ache in her throat and the bruises on her ribs, she'd been feeling pretty good. She'd had no way of knowing just how abused she looked. Her nicked cheek had gotten puffy, the little cuts congealed into a warm knot whose swelling reached to the outside corner of her eye. She'd bled just slightly from a small wound at the back of her scalp, and her hair was stuck to the blood like a bandage. The handprints on her neck had smudged and spread and darkened to a queasy unnatural violet.

She felt herself starting to cry. It wasn't from pain, and wasn't from vanity, but rather, from pity for the woman in the mirror, who seemed like someone else, the sort of universal victim that Suki never imagined she would be. But she didn't want to cry, she didn't see the point. She bit her lip and choked back the impulse that was riding up her ravaged gullet. The effort made her ears ring but her voice was almost normal when she said, "I've got to get cleaned up."

"No running water," Piney said. "But we've got a barrel and a basin. Works pretty good."

Suki nodded, tore her eyes away from the broken mirror. "Any chance of a needle and thread?"

"Has Suki come in?" asked Aaron Katz.

He was sitting in the kitchen at the Mangrove Arms, a damp cordless phone pressed against his ear. In front of him was a plate of cold eggs he hadn't got around to eating and a lukewarm cup of coffee he pecked at now and then.

"No," said a voice that was harried and impatient even through the drawl. "She should have but she hasn't."

"Do you know if she's out selling?"

Donald Egan fiddled with his cheap cigar, rounded the ash against the edge of the ashtray. "I wish I knew what my staff was doing. I wish my staff knew what my staff was doing. Is this about an ad?"

"It's a personal call," said Aaron.

Egan looked around the converted classroom that was his office. It was almost eleven, and not one of his underpaid employees had come in. The computers were switched off, vacant desks were topped with random scraps of paper and winding chains of paper clips. Wanting badly to believe that it was true, he said, "This is a place of business. We try to discourage personal calls."

"I'm afraid she might be in trouble," Aaron said.

"Wouldn't surprise me," the publisher blithely answered. He didn't know exactly what he meant by it. It was just the sort of thing he said to show that he was worldly and tough-minded, like a real newspaperman had to be.

Aaron didn't remember standing up but he was pacing now, his coffee sloshing in the mug. "I mean real trouble. Like danger. Don't you even give a shit?"

Too late as usual, Egan's humanity woke up. He said, "Look, if you have reason to believe—"

Aaron Katz hung up on him, slid his coffee mug along the table. He paced some more and his burgeoning frustration and responsibility surprised him, filled him with a reckless prideful need to act.

He found that he was headed for the door. He didn't know where he was going or what he'd do, just that he had to feel like he was helping, doing something, if only wandering blindly through a town he was still learning, on an uninvited crusade to help a woman whom he barely knew.

SEVENTEEN

"Attempted murder?" said the sergeant who answered the phone for Key West's one-man homicide squad. "We're kind of busy with a successful one right now. 'Zit an emergency?"

This struck Suki as an odd question, and she was less sure than ever that calling the local cops was really such a good idea. "I'm supposed to be dead," she said.

"Is it a domestic situation?" asked the cop.

"I've learned a good way to avoid domestic violence," Suki said. "I live alone."

"Are you in danger at this moment?"

"I wish I knew."

"Don't we all. Hold on a minute." He vanished from the line.

Suki was standing at a pay phone whose base was sunk in a square hole in concrete just inside the seawall. She looked down at the ocean. Tiny birds were pecking bubbles at the shoreline; farther out, egrets were stalking, their necks as fast as snakes. She'd sewn her dress and washed her hair, and now she felt it drying in the sun.

After a while another voice came on the line. "Lieutenant Stubbs," it said. "Can I help you?"

Suki repeated her complaint.

"Attempted murder is a very heavy charge," said Stubbs. "Are we talking battery? Are you saying someone hit you?"

"I'm saying someone strangled me, gave me up for dead, then tried to drown me in a car."

"Sounds like more than battery."

"Thank you."

"And your assailant, you know him?"

"Thought I did. Yes."

"His name?"

"Lazslo."

"Lazslo?"

"Lazslo Kalynin. Runs the T-shirt shops."

There was a pause. Suki heard a scratching sound as the phone was rubbed against a shirt. When Stubbs came on again, he said, "Where are you? I'll come talk with you in person."

"I'm at a pay phone," Suki said.

"Where do you live?" said Stubbs.

"I live on Newton Street, but I'm afraid to go there. I'm staying with some friends."

"And where do they live?" Stubbs asked, with a patience that did not come naturally.

Suki hesitated, looked out at the ocean. Pelicans were diving, then shaking water off their heads like dogs. "Lieutenant, look," she said, "the place they live, it's not exactly legal. I wouldn't want to cause them any—"

"Lady," said Stubbs, "this is homicide, not the building department. Just tell me where you'll be in fifteen minutes."

Lieutenant Gary Stubbs was leaning back against the sauerkraut steamer, a pocket-size spiral notebook in his hand. He didn't wear a uniform, but a rumpled khaki suit that creased up like a concertina behind the knees and at the elbows. He was more thickly built than was ideal for the climate, with a bullish neck that always chafed against his collar. He had a squashed nose and shadowed jowls that never looked quite shaved. He riffled backward through his notes and said, "Let's make sure I have this right. You met him in the course of selling ads?"

"That's right," said Suki. "Six, eight weeks ago." She was sitting in the hot dog's only chair, a fifties dinette job with rusted legs and a torn red vinyl seat. Fred and Pineapple, congenitally shy of cops, had gone for a stroll by the ocean.

"And he was interested in you. Romantically."

"Apparently," she said.

"But what you wanted from him—"

"Look, Lieutenant," Suki interrupted. "It was dumb. I told you that. I thought if I could get a really down-and-dirty story about the T-shirt shops—"

"They'd fold their tents and go away," said Stubbs, "and Duval Street would be a funky locals' drag again."

"That was the fantasy, I guess," said Suki.

"And in the meantime," said the cop, "you could stop selling ads for a living."

"Exactly. Be a reporter instead."

"That's a move up?" asked Stubbs.

"Everything's relative. To me it is."

"Lois Lane."

Suki gestured upward toward the concave wiener in the roll. "Except when I needed rescuing I got Pineapple and Fred instead of Superman. And things blew up before I could file my story."

"Your story," said Stubbs, frowning at his notes. He leaned more heavily against the steamer, shifted the cross of his ankles. "That's the part that sort of loses me. Russian gangsters? Money laundering?"

"Those stores," said Suki, "the rents they pay. They can't be making money."

"I've heard that theory before," said Stubbs. "Look, Ms. Sperakis, no offense but you're a typical Key Wester. You can't stand change. Whenever something comes along—"

"This isn't just something coming along, Lieutenant. This isn't a McDonald's where there used to be a fritter stand. This is organized crime. The things he said to me—"

"While trying to seduce you, Ms. Sperakis. Let's be frank, okay? Men have been known to fling an awful lot of bullshit while trying to seduce a woman."

"Let's be frank, Lieutenant: Every woman past the age of twelve is well aware of that . . . And for a while, yeah, he was bullshitting, I totally agree. But then it changed. He was opening up, cleaning out—"

"Ms. Sperakis," said the cop, "did he ever say to you, 'I, Lazslo Kalynin, am a member of the Russian Mafia'?"

"Well no, of course he—"

"Did he ever say, 'My uncle is a mobster. These stores are fronts for something else'?"

"Of course he wouldn't 've—"

"He was talking headlines, generalities. Bragging. Trying to sound interesting."

"He succeeded. He said they had plutonium."

"Plutonium? He told you that?"

"He hinted at it."

"Hinted. Ah."

Suki hesitated, bit her lip. Then she leaned far forward on her dinette chair and wrapped both hands around her battered violet throat. "Lieutenant," she said, "if I wasn't onto something, why did this happen to me?"

The homicide detective looked away a moment, ran an index finger back and forth beneath his nose. "Ms. Sperakis—"

"And stop calling me Ms. Sperakis. My name is Suki."

"Suki," he said, and he blew air between his teeth. "If I knew why people hurt people I could show them how to stop, and then I'd win the Nobel Prize and could retire."

"This happened because he'd said too much to me and I think you should call the FBI."

"The FBI?" said Stubbs, and despite himself he gave a mirthless and percussive laugh. "The FBI? Suki, jam-packed 747s are falling from the sky, large public buildings are being blown off their foundations, small wars are being fought against skinhead lunatics in Idaho and Texas, and I'm supposed to call the FBI because you don't like the T-shirt shops?"

Suki stewed a minute, her swollen face throbbed underneath her eye. Then she said, "You call me typical because I don't like change? I call *you* typical because you don't believe the outside world could really touch this place, that anything big could happen—"

He shushed her with a raise of his hand, said, "Suki, let's not argue . . . On a slightly different subject, do you believe in karma?"

"Karma?" she said, and she twisted up her mouth. Okay, this was Key West, but still, you didn't expect to be talking karma with a cop. "I'm like most people, I guess. I believe in it when it proves me right."

"Lazslo Kalynin was killed sometime last night."

"What?"

"Burglary. Looks like he came home at the wrong time, got his throat cut."

Suki swallowed, searched her heart for sympathy or vindication. She found neither, just hollowness and bafflement. "Burglary," she said. "Funny coincidence."

"Place was ransacked. Jewelry missing, wallet taken. Seems like there was a pretty good fight. He had lacerations on his face, contusions on his ribs and shins, a deep bruise in his groin."

"I did that," said Suki.

"Good shot," said the cop.

"Look, anyone can fake a burglary."

"His uncle came down to identify the body," said the cop. "Cried like a baby. Almost fainted."

"So what does that prove?" Suki said. "Mobsters don't faint? Criminals don't cry? . . . Look, he talked too much, they killed him. Isn't that—?"

"Suki, listen," said the cop. "I'm sorry for what happened to you, but the person who attacked you is dead, and his death is being treated as a burglary gone wrong. End of story."

Suki swiveled on the dinette seat, raked fingers through her thick black hair, looked disgustedly away. She expelled a deep and angry sigh and said, "I knew I shouldn't 've called the goddam locals."

It was meant to sting, and it did. Stubbs's pink face took on the red of steak, his neck swelled against his cinching collar. For a moment his face sucked inwards like he was swallowing his teeth, but the seditious words escaped. Softly, with an anguished wryness, he said, "You don't think I agree with you?"

There was a silence. Suki turned toward him once more. His flush was gradually subsiding but his hands were white as they squeezed the metal counter.

He went on, "It goes no farther, right? The department is a goddam mess. Politics. Butt covering. PR. They want it murmured there's a Mafia in town? Something they couldn't possibly handle? I'm homicide, Suki, not administration. I don't decide what things get called. Motive: burglary. Officially, that's the story."

Suki's stare grabbed out for his eyes. "And unofficially?"

He looked down at his feet. "There is no unofficially. So what'll you do from here?"

"I don't know. I'm afraid to go home."

"I'll bring you home," Stubbs offered.

"And what then? What happens when they find out Lazslo botched his job and the woman he spilled his guts to is still alive and talking? What then, Lieutenant?"

Stubbs didn't answer.

Suki settled back against the rusty dinette chair, gestured toward the pronged rotisserie, the little propane fridge. "With the protection of the Key West cops I guess I'll stay right here."

Stubbs looked around at the torn screen door, the leaning sack of garbage with some unnameable fluid dampening its bottom. "Look," he said, "you can't stay—"

Suki said, "And if you can't do anything to help me, at least keep it to yourself that I'm alive."

The lieutenant sucked his teeth, pocketed his notebook, pushed his bulky body up from the sauerkraut steamer. He stepped over Pineapple's bedroll and headed for the door. "This job really sucks sometimes," he said. "You never heard me say this but I'll see what I can do."

EIGHTEEN

By early afternoon, Gennady Petrovich Markov had polished off a quart of vodka, and though his stomach burned and his living room swayed under him and his eyes pulsed in and out of focus, his mind evinced a stubborn and perverse refusal to be drunk.

With ruthless clarity he saw his nephew stretched out on the gurney, bloodless and just faintly blue, his sundered neck appalling, his face as waxy and pearlescent as a squid. He smelled the stink that tried to cover death, the antiseptics and preservatives. He heard the voices of the cops and coroner, gruff and clumsy in their sympathies in spite of all their practice. He kept drinking. His ears rang and his vision blurred but the things he didn't want to think about just got more cruelly vivid.

Around two o'clock Ivan Fyodorovich Cherkassky came by to offer his condolences. Silently, he slipped into the living room; silently, he sat at the end of the sofa, his slight stiff body barely denting the cushion. The two men stared blankly at one another, and after a moment Cherkassky said, "A terrible thing. I am sorry."

Markov was hunkered in an enormous leather armchair, sunk so deep that it was hard to tell where the chair ended and its occupant began. He tried to fix his gaze on his old comrade, but nothing would hold its proper shape. Cherkassky's waferish body rippled as in reflecting water. His scooped-out face shrank inward like a drying apple. Markov said to him, "You are not sorry. You hated him."

Cherkassky took no umbrage, just strove to be precise. "I did not hate him. He worried me. He was too careless, too American."

"And so you had him killed."

"You think I did this thing?" Cherkassky said, his voice rising by just the slightest increment. "In this wiolent country of drugs and guns and shooting while you change a tire on your car, you think I did this thing?"

Markov seemed to bloat up in his chair, his fingertips clawed the arc of brass tacks that pinned down the upholstery. "You made him kill the girl. That was punishment enough."

"Yes, it was," Cherkassky said. "For him."

"For him? What is it you are saying, Ivan?"

Cherkassky turned away a moment, looked through the window and across the garden to the Gulf, to mangrove islands hovering on pillows of distant glare. "I am saying nothing. Only I agree. To kill the girl, that was punishment enough."

With difficulty, Gennady Markov reached across his heaving chest, retrieved the glass of vodka from the table next to him. He drank. He said, "Ivan, if you have done this thing, to punish me, no matter why, I will never forgive you. Never. You will be my enemy till one of us is dead."

Cherkassky listened. His scooped-out face wobbled in Markov's vision but its expression didn't change. After a moment, he said, "Gennady, you are sad, you are drunk. I understand and I take no offense at what you say, these accusations. Tomorrow you will apologize and of course, as we are old friends, I will accept."

Markov tried to turn away. The ripples of his shirt twisted up across his belly and his bottom squeaked against the leather seat, but he couldn't really move. He stayed silent and looked down at the floor.

"And I will tell you one more thing," Cherkassky softly said. "You will not hear it now but when you are ready you will hear it. This terrible thing that has happened, it is a grief that will end, and that will spare you far more heartache than it caused. Believe me, I know. Life will become much easier for you, Gennady. You will have one less thing to care about."

Aaron Katz was unaccustomed to wandering the streets.

He worked day and night. He was organized and disciplined. He went to places when he had a reason to go to them, and unlike many in Key West, he usually went to them directly.

But now it was the middle of a working day and he was wandering. He wandered past Hemingway House, tour buses lined up along its slapdash brick wall; past Southernmost Point with its Indians selling conch shells; up to the gay end of Duval Street, past the elegant and well-run and fully booked guest houses such as his would never be.

He wandered, and he tried to figure out just why he was doing it. Was he being chivalrous or pigheaded? Maybe, at the end of this sleeplessness and disruption, it would turn out, pure and simple, that Suki had stood him up. Changed her mind. Got a better offer. Happened to some poor lonely bastard every day.

But he kept going. Past sunglass shops and ice cream stores, places that sold pornography and bathing suits. Tourists spun postcard racks in front of him, or sat on patios in silly hats, sipping cappuccino.

Then he saw something that didn't quite register until after he'd strolled past it: a shop that wasn't open.

It was a busy day in the midst of tourist season, pale visitors were milling and buying, and this one store was closed up tight and dark. Aaron backed up to look at it more closely. In its dim window were racks and racks of T-shirts. Some had spangles, some had pictures, some had slogans. Some racks said SPECIAL TODAY and some said DECALS

FREE. On the big glass pane of the front door of the store, a hand-scrawled cardboard sign had been crookedly taped up. It said: CLOSE DUE TO DETH.

The message was only four words long, but Aaron read it several times, as if it held a nagging and laconic riddle. Suki was involved with Lazslo, and Lazslo ran the T-shirt shops. The T-shirt shop was closed and Suki had not been heard from and somebody had died. He walked on, turning the riddle this way and that, looking for the strand of logic that would make it all come clear. He walked past smoothie stands and bars, galleries and restaurants. Yellow sun bounced off metal roofs and a line of shadow ran down the middle of the street.

On the next block there was another T-shirt store. It too was closed and dim. It too had a cardboard sign in the window of the recessed front door. This one said: DEATH IN FAMILY—NOT TODAY.

But as Aaron was walking past, the door swung open and a young man stepped out, turning around to lock the place behind him. Aaron studied him a moment. He wasn't especially tall, but his arms were huge and his back muscles quaked with even the smallest move-ments. He wore no shirt, just thick suspenders crisscrossed on his massive shoulders. His hair was long and tangled; at the nape of his neck it merged indistinctly with the soft fur that grew in patches down to his waist.

His back looked unfriendly, show-offish, menacing. Aaron strug-gled against a reluctance born partly of shyness and partly of an idi-otic jealousy, and approached him as the second lock was clicking shut. He said, "Excuse me. By any chance, is your name Lazslo?"

The fellow spun toward him. His eyes were hard and narrow. For an instant they flashed suspicious or maybe spooked. He said a sim-ple no and began to walk away.

Aaron followed, gesturing backward toward the sign. "Who died?"

The muscular man was breaking into the heavy flow of walking traffic on Duval. Grudgingly, a little off the beat, with a slightly gut-tural *h* and langorous vowels, he said, "Soon everyone will hear."

They were moving down the busy sidewalk now, Aaron dodging tourists and racks of souvenirs as he tried to keep pace with the other man's bounding steps. "Hear what?" he said. "This is what I'm asking."

The man with the suspenders kept rolling. Couples parted to let him pass between them. Without looking at Aaron, he said, "Is not your business. Leaf me alone."

"But—"

"I tell you go away."

Aaron didn't go away. He wanted to know and he made a mistake. He put his hand on the young man's shoulder, said, "Look, all I'm asking—"

The other man was tired of the questions and it made him angry that this annoying stranger had touched him. With the coiled economy of the practiced fighter, he pivoted quickly, almost nonchalantly, and grabbed two handfuls of Aaron's shirt.

Aaron just barely had time to be befuddled. He hadn't been in a fight since junior high school; he'd had neither strength nor conviction for it even then; fighting, he felt, was for kids whose fathers hadn't taught them reason. But now, by reflex, he defensively reached out and held the other man's arms. The arms were thick as fence posts and fibrous as snakes and they could not be held.

The man looked at Aaron with a calm, impersonal malice, gave a quick sharp pull and then a shove.

Aaron's head whipped forward as his torso rocked back, and he stumbled for a step or two until a parking meter caught him square between the shoulder blades. The impact knocked some air out of his lungs, sent arrows of hot pain up to his brain stem and down to his kidneys.

Nauseating starbursts appeared at the edges of his vision, and by the time his eyes had cleared, a sparse ring of passersby had gathered. They were staring at him. Not in sympathy but with embarrassed fascination for the loser. He'd become a part of their vacations,

something they'd remember; a victim of the kind of brief and pointless sidewalk brawl that Duval Street was famous for.

As for the young man with the suspenders and the giant arms, he
was half a block away, walking neither faster nor slower than he'd
walked before. Aaron did not go after him.

NINETEEN

He went back home instead, and the first thing he saw as he walked into the office of the Mangrove Arms was a crippled blind chihuahua curled up on the front desk, its scaly black nose resting against the cool metal of the service bell. The dog just barely lifted up its hoary head as Aaron entered. Its white eyes panned futilely as its twitching nostrils tested the air to find the new arrival.

Sam Katz was sitting in a chair behind the desk. His new friend Bert was sitting next to him, wearing a shirt of emerald green with a navy chalk stripe and a collar whose wings came halfway down his chest. The two old men were in the middle of a game of gin. Each had a stack of quarters at his elbow, and a ragged pile of cards was spilling over between them. Sam said, "Ah, here he is."

Bert stood up, gnarly hand extended. He said, "I come to visit the old man."

Aaron reached across the counter to shake his hand; the motion stretched the lingering pain down from the valley between his shoulder blades. Distractedly, he said, "Great. That's great."

Sam said, "You went out, I didn't know you went."

It was not an accusation, not exactly, but Aaron, good son, felt guilty nonetheless. "Had a couple things to do," he said. Absently, he petted the chihuahua. With every stroke, hairs the length of eyelashes fluttered from its scalp.

His father looked at him. Sam Katz forgot a lot of things, and a lot of other things passed him by entirely. But he knew his son. He said, "Aaron, something wrong?"

Aaron, a pathetic liar, said, "No, Pop. No."

There was a pause. The dog had exhausted itself, it wheezed and lay down flat again. Then Bert said, "There was a call for you. A guy Evans, Edwards, something like that."

"We wrote it down," said Sam. "Better we should write it down. Where'd I put the paper?"

He patted pockets till he found it, handed it to Aaron. Aaron looked at it then headed for the door behind the desk.

The old men went back to their game of gin.

Sam fiddled with his hearing aid, said, "Wait a second. Been too long, now I can't remember what's been played."

His friend said, "Tough titty, we're playin' cards heah."

"But I'll throw what you picked up already," Sam complained.

"Then I guess I'm gonna win," said Bert.

"It isn't fair," said Sam.

"How sweet it is," said Bert, and he reached out to pet his dog for luck.

"No way," said Suki. "Forget about it."

It was late afternoon. Inside the hot dog the light was getting slanty and yellow, motes of dust gleamed golden against the dull chrome of the counters. Pineapple was moving with his bedroll toward the ripped screen door. "We sleep outside a lot of the time," he said. "Really. Don't we, Fred?"

"Yeah," said Fred, halfheartedly. In October they did, or April. But this was January. Sunsets were early and the ground was cold by midnight. Sometimes a low silver mist, just barely visible, curled up from the salt puddles in the moonlight. Noses ran. Fred's knees were still stiff from the night before.

Pineapple said, "You'll have more room. A little privacy."

"I don't need more room," said Suki, though, looking around the wiener she had to admit it would be very cramped for three. A face next to the propane fridge. A backside folded to fit under the sink. The leaning sack of trash, at least, would have to go. "I can sleep up on the counter."

"You roll over," said Fred, "it's the 'kraut on one side and a long drop on the other."

"It's all settled," said Pineapple, though the truth was that neither he nor Fred was moving toward the screen door all that fast.

"Look," Suki said. "Why not wait till nighttime to decide? See how cold it gets."

Fred looked hopefully at Piney. Piney just tugged lightly at his scraggly beard.

Suki took advantage of their hesitation. "Good," she said. "And in the meantime, could I ask someone to do me a big favor?"

"Name it," Piney said.

Her mouth began to open but then she seemed to think again. "No," she said. "Forget it. It isn't fair to ask."

"What?" said Piney.

Suki had been standing. She plopped down now on the edge of the dinette chair, leaned an elbow on her knee. She said. "What if they have someone watching my apartment? To see if I come home."

Piney said, "Why would they expect you home? You're supposed to be . . . ya know . . . "

Fred said, "Even Lazslo thought you were . . . ya know—"

"Even so—" said Suki.

"What's the favor?" Piney asked.

Suki breathed deep through her battered throat. "I would dearly love," she said, "some clean clothes and a toothbrush and a lipstick."

*   *   *

Aaron, alone in his room, was dazed when he got off the phone with Donald Egan.

There was too much he didn't understand, too much he had to swallow all at once. Lazslo Kalynin had been murdered. Egan had learned of it from a contact in the coroner's office. The news reminded the publisher that Suki had been leaning on him to do an investigative story about the T-shirt shops and the shadowy foreigners who ran them. Organized crime, she'd suggested. Russian Mafia. Crazy stuff. Egan had pooh-poohed it, called it paranoid and xenophobic. Now Lazslo was dead and Suki was AWOL. Probably there was no connection, no connection whatsoever. But Egan thought that since Aaron seemed to be a friend, seemed to be concerned, he should be aware at least.

So now he was aware, and felt the burden of awareness.

He put the phone down and paced. Pacing, he felt the ache between his shoulder blades travel up and down his spine. He paced to his bed and sat a moment. The bed ejected him and he paced some more. Unaware of choosing a direction, he paced through the door of his room and down the hallway to the kitchen, and through the kitchen to the office.

He found himself leaning against the front desk counter, where the ancient chihuahua was still reclining with its nose against the bell. The old men were still playing gin. Bert's stack of quarters had grown, Sam's had dwindled. Sam threw a picture card and Bert quickly scooped it up.

"Shit!" said Sam. He glanced at Aaron. "He playing jacks, or clubs?"

Then he looked at his son more closely. There was a tightness around his mouth and a slight twitch beneath the skin at the corner of his right eye. "Aaron, something's wrong," he said. "What is it? Tell me."

Aaron slumped, put more weight onto his elbow. He wasn't quite sure how he'd gotten to the office and he didn't see the point of sharing his worries with the two old men. Talking things over with his father, though—it was a habit of long standing, and old habits dug troughs that survived the deaths of many brain cells; they didn't change just because time juggled the balances of strength and comprehension and stature in the world. Aaron opened his mouth. What came out was a helpless exhalation somewhere between a sigh and a snort. He tried again, said, "It's nothing. It's too complicated."

"Nothing and too complicated," said Sam. "That's two different things."

"Complicated?" said Bert. "Hey, the whole idea of bein' here is that this is supposed to be a simple town."

"That's what I thought," Aaron said. "Till now."

"Till what?" said Sam.

Aaron sucked a deep breath in, blew it through his teeth. "Till I tried to have a bowl of pasta with a woman, and a guy I decided I was jealous of got killed, and the woman disappeared, and everybody starting whispering about a Russian Mafia."

Bert shrank down just a little at the final word, raised his cards a few inches higher. Sam didn't notice. He dropped his own hand; he'd forgotten he'd been playing gin. He said, "Mafia? Whaddya know. Bert was Mafia."

His friend said nothing, just cinched together his silver brows and shot a look at Sam.

Sam said, "What? You told me yourself. I'm not supposed to say?"

To no one in particular, Bert said, "Everything else, the man forgets. This he has to remember."

"Who could forget a thing like that?" said Sam.

"Okay, okay," said Bert. "But it's not the kinda thing ya hang a sign."

Aaron stood there. He squeezed the counter, tested its solidity. He looked through the window at the hibiscus hedge, the familiar rustling palms. The veneers of his universe were coming unglued, he needed some assurance that the planet he inhabited at that moment was still the same one that he'd lived on all his life. At last he said, "Bert—you're a mafioso?"

"Used to be," admitted Bert. He looked down but could not quite squelch a piece of smile at one end of his mouth. "They called me

Bert the Shirt. Knew how ta dress, ya know? But I been outa that game a long time now."

Aaron tried his best to look worldly and unshockable. His father playing gin with a gangster. Soviet desperadoes getting their throats cut half a dozen blocks away. Okay, no problem. Casually he said, "Know anything about the Russians?"

Bert reached out to pet his dog, short pale hairs rained down from its knobby head. "Not really. I was already out when they were comin' in. But ya think about it, how different could it be?"

"I have no idea," said Aaron.

"Customs," said Bert. "Cultures. I'm sure there's differences. But the basics are the basics. Gotta be. Loyalty. Secrecy. Revenge."

Sam said, "Revenge?"

"Can't hold the thing together wit'out revenge. Pretty basic, that."

Aaron nodded, but then his attention was diverted by his father, who was squinting upward toward the ceiling, pulling lightly on his translucent tufts of Einstein hair. "Shit," he said at last. "My Russian's going too."

"What, Pop?"

"I was trying to remember the Russian word for mafia."

Aaron said, "I think the Russian word for mafia is *mafiya.*"

Bert lifted half an eyebrow, reached out to pet his dog. "See dat?" he said. "Same word and everything. How different could they be?"

TWENTY

The worst crimes that Pineapple had ever committed were vagrancy, loitering, and, back before he'd sworn off alcohol, the occasional bout of public drunkenness. He never stole. In this he differed from Fred, who was not above slipping a couple of Slim-Jims into his pocket if the prong that held the packages was concealed by the lip of the convenience-store counter, or glomming some cigarettes if, by luck, the wire rack was left briefly unattended. Piney didn't do that. He had a superstitious dread of doing wrong and getting caught; a dread that in more solid citizens was recognized as virtue.

Still, he knew very well what it was to feel like a criminal. He understood the vague shame that descended when a storekeeper, his hard stare righteous and rude, dogged him as he made his way up and down the aisles. He knew the fugitive edginess that resulted from a cop car going by, the passenger-side cop giving him a long smirking glance as he sat there on the curb. The feeling was like confronting a blank demerit sheet that hinted nonetheless at grievous faults; a floating guilt waiting only for some act to be attached to.

He felt those things now, as he leaned his rusted bicycle with its corroded metal basket against the picket fence in front of Suki's house.

It was dusk. The street lamps were just coming on. They buzzed slightly and their salmon-colored light was brittle and metallic against the plush blue of the fading sky. Daytime flowers were closing up, their edges crinkly, like eyelids at the cusp of sleep. A few people were about, doing the things that people who lived in houses did. A woman on skates trailed a pair of cocker spaniels on a leash. Another woman carried a bag of groceries, a bouquet of lettuces poking out the top. Half a block away, a man parked his car and then emerged, his posture saying he had every right to be there.

Feeling like an intruder and a thief, Pineapple unlatched the gate that gave onto the walkway that led to Suki's porch. On either side of the wooden stairs, shrubbery beds were planted with crotons and jasmine; their dense foliage swallowed up the light, and partly masked Piney as he climbed the steps. Still, he felt like eyes were on his back as he made his way along the porch to the apartment on the ground floor left. He could not help looking over his shoulder as he skulked along, and the furtive gesture only made him feel more furtive.

As Suki had described, her door was flanked by rows of flower pots—pansies, basil, blue daze. Bending quickly, ducking his head below the level of the shrubs, Piney lifted the third pot on the right. Beneath it were a few crumbles of soft dirt and a house key. The key gleamed slightly and Pineapple found it terrifying. He hated keys— the guilty summaries of all things owned and guarded. He was here at Suki's request; he was doing her a favor. Still, to seize somebody else's key and open up a door to someone's home—the enormity of it made his mouth go dry.

His hand trembled as he fitted the key to the lock. It seemed to him that the click of the bolt could be heard all over the neighborhood. He opened the door no wider than he had to, and as soon as he had squeezed through he shut it firmly behind him. He was standing in her living room.

Vacant for only a single day, the apartment had the exaggerated stillness of a place long uninhabited. Echoes had settled. Nothing hummed. The pictures on the walls seemed lonesome, like paintings at a closed museum. The place was very dim but Piney didn't want to turn a light on.

He felt his way to Suki's bedroom, found her closet door. A plastic shopping bag caught his eye; randomly he started filling it with clothes and shoes. He moved on to her bureau, filled another sack. Suki needed underthings; Piney plucked at bras and panties. He'd been with a woman a few times in his life, though not in many years. Lacy cups and silky briefs were, for him, too foreign to be titillating; obscure artifacts from some other dimension. He crammed them into the shopping bag and slunk on toward the bathroom, grabbed her toothbrush and some lipsticks, tossed in jars and tubes and vials of things he didn't know the names of.

By now his heart was hammering and his armpits were wet. A bum in someone else's house clutching bags of someone else's things. A thief, what else? He didn't fear the Russian Mafia. He feared the neighbors, and their righteous and remorseless dogs. Someone would see him. Someone would shout. The police would come and Piney would be hurt and handcuffed before he could explain.

He breathed deep, tried without success to stretch his cramping ribs. He pressed the shopping bags against his chest then reasoned he would look less guilty if he held them by the handles.

He moved back through the living room and toward the door. With the lonesome pictures looking on, he opened it a crack. The dusk had deepened and the street lamps had grown more acid bright, they threw hard-edged shadows of fences and palms, lined the porch with dark bars that stretched out from the newels of the railing. Somewhere a television was blaring; somewhere a big dog barked. Piney held his breath, stepped outside, and locked the door behind him as quietly as he could. He pocketed the dreadful key; it was cold against his leg.

Planks creaked underfoot as he crept along the porch. His bike still leaned against the fence; he looked longingly toward it, his means of escape from the blame of locks and back into the safety of the unowned streets. A cat slunk out from underneath a car. He kept the shopping bags below the level of the shrubbery.

He reached the stairs. There were three of them, painted lumpy gray. A shadow slashed across them, and then there was a swath of naked light. Piney yearned to jump the steps and run but that would look suspicious. He moved deliberately, his eyes straight forward. His right foot was in midair, descending toward the concrete walkway, when a crouched dark form sprang up from the bushes and rammed him with a shoulder.

Piney grunted as his chest compressed and his body warped into a boomerang shape. His fingers opened up and Suki's things went flying, bras and blouses and lipsticks skittering across the yard or catching on low branches, hanging there like laundry. Piney crumpled then tumbled to the ground ahead of his attacker, and in the damp and wormy dirt at the edge of the shrubs, he did what he had long ago learned to do when someone was about to beat on him. He curled up like a baby, his bent arms cradling his face and skull, his guts and groin tucked in as far as the geography of his skinny frame allowed. He lay there and waited for the fists and feet or the knife or gun butt to start punishing his back and sides.

Gennady Petrovich Markov lay back on his feather pillows, pulled his satin sheet up snug beneath his sagging chin, and tried to quell the feeling that his bed was tipping over. If he sought balance by opening his eyes to gaze at some fixed point, he saw sickening undulations along the creases where the walls and ceiling met. If he closed his eyes to stop the rocking, he saw the murdered Lazslo. Vapors of rancid vodka were seeping from his pores and souring the room. He belched and tasted juices like the stink of the morgue.

Silently, he started once again to weep. In his drunkenness, his grief became not just a feeling but an object with weight and a geography. He pictured it as a sort of dark dense hub with many avenues leading out from it, like roads from the center of a city. His fevered mind sought to name these avenues, so that he might pick one to travel on. But all the roads save one stayed dim and featureless. The only pathway he could name was vengeance.

Ivan Fyodorovich had had his nephew killed. Of that he was nearly certain. Lazslo's vitality had made him dangerous. His transgression was that he had taken some joy in life, had had warm blood and thick semen in his tubing. The police, in their lazy embrace of the obvious, might see his murder as a side effect of robbery; and that was just as well. A Russian slain by Russians. What had the American authorities to do with that?

But if it was an affair among Russians alone, what role was left for him, Gennady Markov? He blinked wetly and considered. His life had been one dereliction after another. Dereliction of party, of country. Betrayal of the early promise of his own career in science, of the wisdom of equations, their capsules of insight as spare and beautiful as proverbs. He had always been a shirker and a coward. He knew that about himself, more or less accepted it, and went about his business; self-respect was not required for good digestion. But his handsome, avid nephew had been the only person he loved. To let his murder go unrevenged—even for a man like him, that might be one dereliction too many.

So what would he do? Ivan Fyodorovich, who despised him as only an old friend could, believed he would recant his rash words of that afternoon, and apologize.

Well, maybe he would. Apologize and reclaim his old buffoonish mildness and bide his time. He had less to care about now; Cherkassky had been kind enough to point that out. He could afford to wait. He didn't have a plan, but he had certain knowledge that his superior did not have, certain technical skills that might earn him the last word.

He would wait, and remember the bloodless Lazslo on the slab, and pick a time when he could make more trouble for Cherkassky than such a careful man should ever have to face.

TWENTY-ONE

Piney, resigned and braced, lay there for a long moment on the moist cool ground, his knees drawn up, the air growing stale in his unflexing lungs. Heartbeats slammed by, crickets marked the time, and he was almost as baffled as relieved when the dreaded kicks and slashes failed to start.

Holding his tuck, he took a deep but guarded breath that smelled of grass and stone, then moved his forearm just enough to catch a sideways look at the man who'd knocked him down and now was kneeling over him. Harsh and jagged shadows played over the man, but even so, he did not look very big or very mean or very angry. His arms hung at his sides and his hands were not balled into fists. His face looked almost as scared as Piney knew his own must look. Very tentatively, he started to uncradle.

Aaron Katz looked down, saw the scraggly beard, the slot of a mouth. Trying hard to sound commanding, to keep the quaver out of his voice, he said, "Who the hell are you?"

Piney did not presume to get up from the ground, but lay there among the broken shadows of the shrubs. "Name's Pineapple," he said.

"Why are you here? What are you doing?"

Piney blinked and squirmed. He almost started to answer, then remembered that Suki was supposed to be dead. This complicated things a lot. "You a Russian?" he asked the man who hovered over him.

"What are you talking about?" said Aaron. "What do you know about Russians?"

Piney didn't answer but he knew he'd made things worse.

Aaron said, "Look, do you tell me why the hell you're here, or do I call the cops?"

Pineapple flicked a dry tongue over dry lips, glanced around himself at the ladies' garments that festooned the yard. He'd been caught red-handed with sacks of skirts and panties and lipstick. The authorities would frown on this and the nature of the crime would not earn him the respect of the other guys in the lockup. He said, "Please don't call the cops. I ain't done nothing wrong."

Aaron hesitated, sighed, said, "Let's start over then. Why are you here?"

"Mind if I sit up?"

Aaron said nothing and Piney raised himself. Absently he began retrieving clothes and cosmetics and putting them back in the bags. Finally he said, "I can't tell you why I'm here, okay? But I'm not a thief. I have a key."

"Plenty of thieves have keys," said Aaron. But he was watching Piney put things into the shopping bag, and there was something in the almost dainty care he took that told him this man was not a burglar.

There was a pause. Aaron became acutely aware of the dampness of the earth beneath his knees. His own pulse was just now getting back to normal, the adrenaline just retreating from the edges of his twitchy muscles. He was surprised at himself for coming here, shocked at his nerve in staking out the bushes when he'd seen the sneaking figure on the porch, amazed that he'd had the chutzpah to bowl him over.

Finally he said, "Listen, I'm not looking to make trouble for you. I'm a friend of the woman that lives here."

Pineapple was freeing a bra whose strap had caught on a croton branch. "So am I," he said.

Aaron thought this doubtful. Key West was a loose town, and the climate had a way of leveling things out between the citizens and the vagrants, but there were limits here, as everywhere. He let it slide. "I'd really like to find her."

"Why?"

Aaron wondered what a tougher guy would say to that. "You're not the one to ask the questions," he said.

Piney just kept putting Suki's things back into the bags.

"Because she was supposed to meet me for dinner last night," Aaron said, "and she didn't show, and I'm worried. Okay?"

The moon had risen, it poured a milky brightness on the stamped tin panels of the roofs and threw a cool light that nibbled at the shadows from the street lamps. The woman with the cocker spaniels skated past, saw two men kneeling in the yard around assorted female garments. It didn't register as that unusual, she kept on skating.

Piney said, "You had a date with her? What's your name?"

"Aaron."

Pineapple remembered something then. He remembered the day, back before he and Suki had ever spoken, when she'd come out of a guest house on the corner of Whitehead and Rebecca, and rode past him as he sat there on the curb, and he noticed that her face had changed since the time that she'd gone in. "Aaron, can I ask you where you live?"

He told him.

"She likes you," Piney said.

"She does?"

Piney tucked the last of her things back into the shopping bags. "You sure you're not a Russian? You swear to God?"

"Swear," said Aaron.

Stiffly, Piney rose up from the ground. "I wish I knew what I should do."

"She's okay?" said Aaron, still kneeling on the cool ground. "You know that she's okay?"

Piney probed his eyes. At last he said, "She's okay, sort of. Follow me. I hope I'm doing right."

"Oh, Christ," said Suki, "I look like hell."

Though the truth was that, in the dim and flickering light of three candles spread around the hot dog, she didn't look like much of anything. It could vaguely be seen that the fabric of her dress was puckered where it had been ripped and sewn. The swelling in her cheek was softened by the dimness, and the discolorations on her throat were the same deep greenish lavender as the rest of the shadows.

Aaron said, "Pineapple told me what happened. God Almighty."

Suki shook her head. "Lazslo. You hated his guts from the first time I mentioned him. Good judge of character."

Aaron said, "I was jealous, that's all. You've spoken to the cops?"

Suki looked away, blew air between her lips. "Don't know why I bothered. Their theory is I got attacked, my attacker got unlucky. By coincidence. The rest is my imagination."

"Bozo cops are on the take," said Fred. He was perched atop the propane fridge, and the underlighting from the candles gave his face the smudges and furrows of a miner's face.

"Possible," said Suki. "Or maybe just your basic Key West blindness. Big things only happen from Miami north. Down here we're puny even in our criminals."

Aaron rubbed his chin. He hadn't got around to shaving that day and the sound of beard filled the small space of the hot dog. He said, "So what'll you do?"

Suki didn't have a good answer so she changed the subject. "Hey, I never apologized for standing you up . . . I stood you up and you looked for me. I can't believe it."

"Why not?"

She looked at Aaron but then went back to the question before. "I guess I'll hide," she said. "Till I figure something out."

Aaron glanced around the wiener. "Hide here?"

"Here or sneak out of town and go back to Jersey. And that, I'd just as soon get strangled."

Pineapple was leaning against the pronged rotisserie. He said, "You stay right here as long as you want."

Suki shot back, "Not if it means you guys sleep outside."

Aaron pressed his lips together, twined and untwined his fingers. Life was a matter of holding back or plunging in. It was like that at each and every moment, but there were only rare occasions when the choice came quite so clear. He looked at Suki from under his eyebrows and finally he said, "I've got a whole empty guest house."

It took Suki a moment to realize what was being offered. She bit her lip, the upper one. She said, "I couldn't do that."

Aaron stood there in the candlelight, still tasting the words in his mouth. The words were dangerous and tasted salty.

"It's your business," Suki said, "your livelihood."

Aaron could not hold back a squirt of nervous laughter. "Believe me, it bears only very faint resemblance to a business."

"Thank you but forget about it, there's no way."

"Electricity. Hot showers."

Suki gazed off through the service window, gave in to a brief fantasy of endless suds cascading over her skin, a warm stream drumming on the tense place at the top of her spine. But then her aching throat clamped down, a thwarted sigh squeezed through it. "Aaron," she said, "it's not about hot showers. Don't you understand? They want me dead. I'm trouble."

"I do understand," he said, and meant it, though the truth was that the understanding, like a blood red stain on cotton, was seeping into him only gradually.

They locked eyes and then she looked away. "I'm staying here. I have friends here."

Aaron did not take time to think about his customers' reaction to shoeless vagrants wandering the premises. He said, "Your friends could visit . . . Besides—I'm not a friend?"

Suki started to smile but then it was erased. "What you are, Aaron . . . I don't know what you are, and to tell the truth it sort of scares me."

Aaron drank that in but didn't answer.

Suki said, "It isn't fair to pull you into this."

Aaron had been hearing his own voice bouncing off the hot dog's fiber walls. "Sounds to me," he said, "like I'm asking to be pulled in."

Suki lifted her gaze toward him. Her irises had candles in them, and her face was a puzzle of bruise and shadow. She said, "Aaron, like your old man says, you are a mensch. But no, I'm staying here."

TWENTY-TWO

Aaron chose the route along the ocean and drove home very slowly.

It was a mild night, clear but with that loamy greenhouse moistness that is always there in southern Florida. A swelling moon obscured the stars around it; the farther constellations burned a winter blue. Some of the palms hung limp and black while others tossed seemingly at random in little disconnected scraps of breeze. Aaron drove and tried to figure out the faint but chafing sense of failure that had come upon him.

He'd managed to find Suki, but the fact that he'd found her had done her no good at all. Her situation was the same as if he'd done nothing whatsoever. He'd tried to get involved, but he couldn't help feeling that he hadn't tried quite hard enough; worse, he couldn't quite deny an abashing and ambivalent relief that his offer had been refused. Maybe at bottom he'd been doing nothing more than trying to trick his conscience, sidestep some inchoate blame.

But blame for what? How much did a person have to do? He had a father who needed watching and an anemic business that required constant care and feeding. He wasn't sleeping with Suki, they had no history together; he'd made her no promises, owed her no allegiance.

Why should he adopt this lunatic jeopardy in which she'd placed her-self? And yet ...

And yet, in some unreasonable and undodgeable way, he felt responsible. Not because of anything he'd done. That was the bitch of it. He was not only blameless but incidental. He'd been cruising along and, like the guy who sees a crawling turtle in the middle of the road, was confronted by a clear and necessary duty. Such duties fell across the paths of decent people all the time. But usually the rescues required were small and quick—ease the tied-up dog tangled in its leash, save the bird being harried by a cat. Luck of the draw that the charge which fell to Aaron involved not a turtle or a sparrow but a human being; and not just any human being, but a woman he hap-pened to find beautiful.

He drove, and he did not remember turning right on White Street.

Once on White, he could have taken Truman to head downtown, but when he got to Truman he didn't turn. His hands and feet realized before his mind did that he was heading back to Suki's.

He didn't know why he was going there, except perhaps to allay, if only for a moment, the shameful feeling that he was letting himself off too easily. He would see again the thick shrubs where he'd been brave enough to wait in ambush, the ratty patch of lawn on which he'd tackled poor Pineapple. He turned right on Newton Street.

From a distance off, he looked at Suki's house, the unlit windows, the dark porch under gingerbreaded eaves.

But then his attention was diverted by something he just barely glimpsed on the opposite side of the street. An elbow. An elbow propped on the window frame of a car parked across from Suki's house. The car was a poor choice for stealth—an electric blue Camaro, some nonproduction color, with a molded skirt stuck onto the bottom of the frame. It hunkered just outside the main splash of orange brightness from a street lamp.

Aaron took his foot off the accelerator, crept along as slowly as he dared. He didn't have the nerve to turn his head, but as he passed the parked car he saw out of the corner of his eye a dark suspender cinched down on a muscular and shirtless shoulder, a tangle of unruly hair falling on a massive neck.

Praying that his face had not been noticed, hoping that his leg would not slam down on the gas and draw attention, Aaron kept on. Hands damp around the steering wheel, he hung a left on Eisenhower Drive and headed home to the Mangrove Arms, trying not to imagine what might have happened had the strongman from the T-shirt shop staked out Suki's place an hour sooner.

Pineapple waited until he thought Suki was asleep, then quietly started gathering up the edges of his bedroll.

Sitting, he tucked his pillow in among the folds, then tried to stand without shouldering the sauerkraut steamer or stepping on Fred, who was snoring with his head beneath the sink. Stepping barefoot over Suki, who'd been given the choice spot next to the propane fridge, he opened the screen door as gently as he could and escaped down the piled cinder blocks into the uncluttered night, to sleep among the mangrove roots and the animate puddles that survived somehow in every hollow.

When he had gone, Suki let her eyes spring open.

From floor level, she looked at the moonlit rusted legs of the single dinette chair, the dust-caked recesses at the base of the idle appliances. She had a pillow and two blankets and a sleeping pad. She was not uncomfortable but she was getting more disheartened every minute. What was gnawing at her was the gradual understanding that, strangled, half-drowned, and rescued, she was not at the end of her trials but only the beginning.

Terror had come and gone and probably would come again— but terror was a fast emotion, and mercifully impossible to remember fully. What confronted her now was a slower and more grinding dilemma: How did she continue her life in the face of what had happened?

She couldn't stay long at the hot dog; that was clear. So what were her options? She could leave Key West, abandon Florida; a long retreat, she imagined, would be adequate to keep her safe. But goddamit, she didn't want to leave. She liked it here. The home-made boats, plywood painted lavender and green. The old Cuban guys playing dominoes in shady doorways. The funk and the geeks that made it feel like home. It was bad enough that fear of crime made you have to lock your bicycle; she was damned if fear of crime would make her give up the whole entire archipelago of Keys.

But if she stayed, what then? The cops could not be counted on. Her boss, for all his cheap cigars and city-room gruffness, quailed in the face of a real story as though it were a fatal infection. Which, per-haps, it was. Who, then, had the guts to risk contamination? Pineapple and Fred.

And maybe Aaron. But Suki hated the idea of involving him. What she'd liked about him from the start was precisely that he did not seem tough, did not have the Key West thorniness engendered by the climate and the transience, a passive hardness that defeated joy by expecting . . . not the worst, exactly, but just not much of any-thing. A cuticle around the heart like around the leaves of tropic plants. Aaron seemed free of it. His gaze was unguarded. He was actually trying to accomplish something here, and, amazingly enough, he seemed to believe in the value of his efforts. A long siege in the hot sun would probably simmer the tenderness and the belief right out of him.

Suki rolled over, faced the little fridge. Through the cracking propane hose she caught a faint whiff of the tracer gas they mix in with the fuel. Across the way, Fred's snoring had changed from a steady, almost restful purr to a syncopated rasping, a sort of nasal jazz. She couldn't stay here very long. But could she bring herself to go to Aaron's place? If he asked again, that is?

She tried to banish the possibility; it wouldn't go away. She imag-ined a hot bath. She imagined a window with a curtain on it, moving in a yellow breeze. She imagined Aaron's curly hair, the earnest tilt he gave to his head when he was puzzling something out. She could see herself at Aaron's place, it was pointless to deny it. And for just a fleeting second she admitted something else as well. She could see herself, maybe sometime far from now when all of this was settled, in Aaron's arms.

TWENTY-THREE

"Ya see," said Bert the Shirt d'Ambrosia, "this is the part I don't like."

"Which part?" Aaron said.

It was morning at the Paradiso. Long shadows sprouted from the palms. A few old people were walking laps around the pool, none of them could exactly straighten out their knees. The pock of tennis balls echoed between the buildings of the complex; the tinny plunk of golf balls issued forth from the putting green.

Aaron had slept badly once again, he'd awakened in a sweat. He needed to do more for Suki and he had no idea what he should do. He woke up with the thought that *mafiya* was Mafia. That's what old man Bert had said, and it seemed that Bert should know. Besides, who else could Aaron talk to? Who'd had more practice keeping secrets? So he'd roused his father with a cup of tea and off they'd gone.

"The part I don't like," the retired mobster was replying now, "is this burglary bullshit. The part where the dead guy, what's his name?"

"Lazslo."

"Where Lazslo, they make it look like it's a robbery."

"You don't believe it?" said Aaron.

"Come on," said Bert, his silver eyebrows arching skyward. "On that night of all the nights? They rubbed him out. Course they did. But the way they did it—chickenshit. No class."

Sam Katz was gradually waking up. In the mornings his mind came back to him in jigsaw pieces that slowly combined to make a map. Some days the map had rougher seams than other days. He said, "You cut somebody's throat. There's a classy way to do it?"

Bert petted his dog, which was splayed out like a Chinese duck on the metal table where the three of them were sitting. "My people," he said, "when they were faced with the unfortunate necessity of someone he had to be rubbed out, at least we tried to make a lesson of it, a learning experience. We left a calling card. A symbol. Bag a fish. The guy's tongue. Whatever. Sometimes, okay, the symbols got a little, like, mysterious. One guy he was found frozen in a car trunk wit' a candelabra on his head. Don't ask me. But the point is we didn't bullshit, make it look like something which it wasn't."

Sam ran a hand through the little pillows of his Einstein hair. "So maybe," he said, "these people aren't so much like your people after all."

Bert thought that over, tugged on the placket of his shirt. The shirt was somewhere between pink and red, the color of water-melon, in a shiny material that looked wet. "Similarities and differ-ences," he said at last. "This robbery bullshit, okay, that's a difference. But the guy shoots his mouth off and gets dead, that's the same."

Aaron's mouth was very dry. His hairline itched. He said, "So where does that leave Suki?"

Bert frowned. He petted his chihuahua and watched short and brittle hairs flutter off its back and float in swaths of sunshine. "Aaron," he said, "remember that jerkoff, what's his name, he said something bad about God and the Moslems were gonna kill 'im and then they backed off and made him famous 'stead of dead? Well, if these people are anything like my people, it isn't gonna work like that. They follow through. Have to. Credibility. Ya know. If she's been sentenced, well, it isn't good."

"She's not a threat to them," said Aaron.

"They probably would disagree," said Bert.

"The cops, her own newspaper—no one'll listen to her," Aaron said. "She couldn't hurt them if she tried."

"And who's gonna tell the Russians that?" asked Bert. "Who's gonna convince them?"

Aaron's voice was getting ready to answer but then he began to see the problem.

"The person who tells them," Bert went on, "he knows the same stuff she does. Same knowledge, same sentence. *Capeesh?*"

There was a silence. People did their laps around the pool. A curse came from the tennis court.

Bert leaned lower across the metal table, his watermelon-colored shirt stretched along his skinny chest. He put his hand on Aaron's wrist, said, "Wit' due respect to your father here, I'm gonna talk like you were my own son. My world, Aaron, any world I guess, we had to learn that nobody could save nobody else. Hard thing, but true. Eh?"

He held Aaron's eyes till Aaron reluctantly nodded. Then he went on.

"Somebody got sentenced—Mafia, cancer, what the hell's the difference how it happens?—we had to learn to say goo'bye. Say it in our heart, wit' no words coming out and nothing showing on our face. Y'unnerstand? Shitty sometimes, but there it is. Ya see?"

He stared at Aaron till the younger man looked off, his smarting eyes stung further by the glare from the pool. "I see."

Driving away, Aaron said, "Pop, you understand what's going on?"

Sam Katz didn't answer right away. There was a certain bleak equity in what was happening to his brain. As he remembered less, he cared less, there was a balance to it. But there were moments when he had to care, and then it took a monumental effort to keep the understanding in proportion. "I think I do," he said at last. "But Aaron, is it me, or is this all a little crazy?"

"It isn't you, Pop," Aaron said.

They cruised up Smathers Beach. Vending trucks were already selling french fries, sno-cones. It was a carefree place. You could take a parachute ride hitched to a motorboat and float weightlessly above the twinkling ocean.

After a moment Aaron said, "Bert's telling me to walk away. Whadda you think, Pop?"

Sam was slipping but he'd seen a lot of life and raised a son and he still knew things that Aaron didn't know. He said, "He's not telling you to walk away. He's saying it's okay if you walk away. He's giving you permission, freeing you."

Aaron drove and rubbed his cheeks. "And whadda you say?"

Sam looked out the window. The ocean was on his side of the car. "Isn't home the other way?"

"Yeah, it is," said Aaron. They were driving past the airport, the fenced-in stand of mangroves at the east end of the runway.

Sam said, "Wait a second. My hearing aid, it's acting funny. Funny noises, like."

He pulled out the device, squinted at it, turned it over and over in his hand. Aaron said, "If you'd stop experimenting on it—"

"What?" He put the hearing aid back in. "Better now," he said. "About this girl, this Suki, she have anybody else could do a better job of helping her?"

Aaron didn't answer.

Sam looked out the window. The island was curving, the ocean scouring through toward Cow Key Channel. "We going where she is?"

Aaron didn't move his eyes. "I guess that's where I'm heading."

His father watched the water and the wheeling sky. Then he reached across the car and put a hand on Aaron's shoulder. "I'm proud of you," he said. "The whole thing's crazy but I'm proud of you."

* * *

Suki was washing her hair in a bucket.

Aaron had walked in from the road and was standing in the shadows of the foliage. He saw her before she noticed him, and the whole scene reminded him of something from another century. A driftwood fire burning. The dented pail lifted up on rocks. Thin suds being wrung out of her hair in sunshine.

He entered the clearing. She looked up and saw him. They both had tired eyes, there was an intimacy in the heavy lids, the shadowed sockets. The bruise on Suki's face had mellowed to a pale chartreuse; you had to look twice to see the marks on her neck. He said good morning.

She wrung her hair, water streamed onto her shoulder. "You're always showing up when I'm at my very worst."

Aaron said, "I don't think you have a very worst."

Suki tried to smile at the compliment but her lips wouldn't budge and, absurdly, the back of her throat closed down.

Aaron pawed the stony ground. "I'm here to bring you home. Do I have to drag you or will you come along?"

Suki tilted her head. Drops of water slapped into the bucket. Looking down, she said, "You don't have to do this."

"Oh yes I do."

She tossed damp hair across her shoulder and searched his sleepy face. After a moment she said, "You slept as bad as I did."

"Maybe worse."

"I'll get my things," she said.

Part
Three

TWENTY-FOUR

A couple of mornings later, two old Soviets were brooding in their separate houses on Key Haven, thinking thoughts that wound around each other like strands of oily rope.

Gennady Markov had wriggled higher on his feather pillows and reached out for the cup of coffee that his housekeeper presented. He'd taken a couple of small but noisy sips when he noticed with surprise that, for the first morning in what seemed a long, long time, he didn't have a headache.

Gingerly he let his eyelids open wider. His mind seemed clear, although it was the illusive clarity that reflects off the bottom of a long hangover—a morbid compromise between his recent grief and rage, and the pathetic geniality of his life before. He felt almost cheerful, with the bleak cheer of the nihilist. Somehow, overnight, it had gotten through to him that nothing mattered. Blood and consequences had been drained from life; what was left was, so to speak, schematic. Thrusts and parries. Attacks and defenses. The hellish triumph of laughing last.

Laughing last—God knew that people kept on living for the sake of paltrier satisfactions. Markov thought about it and worked his shoulder blades deeper into the yielding pillows.

At the same moment, Ivan Cherkassky, Markov's only friend and now his mortal enemy, was perching weightlessly on the edge of his sofa, drinking tea and fretting.

With Lazslo dead and Gennady in an ugly sulk, the illicit empire that he managed in Key West seemed, quite suddenly, overwhelmingly complex and burdensome.

There were bribes to dole out, phony immigration papers to distribute. There was the irksome necessity of filling Lazslo's mock-important job. There was a network of informers to monitor— busboys, housekeepers, taxi drivers, clerks. Money in need of laundering kept flowing in; couriers in mirrored sunglasses shuttled here and there among the rogue nations of the world.

Keeping an unwritten record of it all was a staggering task— though that was not the aspect of the business that troubled Cherkassky this morning. He'd been an upper-level bureaucrat under Brezhnev; nothing could throw him in terms of covering a trail. Rather, it was the human element that burdened him—that made him, uncharacteristically, second-guess his wisdom in having Lazslo killed.

Emotions! he thought with disgust. Damned, wretched, ludicrous emotions. All he'd ever wanted from life was rationality and predictability and calm. But emotions always intruded. Not one's own emotions, of course, which were easily enough controlled, but the whims and unreasonableness of others. Now it was Gennady, getting sullen and neurotic over the loss of his misbegotten nephew. His reaction was much more virulent than Cherkassky had imagined; much more virulent than made any sense at all.

Gennady Markov, too, was just then thinking about his murdered ward, and his own reaction to his death. He understood that the real-life Lazslo—the Lazslo whose strong forearm he used to stroke, whose open shirts delighted him—was already fading, becoming shimmery and insubstantial, like a distant ship sliding down the curve of the world. He was ceasing to be a person and becoming little more than a marker in a game.

A game, Markov reflected, that he was losing. Why? He sipped coffee, peered at the dampened light that filtered through the curtains, and tried to recapture a scientific attitude, a set of mind that swept away the nonessentials and cut through to what was crucial. Why was Cherkassky decisive and effective and he himself ridiculous? Why was Cherkassky master of his fate and he himself a victim?

There were a thousand differences between the two of them, of course. But the difference that underlay all others and that determined their relative positions seemed to be precisely this: Cherkassky was capable of killing. He saw his own survival as infinitely more legitimate than the survival of all others, and therefore he put no limits on his actions. That, finally, was his advantage.

It followed, therefore, as logically as a geometric proof, that he, Gennady, if he ever hoped to pull even in this game, must also kill. Moreover, if he wanted not just to equal his old comrade but surpass him, he could do so by killing not through the agency of others, but with his own two hands. The thought terrified and warmed him, he tossed aside his satin sheet.

Cherkassky, thin and rigid on his sofa, moved just slightly to avoid the shifting sun. Yes, he mused, Gennady was taking it stupidly hard. And this was bad, because Gennady still had something that Cherkassky badly needed: expertise in physics. Gennady knew how neutrons would behave, how isotopes would decay, one element into another. He knew how to mix and store and transport the treasure that the two old friends had smuggled out of Russia—sheathed in exotic foils and concealed in the hollowed out innards of a car shipped through Miami—and that represented Cherkassky's ultimate security.

His ultimate security—and yet Gennady Markov, scientist and hysteric, knew how to make it work, while he, Cherkassky, bureaucrat and planner, did not. How had he allowed himself to land in such a grotesquely dependent position? An appalling situation.

An appalling situation, echoed Markov, thinking of his long subservience. But now, with the serene pleasure of someone who has just worked out an elegant equation, he'd found the way to be an equal.

But who should he kill? Sadly, since Cherkassky cared for no one, there was nobody whose demise would wound him as deeply as Lazslo's had hurt *him*. Then again, Cherkassky being as he was, the most potent poison to be used against him would be not grief but paranoia. Destroy his peace of mind. Commit a murder that he would know, deep down, was in fact a killing aimed at him.

Fine—but who should be the corpse?

Leaning on his feather pillows, Markov looked down at his hands. They were white; they were plump; they were soft. And he could not help admitting something to himself. He was desperate, he was damned, perhaps he was on his way to going mad, but he was still fundamentally a weakling and a coward. Whoever he killed would have to be somebody easy.

Still, picking a victim gave him something to think about, and the act of thinking summoned back the immoderate appetite that had been strangely absent these past few days. He decided on berries and sour cream for breakfast. Eggs to follow. Cinnamon toast alongside. He rang for the housekeeper to bring it.

Unblessed and untroubled by appetite, Ivan Cherkassky shook his head at the absurdity of being hostage to Gennady's expertise. It was a big problem.

Or maybe not. Probably Gennady would come around, put aside his grief and his offense, slide fatly into his old persona as a shallow and gluttonous clown. He lacked the strength to hold a grudge, would be seduced away from sorrow and purpose by every slab of beef or wedge of fragrant Camembert.

Still, it was a nuisance to have to worry about, and Cherkassky sighed as he sat there on his undented sofa. He looked through his window at the frivolous and stupid mint-green house on the other side of the canal, and he marveled at how different life must seem to different people.

The green house was a rental. Sometimes it was empty and sometimes crammed to bursting with vacationers. When the opportunity offered, Cherkassky studied the tourists like an anthropologist among the savages.

They were always laughing, these primitives in pastels and plaids. They laughed when meat caught fire in the barbecue. They laughed as they jumped into the canal wearing fins that made them look like hairy ducks. Their obese children laughed with their mouths full of food, and everybody kept on laughing well into the night.

It was a mystery. Was everything so funny, or did laughing simply take the place of thinking for these people?—these people whose every chuckle revealed an unexamined trust that everything would turn out fine, that life would not betray them. So barbarous and unevolved, that brainless trust. So typically American.

TWENTY-FIVE

Suki's room at Mangrove Arms was in a turret that was above the second floor but wasn't quite the third.

It was hexagon-shaped and had a sloping ceiling; triangles of roof came slicing down and met the walls at wavy seams that crazed the paint. The bathroom floor sagged beneath a claw-foot tub that had lost some puzzle pieces of enamel. The white muslin curtains had been worn down to a perfect thinness by years of sun and wind and washing to remove the salt.

The bed was squeaky and soft, and Suki, somewhat to her own befuddlement, slept in it alone.

A peculiar situation. What had brought her to Aaron's place was a weird mix of danger and attraction, decency and need. But survival took precedence over romance, and now that she was here, a polite and caring but ultimately false reticence was taking root between the two of them. Bruised and exhausted, Suki felt unlovely; afraid and under siege, she dreaded the humiliating error of mistaking gratitude for desire.

As for Aaron, he was trying to be gallant, and gallantry meant you couldn't exploit the role of rescuer to win the role of lover. He had offered her a haven, and could not live with the idea of either of them feeling that the offer came with strings.

So he kept his distance, and Suki healed herself through a series of prodigious sleeps. Hour by hour, her bruises faded and shrank inward like evaporating puddles. Pain lost its sear, became abstract, a lesson.

Between stretches of oblivion, she spent much of her time out on the widow's walk that wrapped around her little tower. The walkway's planks were grooved and burnished with ancient footsteps. The drooping foliage of a fig tree tickled its railings, and light came through in patches and dabs. The widow's walk was a serene place, out in the world and yet removed, above it, and in its cozy shadows, mostly hidden from the courtyard and the street, she could reflect almost calmly on her situation.

Her problems had not even begun to be solved; that, she had no choice but to acknowledge. She couldn't hide forever in her turret. Nor could she emerge while her enemies were at large. She was only stealing time.

Still, there was a certain peace in being cloistered away and given up for dead. No one bothered to hunt the dead, and eventually the dead were all forgotten. In the meantime, she was as comfortable as any threatened damsel, and safe beneath the munchkin ceiling of her room.

Or so it seemed for the short space of a couple days.

Pete and Clam weren't trying to make trouble. They were stoned and harmless guys, locals from Big Coppitt, and all they were trying to do was round up shrimp.

They'd gone out on the evening just before the moon was full, when shrimp were running through every cut and channel in the lower Keys. Shrimp coursed under bridges, steering with spit and flicks of their tails; shrimp traced out the curves of beaches, funneling and tumbling in their millions. Catching them was easy; took no more than a flashlight and a net, a mask and snorkel if you wanted to get fancy. The big shrimp you could eat and the little ones were bait.

So Pete and Clam smoked a joint as they waited for dusk to settle and the moon to get some height, then they piled in Pete's truck, crossed the highway, and smoked another as they drove a bumpy road that wound and scratched through mangroves, until they reached their shrimping spot. They saw tire tracks and the remnants of a campfire in the little clearing that gave onto the water, but made nothing of it at the time. Other locals used the spot for fishing. Kids got hand jobs there. Tire tracks were nothing that unusual. It didn't really register that the tracks went straight into the ocean.

They started shrimping. Pete waded in thigh-deep, and his flash-light beam almost immediately discovered translucent clouds of shrimp, their bodies so sheer that he might have looked right through them except for their stalked unearthly eyes that wiggled like paired periscopes and gleamed an orangy pink. He snagged them with a net and dumped them into a mesh bag he carried on his shoulder.

Clam used a different method. He put on fins and a mask, and he rigged his flashlight through the mask straps so that it sat behind his ear like a giant cigarette. He waded out maybe thirty yards, then pan-caked into a lazy float, his net poised at his side as his beacon shone straight down. Swimming after shrimp was no more productive than just standing there, but Clam was pretty ripped and felt like looking through the water. A baby bonnet shark slipped past, its head flat as a catfish. A sergeant-major scudded by, its yellow stripes almost disap-pearing against the sand, its black bars disconnected.

Clam kicked himself a little farther out and scored some shrimp. He was just jiggling them into his pouch when he saw an angelfish whose iridescent blue flashed a weird magenta against some car upholstery.

For just an instant it did not compute that there was something off about car upholstery, a dashboard, a steering wheel at the bottom of the ocean. Clam blinked inside his mask and held his breath. Current carried him past the windshield and directly over the Caddy's hood ornament, its chrome not yet corroded. The drowned logo finally persuaded him that something very unusual was going on. He raised his head and called his buddy.

They swam around the car together, stood on the sodden boot, agreed that it was really there.

Not much happened on Big Coppitt. When something did happen, and it happened to *you*, you played it up, because it made you briefly a celebrity. Pete and Clam put their shrimp in the cooler, smoked a joint, then headed to the bar at Egret Key, to tell everyone what they had found.

The sunken Cadillac spawned theories all up and down the bar. Better ditched than repo'd, one suggestion went. Or someone stole it then got scared. Or a jilted girlfriend trashed it for revenge.

"Y'oughta call the paper," someone said.

Discreetly, the sober bartender advised, "I was you, I'd call the cops."

Clam sucked some beer. He didn't really like to deal with cops, but probably the bartender was right. Civic duty and all. Maybe a reward. He looked at Pete. "Any more shit in the truck?"

Pete shook his head. "Clean," he said. "We smoked it all."

And so by nine o'clock the Monroe County sheriffs had run the tag on Lazslo's sunken Caddy, and by eleven the car had been dredged up from the bottom, wet sand streaming from its doors; and by seven the next morning the whole thing was in the paper: Unsolved sinking of the car of the victim of an unsolved murder. Unsolved puzzle as to how the car got a dozen miles from the body of its owner.

For almost everyone who read the story, it was a head-scratcher but no more, just one more instance of the kind of loony and inscrutable misadventures that happened in the Keys. You slapped the paper then went back to your breakfast.

Some few people took the story much more seriously, however. Some few people were surprised and disappointed and very much annoyed that there was no mention whatsoever of a woman's body in the trunk.

TWENTY-SIX

Sergei "Tarzan" Abramowitz, the muscular young man who always wore suspenders, paced athletically along the length of Ivan Cherkassky's sofa. The ridge above his eyes was furrowed; tangled hair bounced against his neck. He moved his heavy jaw and spoke in Russian. "That *prozhny vorchnoi*," he snarled, calling the dead Lazslo an eliminatory organ of low social status, "he screwed it up but good."

Cherkassky didn't answer right away. He crossed his skinny legs, gazed out the picture window at the yellow morning light, and wondered briefly if Abramowitz's gait was naturally that springy or if it was one more way of showing off. At last he said, "You're sure? You're absolutely sure?"

Tarzan's walk became more acrobatic still, his knees flexed, his thigh muscles bulged, it seemed he might do a back flip any moment. "Ivan Fyodorovich, I am sure. Practically the last words of that out-of-wedlock child who has sex with his mother. We are holding him down. He says Why? Why? I did my job, I swear. The knife, we bring it closer. He says, The bitch is dead, she's dead. The blade is now against his neck. He tries to shrink, he cries, the cockroach with no testicles. The car, he says. Even now the car goes down, she disappears forever. I did my job, I swear."

Ivan Cherkassky hunkered forward across his knobby knees. His scooped-out melon face seemed to grow a little hollower, chin and forehead cinching in with concentration. "The car," he said. "Who helps him? Who makes it disappear?"

Tarzan pivoted, fisted hands swinging low against his legs. "This he did not say."

Resignedly, Cherkassky nodded. "Of course not. Because it would be good to know."

The young man in suspenders burst forward once again like a sprinter from the blocks. "Yes," he said. "It would."

"And the girl—you think she lives?"

"If she is not in trunk, I fear she does."

"*Pyutchni streshkaya!*" Cherkassky murmured in disgust. "Still we must clean up after this ragpicker who is incontinent."

"You want I find the girl?" said Tarzan.

"She cannot live," Cherkassky said. "Is clear."

"*A flotl defioreski khrichevskov!*" Tarzan hissed. "I find her, I send her to meet Lazslo, they have oral sex in hell."

At the Mangrove Arms that morning, things got too busy too early for anyone to read the paper.

At eight A.M. Suki was leaning over her widow's walk railing, peeling an orange and looking through the leaf curtain to the street, when she saw a taxi pull up and disgorge a pale and harried-looking couple.

Barely had the couple bumped their luggage up the porch steps when another taxi approached from the opposite direction, dropping off another pair of white and rumpled visitors.

From anything that Suki had so far seen or heard, two couples arriving at the Mangrove Arms on the same morning was a record. Without thinking about it very much, she stepped inside and went downstairs to see if she could help.

She found Aaron bustling around the kitchen. He was slapping coffee cups onto a tray, his hair was wet, and he was sweating. "Town's packed," he said without looking up at her. "Business finally trickling down to me. Last resort. No reservations. Not ready for the rush."

Two couples. To Suki it didn't seem like that much of a rush, but she kept it to herself. She said, "What can I do to help?"

Aaron, frantic, didn't seem to hear her. He arced around his father, who was sitting calmly, sipping tea. Pouring milk into a pitcher, Aaron rambled. "Beds unmade. Towels balled up in the dryer. Drop cloths in the hallway. Paint chips."

"So what should I do?" said Suki.

Aaron's hands were not quite steady, milk splashed on the floor. "The breakfast person, out sick again. Not the hemorrhaging tattoo this time. The bellybutton. Pierced. Abscessed. Dripping she said."

He was heading for the doorway to bring coffee to the waiting customers, when Suki said, "So should I cook or should I make up rooms?"

Finally he heard her, and looked up. Without question she was recuperating well, but she had a ways to go. There was still a heaviness around her eyes, her ravaged neck was still discolored. Aaron said, "Look, you're not indentured labor."

"I'll cook," she said.

"You're here to rest."

"Rest," she said, with breezy contempt. "I work. I'm Greek, I grew up in my father's diner. Plato's."

Aaron said, "I'm not even sure it's a good idea you came downstairs."

Sam Katz said, "Your father's name is Plato?"

"My father's name is George."

"Plato sounds more Greek," Sam said.

"Voilà," said Suki, then stepped toward Aaron and reached out to take the tray. "You go make up the rooms."

"But the guests—"

Suki said, "I've done this job, Aaron. Hostessed. Waitressed. I'll talk to them, tell them what a fabulous time they're gonna have."

"What if someone recognizes—"

She lowered her voice. "These are tourists, Aaron. Tourists don't know diddly. Besides, I'm dead. Remember? Now go make up the rooms."

He hesitated just a moment, leaning so far forward that his toes began to hurt. They were staring at each other across the coffee cups, the milk. He handed her the tray and the two of them went off in opposite directions.

When they'd gone, Sam Katz sat alone in the kitchen and sipped his cooling tea.

He thought about the old country and he smiled. He didn't really remember the old country, not at all, but at some point what pretended to be memory became instead a sense of what was right and fitting; nostalgia as a softer word for morality.

Sam liked it that a man and woman worked together side by side. Helpmates. That old word. Work, and purpose. It was nice, thought Sam, nodding to himself. It was the basis of good things. He finished his tea, fished the wedge of lemon from the bottom of the cup, and puckered up contentedly as he nibbled along the inside of the rind.

Bert the Shirt's mornings tended to be slow and lonely.

He woke up earlier than most people; there was nothing to do and nobody to talk to. In monogrammed pajamas that had grown too large, he wandered around the apartment still cluttered with his dead wife's fancy lamps and gewgaws, and he rationed his activities to fill the time. One by one, he counted out the dog's pills and his own; he counted them again. He made old-fashioned oatmeal, not the instant kind. And he always read the paper thoroughly, from the headlines to the classifieds. This morning he did not like what he saw.

He finished up his cereal, took Don Giovanni for an only partially successful walk on Smathers Beach, then drove down to the Mangrove Arms to strategize.

He gathered everyone around a wire-mesh table in the courtyard, made sure that the hotel guests—arrayed on lounges in their garish bathing suits, their skins already blossoming a pebbly irritated pink—were out of earshot. Then he spread open the paper, pointed. "This here," he said, "it like changes the whole complexion a the thing."

The others read the article.

Suki felt the columns of type sticking in her throat. Her brief sense of belonging here at Mangrove Arms imploded; her belief that she could help now loomed up as fake and selfish. She should not have come; it was reckless and unfair. She'd been foolish to imagine she could dodge the threat against her, and now she was a threat to others, to everyone around her.

Bert's voice snapped her back into the practical. "Wit' out this," he said, "we coulda stood and waited. Pressure was off. Time was on our side."

"And now?" said Suki.

Bert pushed his lips out, stroked his dog. "A job half-done," he said. "That doesn't sit so well wit' guys like this . . . I think we gotta get more active like, aggressive."

"Aggressive?" Aaron said. They were two old men, a youngish man who was not tough, and a woman who'd already come close enough to dying. Against a Mafia, just how aggressive were they supposed to be?

"Like learn more what we're up against at least," said Bert. "How they do things. Who's in charge."

Suki said, "The uncle. He's in charge."

Bert's chihuahua was splayed out on the table and the mesh was stamping a waffle pattern in the short fur of its belly. The old mafioso lightly drummed his fingers on the steel. "And how do we know this?" he asked.

Suki started to answer, then realized that all she knew was what she'd heard, and what she'd heard had been rumors passed along by people no less remote than she. The slyness of Bert's question sank in around the table, and suddenly, louder than necessary and off the beat, Sam Katz said, "Aha!"

Suki put in without confidence, "It's just the way it seems."

"Exactly," Bert said. "Just like it used to seem like Luciano ran Havana, when really it was Lansky. Or the way it looked like Fat Tony was boss of the Genovese family when really it was Vinnie Chin."

Aaron raised his eyes from the unplanted shrubs strewn along his property, their thwarted roots poking through the burlap swaddling. "So you're saying—"

"I'm saying," Bert went on, "that unless the head guy is a knuckle-head egomaniac like Gotti, he don't want it should look to all the world like he's in charge. Old Sicilian saying: Ya got the biggest balls, ya don't need the tallest antlers. 'Scuse me."

"No problem," Suki said. "But then who—?"

Bert shrugged and petted his dog, little diamonds of whose abdomen seemed to be slipping through the table's metal mesh like strands of melting cheese. "I have no idea," he said. "I'm only saying don't trust the way things seem or you'll get confused before y'even start."

"I'm confused," said Sam, and he fiddled with his hearing aid.

"Ya think about it though," Bert resumed, "a hit on his own nephew? Flesh and blood, they usually get some extra slack."

"Flesh and blood," said Sam. "How could anybody do that?"

"So say it's not the uncle," Suki said. "Who else . . . ?"

Bert stroked his waffled dog, raised his shoulders almost to his long and fleshy earlobes. "Maybe we never find 'at out," he said. "Wit'out we infiltrate."

"Infiltrate?" said Sam.

"Ya know, like get inside."

"I know what infiltrate means. But how—?"

"Hey," said Bert, "we're talkin' just, like hypot'etical heah. Just thinkin' things through."

Sam looked a little disappointed, tugged his Einstein hair. "Infiltrate," he murmured. "Spies, like."

A pack of motorcycles roared up Whitehead Street, a plane banked low and clattered in its final approach to the airport. The din reached a harsh crescendo then subsided, and a soft whoosh of fronds soon erased the memory of it; in Key West, peace and quiet were shattered and restored a thousand times a day.

"And say they're lookin' for you," the Shirt said to Suki. "Where they gonna look? They got no reason to look here. Not so far at least. Who they gonna squeeze? How hard they gonna squeeze 'em? These are things I think we gotta find 'em out."

Suki bit her upper lip, looked down.

Aaron rubbed his forehead. He'd always been taught that an enterprise could not succeed without a plan, that you didn't just embark on a journey without a strand of logic laid out like bread-crumbs in the forest. He said, "Bert, so say we figure out those things. Then what?"

"Then what *what*?" the old man fired back.

"Do we know where we're going with all this? Longer term, I mean?"

Bert the Shirt scratched his dog behind the ears. "Longer term?" he echoed.

The phrase coaxed his lips into a rueful smile. He was seventy-eight years old. He'd been dead once. He kept thinking he was retired, then life would throw some caper or crusade across his path, and he would realize that retirement was a ludicrous concept. No one breathing was retired. Life didn't work the way young people thought it did. It didn't go in one straight line, with stages and events notched out like inches on a ruler. Results didn't squirt out clean and parallel from causes like jet trails from an airplane. Life was crazier and richer and less fair than that. But how did you explain that to someone young enough to hold sacred the idea of future, a person in thrall to a fascination with what would happen next?

"Longer term," he said again, "I guess we'll just have to see what happens in a bunch of shorter terms."

TWENTY-SEVEN

I t was over a late lunch that day—cold lamb and potato pancakes, eaten at the shaded table on his patio—that Gennady Markov decided on a victim. His choice satisfied him in every way, and he celebrated with an extra Key lime tart.

First and foremost, this victim would be easy. Second, the killing would be one whose significance would be lost on everyone except Ivan Cherkassky. Finally, Markov might even be able to work up a bit of moral umbrage to underpin his questionably sane resolve, since this person had played an undeniable role in the death of Lazslo.

Excited but not impatient, he finished his meal and blotted his flubbery lips on a napkin. Not without difficulty, he pushed back from the table, then strolled through his garden, past oleanders and lemon trees and palmettos, to the seawall. Sharp western light was skidding off the Gulf, little tufts of mangrove dotted the horizon, and Markov reflected that, of all of humankind's gizmos and contraptions, the seawall was among the saddest and the most futile. A tissue of cement against a universe of seep and surge; a draughtsman's tracing of hard edge sketched atop a ceaseless maelstrom. Blink an eye, your seawall is gone, a coastline rearranged, your attempt at a boundary mocked and undone. So much for security.

He moved to the very edge of the wall and looked down through the clear green water. Tiny fish with needle noses were sucking algae off the concrete. Old storms and the tug of the moon had raised miniature dunes in the sandy bottom, six feet from the surface. He tore a few leaves from a buttonwood shrub and threw them into the water, studying the tide.

It seemed to be near the end of its oozing ebb from gulf to ocean. Soon the water would be slack, stalled so utterly as to make it seem impossible that the machinery of tides would ever start again. But the flood would come, softly at first, like drizzle before a hammering downpour, then swelling in volume and lurching in pace, becoming a gale of water that would shred the tops of seaweeds and pull the anchor lines of boats as taut as cables on a bridge, and would carry unmoored things—bottles, branches, bodies—miles to the north and west, deep into the Gulf, among the coiling shallows and the nameless knots of mangrove.

The peak of it, Gennady Markov figured, would come the hour after dark. He went inside and told his housekeeper to take the evening off. Then he composed himself and made a phone call, summoning his victim to Key Haven.

On another seawall, this one near the airport, facing south and east across the straits, Pineapple and Fred were sitting, dimly and mysteriously depressed.

Until just recently, their lives had been ticking along, basically rock-steady, not like a heartbeat but a watch. You wouldn't say they were terrific lives, but Piney and Fred were used to them, they fit. Then Suki came along and rippled everything, and then she left and the ripples started to subside, and the exact same mild flatness that had suited them before no longer seemed to satisfy.

So they sat there on the seawall and they didn't talk. Fred smoked, his inhaling powered by frustration, a gruff wistfulness being vented on the out-breath. Piney dangled his bare feet close enough to the water to feel its coolness reaching up between his toes. Finally, apropos of nothing, he said, "Ya think he really meant it?"

Fred welcomed the opportunity to get grumpy. He said, "You always fuckin' start a conversation in the middle. You realize 'at?"

Piney didn't answer, just watched a small barracuda, implausibly motionless as a school of pinfish wafted toward him.

Fred gave in, said, "Do I think that who meant what?"

Piney watched the school of fish, the extraordinary way they banked and turned as one. There was a certain distance from the 'cuda inside of which the little guys were doomed. If they didn't see or smell him before they swam into that circle, one or two of them would disappear so fast that no human eye could ever track them being swallowed. Without looking up, Piney said, "Aaron. He said that we could visit."

Fred sucked hard on his cigarette, his whole face scrunched up with the fury of the puff. "Yeah. He said that."

"You don't think he meant it?"

Fred blew exhaust from both nostrils. "Piney, " he said, "say you're a rich guy owns a hotel. Guests come in—credit cards, matching luggage. 'Ah, welcome, Mr. Fuckface, Mrs. Tit.' You want guys like us around?"

Piney looked up. A second later there was a splash from where the 'cuda had been lurking. Probably a fish or two had gotten scarfed, but he would never know for sure. He said, "What's so bad about us?"

Fred just kept on smoking.

"We wash," Pineapple said. "We don't ask for money."

Fred shook his head and looked toward the horizon. Grudgingly he admitted to himself that it was nice to look east when the sun was in the west. The sky just glowed, it didn't burn; the ripples in the water shone an even green with a cool white filament on top.

After a silence Piney softly said, "I miss her."

Fred took a long moment to swivel first his hips, then his shoulders, and finally his head toward his friend. He broke into a taunting smile that made parts of his face look twelve years old. "I think you got a crush on 'er," he said.

Piney looked down at his dangling feet. "I just think maybe there's more that we should do."

Fred hadn't quite got over feeling guilty about taking money to sink a car with a woman in the trunk. But he wouldn't admit it, and unadmitted guilt was making him feisty. He said, "More? Fuck should we do more?"

Piney raised his face again. Sun came over his shoulder and sliced through his scraggly beard like a golden comb. "Because we've done some stuff already."

"Now that don't make no sense," said Fred.

"Course it does. Ya help somebody once, ya got a obligation. Ya don't just stop."

Fred found this line of thought exasperating. "Piney," he said, "we saved this woman's life. She owes *us*. We don't owe her."

Piney gave a little shrug and said with infuriating calm, "I guess this is just exactly where we disagree."

"Bullshit," said Fred, and sucked so hard on his cigarette that the paper almost flamed. Expelling smoke along with words, he said, "You got a crush on her. That's the only explanation."

TWENTY-EIGHT

There was something uncanny, witchlike, about the sight of Ludmila the Belorussian housekeeper on her red motor scooter.

She wore square black shoes that looked absurd against the shifter pedal. Her wide coarse skirt was gathered up and bunched between her squat and parted thighs. Beneath a pilled and shapeless sweater, her flaccid breasts quaked with every bump and shiver of the noisy little machine. Random bundles of chopped gray hair poked out of the helmet that framed bulbous cheeks and a fleshy nose as she rode to meet her death.

She pulled into Gennady Markov's curving gravel driveway, cut the engine on the scooter, took her helmet off. She started walking toward the big front door behind its porte cochere, then stopped, unsure whether she should use the main entrance. It was dusk and she scanned the dimness for some lesser portal, a servants' wing maybe. She was still standing there, her square shoes and stocky legs uneasy on the stones, when Markov appeared in the doorway and greeted her.

Tentatively, she greeted him in return.

Moving toward her, he said, "Is beautiful evening. Perhaps we talk outside."

Obedient, the housekeeper nodded, and followed him as he

moved around the corner of the house, past trellises and hedges and
fragrant citrus trees. To the smell of powdery lemon was added the
smarting tang of iodine as they moved closer to the seawall. A table
stood very near the water's boundary, a bottle of vodka and two
glasses on it. Gennady Markov sidled toward the seat on the landward
end of the table. Casually, he motioned Ludmila toward a chair whose
back legs stood several inches from the manmade edge of the thirsty
Gulf that was drinking deeply of the ocean.

He poured vodka for both of them and then studied her a
moment. She had a mole that seemed to bind the edge of her left nos-
tril to her cheek. Her thick forearms were flat on the table and there
were creases of fat at her wrists. She didn't touch her glass till he
touched his. Then, when Markov tossed his vodka back, she tossed
back hers as well, tossed it back in one good swallow.

He refilled their glasses and spoke at last. "You like it here, Ludmila?"

Ludmila was a very cautious person. She hated to answer any
question, especially a question she wasn't absolutely sure she understood. "Here?"

"In America," he said. "Key West."

She thought about it. She cleaned houses. She lived alone in a trailer
on Stock Island, next to an auto body shop. She did what people told
her and she lived in fear. She'd carried the fear from Russia to America
and would carry it all the way to heaven because she simply couldn't
imagine that things might ever be different anywhere. But the bread
was fresh here and the weather was good. "Is better, yes," she said.

Markov drank his vodka. Ludmila drank hers. Her chin shook as
she swallowed and then her face regained its doughy impassivity.

He looked past her to starlight on the water. Current was invisi-
ble and silent and yet it had a weight and a presence; somewhere
very deep people were aware when the tides were running strong.
Markov smiled, said, "You go to beach? You swim?"

Maybe it was the vodka or maybe the chance to complain.
Ludmila grew briefly talkative. "Beach? Who has time for beach?
Swim? No. No place swim in Belorusse."

"Ah," said Markov, and refilled the glasses. Offhandedly he added, "You have more time, now you don't clean for Lazslo."

Ludmila had been waiting patiently, obediently for some indication of why she'd been called here. Now she understood. She said, "So you want I clean for you?"

Instead of answering, Markov said, "Very sad what happened to Lazslo." He emptied his glass.

Ludmila left hers alone. She lowered her flat gray eyes and became aware that the air was cooler at her back than on her face.

"Now you do not drink?" he said.

She didn't answer. Secretly she tried to scoot her chair a little forward. Its legs were pegged in small white decorative stones. It didn't budge.

Markov poured himself more vodka. "Still," he went on, "what Lazslo did, the things he said . . . Ivan Fyodorovich played the tapes for me, of course."

Ludmila reached for her glass, stopped her hand midway. For her there were many kinds of fear and each sent a different flavor climbing up her throat. Ordinary fear, the kind she felt every day, tasted of salt and bile. Now she tasted curdled milk and vinegar. She tried to choke it back then grabbed her vodka after all in an attempt to wash it down.

The liquor was still in her gullet when Markov softly asked, "How did you plant the tapes, Ludmila?"

She said nothing and he stared at her. Her eyes were blank, her cheeks a doughy graceless blur, her mouth weak and loose and stupid. Markov tried to feel hatred for her but could manage no more than a disgust that splattered filthily and stained himself as well. He stared, and fixed her in the stare like an animal in headlights. Behind Ludmila the water was flat, and yet the very starlight seemed swept up by the tide, there was an illusion of reflections stretched and smeared by the current's northward rush.

Moving deliberately, his eyes set now on the water, Markov put the heels of his hands against the corners of the table and pushed as hard as he could.

The far edge caught Ludmila in the chest and she started going over. Her shoulders shot back, the front legs of her chair pulled free of the stones, her chopped gray hair stood on end as it broke the plane of the seawall. For an endless moment she teetered there above the Gulf, thick arms pinwheeling for balance, squat thighs flailing for the ground.

Terrified she would not fall, Markov bumped her once again.

The vodka bottle tumbled, the glasses clattered to the ground. Ludmila's hardened hands grabbed the table's edge and the absurdest sort of equilibrium was briefly reached. Her feet were kicking inside the square black shoes, she tried to claw and slither her way onto the surface of the table as if the table was a lifeboat. Her tongue stuck out, she grunted, she wobbled like a bowling pin but would not fall, and Markov, straining, sweating, horrified, at length realized that the only way to end the grotesque and ludicrous stalemate was to lift the whole damn table and throw it in on top of her.

He upended it and shoved, and Ludmila, still cradled in her chair, somersaulted backward and entered the water like a scuba diver.

The table landed flat atop her splash, sealed it like a manhole cover. She disappeared immediately.

Then she surfaced a dozen feet away.

Her coarse wide skirt had filled with air, she'd become her own pontoon. She bobbed, she flailed, but the more she struggled, the more her skirt deflated, sea encroaching as air leaked out, until the material began to undulate like the body of a squid, and the fast water grabbed her as if it were armed with hooks, and her single unheard scream ended in a gurgle as she was carried out and down.

Gennady Markov stood at the edge of the seawall, panting and sweating as the body was trundled northward and then submerged. He felt no remorse, but a deep discouragement. If it was this exhausting to murder even a weak old woman, how could he ever hope to equal the efficiency of Cherkassky and his minions?

Ludmila had kicked off one of her square black shoes, it lay derelict and mute against the cool white stones. Markov picked it up, along with the glasses and the uncapped vodka bottle that was lying on its side. There was a shallow pool of liquor that had not spilled out, and he drank it as he strolled back to the house.

TWENTY-NINE

"So Aaron," Suki said, trying to steer the conversation clear of Russians and tactics and dread, "when did you first hatch this dream of owning a guest house?"

The two of them were having dinner—bowls of pasta, finally—in the kitchen of the Mangrove Arms. Aaron had a forkful of fusilli halfway to his face. He thought a moment, then said, "I didn't hatch it. I caught it."

"Caught it?"

The kitchen was not romantic. Its surfaces were mostly stainless steel, per the Board of Health. Outsize pots and pans hung from hooks above the counters; it was hard to stop seeing the big aluminum sink and huge black iron range.

"Dreams are catchy," Aaron said. "Contagious as the flu."

"So who'd you catch it from?"

"I was afraid you'd ask me that. My wife," he said. "Ex-wife."

Suki nodded. Most people, by her age, had an ex-spouse or two. They'd had chicken pox, broken bones, crashed a car, been married. What had Suki had? Some boyfriends who in retrospect were clearly jerks and one measly attempted murder. Just occasionally she wondered what she'd missed. She sipped some wine. "She wanted a guest house?"

"No. She only pretended she did. Very convincingly. That was the problem."

Suki ate some pasta. They'd made it together. Aaron chopped the garlic, she shredded the basil. The kitchen was not romantic but it was nice to be cooking side by side, their elbows close and fingers busy as good smells wafted up between them.

Aaron blotted his lips. He hadn't intended to go on, but he heard himself say, "It's a thing with city people, a safety valve. The fantasy of escape, of change."

Suki sipped some wine. "But most people stay. And stay the same."

Aaron nodded, ate.

Suki said, "You sorry?"

"Sorry?"

"About your marriage. Leaving."

He ran a hand through his hair. Suki watched the curls wrap around his fingers, one by one. "No," he said. "Not at all."

He put his fork down for a moment and looked at Suki's face. Her unlikely blue eyes were toned down to slate gray in the dimness, her lips stayed just slightly parted, as though she herself was speaking, as if listening had a breath and a language of its own. Looking at her, it seemed suddenly to Aaron that it had been a long, long time since he'd really spoken with anyone.

"One thing bugs me, though," he said, refilling both their glasses. "I don't think I ever made her understand."

"Understand?" said Suki. "Or want the same thing you did?"

"Okay, okay, fair enough. But there's one conversation I remember, it still frustrates me no end . . . But wait a second, you don't wanna hear this."

"I do," said Suki. "Really."

"Really? . . . Well . . . I guess it was one of those conversations that couples sort of have a thousand times, and then one night they *really* have it. I said, 'Okay, that little B&B we always talk about it, let's go for it, let's do it now.' She looked at me like I was nuts. 'Now?' she said. 'Not now. Much later, when we retire.' 'When's that?' I said. 'Come on, let's leave our jobs, leave Manhattan ...' And she freaked of course, turned the whole thing upside down. 'Why are you so frightened by success?' 'Frightened by success?!' I said. 'I'm frightened, yeah. Wanna know what scares me? What scares me is that I'm barely forty, and I don't want the whole rest of my life to consist of a few dumb things I already know I'm good at. T-bills. Matching my socks to my tie. Which crosstown streets to take. Twenty years from now I know nothing but those same few things? I wanna do some things I'm bad at. Hammer boards and see them crack. Plant shrubs and watch them die...' "

"And she said—?"

Aaron pushed some pasta around his plate. "She told me I was having a midlife crisis."

With a vehemence that surprised them both, Suki said, "Now that's an evil deadly phrase."

Aaron had to smile. "It is, now that you mention it."

Suki got more Mediterranean; her arms came up, her shoulders dimpled as she gestured. "Someone wants to change his life, it must just be a nervous breakdown. Give it a label and stop listening. Otherwise . . . otherwise, change might get contagious too, and wouldn't that be terrifying?"

Aaron sipped wine. "You sound like someone who's heard that stuff herself."

"Something like it," Suki said. "A long time ago. You had a midlife crisis. I was a dropout. Same kind of thing, I guess. A tag that's in style to explain away the crazies and the misfits who don't want what other people want. Hey, face it—there's gotta be something wrong with someone who doesn't want a house with a garage and a baby dressed in Gap and the kind of job that gets you frequent-flyer miles."

Aaron said, "So when you left that, was it hard?"

"Leaving Jersey? Hard?! Pfuh. I was a kid. Parts of it were hard, I guess. Hard to tell my folks I wasn't gonna finish college. That was a big deal to them. Slinging all that hash to help with the tuition. The

rest? I didn't really have a life yet. What did I have to leave? You—you
had a lot."

"Seemed that way at the time," admitted Aaron. He reached up,
scratched his neck. He looked at Suki. The kitchen was not romantic.
The light was flat and neutral, there were no cut flowers on the table.
He said, "But it doesn't matter what you leave. It only matters what
you find."

"I'll drink to that," said Suki.

She raised her glass. They clinked. The glasses were not crystal,
there was no one to clear away the dishes and leave them staring
soulfully at one another. They looked at one another anyway, until
Aaron was defeated by her improbable blue eyes and dropped his
glance. And if the kitchen hadn't been so unromantic, and if the
threat of murderous Russians wasn't looming over their emotions, it
might have dawned on them to reflect on how extraordinary it was,
how quaint and ripe with promise, that they were sharing a roof and
sharing food and telling stories, and weren't lovers yet.

The big school windows of the *Island Frigate* office had a crisscross
pattern of iron bars in front of them, and Tarzan Abramowitz was
briefly stymied in his determination to break in.

He stood a moment on the metal landing, his crowbar tapping
edgily against his thigh, the strap of a leather satchel paralleling the
wide suspender on his shoulder. Above and behind him, the light of a
bright orange street lamp was swallowed up by the leaves of a
banyan tree; below him the street was quiet. He cursed the windows
and worked his crowbar between the door frame and the door.

The process lacked subtlety, but Key West break-ins didn't require
a great deal of finesse. Alarms were few; back alleys were many;
police response time was on an island schedule. Tarzan got a grip
and started prying with his beefy arms. Paint twanged off the jamb,
you could see a lot of different colors beneath the present gray. The
molding bowed and started breaking free, and then the bar bit

deeper, down to where the wood was too sodden and decayed to splinter, but could be scraped away, grated almost, like a raw potato. Abramowitz grunted and squeezed, and when the door fell open the lock was still intact, just not attached to anything.

Inside, the office was dark save for the sickly glow of a computer monitor that Peter Haas, the restaurant reviewer, had neglected to turn off. His screensaver had flying toasters on it and these annoyed Tarzan Abramowitz. He smashed the computer with his crowbar. The toasters shattered along with the glass and left behind a fugitive green glow that seemed to come from nowhere, that hovered in the air like fog then flashed and faded like a lightning bug smeared against a sidewalk.

He turned his flashlight on and tried to determine which desk belonged to the woman who could not live.

On one desk he found a cupful of cigars; he cleared the surface with his elbow, monitor, smokes and all. At another he found drawers full of old Playbills, which he dumped out on the floor. Finally he turned his beam on a desk that was topped with little stacks of invoices and proofs of ads. He scanned it quickly for a note pad, an appointment book. Finding nothing that gave an immediate hint of Suki's whereabouts, he started stuffing things—business cards, receipts, her Rolodex—into the leather satchel.

Then, without particular hurry, he headed for the sundered door. Halfway there he stopped, like a man who's forgotten his hat. He'd decided to smash one more computer. He cocked his crowbar and savored the shatter, then walked unharassed down the metal stairway and around the corner to his blue Camaro.

THIRTY

"Look," said Officer Carol Lopez, "it's just a break-in. Why you wanna talk to homicide?"

"Just a break-in," Donald Egan murmured.

It was morning. He'd arrived at work with a double Cuban coffee in one hand and a sheaf of papers in the other. He'd seen the front door hanging open just a crack, and his first thought was, *Good, someone came in early for a change*; he wouldn't have to rearrange his hands, he could simply push through with his shoulder. That's when he noticed that both halves of the lock were sticking to the door, and the door frame had been hollowed out.

"It isn't just a break-in," the editor went on. "That's the point."

Lopez was a woman but she had the same flat but spreading ass that male cops always had. Maybe it was the pants they made them wear, or maybe the weight of the holster on the hips. "If it's not a break-in—" she began.

"There's nothing here worth stealing," the editor interrupted. "No cash, no drugs, no television sets—"

"A grudge then?" said the cop. "A controversy? Like a white trash letter to the editor?"

"Getting warmer," Egan said.

"Still. A grudge, I don't see where that's homicide."

Egan patted the empty pocket of his shirt. He badly wanted a cigar. He squatted down and combed through the rubble around his desk—the papers and folders and dangling wires—until he found one. Straightening up, he said, "I think it's connected to an unsolved murder on your books. Lazslo Kalynin."

Lopez used her forearm to push her hat back farther from her brow. "Lazslo Kalynin. I saw that stiff. Wasn't pretty. But the connection, there you lose me."

Donald Egan lit up, pulled cigar smoke deeper down his lungs than cigar smoke was supposed to go. He looked around his trashed premises as the vapor hit his bloodstream. Smashed monitors glowered back at him like vacant eye sockets, and he knew his leveraged business was going down the tubes. Yet in that moment, with the rank nipple of tobacco tickling his gums and the narcotic sting of smoke scratching at his passageways, this failed and disappointed man was almost happy. This was the beauty, the near-salvation, of addiction. With sudden calm, he said, "I know I lose you there. This is why I want to talk to homicide."

Officer Lopez frowned. People tended not to take her as seriously as she thought she should be taken, and she didn't know if it was because she was a woman, or because she was only a patrol cop, or because she was a woman patrol cop in a town where people didn't take much seriously. She sighed and raised a clipboard.

She started filling out a form. Egan smoked. He narrowed his eyes, clamped his throat shut to hold the precious cargo in his chest. The universe shrank down to that wet red horizon where the welcome poisons rubbed against his membranes.

"A report," said Lopez, tearing the top sheet off a triplicate and handing it to him. "You'll need it for insurance."

Egan blinked at dead computers, battered furniture. "I don't have insurance."

"Boy, you really should." She reached into a back pocket and came out with a pamphlet. She handed it to Egan.

"Victims Rights," he read. He spit a fleck of tobacco onto the littered floor. "Bet you hand out more of these than I distribute papers."

"Better reading maybe," Carol Lopez said. "I'll ask Lieutenant Stubbs to stop by later."

Pineapple had never been to a hotel before, and he didn't know how to act.

That, and his shoelessness, and the fact that he was carrying his sign with PARKING written on it, was making him extremely selfconscious. But he was determined to visit Suki, to see how she was and to ask if there was any more that he could do for her. So he screwed up his courage and climbed the porch steps of the Mangrove Arms.

He hoped to see Aaron before he had to talk to anybody else, but, instead, there was an old man sitting at the desk. Piney considered fleeing, but fought the impulse. He hesitated just an instant then shuffled quickly toward the counter, trying to hide his crusty feet before the old man saw them. "Hi," he said. "My name's Pineapple."

Sam Katz looked up and smiled.

His own life had changed invisibly but dramatically over the past few days. The guest house finally had some customers; they were harboring a refugee; and he felt that Aaron needed him. This belief was bracing beyond words, more galvanizing than some exotic medication. So Sam had been begging his brain to concentrate, pleading with his circuitry to carry messages truly, so that he might be of help. He was determined to be alert and businesslike behind the desk. He said, "Ah, Mr. Pineapple, welcome. You have a reservation?"

This flustered Piney, he changed the angle of his PARKING sign. "First name," he mumbled. "First name's Pineapple."

Sam smiled benignly. "How interesting. Were all the children in your family named for fruits?"

"Didn't really have a family," Piney said.

"Ah," said Sam. He tried to give comfort. "Sometimes, ya know, it's really just as well. So. What can I do for you?"

Piney's feet were damp against the sisal rug. He leaned across the counter with an elbow very near the little silver bell. Softly he said, "I'd like to please see Suki for a minute if I could."

Sam froze. His heart bounced around inside his skinny chest. His eyeballs itched. Suki wasn't there. That was the first, main, most important thing he had to remember. No Suki. Never heard of her. Now here's this person asking for her. Either it was some kind of a crazy test or it was big-time trouble. He tugged a tuft of hair, fiddled with his hearing aid. "Suki?"

"Ya know," said Piney. "Aaron's friend."

Sam thought fast. "Aaron?"

"The owner. He brought her here. She stayed with us before. Me and Fred."

"Oh yeah? And where do you live?"

"In a hot dog."

"Hot dog?"

"In the mangroves. Old military property. By the airport."

Sam remembered, sort of, driving past the airport on the morning they picked Suki up. But he wasn't quite convinced. He narrowed his eyes, said, "*Shkulski pudenska.*"

Piney said, "Wha'?"

"I called you a filthy name in Russian. You didn't flinch."

"Why would I?" Piney said.

Slowly, Sam got up from his chair. "Wait here a minute. But I have to tell you, Cantaloupe, you scared the shit outa me."

"Found the car?" said Piney. "I kept telling Fred we oughta find a better swamp."

"Better swamp," said Suki, "I would've drowned."

"God. I didn't think of that."

They were standing on the widow's walk outside of Suki's room. The fig tree threw a dappled shade, leaves scratched dryly at the railing when the breeze blew. Piney leaned far over, craned his neck toward Whitehead Street. "I change the place I sit a little ways," he said, "we could wave to each other."

"I'd like that," Suki said.

There was a pause. A plane went by. Piney said, "So I guess you're sort of stuck here, huh?"

"Looks that way."

"I'd do anything to help, ya know."

"I know you would. Thank you."

Piney looked away, grabbed a little dangling branch and let the leaves rub on his shoulder. "Fred says it's 'cause I got a crush on you, but it isn't. It's philosophy."

For that Suki had no answer. A breeze moved the shadow she was standing in and sunshine warmed her face.

Piney went on, "Fred'll help too. He says he won't but he will. That's just Fred."

Suki nodded and Piney turned around to face her. He met her eyes for just a second and then he dropped his head a little and looked beneath her chin. Thin strands of muscle were moving in her neck, and watching very closely he could see the pulse surging underneath her skin. "Healin' up nice," he said.

"Coming along," said Suki.

"Well, gotta go," said Piney, and he gathered up the PARKING sign that he'd leaned against the railing. "I'll wave to you."

"I'll wave back," Suki said.

"You need anything," he said, "I'm sitting there."

THIRTY-ONE

" 'N other donut?" said Dunkin' Dave.

"Fuck yourself another donut," said the thickly built Lieutenant Gary Stubbs. Since Dunkin' Donuts moved to Southard Street, just around the corner from the station, the waistband of his pants had started folding down across the top half of his belt, his thighs had filled in the last pucker of his boxer shorts, and he walked around all day with an oily feeling at the corners of his mouth.

"Come on," said Dave. "'Sa last one onna tray."

Stubbs looked at the donut. Hot grease had pocked its surface beautifully, it had a perfect mix of sheen and craters. He took it. "Only 'cause I'm having such a shitty day."

It was a slow time, just around eleven in the morning. Cops had crazy schedules, that's why Dave could talk to them. He rested the corner of the tray against the counter. "How come shitty?"

Stubbs had dunked his donut, coffee dripped back out of its honeycombed insides. "Ever had a cat sleep in your motor?"

"Huh?"

"Cool nights like lately," said Stubbs, "the strays, they climb up underneath your car and sleep on top the motor."

Dave rearranged the angle of his paper hat. "Whaddya know."

"'Cept this morning," Stubbs went on, "some asshole cat, he's sleeping in the fan. Go to start 'er up ... "

"Oh shit," said Dave.

Stubbs made a clattering but glutted sound.

"Cut 'im right in half?"

"Thirds," said the lieutenant. "His tail was wrapped around. Some fuckin' way to start the day, huh? Pieces a cat glued to the radiator. Then they find a body out around Cottrell."

"Cottrell? Way out in the Gulf?"

"Fishermen found 'er. Thought she was a bundle a rags. Red sweater, gray skirt. One black shoe. Ever seen a body been drowned a coupla days?"

Dave shook his head. Making donuts all night long wasn't any picnic but it was better than a lot of jobs.

"'S weird," the cop went on. "No two are alike. Sometimes the skin pops open. Ya know, like a plum that's overripe. Usually there's pieces missing. Shark eats a leg, the nose is nibbled off. Eyes, the gulls sometimes—"

Dave hadn't eaten since last night, he had a lot of acid in his stomach. He raised a hand. "Accident or someone killed her?"

"Hard to say," said Stubbs. "Had one big bruise across her chest. Narrow, even—not like from a punch. Too high up to be a gunwale. Coulda been a boom swinging across, but she wasn't dressed for sailing. No other signs of struggle and she was breathing when she hit the water."

"Any idea who she was?"

"No ID," said Stubbs. "Not much face to tell the truth. One little kinda crazy clue."

"What's that?" asked Dunkin' Dave.

"Her underpants."

"Underpants?"

"The label," said the cop. "Seems to be in Russian."

Dave had been at work since midnight, sweating under bare light bulbs, tending fryers big as kiddie pools, squirting jelly, squirting cream. By late morning he sometimes got a little giddy. "Exhibit A," he said. "The victim's underpants."

"Not funny," said Stubbs. He dunked his donut deep down in his tepid coffee, and then his cell phone started ringing.

Dunkin' Dave picked up his tray and moved discreetly toward the kitchen, going slow enough to hear the homicide detective curse then drop some money on the counter.

Gary Stubbs and Donald Egan knew each other vaguely, in the way that cops and newspaper guys were acquainted. They were usually cordial and they didn't trust each other worth a damn; they traded information and if the swap was even someone felt like he had lost. Cops were big on order; editors made their livings from freedom; they were dogs latched on to opposite ends of the gristly bone of power, and neither dog was programmed to let go.

Now Stubbs stood in the wrecked old classroom as Egan began his story, and after listening for a while the cop said, "Is the Cold War back or what? I am all of a sudden hearing altogether too much bull-shit about Russians."

Egan was sucking a cigar. Smoke was painting his lungs like a satin roller on a wall. "Oh yeah? What else are you hearing?"

"First you show me yours," said Stubbs.

The editor picked tobacco off his tongue. He was sitting on a rolling chair in the middle of the room, and he gestured at the mess around him. "My desk," he said. "Vandalized. Nothing taken." He pointed to his right. "Reporters' desks. Ditto." He pointed to his left. "Ad sales desk. Suki Sperakis, woman's name is. Drawers rifled. Stuff taken. Names, addresses."

Stubbs said, "So?"

"She was playing journalist. Wanted to do an article on the T-shirt shops. Russian Mafia, she said. Went out with Lazslo Kalynin. Hasn't been seen since the night he died."

Egan thought he was being pretty damned forthright and informative. He expected a show of interest. Take a notebook out. Lean closer. Something. Stubbs just stood there. Then he said, "Now tell me something I don't already know."

The editor got flustered, his cigar made circles in the air. "How d'you—"

"Like for starters," the cop interrupted, "she's been missing, what, almost a week now, and you don't think to report her missing?"

"I didn't think . . . " Egan began. "I didn't want—"

"Didn't want to get involved," said Stubbs. "Didn't want the inconvenience. I know the type . . . But now you're being inconvenienced and maybe now you're scared, and now that it's not just a question of the ad person being dead or not, but your papers being dumped out on the floor, now you're starting to believe there really is a Russian Mob."

Egan didn't take offense. He smoked instead. Then he said, "Well, yeah, I sort of am. Aren't you?"

Stubbs started pacing through the rubble. "Doesn't seem to matter much, what I believe."

Quite suddenly he was thoroughly pissed off. He couldn't put his finger on just why. He catalogued the day's annoyances. The trisected cat, its neck vertebrae protruding like something meant for soup. The drowned woman with her noseless nostrils. The second donut he should not have eaten, and now this typical solid citizen who didn't want to get involved.

Irritations all—but with each step Stubbs took in his futile little march around the ancient classroom, he realized that none of them was to the point. He was pissed off because he too was at fault. Egan's guilt was his guilt. He hadn't wanted to believe, either. He pictured the battered Suki holed up in the vending truck. Why was she there? Because she cared about the town, tried to fight back against something that was ruining it; and when the whole thing blew up in her face, no one wanted to get involved. Bad for business at the *Island Frigate*. Bad PR for the police department, a headache for the tourism flacks . . .

Now there was a dead woman with a Russian label in her panties. That seemed to make it two dead Russians and someone nearly strangled *by* a Russian. Money laundering probably. Plutonium dealing, just maybe. How much weirdness made a Mafia? And if there was a Mafia in town, what then? Stubbs didn't have the manpower or the knowledge to fight it, and the thought of killers that he could not fight frustrated him to the point of tantrums. So he paced, and he glared at the hangdog editor sitting in his wreath of smoke, and then without a word he kicked aside some Playbills and some broken glass and headed for the door.

"Wait! You never showed me yours!" protested Donald Egan.

Gary Stubbs kept going, and his footsteps were heavy on the metal stairs on the outside of the building.

THIRTY-TWO

Suki had no patience for sitting still, lacked the prudent meekness to stay hidden in her turret. At the Mangrove Arms that afternoon, she and Aaron were planting shrubs out in the courtyard.

They were working side by side and on their knees. Suki's hair was tied up in a red bandanna, her shoulders were covered by a big workshirt knotted at the midriff. She wore gardening gloves, and where they ended the sinews of her wrists were flickering. Dirt flew from her trowel as if kicked back by a terrier, and her forehead was pebbled with sweat at the hairline.

Aaron's shovel bit in next to hers, and when the hole was ready, he lifted the shrub by the base of its stem, the hairs of its roots protruding from the shredding burlap, and Suki helped to center it and nestle it in. Leaning across to tamp down the soil, their faces were very close, they smelled each other's skin, and they pretended that the closeness was an accident, nothing but a circumstance of labor, a gesture from some archaic time when life was tenuous and basic and people didn't speak of love, but rather sowed it, pruned it, proclaimed connection with muscles not with words. Suki dragged an arm across her forehead. Aaron stared an instant at her mouth. They scuttled side by side to the next place in the line of shrubs.

They were tamping dirt, serene, cares put aside, when a squat distorted shadow slashed suddenly between them.

The shadow stained the upturned soil the brickish brown of drying liver, and in a heartbeat it brought an unnatural and unwholesome coolness to the air. The wheeze of labored breathing scratched through the whisper of the palms; some sinister note in the rasp of it sent adrenaline squirting into Aaron's blood.

On some dormant heroic impulse that lived not in the brain but the spine, he clutched his shovel harder, ready for defense. His haunches tightened, set to spring. From under resolute brows he raised his eyes.

He saw Fred standing there, breathing hard and sweating through his ragged shirt.

Fred said, "Biked down pretty fast. Thought I'd better talk to you."

Aaron exhaled, dropped the shovel, muttered, "Jesus Christ."

Suki rolled off her knees, sat down on the ground. "What is it, Fred?"

"That cop guy, Stubbs," Fred wheezed, "he came up to the hot dog. Looking for you. I didn't know if I should tell him where you were. Told him I could get a message to you."

"So what's the message?" she asked.

Fred gestured for time-out. He patted his damp pockets, looking for a cigarette. Still trying to catch his breath, he lit up, filtered vapor through his nicotine-colored moustache. "Said a woman got murdered. Seems to be a Russian. And the *Frigate* office got all busted up. Whoever did it took papers from your desk. He thinks they're looking for you. He thinks you oughta talk to him."

Suki bit her lip, the upper one. "*Now* he thinks that."

Fred blew smoke out of his nose. "Said he's sorry. He believes you now. Unofficially, he said."

Suki shook her head, looked along the ground at the line of shrubs they'd just put in, the churned and reworked earth. Life was supposed to be much simpler than it was turning out to be. Plant shrubs, cook meals. Sip wine and watch the sun go down. She said, "I just don't know anymore what I should do."

Aaron started getting to his feet. He stood up too fast and blood drained from his skull. His vision went blank silver at the edges and the solid earth felt like batter underneath him. He said, "You know, it's very strange. I'm a law-abiding person, I believed what I was taught in civics class. But my gut is saying that before we talk to the police, we really ought to talk with Bert the Shirt."

On Key Haven, in a study with narrow windows and snug-fitting blinds, Ivan Cherkassky and Tarzan Abramowitz were trying to make sense of Suki's pilfered papers.

"A mess," Cherkassky said disgustedly. "Here she puts a circle, there she puts an arrow. Over here she draws a line goes right off the page. Where it goes, this line? Is disorganized. I see nothing here."

Tarzan Abramowitz, leaning on a thick bare arm, was looking over his boss's shoulder. "A doodler," he said.

"Doodler?" said Cherkassky. "What is doodler?" He didn't like the nearness of the other man, the dampness of his armpit near his face. He tried to shrink down lower in his chair.

"Doodler. Squiggles she makes. Airplanes. Little men."

"Disorganized," Cherkassky said again, and elbowed the most recent batch of papers to the edge of his desk blotter, where they shuffled in with many others. Unpaid invoices that were three months old. Mechanicals from ads for sunglass shops, porno stores. A Rolodex written in the various hands of half a dozen people who'd come to understand that they couldn't make a living selling space for *Island Frigate*. Nothing so far about the sentenced woman's private life, who she saw, where she went, nothing that might give a hint as to her hiding place.

Cherkassky reached into the leather satchel for another handful of papers. The two men, mystified, pored through them. Wands of light squeezed through the small gaps at the edges of the blinds; motes of golden dust floated in the air.

At length Abramowitz, his massive jaw almost nuzzling his boss's ear, pointed at a paper not unlike the hundred others that had gone before, and said, "Aha!"

"Aha?" Cherkassky said.

Tarzan pointed with a thick and hairy finger. "Look! A small thing only, but perhaps ... This paper is, how you call, paste-down for an ad."

"Paste-down," Cherkassky echoed. "Yes."

"Copy of what goes to printer," Tarzan said.

"I understand."

"But look the date," said Abramowitz. "Day before she goes with Lazslo."

"Ah," Cherkassky said. "Only one day. Good."

"Now here," said the assassin. "You see here she doodles the circles, arrows, little fish? Here she writes 'Lucia's 8.' "

Cherkassky bit his knuckles. "We know who this Lucia is?"

"Is restaurant," said Abramowitz. "Nice restaurant. Perhaps she is going there for dinner."

"But by dinner time she is—"

"She does not arrive. No dinner, very sad ... But perhaps there is someone waits for her. Friend. Boyfriend. Someone she tells things to."

Cherkassky swiveled in his seat. "We have busboy at Lucia's?"

"Of course," said Tarzan Abramowitz.

Cherkassky sighed. "Is how you say long chance."

"Long shot," said Abramowitz.

"But okay, is a start."

THIRTY-THREE

" Cops ain't subtle is the problem," Bert the Shirt was saying. Aaron had fetched him from poolside at the Paradiso, and now he was sitting poolside at the Mangrove Arms. Life in Florida—largely a matter of moving from pool to pool, staying within the radius of the waft of chlorine. He was wearing an ice-blue guayabera and stroking the hard and bound-up belly of his comatose chihuahua.

"The whole idea," the old mobster went on, "is layin' low, right?—and wit' the cops right away it's flashing lights and sirens, motorcades and tear gas. No patience. No subtlety. All 'ey do, they draw attention. The cops, I seen 'em protect a person right ta death . . . Guess I shouldn't say that. But hey, wha' do I know? Face it, when it comes to cops, I'm like prejudice."

The others, daunted and inexpert at tactics, moped around the wire mesh table. Aaron rubbed soil from the creases in his knuckles. Suki looked with yearning toward the fresh half-finished plantings. Fred plucked at his damp shirt and lit another cigarette.

Somewhere a motorcycle revved. Then Sam Katz matter-of-factly said, "Sounds to me like the time has come we gotta infiltrate."

It was sometimes hard to tell if Sam was listening. It was always hard to tell if he was following what was said. No one had expected him to weigh in with an opinion. After a baffled pause, Aaron said, "What?"

Sam said, "Infiltrate. Like get inside."

Aaron said, "I know what infiltrate—"

Bert said, "Hol' on. Didn't I say this days ago?"

Suki said, "Now let's not get any—"

But Sam Katz leaned down on his elbows, tugged his Einstein hair and moved slowly, resolutely forward. "Look. Going to the police—no good. Just sitting here—no good. They're going after Suki, we're going after them."

"And who's this *we?*" said Aaron.

Sam hadn't gotten quite that far. He fiddled with his hearing aid.

Fred surprised himself by speaking up. "Me and Piney. I guess that we could do it."

"Do *what?*" said Suki. "Am I missing something or is this all a little—"

"No offense," Bert said to Fred, "but no, ya couldn't do it. 'S gotta be somebody that could blend."

Aaron pulled his hair, was abashed to realize it was his father's gesture. "Look, these are killers. There's no one that could blend. Forget about it."

Sam Katz said, "Like us. Like me and Bert."

"Forget it, Sam," said Suki, "it isn't your—"

Sam just then remembered something very stirring that he had heard or read many decades before. He raised his finger grandly and intoned: " 'If I am only for myself, what am I?' I think that's from the Talmud."

"Pop, it just isn't realistic."

Sam Katz shook his head and looked at Bert. "Kids," he said. "They think they have a lock on realistic. Like realistic stops when Medicare starts? They think they're the only ones can accomplish anything."

Bert stroked his fading dog, watched as ghostly hairs came unstuck and fluttered through the table's wire mesh. "The uncle," he said at last. "Probably an old guy. Maybe near as old as we are."

"But with young guys," Aaron pointed out, "to do the murdering."

Bert and Sam ignored him. Friends, coevals, they were now on a circuit of their own. Sam said, "S'okay. We find out where he lives—"

"He lives up on Key Haven," blurted Suki, then wished at once she hadn't said it.

"Key Haven," said Fred, picking a tobacco fleck from his tongue. "People up there, they see you hanging around, they call the cops. Me and Piney, we couldn't blend so good up there."

Bert finished Sam's thought for him. ". . . And we rent a house nearby."

"Bert, Pop," said Aaron, "don't even start—"

"We need a cover," Bert went on.

"Cover?" said Sam. His brain was itching and he was leaning so far forward that his nose was almost on the table.

"A story. Ya know, who we are . . . How 'bout . . . How 'bout we're a coupla old gay guys."

"Gay?" said Sam. "We gotta be gay?"

"Gotta blend," said Bert. "Dignified old gay guys. Like a sweet old married couple. Partners a long, long time."

Sam Katz thought it over, wound a finger through a tuft of sun-shot hair, and shrugged. "Okay, podnah."

"Not podnah," said the Shirt. "Podnah, that's cowboys. Gay guys, it's *part*ner."

"Look," said Aaron, "there is not a chance in hell—"

His father wasn't listening. He'd stood up from his chair, his finger-tips, for balance, splayed across the table. He said, "Okay. Gay guys. Partners. So much planning, I'm exhausted."

Aaron went on even though he was no longer sure who he was talking to. "This is absolutely out of the question."

"Totally," said Suki. "Totally."

Bert the Shirt was scratching his dog like the dog was his own chin. "Infiltrate," he said. "Check 'em out. Me and Sam. Anyone got a better idea, I'm listening."

* * *

Not long after Tarzan Abramowitz left Ivan Cherkassky's house, there was a knock at the scoop-faced Russian's door.

The door was double-locked, of course, and the old Soviet's impulse was to ignore the visitor—a brat selling cookies, most likely, or a cheaply dressed fanatic handing out religious leaflets. But the knock was repeated, then again more loudly, and finally a familiar voice boomed through. "Ivan Fyodorovich! Ivan Fyodorovich!"

Cherkassky cocked his head. His pinched-in face stretched outward just a notch, and for a second he nearly smiled.

So—Gennady was coming out of his week-long sulk and was ready to resume his role of clown and figurehead and scientist and payer-out of bribes. This was a relief, though it only confirmed what Cherkassky had long known: that people, however whipped and humiliated and badly used, would come limping, crawling back to the life they knew, because being mortified, spat upon, was less appalling than the chore of finding a different life.

Cherkassky smoothed his shirt and headed for the entryway, determined to be as conciliatory and gracious as his old comrade would let him be. Opening the door, he slightly raised his hands in a gesture that was for him expansive, and said, "Gennady Petrovich, how good to see you up and out."

Markov stood in the doorway and did an absurd little pantomime of a man just freed from prison or the hospital, flared nostrils gulping in air, fat spread arms embracing the landscape, wattly chin quivering as it turned up toward the sky.

Reassured by these fresh signs of buffoonery, Cherkassky said, "Come in, come in. Tell me how you have been."

"How I have been?" said Markov, when he'd moved into the living room and settled deeply into the softest chair. "I've been drunk. I've been weeping. I've been angry. Maybe I am better now."

Cherkassky studied him. But Markov didn't want to be studied, and a buffoonish yet melancholy grin was as good a mask as any. The thin man said, "Maybe?"

Markov shrugged, lightly drummed his fingers on the chair arms.

Cherkassky studied him some more. He wanted to be delicate but he did not believe in coddling. He said, "So you are ready to get back to work?"

Markov flashed a bland and fleeting smirk, and shrugged again.

Cherkassky squirmed in response. He was accustomed to hearing Markov talk too much, blab out whatever was on his mind or in his sloppy sentimental heart. These inscrutable smiles, these stubborn silences unsettled him, as Markov knew they would.

"A new shipment needs preparing," Cherkassky said. "Libya. Twenty kilos, oxide form. Sent in pigment canisters. You can do?"

Yet again the fat man shrugged and smiled. Yes, he could do it. Take metallic plutonium, bind it to oxygen with strong acid and electric current. Easy, if you knew how. And that was his edge. He was on terms with the atom. Plutonium—people feared it like they feared whatever they did not understand. Science fiction and propaganda made them think it was much more mysterious and dangerous than it was. In fact you could carry plutonium in your briefcase; you could hold it in your hand. Do anything but breathe it in. Markov's special knowledge made him serene; his serenity made the other man fretful and fidgety.

Cherkassky leaned forward with his elbows on his knees. Uncertainty was poison to him; he felt he had to test Markov somehow, elicit some reaction he could read. Sucking in his face, he said, "Now that you are back, Gennady, there is some bad news I must tell you."

Markov sat with the stony calm of someone who's already heard the worst news he will ever hear, been visited by a calamity that could not be topped.

"The woman is alive," Cherkassky said.

This took a moment to sink in. Markov's eyes went soupy, and he stared unseeing through the picture window at the still canal and the mint-green house beyond it. The woman? Alive? Impossible. "Ludmila?"

Cherkassky blinked. His eyebrows crept together but his voice was less suspicious than confused. "Ludmila?"

Markov scratched his belly, dragged his tongue along his flubbery lips. "I only mean," he said, "what woman? What woman is alive?"

Cherkassky turned away. Too late, he realized that opening this subject had been a mistake, that Markov's goading passivity had pushed him toward a misplay. He steeled himself and said, "The woman that Lazslo was supposed to kill."

Lazslo. The name itself, in memory, had taken on for Markov an echo of the mythic, nearly the sacred. He hid his deep offense at Cherkassky's mention of it. He hid, as well, the unexpected ambivalence he felt at learning that his nephew's last squeeze was still alive. She was dangerous, of course, an awful liability; yet she was also a link to the dear passionate departed. Lazslo had desired her, and part of Markov was glad she still existed. He said, "Never the boy was meant to be a killer. I told you that, Ivan."

Cherkassky pulled on the pitted crescent of his face and made a huge concession. "And perhaps you were right, Gennady . . . But now the job needs finishing. Surely you agree."

Markov pushed his tongue against his teeth, said nothing.

Cherkassky paused, then launched into the effort of smiling. His eyes twitched at the outside corners. Skin crawled at his hairline. His lips stretched briefly, their surface shiny and dry as cellophane. He said, "And surely you understand we are together till the end. Are we friends again, Gennady?"

Markov drummed his chair arms. "Of course, Ivan," he said. "How could we ever be anything but friends?"

THIRTY-FOUR

N ick Sorrento, the maitre d' at Lucia's, had a suave but modest smile, a manner that was confident yet deferential, and just a hint of an Italian accent.

Or at least he did when customers were present. But now it was five P.M. and the door was locked. The floor was being mopped, the bar was being polished. The evening's flowers were being divvied up into many little vases, and Sorrento, in an accent direct from an Italian neighborhood in Queens, was screaming at the top of his lungs, "Where the fuck's the reservation book?"

Yussel Lupinski, the busboy from Minsk, kept his mop in steady motion, and stared down at the red and golden highlights in the hardwood floor. The reservation book was in his pants. One end of it was tickling his pubic hair and the other was poking past his belt but was covered by his apron. He stayed hunched over so the corners wouldn't show.

"We are really fucked wit'out that book!" Sorrento screamed. "Fucking chaos! Fucking madhouse!"

Swaying on his mop like a hockey player on his stick, Yussel skated back toward the kitchen. The book's edges dug into the lymph nodes in his groin.

Nick Sorrento rummaged through the shelves beneath his

podium. "I find the asshole moved that book I'm gonna fire his sorry ass."

Yussel mopped straight through the swinging kitchen door. He mopped past the ranges and the ovens and the dishwashers with their big round wire racks, to the side exit where the garbage was put out. Tarzan Abramowitz was waiting in the alley. He took the book and bounded off.

Lupinski went back to his mopping.

Sorrento kept on screaming. By five-thirty he was so hoarse he could barely croak out a *buona sera.*

But by six-fifteen the reservation book had miraculously been found, underneath some menus at the end of a banquette, where Yussel Lupinski had been setting tables. Sorrento looked daggers at the quiet busboy as he handed it over with no expression on his pallid face.

"Wait," said Sam Katz, "again it's making noises." He yanked out his hearing aid, started fiddling with it in his lap.

Aaron rolled his eyes. It was dusk, and he was giving Fred a lift back to the hot dog. Fred was in the backseat and his bike was mostly in the trunk, its front tire hanging out and spinning slowly, last light glinting off the spokes. Aaron said to his father, "If you'd stop taking it apart and putting it back together ... "

"What?"

They'd passed the airport, were rounding the curve where the mangroves were fenced in. "Either that," said Aaron, "or you just don't want to listen."

"I'm listening, I'm listening," said Sam, still twisting and turning the little gizmo in his hands.

"All right, then," Aaron said. "This infiltration nonsense, just get it off your mind."

"What?"

Fred said, "Hey Aaron, how about we stop for ice cream?"

"Ice cream, yeah," Sam said.

Fred slapped his knee. "I knew it! I had a grandmother was exactly the same. Deaf as a post till someone mentioned ice cream."

Sam put the hearing aid back in. "Better now. Must be something from the airport. We really going for ice cream?"

"Pop," said Aaron, "this infiltration craziness, I really want you to forget about it."

"Don't tell your father what to do."

They'd reached the place where the mangroves gapped and a narrow path led back to the hot dog. Aaron pulled off the road.

"Basic respect," Sam went on. "I'm not so old I shouldn't be allowed to make my own mistakes."

"But there's mistakes and there's mistakes," said Aaron. "Some mistakes you don't recover from."

Sam looked out the window. Color was fading from the water and the sky. It was time for that to happen and Sam was not saddened by the change. He said, "Aaron, worst case, what? My life is worth so much?"

"To me it is, okay?"

Leaning forward in the backseat, Fred said, "Ninety-eight cents."

Aaron said, "Excuse me?"

"Something I heard a long, long time ago," said Fred. "Really made an impression. Take the chemicals and stuff from a human body, it's worth ninety-eight cents. Maybe three bucks by now . . . Wanna come in for a beer?"

"Not a beer," said Sam. "Some ice cream maybe?"

"Can't help ya there," said Fred.

"Another time," said Aaron, and as Fred climbed out and lifted his old bike from the trunk, he looked through the windshield at the darkening ocean and the thickening sky. Young and unresigned, he saw with fear and sorrow the closing jaws of mortality in the sealing of the seam between them.

* * *

Tarzan Abramowitz leaned over Ivan Cherkassky's shoulder and failed to notice that the older man was shrinking from his nearness, from his breath. The killer peered down at the photocopied page from Lucia's reservation book, and said, "Jesus Christ, where to start I can't tell nothing."

Cherkassky just pulled hard on his scooped-out face; in the exaggerated shadows from the desk lamp, it looked like pieces of nose and chin might come off in his hand. He studied the names and numbers and check marks and cross outs on the sheet of paper, looking for some logical pattern that would make everything come clear. He found instead the same carelessness and disorganization that so often irritated him in America.

"Too he doodles," the thin man said at last, pointing to spirals and solar systems at the corner of the page.

"Is boring job," said Abramowitz. "Stand there, have to smile."

"Smile, feh," Cherkassky said. "And look, sometimes there is phone number, sometimes there is not."

There were thirty-two tables at Lucia's, and eleven of them, according to the reservation book, had turned at eight P.M. on the evening that Suki was supposed to have died. There were reservations under Cardenas and Berman, Woods and Pescatello, under Robertson and under Katz; these had contact numbers written next to them. Two tables, regulars presumably, were booked by first name only. Some reservations had hotel names appended, with initials duly noted so that the concierge might get his kickback. In all, there were six tables booked for two, one three, three fours, and a six. The maitre d' had scratched off each name as the tables had been filled; no note was made of parties that were incomplete.

Abramowitz said, "Is useless, so many people."

Cherkassky picked up a fountain pen. It was silver and engraved and wrote with elegant precision. He started crossing people out. "Is not so many. Hotels, forget hotels. Tourists. Tourists matter nothing."

That left eight tables.

He put question marks next to the regulars. "These," he said. "Only first name. Local people. Maybe her friends. We eliminate the others to find out."

Now it was down to six parties with phone numbers written down. "These you call," Cherkassky said.

"Call?" said Abramowitz. The prospect made him uncomfortable. He was handy with a knife or crowbar or wire, but talking was not what he was good at.

"Is bad too many people see you," said Cherkassky. "You call from pay phone and ask for her."

"Ask for her? But—"

"Someone will be afraid," Cherkassky said. "Will be afraid and make mistake. You will hear. One thing in America you can depend. Someone will be careless, will trust too much. Will make mistake."

THIRTY-FIVE

"You gay?" said Sam Katz to the realtor who was driving them around Key Haven the next morning.

Sam was sitting in the backseat. He leaned forward and spread his elbows near Bert's shoulders, his eyes meeting the young man's in the rearview mirror.

The realtor had short moussed platinum hair above jet black eyebrows. He had a diamond stud in his right ear and wore a shirt of polka-dotted silk. "Well yes," he said, "I am."

"Very nice," said Sam. "We're gay too. Been together, what is it now, honey—forty years?"

Bert stroked the chihuahua in his lap and stifled a grimace. "Fawty-one."

"Forty-one years," the realtor said. "Me, I've been lucky if a relationship lasts the weekend. And you've been out all that time?"

"Out?" said Sam.

Reluctantly, Bert picked up the thread. "New Yawk. Ya know, the Village. No one gave a shit."

"Here neither," said the realtor.

"Except my father," Sam rolled on. "I thought he'd *plotz*. My boy, my Sam, a *faygela*. Took years before—"

"Sam," Bert cut him off, "this gentleman doesn't really wanna hear the story of our lives."

"*Au contraire*," the realtor said. "I'll bet you were at Stonewall. It's like a link to history."

"There," said Sam. "You see? Now where was I? . . . Forty years he does this to me, makes me lose my train of thought . . . "

It was a weekday and the streets were as quiet as a suburb anywhere. Houses crouched behind hedges of buttonwood and jasmine, awnings threw parallelograms of shade across mute windows. Here and there a yard crew worked, a pool man stood beside his truck and wrapped himself in underwater vacuum-cleaner hose.

The realtor turned around in gravel cul-de-sacs, leaned low across the steering wheel as he pointed out his listings. At length the three of them were standing in the kitchen of a pink stucco cottage, when Bert said, "I'm curious about the neighborhood. Who lives up here?"

The faucet in the sink was dripping. The realtor discreetly tried to make it stop. "Very mixed," he said. "Better-off Conch families—big move up for them. Professionals, doctors from the hospital. Snowbirds who don't like the noise in Old Town."

"Ah," said Bert, picking lint from the dog that was hanging from his hand. "We heard there were some Russians lived up here. The guys with all the T-shirts."

"Markov," said the realtor, with an insider's quiet certainty. "Very wealthy man. A few others. Very quiet, keep to themselves. Live out farther toward the point."

"Maybe we should look out there," Bert said.

"Pricey," warned the realtor.

Sam Katz had been looking in the microwave, checking where the rays came out. Such a simple invention; he wished he'd thought of it. He said, "Two pensions, no babies. Pricey doesn't matter."

So they got back in the car and headed toward the Gulf. The lots got bigger, the houses sprouted breezeways, guest wings. When swaths of open water appeared past barricades on dead-end streets, Bert said, "Ya mind we swing by Markov's place? I hear it's a helluva house."

The realtor turned left, then right, then pointed toward a large establishment that looked confused. Brick pillars guarded both ends of a horseshoe gravel driveway. Trellises of bougainvillea were squandered on a huge garage. An orange tile roof was slashed open by a stone chimney. The informality of a shady porch slammed into the pomp of an entranceway with columns.

"What helluva house?" said Sam Katz. "Borax. A mishmosh."

Confidentially, the realtor said, "Money can't buy taste."

"And happiness can't buy money," said Bert. "Ya got anything on this street?"

The realtor put on the brakes, considered. "This street, no. Closest thing, around the corner. On a side canal. Eccentric little house."

"We're on the eccentric side ourselves," said Sam.

"Kitsch with attitude," the realtor said. "Between us, sort of homo barocco."

So they went around the corner and pulled into the driveway of a mint-green house that seemed to have been built by someone with a fetish for tile. A tile walkway led to the front door, which in turn was framed in tile. The entryway floor was tile in a sunburst pattern. The countertops were tile, a wide band of tile went all around the kitchen like a belt. A path of tile meandered through the living room; Bert put his dog down and the creature's tiny claws made a bone-dry ticking sound. The tile flowed beneath the sliding glass back door to form a tile patio that extended halfway to the seawall.

Sam Katz ran his hand along a coffee table topped in tile and said, "Looks like the men's room in Grand Central."

"Easy to keep clean," said the realtor. "No mildew. Good if you have a problem with mold."

"Problem wit' mold," said Bert the Shirt, "I'd be dead ten times already." He gestured all around himself. "Who else is onna street, across the way?"

"Don't know," said the realtor. "But it's mostly owner-occupied. Very quiet, I assure you."

Bert said to Sam, "Take it for a month?"

Sam said, "We haven't seen the bedroom, the bath."

Bert rolled his eyes. "Okay, Sam. Go look at the bathroom."

Sam followed a line of tile down the hallway. Bert lightly drummed his fingers on a mosaic-sided hutch.

After a moment Sam's voice came reverberating as though from a dormitory shower. "Tile," he reported. "Tile up the *poopik.*"

"We'll take it for a month," Bert said to the realtor.

Lieutenant Gary Stubbs sat in his cramped and dingy office, watching water droplets dribble from his ancient air conditioner and arc gently to the floor.

Before him on his scratched-up desk were two manila envelopes, which together comprised what he'd come to think of as the Dead Russians in Paradise file. Lazslo Kalynin. Throat cut in a purported burglary. Except no one but the department politicians believed it. Burglars in this town were crack heads, coke fiends. They were strung out and they were amateurs. They left fingerprints, and if they had to kill someone, they hacked him thirty, forty times, poking till they found an artery. Kalynin's killers had made no errors and their killing was as neat as surgery.

Then there was Jane Doe of the Russian undergarments. Not a clue on her, other than two lungsful of saltwater, proving that she'd gone down breathing. Suicide was possible, though that long thin bruise across her chest didn't go with suicide. Besides, who drowned themselves with shoes on?

Stubbs shuffled the folders, laid them side by side, put a palm on each of them. He wanted the two dead Russians to be connected, and then again he didn't want them to. Connecting them might turn two unsolved cases into only one, and he might feel only half as bad. Then again, police work was about the possible, and if the two stiffs were connected, that argued that there was in fact a Mafia involved, and if there was a Mafia Stubbs might very well be stymied altogether and end up feeling twice as bad.

He got up from his desk and paced. He was hungry. He thought about the coffee-sodden weight of a donut. Then he remembered something that he'd only half-noticed before. He opened the Lazslo Kalynin folder. The body had been found by a housekeeper. The cop who'd first arrived at the crime scene was Carol Lopez.

He raised her on the radio and asked her to meet him at the morgue in half an hour.

"Little hard to tell without the nose," said Lopez, when Ludmila had been slid out on her slab. "But yeah, height, shape, I'd lay a bet that's her."

Stubbs looked down at the blue skin, the matted tangled hair. "She say anything you remember? Anything at all?"

Lopez pushed her hat back with her forearm. "Barely spoke English. Said hello and pointed. I sent her home."

"Very upset?" said Stubbs.

"No," said Lopez. "Not that showed."

"Maybe she saw something she shouldn't have seen."

Carol Lopez shrugged. "Wonder what got the nose."

"Grab a donut?" said the homicide detective.

An attendant slid the corpse back into place. The slab locked in like a file drawer.

Stubbs said mostly to himself, "Maybe I'll see if Markov can ID the body. Gimme an excuse to talk to him again at least."

THIRTY-SIX

The Mangrove Arms was strangely quiet.

The woman who occasionally appeared to do the breakfast had straightened up and left. The few guests had had their fresh-squeezed juice and their muffins and their sliced papaya, and had gone out to sightsee or were lazily baking at the edge of the pool. Aaron and Suki—faces close, arms intertwined—had been nailing down a puckered runner on a stairway, and now they took a break for coffee.

They sat down in the unromantic kitchen, and Suki counted Band-Aids on Aaron's hands. "Only four today," she said.

"Getting better with the hammer." He tried to smile but it didn't quite work. He looked at her. The undaunted gleam was back in her unlikely eyes. Her bruises were healed and her tanned neck flowed down to rosewood shoulders. They were alone and it should have been wonderful, but Aaron was fretful and preoccupied.

Suki, in his house and not his lover, could not help wondering if it was because he regretted inviting her to stay. She sipped some coffee, hid her face behind the cup. "Something wrong?"

"Wrong?" said Aaron. A pathetic evasion. Even in business he'd never got comfortable with fibbing. "Guess I miss my father. Can't help being worried."

Suki wrestled with an impulse. She wanted to put her hand on his. But touch was not a simple thing. Between a man and woman who were not lovers, it could easily go wrong, or go too right; a gift of comfort could seem too bold, a gesture of solace could cross over into awkwardness. She held her coffee mug and the moment slipped away.

Aaron said, "You think it's weird? How close we are?"

"I think it's great," said Suki. "I can't imagine wanting family in my face, but the two of you, I think it's great."

Aaron drank some coffee, glanced at the outsize pots and pans hanging from their racks. "Growing up," he said, "all my friends, their fathers worked too hard. Never around. Or around and exhausted. Everyone felt gypped. I didn't. My father was around. We did things. He taught me stuff."

"My old man taught me stuff too," said Suki. "Pour boiling water on roast beef if people said it was too rare. Check dinner rolls for bite marks before putting them in the next guy's basket . . . Wha'd he teach you?"

Aaron pushed his lips out, searched for a way to sum up the oblique and scattered and half-learned lessons of a childhood. Finally he said, "He taught me to make the most of what I had."

"Example?"

Aaron pondered, looked out the French doors to the glaring water of the pool. "Pitching."

"Pitching?"

"Pitching. Baseball. I was a skinny kid. Smallish. Weak. But I loved to play. I wanted to pitch. My father said, 'We'll study up.' We watched the little guys, the Whitey Fords, the Bobby Shantzes. So great, watching Whitey Ford with my father's arm around my shoulder. My father said, 'Aha! Mechanics and control! You don't have to be a *shtarker*—'"

"*Shtarker?*" Suki said.

"Strong guy. Yiddish." Aaron got up from his chair, measured empty space around himself. He went into an exaggerated slow-motion windup that looked more like martial arts than baseball.

"'Look,' he told me, 'the power, it all comes from the middle. Not the arm. And the pitch—a million miles an hour it doesn't have to be. Location. Pinpoint. That's what we'll work on.'"

Aaron's arm was back now, his shoulders turned as though he were about to chuck a spear. "And we did," he went on. "And I pitched. Little League. Junior High. Was I great? No. Lack of talent takes you just so far. But I had excellent control."

He was just going into his delivery when he saw the misshapen mango muffin on the counter. With hardly a hitch in his motion, he picked it up in battered fingers. Then his arm came forward, pulled by the uncoiling of his middle, and the muffin flew across the room and landed cleanly in the garbage can.

Suki said, "Strike three."

And the telephone rang.

Aaron, slightly abashed at finding himself in the middle of the kitchen with muffin crumbs between his fingers, let it ring another time then moved to answer it. Out of Little-League mode and back in somber adulthood, he said, "Good morning, Mangrove Arms."

There was a brief but ragged silence on the other end, a beat with some clumsy fraction added. Then a male voice echoed, "Mangrove Arms?"

There was something odd about the voice, a stilted precision that Aaron could not place at first. "Yes, Mangrove Arms," he said. "May I help you?"

Again, a pause with jarring syncopation. Then the single careful word: "Hotel?"

A rolling cramp climbed up Aaron's back. His spine was registering the wrongness even as his brain was denying that anything was wrong, claiming only that Key West was a city of misdialed numbers, of people who were lost, of drunken fingers that couldn't find the buttons. But that careful voice—the h had too much breath; the o was too perfectly round. This was someone laboring to hide an accent. Perhaps a Russian accent. Aaron swallowed, turned his too-revealing face away from Suki, urged a steadfast neutrality on his tightening throat. "Hotel, yes. Bed and breakfast. May I help you?"

A final mistimed pause, then he heard a click.

He held the receiver an extra moment then replaced it slowly in the cradle. He put off turning around because he didn't know what he would say to the woman the Russian Mafia was looking for.

When he finally met Suki's eyes, the coffee cup was at her mouth, it made a kind of veil. Looking at her, he felt the thwarted helplessness that turned people reckless, that drove them to acts of flamboyant but unhelpful martyrdom. His father was out there somewhere, blundering through the world; Suki was in here, hidden only by some scraps of hedge and a rotting picket fence; and he, to mask his own anxieties, was clowning, combing through boyhood for clues about what it was to be a man. He was in the prime of life and not devoid of courage. But what did it take to protect another person, to keep somebody safe? Did only freaks of opportunity make heroes, or did heroism call for things he couldn't see because he didn't have them?

He looked at Suki, the surprising dark blue eyes beneath the coarse and wild hair. "Wrong number," was all he said to her.

"Fred," said Piney, "ya know what I sometimes wonder about?"

It was late afternoon and they were wandering through the unearthly no-man's-land that stretched back from their clearing, just north of the airport, where the mangroves were fenced in. It was weird back there in every way. In a jam-packed little town where strangers' beach towels touched at the edges, and visitors piled up three-deep at the bars, here was an expanse where almost no one went. On a tiny island where building lots kept doubling in price, here was a tract the developers didn't bother trying to grab. Certain people might have found it beautiful but for the most part it was ugly. Colorless crumbled coral that passed for soil. Salt puddles ringed with dusty shrubs whose leaves could slice through skin. Greedy gulls shaking dying tadpoles in their beaks.

Piney gave Fred a few seconds to ignore him, then answered his own question. "Air raid drills."

"Air raid drills?" said Fred.

They strolled, skirting puddles. An egret landed, wings whooshing, and for a moment it seemed like they were very far from anywhere; then a gap opened in the mangroves and they could see the airport runway, not three hundred yards beyond.

"Like in grade school," Piney said. "Remember?"

Grade school was the only school that either of them knew, but Fred didn't like to think about it. "Fuckin' school," he said.

"That bell," said Pineapple. "Different from the fire bell. No, not a bell now that I think of it. More like a horn. Trumpet. So loud it was. Made the walls ring. Made your pencils rattle on the desk. Remember?"

They walked. Part of this land was federal, and part was state, and part was city, and no one seemed to care enough to mark down where the bounds were. Bums slept and kids partied sometimes on the bigger chunks of higher land. Rusted cans and broken bottles collected on the edges of those places; underpants and condoms and shreds of torn-up blankets wrapped themselves around the scaly stems of mangrove.

"They took us down the basement," Piney said. "Remember? Down the stairs with that big horn blowing. Kids dragged their hand along the banister, the varnish was worn off. Got colder every step you took."

Fred lit a cigarette. They walked. Off to their right there was a quarter-acre of cracked cement behind a rusted fence, its gate gradually collapsing on corroded hinges. Here and there the cement was raised into little platforms; here and there the earth was hollowed. In 1962, Nike missiles had been standing on those platforms, their scaffolds anchored in the hollows, their warheads pointed at Havana. In Havana, missiles overseen by Russian scientists had been pointed at Key West.

"Was crowded down the basement," Piney said. "Walls were cinder block with like some rubber paint. Freezing cold, the walls. We all sat down, the floor was cold and gritty. And they told us to put our arms up to protect our heads. Fred, remember how skinny your arms were as a kid?"

Fred didn't answer, just smoked. They skirted puddles, kicked at porous rocks. Ahead, by far the highest land in sight though it wasn't very high, loomed a ragged flat-topped pyramid. It was made of crumbled rock which the years had ground almost into powder. Tufts of coarse gray grass sprouted up through it. Stunted shrubs clung to its flanks.

"You sat there and your butt was cold, and your arms got tired being held up in the air, and you got this milky feeling in your stomach. Remember, Fred?"

Fred picked tobacco off his lip, finally spoke. "Where we goin' with this, Piney?"

They walked close to the pyramid. The pyramid had a doorway and it used to have a door. The door had been sheathed in lead to keep the radiation out. When the bombs from Cuba started falling, people were supposed to go inside this low, small, scrubby pyramid and wait. In 1962 there were lights inside, and drinking water, and cans of tuna fish.

Piney said, "Those drills. They said we did 'em so we'd know just what to do, so we'd feel safe."

He was standing in front of the pyramid's vacant doorway. Slanting sunlight squeezed through a little ways, then stalled. People slept in there sometimes. Trash built up and there were rats.

"Thing is though," Pineapple went on, "they didn't make us feel safe, they made us more scared. That horn. The cold."

Fred flicked his stub of cigarette through the doorway, it glowed against the shadowed ground.

"And they had to know that all along," said Piney. "They were grown-ups. We were kids. They had to know it'd only make us more afraid."

Fred had turned to walk away. Piney stood there at the black entrance to the pyramid.

"They wanted us to be afraid," he said. "You think about it, that's the only explanation. But why would they do that, Fred? Why would they want us to grow up afraid?"

THIRTY-SEVEN

"Sam," said Bert the Shirt. "About this gay stuff. We really don't have to make it point one of what we say to people."

It was an hour before sunset, and they were sitting on their tile patio. They'd laid in groceries, made up beds. It was a lot for two old men to do and they were happy to sit down. But Sam was not just sitting there. He'd taken the casing off his yellow Walkman, and with a tiny screwdriver meant for fixing glasses, he was fiddling with the guts of it.

A little stung by Bert's comment, even though Bert had said it as gently as he could, he looked up and said, "I thought that was our cover."

"It is, it is," said Bert. "But like, how many people you meet where, right off, first thing they tell you is they're gay? It doesn't sound, like, normal. It should be just, ya know, inna background."

Trying not to whine, Sam said, "I was just rehearsing. Getting into character."

The table at which the two men sat had a mosaic on the top, and Bert's chihuahua was laid out on the tiles like a meat loaf. Bert stroked the dog with one hand, and with the other he patted Sam's wrist. "No harm done, Sam. No harm."

They sat in silence for a while. Bert sipped a beer, Sam went back to his fiddling. He cheered up right away. A good thing about his slip-page was that he didn't remember annoyances or slights long enough to sulk or hold a grudge. "Pleasant here," he said.

Bert didn't care for it but held his tongue. Disagreeing, contradict-ing—it too easily got to be a bad habit with a couple. But, a city guy at heart, Bert liked more activity around him. The Paradiso—people were always jumping in the pool, practicing their putting, playing cards. Here it was all fences, hedges . . .

Adrift in his own thoughts, it took Bert an instant to respond when Sam grabbed his wrist. "Don't look now," he whispered, "but there's a Russian over there."

"Over where?"

Sam pointed with his eyebrows to the nondescript gray house on the other side of the canal, where, in the shade of an awning at a cor-ner of the patio, a slightly built and crescent-faced man was looking at the water and sipping amber liquid.

Bert stroked his dog, said indulgently, "And what makes you think he's Russian?"

Excitedly Sam whispered, "He's drinking tea from a glass. From a glass he's drinking tea."

Bert looked a little closer. "Okay, so it's a warm day and he's hav-ing a nice ice tea."

"Ice tea my eye. Where's the ice, Bert?" Sam demanded. "Show me the ice."

It was a little far away to see an ice cube, but it was true there was no telltale shimmer, no prisms in the tea.

"Hot tea he's having," Sam said. "Hot tea from a glass. Now look at his left hand."

Bert peered across the patio, and over the seawall, and beyond the small canal, and saw their neighbor bring his left hand briefly to his lips.

"Sugar cube," said Sam. "He nibbles sugar, he drinks hot tea. Russian thing. My parents did it. Only a Russian drinks his tea like that."

Bert said, "Whaddya know," then scratched his dog to help himself think. Half-aloud, he said, "So now what—?"

"So now we go and say hello," said Sam, and he began the creaky process of rising from his chair.

Bert held him by the wrist. "We should have a plan at least."

But Sam's brain was on fire. He was thinking; he was helping; he was thrilled. He didn't want to lose momentum. "Come on," he said, "we'll just go introduce ourselves as neighbors. Doesn't look natural we make a big deal out of it."

So the two men rose, and walked to the end of their patio and across a narrow swath of coarse brown lawn to the seawall. Perched on the edge, Sam Katz turned toward the slim figure underneath the awning and shouted a hello.

Ivan Cherkassky looked up briefly from his tea, saw two more silly Americans at the rental house. Old men this time. One with clownish tufts of unkempt hair, the other wearing a loud shirt and holding an absurd and useless dog. He felt the dim irritation that goes with utter lack of interest. But rudeness drew attention so he tried not to be rude. He returned the hello, no encouragement attached.

Bert cleared his throat. "Just moved in, thought we'd introduce ourselves. I'm Bert d'Ambrosia. This is Sam Katz."

"Nice to meet you," said Cherkassky blandly. He didn't offer his own name, didn't get up from his chair, didn't move out of the shade.

There was a pause. Water sloshed very softly against the seawall, the late sun threw a round warmth that seemed to come from nowhere. The Russian decided he had held the strangers' eyes long enough to be polite, and he went back to his tea.

Sam Katz, feverish with thought, pawed the ground, groped for some way, any way, to keep the conversation going.

Finally he blurted, "I'm not supposed to say this, but we're gay. Welcome to America."

Ivan Cherkassky said, "Excuse me?"

"You're Russian, I believe," said Sam.

This was enough to pique Cherkassky's paranoia. Who told them?

Why did they care? He said nothing but now he held his neighbors' gaze.

"The tea," said Sam, pointing vaguely. "So, are you finding opportunity here in the United States?"

"Opportunity?" Cherkassky said suspiciously, and he started rising from his chair. "No. Seeking peace and quiet only."

"Come by and have a drink sometime," said Bert the Shirt.

"Sometime perhaps," said the old Soviet, moving toward his house. "Now if you'll excuse me . . . "

He slipped into his kitchen, disappeared at once into its dimness, and the sliding door slid closed behind him.

Bert and Sam stood there a moment in the diffuse and buttery sunshine, then turned back toward their tiled patio.

On the brief walk across the lawn, Bert said, "Guy makes ya feel 'bout as welcome as a turd in a punch bowl."

"We broke the ice," said Sam, tugging on his Einstein hair.

"All ice, that guy is."

"Important thing, we broke the ice."

Suki Sperakis settled back in her claw-foot bathtub and caught herself wondering when, if ever, she and Aaron would make love.

She soaped her arms, sponged water on the tired muscles of her neck. It was time, it seemed to her. There'd been gazes, meals together, conversations that plunged quite suddenly beneath the skin of the safe and the polite. They'd glimpsed intimacy the way people glimpse stars behind swiftly scudding clouds.

Maybe that was the problem, she reflected, as she scrubbed the tiny webbings at the bases of her fingers, where soil had filtered through the gardening gloves. Maybe too much had already happened, and they'd missed their chance at mutual seduction, because seduction was a dance that strangers did. Circumstance had swept them past that phase, they'd missed it like an exit on the highway, and found themselves a long way down the road. They were friends by now, and friends did not seduce. Friends decided, with their eyes wide open. No teasing and no flinching. An honest yielding to the inevitable. It sounded like the easiest thing in the world. Why did it feel like the hardest?

Stumped, she slid down in the tub to wet her hair. She didn't hear the phone ring on the main line in the kitchen and the office.

Aaron, at the front desk doing paperwork, picked it up, said, "Mangrove Arms."

His adrenaline started coursing before he'd heard a word—as soon as a normal silent beat had passed, and a jarring foreign fraction had begun.

"I am looking for a Mr. Katz," said Tarzan Abramowitz. He'd come up empty the first time through his list of numbers from Lucia's reservation book. He'd reached answering machines, cleaning ladies, gotten numb responses. Now it was early evening and he was trying again.

"This is Aaron Katz."

Out of rhythm, Abramowitz said, "Ah, you are proprietor."

Aaron was itchy at the hairline and his hand was growing damp around the phone. "Who's this calling, please?"

A syncopated pause. Then: "I am looking for a friend. Perhaps she stays there. Suki Sperakis."

Time compressed for Aaron, the way it does when synapses are glowing, nerve endings crackling, when a looming fall or crash rearranges space and puts a freeze on gravity. He pleaded with his voice for steadiness, groped for a cadence that would not sound false to this man of clumsy cadences. "Susie Sperakis?" he said.

"Suki . . . Suki."

Aaron's shirt was clinging to his back, his stare was stuck on the little silver bell on the counter. He paused, like he was looking in his book. "There's no one by that name staying here."

"You go to Lucia's, Mr. Katz?"

"Who is this, please?"

Abramowitz hung up.

Aaron put the phone down, then reached out for the silver bell, didn't ring but squeezed it a long moment, let its coolness and its weight absorb the heat and quaking of his hand.

THIRTY-EIGHT

At the very end of what appeared to be the guest wing of his house, Gennady Markov was working in his lab—mixing a broth of sulfuric acid and iodide salts; doing the prep work, like a chef, for the later concoction of plutonium oxide—when his housekeeper called him on the intercom to tell him a policeman was waiting in the foyer.

The buzzer broke the Russian's concentration, but the news didn't rattle him at all. Key West cops—they cared about parking tickets, cats in trees. Something big and complicated and organized was way beyond them. Why then was he here? Looking for a bribe, no doubt . . . It did not occur to Markov that the cop was here about Ludmila. He didn't know the body had been found; he hadn't imagined it would *ever* be found. And if it was, so what? No one would connect him with Ludmila's death. Where was the motive? No one but Cherkassky would ever figure it out. Besides, who would care about Ludmila? She was joined to no one, made no difference in the world. Her death meant only that some pillowcases might go unchanged until a new cleaning lady had been found; here and there a cobweb might briefly flourish in a corner.

Markov washed his hands, left the lab, and locked the door, walking calmly down the long hallway toward the foyer.

He recognized Lieutenant Stubbs at once—the wrinkled khaki suit, the concertina creases behind the knees—from the day that Stubbs had brought him to identify the murdered Lazslo. He said, "Ah, Lieutenant, you bring news perhaps of my nephew's killers?"

"No, Mr. Markov, I'm afraid I don't."

"Then—"

"There's been another death."

Markov strove to look shocked but not too shocked. He was a man of the world. He'd been through a lot. His reaction should be dignified, muted.

"A woman," Stubbs went on. "Drowned. We think she's Russian."

"Russian?"

"Labels in her clothes," said Stubbs. "Russian labels."

"Ah," said Markov. He hadn't thought about labels in the murdered woman's clothes, and now for the first time he began to wonder what else he hadn't thought about. Ludmila's absurd red scooter was in his vast garage, covered only with a tarp. Her lost shoe was stuffed into her helmet. He'd thought no one would care.

"And the officer who answered the call about . . . about your nephew," Stubbs continued. "She met his housekeeper. That's who found the body. The officer thinks that's maybe who the murdered woman is."

Markov blinked, a quick shiver ran through the pads of fat beneath his eyes. He hadn't thought about the cops connecting Lazslo with Ludmila. He hadn't realized anyone had seen her.

"Did you know your nephew's housekeeper, Mr. Markov?"

The Russian thought back to the days when he had planned his crime. Drunken days, days of grief and rage amok, wildly incautious days. Now belatedly he groped after caution. "A little. I've met her, yes."

"Her name?"

"I think . . . Ludmila. Ludmila, yes."

"Last name?"

Markov shrugged.

"You'd know her if you saw her? At the morgue, I mean?"

"I think I would. Not sure."

"I hate to ask you, but—"

Markov, man of the world, waved away the cop's compunction. He realized now how sloppy he'd been, how foolish to imagine that the very puniness of his crime sufficed to make it unsolvable. If returning to the morgue allowed him to lead the cop away from the garage with the dead woman's things so carelessly hidden, from the seawall with the overturned table sunk in the muck at its base, then he was only too happy to return to the morgue.

"Will be painful to see that place again," he said. "But as citizen of course I will help." And he gestured with Old World graciousness for the lieutenant to precede him out the door.

"Aaron," Suki said, "let's not eat in the kitchen tonight, okay?"

He said nothing, just looked up from the pan in which the grouper was sautéing. Suki was holding a pair of candlesticks; he had no idea where she'd found them. Then again, there were cupboards, crannies in the Mangrove Arms he'd never yet got around to opening, and the old hotel was day by day becoming her place as well as his.

"Nicer," she said.

He looked at her and his throat was closing down. Her hair was drying, not dry all the way, it had a sheen like licorice. Her neck was very tan where it joined her shoulders and tucked beneath her blouse. There was a happiness about her that didn't need to smile, that Aaron almost let himself recognize as desire.

"Maybe the coffee table right out here," she said, pointing through the kitchen doorway to a sitting area where no guests ever sat, and where Suki and Aaron had never taken time to rest.

Aaron couldn't speak just then, he nodded and looked back at the stove, down into the pan where the fillets were nestled in beds of shallot and olives and sweet pepper. Something was happening in the muscles above his knees, they kept tightening then letting go. He turned the fish and thought about his stubborn suffocating gallantry. Was it fair to make love to Suki, trapped there as she was? Was she free to open up her arms, or not to?

She was standing in the doorway now. She smiled and her disconcerting upper lip twitched slightly at the corners. "Looks civilized," she said with satisfaction. Aaron saw candlelight licking at the slatted walls behind her.

She moved into the kitchen once again. "Plates?" she said, and Aaron, strangling on his chivalry, could only nod.

He watched her reach up to the high shelf above the counters, her body lengthening as though in a dream of leaping into flight, heels flexing from the floor, hips lifting as back sinews stretched, shoulders tilting to raise one full tan arm in a ballet of the sublimely ordinary.

He turned off the stove and opened the wine.

Tarzan Abramowitz could not bring himself to face Ivan Cherkassky.

He'd failed. He'd spoken with six, eight people, feeling maladroit and foolish the whole way through, and he'd learned nothing about who Suki was supposed to have joined for dinner at Lucia's.

But of course he'd failed. Listening for the tiniest of glitches in a language not his own—it was impossible, ridiculous. Still, the failure embarrassed him, and feeling embarrassed made him mad. He was mad at Cherkassky, though that was an anger he could not afford; so he got mad, instead, at the people he had called.

He sat on a high stool, his feet impatient on the rungs, in the back room of a T-shirt shop on Duval Street. Behind him loomed stacks of open cardboard cartons, and behind that wall of shirts was stashed the more valuable inventory of cash and gems and art— spinoffs of the traffic in fissionable material. Abramowitz had a phone book on his knees, and he was jotting down addresses.

Cherkassky didn't want him to be seen; well, Cherkassky was still as meek as your basic civil servant. He, Abramowitz, was bold. Let people recognize his suspenders and his muscles and his short legs and his hairy back; he didn't care. He wanted to try things his own way now. Confront; intimidate; punish.

He closed the phone book, folded the paper on which he'd written the addresses, and put it in his pocket. Then he sprang out into the deepening dusk to jump into his electric blue Camaro and see what information he could shake loose not with his voice but his hands.

THIRTY-NINE

Driving his unmarked police car back to Key Haven from the morgue, Gary Stubbs said, "These two deaths, Mr. Markov—you think they could be related in some way?"

Markov had been looking out the window, still seeing the nose holes in Ludmila's gray face. He swiveled fatly in the seat, gave a world-weary shrug. "You are the policeman, Lieutenant. I only wish to know, no matter what, who killed my nephew."

Stubbs drove. Pelicans flew low along the road, their wings lit from above by orange street lamps. After a moment he went on. "But if they *were* related, why would they be?"

Markov said nothing, just sniffed at his clothes. They stank of chemicals and death, he'd change them before tucking in to his waiting veal chop and his Pomerol.

At a red light, Stubbs said casually, "It's very strange. Another woman disappeared on the night your nephew was killed."

"Another woman?" Markov said.

They were on the ugly highway now. Ragged palms were skinny silhouettes behind a curtain of neon, traffic sneaked in and out of gas stations and furtive bars.

"A woman who knew your nephew pretty well. Was dating him, in fact."

"This I did not know," said Markov.

"Never said you did," said Stubbs, and for just an instant his eyes peeled off the road and fixed his passenger.

For a time they didn't talk, the only sound was the tires sucking dryly at the pavement. Then Stubbs said, "Little town like ours, I guess you've heard some of the crazy rumors about a Russian Mafia."

Markov put on the sad wise houndlike face of a man long disappointed in humanity. "I have," he said. "Is disturbing, of course. Even here is a mistrust of foreigners."

"Everybody's foreign somewhere," said the cop.

"Your nation goes away," Markov complained, "you are foreign everywhere."

Stubbs saved his sympathy. "But Mafias," he said, "they're gonna hurt someone, usually, for starters at least, they hurt their own."

Gennady Markov didn't like where the conversation was yanking him but he had no choice except to follow it along. "This means you think a Russian killed my nephew?"

Stubbs didn't answer the question. Instead he said, "And deaths, disappearances that come in clusters—that's a Mafia kind of thing."

Markov hesitated. For just a heartbeat he almost hoped this bumbling policeman with the wrinkled clothes would solve the crimes, that the loathed authorities would win. He pictured Ivan Cherkassky being carted off to jail, hunched and thin and bitter. It would be nice to see; and, with a mocking useless remorse, Markov realized that he might perhaps have seen it with impunity, had he not given in to the lunatic impulse to push the cleaning lady into the ocean. He'd picked the wrong revenge; he could have simply squealed. But as Ludmila went down, so did his chance of getting off easy. He said, "So you assume now that these murderings, they are related?"

"Just a theory." Stubbs drove. The roadside chaos thinned out, mangroves invaded vacant lots.

Markov pointed a fat finger suddenly. "You miss the turn," he said.

"Ah, so I did," said Stubbs.

Markov didn't like that. Policemen drove the streets every day, they didn't make wrong turns.

Still heading north, Stubbs said, "I was thinking about the FBI."

Markov said nothing.

Stubbs gave forth a little nervous laugh. "Every local cop's worst fear, I guess. You call them in, they take right over. Show you how small-time you are. Make you feel like crap for everything you've missed."

The foolishness of his position was pushing Gennady Markov down into the seat, squeezing him against the door. He'd briefly had the upper hand against Cherkassky, and he'd been too drunk and self-pitying to notice. Now the guilt was equal and the punishment was circling. With disgust, he understood that Cherkassky, once again, was right: they *were* together till the end. Trying to sound sage but not dismissive, he said, "This is really such big matter for the FBI?"

Lieutenant Gary Stubbs had driven far enough and had found a place where he could make a U-turn. His arm across the steering wheel, he glanced at Markov, whose face was awash in the fugitive glare of headlights from the oncoming traffic. "A little while ago," he said, "you wanted to do anything to find who killed your nephew."

He pulled into the southbound lane.

At the Mangrove Arms, wisps of breeze slipped through the porous walls and around the unsquare edges of the windows, and flattened and stretched the candle flames. Wax trickled and slowly congealed; shadows billowed up like shaken sheets. Suki and Aaron sat eating dinner, side by side on the edge of the low settee. Their plates were on their knees and their knees were almost touching.

Aaron was saying, "You had a plan when you first moved down here? You knew what you were looking for?"

Suki had sipped some wine, she worked to swallow it before she laughed. "A plan? Me?" Her eyes were wide above the rim of her glass; candle flames danced in her irises. "All I had was a pretty clear idea of what I was running away from. Winter. Brown air. Drizzle and traffic. Feeling like my life was in a tube between the Turnpike and the Parkway."

"Can't have been all bad," Aaron said.

"Wasn't," Suki conceded. Her shoulders lifted and she burgeoned, her presence expanded with promise like rising bread. "But there's a hell of a gap between not all bad, and good."

"So what you wanted—?"

"Had no idea," she said. She put her fork down, picked up her wine. She gestured. Her arms moved wide, her neck bobbed. Space became elastic to accommodate her. "And something I figured out: What you want matters a whole lot less than what you don't want."

Aaron drank wine and pondered that a moment. Then he said, "That make you a pessimist or a mystic?"

"No, really," Suki said, as though he'd contradicted her. "You get rid of the ugliness, the annoyances, the discomforts, the stupid pointless worries . . . and it's really almost enough."

Aaron watched her. She'd put her plate onto the coffee table and she was half-reclining. Candlelight traced her side, the arc of her tilted hip and the sleighride slope of her torso as it rose up toward her shoulder. His eyes grabbed for hers. He said, "Almost?"

Outside, beyond the porous, slatted walls, fronds were rustling, and cats were scuttling under porches, and Tarzan Abramowitz, suspenders spread around his thick ropy neck, was working his way through his list of suspect addresses, looking for someone to hurt. He cruised Key West's dusty streets, the molding of his electric blue Camaro barely clearing the still-warm pavements.

Suki got suddenly shy. She met Aaron's gaze but then her eyelids came slipping down, her mouth tightened at one corner and her voice had trouble turning breath to sound. "Yes," she said at last. "Almost."

He leaned a little toward her then. His face forgot the habit of appearing self-sufficient, it softened to reveal the true and simple thing that people trembled to admit—that they were lonely, that their own sealed skins did not satisfy as their only home. He didn't mean to whisper but he whispered. "What's missing, Suki?"

She didn't answer and she didn't have to. Her chin lifted, her shoulders opened. Her disconcerting upper lip gave a small slow undulating twitch, and he took her in his arms.

They were still kissing, there on the settee, with burned-down candles sputtering, and wavy shadows clutching at the walls, when a bounding step was faintly heard on the old boards of the office stairs, and a heavy hand smacked down on the little silver bell, its bright and singing tone now turned imperious, infernal.

Part Four

FORTY

The woman who sometimes did the breakfast at the Mangrove Arms had tattoos on her ankles and her shoulders, studs through her nose and at the edges of her navel, and bits of mirror glued to the fenders of her bicycle. She believed in ghosts and spirits, cherished unusual beliefs about causes and effects, and saw things that other people didn't see. But in her own way she was very disciplined, even conventional, and when it came to work she had a policy: Some days she showed up, other days she didn't; but she never showed up late.

On the days she went to work, she left her Stump Lane bungalow at a quarter of six. In winter it was still full night. Cats owned the streets. In quiet alleyways, raccoons tested the tops of garbage cans. If it had been windy, broken-backed brown fronds would drape the tops of fences; when it was especially humid, she needed to dry her bike seat with a sleeve.

This particular predawn, however, was dry and still and clear. Street lamps still buzzed, and the crisp stars, like people fated to die young and suddenly, revealed no inkling of their imminent eclipse. She pedaled toward Whitehead Street and thought about the morning's menu. The papayas were a little green; she'd slice kiwis and oranges instead. Banana walnut muffins. Key lime marmalade.

She crossed Duval Street, drained and embarrassed at the end of its nightly debauch. Drunks as trusting as dogs lay stretched full-length in doorways. Transvestites strutted, wigs askew. A tourist woman leaned against a lamppost and wept, grown maudlin and ashamed over something she had said or done or seen her boyfriend say or do, some bleak thing that a too-long evening on Duval had proved about her life.

Whitehead, on the other hand, was peaceful. Tunneling banyans softened the night, as they would soon soften the day. People who worked the early shift at the Aqueduct or the electric company drank coffee on the sidewalk in pools of light in front of countered windows.

The woman who did the breakfast locked her bike and climbed the porch steps of the Mangrove Arms.

She found the front door open, which at that hour it should not have been, but which wasn't that unusual. Guests had keys and guests were careless. Even Aaron, lax like many ex-New Yorkers, as if all crime and danger had been left behind, didn't always bother locking up. She went inside.

The office, over-bright in lights that should have been turned off, was just very slightly, even daintily, trashed. A couple of potted plants had been turned onto their sides, not smashed but tipped; they lay pathetic as flipped turtles, soil spilling on the floor. Papers and brochures were scattered here and there, and the counter itself had been scarred with a jagged, spiteful slash of a knife. Yet, as far as the woman who did the breakfast could tell, nothing had been taken. Random mischief, she decided. An angry kid; a blackout drunk. An unfortunate and unmeaningful visitation.

Bewildered but not yet afraid, she went through the doorway behind the desk, which led on toward the kitchen. In the sitting room that no one ever seemed to use were the remnants of a not quite finished meal. There was something disturbing, something pending and glum about the abandoned dinner. Low pools of wine sat in the bottoms of two glasses; sauce streaked plates like brush strokes. Knives and forks were arrayed in gesturing positions, as if the hands that had put them down had planned on coming back, and were prevented.

The rumpled settee spoke of sudden absence, of weightless abduction. Beyond the curtained window it was still dark, and the stubbornly lingering night called up the primitive terror that there would come a time when the mechanisms of the world would stall, and the sun would fail to rise.

Spooked now, the woman who did the breakfast went into the kitchen, put the lights on as bright as they would go, and tried to beat down her unease with work. When she filled the coffee urn with water, the sound was mournful and hollow, like a splash from deep down at the bottom of a well.

In the mint green tiled house on Key Haven, Bert the Shirt also woke well ahead of dawn. Propped on pillows, he listened to the cooing of doves, the more distant squawk of seagulls. He wanted to get up and make his oatmeal. That was his routine, and routine was vastly important to him; but he was afraid he'd wake his housemate.

He needn't have worried. Sam, lying in a narrow bed on the other side of a thin wall, had been awake for quite a while, or at least he thought he had. Sleeping and waking—for him the states grew ever less distinct. Sleep gained in truth as waking lost the arrogance of certainty. Dreams, three-D and portentous, sported a logic no less satisfactory than that of what, by mere consensus, was called the real. Categories dissolved; things floated free of their names, and a kind of geriatric Buddhism became ever more unquestioned and serene.

At length it was the sound of the dog's paws clicking on the tiled floor that made the two old men confess they were awake.

They got up, put on their baggy bathrobes, and had their cereal. Breakfast eaten, they waged slow and labored campaigns in their respective bathrooms. By the time they were ready to venture out to walk the dog, the clouds had burned away and the sun had topped the trees.

Outside, the streets were bright and vacant. Bert carried a thin pink leash but he didn't put it on; the old chihuahua wasn't going anywhere. It ticked along stiffly, very near its master's shuffling shoes, stopping now and then to lift a leg just slightly. White eyes squinting, the dog toiled to pass urine; mere drops, slow and pendant as the outfall from a runny nose, formed one by one at the tip of its wizened pecker, then broke and dribbled down a blade of grass.

Bert shook his head. "Fuckin' age," he said. "Dog used to be quite the little stud."

Dubious, Sam said nothing.

"Jaunty," Bert went on. "Confident. Did he know he weighed t'ree pounds? Did it stop 'im that his wang was smaller than a cocktail frank? Bullshit. He humped Rottweilers, this guy. Chased away Dobermans. In his heart he was Rin Tin fuckin' Tin."

Don Giovanni knew when he was being talked about. Slowly, creakily, he raised his head. His hoary whiskers drooped in their dry and scaly follicles, his smeared and futile eyes panned through glare and shadow.

They strolled. At the end of their block, they took a low bridge that crossed over the canal. In the thick green water, bits of weed floated dreamily on sluggish current.

On the opposite side, Sam looked down the street and saw a snazzy blue car in the driveway of the dull gray house where the unfriendly Russian lived. The house and the car just didn't match, and Sam fiddled with his hearing aid. "Our neighbor," he said. "You think he'd drive a car like that?"

Bert sized up the Camaro. Tinted windows, extra chrome, tire skirts. The only excuse for having a car like that was youth. "Son, maybe."

Sam pushed out his lips. "Or maybe somebody who works for him."

"Works for him, like cleans, like gardens?"

"Works for him like works for him," said Sam. "Who knows? Maybe, like, a criminal guy, he has to report to headquarters."

"Headquarters," said Bert, and gave an indulgent little smile. Sam tended to get carried away. Also, people who lived together came to mimic one another, and Bert just barely noticed that Sam was beginning to talk Brooklyn. "You don't think Markov's place is headquarters?"

Sam tugged his Einstein hair. "How should I know? You're the one says don't trust how it looks."

Don Giovanni started sniffing the ground and moving in a tiny circle, like he was dancing on a beach ball. "I did say that," conceded Bert.

Heightening sun beat down. The dog hunkered into a hopeful, straining squat, tail lifted, sides pumping like a bellows. Sam said, "I think we gotta try again to get to know our neighbor."

The dog squeezed. Its skin sucked in around its ribs like leather on a drying carcass. It crouched down lower, nearly scraping its chapped asshole on the pavement. Nothing happened. Bert said, "We just go barging in his house? I don't see it, Sam."

The two men stood over the clogged chihuahua like doting uncles above a newborn. The dog lifted up its blind eyes toward them. Looking for help? Sympathy? A miracle? Sam said, "An excuse. An excuse is what we need."

The dog made one last push, then gave up, embarrassed and exhausted. Disingenuously, it pretended to kick some dirt on its nonexistent leavings. It panted. Moved to pity, Bert bent low and swept the little creature into his hands.

Sam said, "Dog looks very, very thirsty."

"No he don't," said Bert. "Just tired, disappointed."

Sam glanced off toward the dull gray house with the snazzy blue Camaro in the driveway. "Thirsty is what I'm saying. I'm saying he needs some water right away."

FORTY-ONE

At the Mangrove Arms, daylight quelled the ancient fear of a night that stuck forever in the groove, but did nothing to dispel the uneasy riddles of the gently roughed-up office, the mute puddles of unfinished wine.

The woman who did the breakfast had put hot muffins on a table near the pool, had rolled out the urn of coffee and the pitchers of juice. Now she was back in the kitchen, cleaning up—and cleaning up more slowly than she needed to, because a voice was telling her she shouldn't leave. Something wasn't right. Aaron was always up by now, making lists, looking for a hammer, losing his coffee in odd places as he bustled around.

His bustling was important, thought the breakfast woman; it somehow neutralized the sort of ghosts that lived in old hotels, that took the form of molds and mildews and creaking doors but whose true substance was failure and sorrow and heartbreaks past remedy. Aaron's bustling subdued those ghosts, shamed them into silence. Without his activity, they clamored, hummed, and the woman who did the breakfast didn't like the sound at all.

So she stood at the sink and made bustling noises of her own, washing mixing bowls and muffin tins. Water rang on metal and she didn't hear the footsteps coming up behind her.

She scoured, she rinsed; the steps grew nearer until, less by hearing than by some vaguer sense of closeness, she became aware of them and swiveled. Her breath caught, her fingers sprang open, a muffin tin clattered to the floor.

"Jeez," she said, "you scared me."

"Sorry," Aaron said.

She looked at him. She was the sort of person who noticed odd details she couldn't always put into words. She noticed that Aaron's arms seemed longer because his shoulders had dropped down farther from his ears. His eyes seemed farther apart because his forehead was less crinkled. She said, "Hey, what happened here last night?"

Aaron blinked at her, had to suppress an unbecoming adolescent grin. He didn't see that it was any of her business. He said, "Excuse me?" He poured himself a cup of coffee.

"The office," said the woman who did the breakfast.

"Office?" He went to look.

He stood mystified before the mess—the toppled plants, the tossed papers just dense enough to grab the eye. A weirdly considerate malice seemed to have been at work; or perhaps the invasion was at bottom a message. Aaron righted the pots, noted the mean damage to his beautiful varnished counter—and only then remembered last night's sharp insistent ringing of the front desk bell.

By reflex he'd started getting up from the settee to answer it. Suki's arms and eyes had sought to hold him where he was. For a heartbeat he was unsure what he should do. But by his next breath several things had been not so much decided as finally understood. They were lovers and had been for a while. The tardy act of making love would be not the initiation, but an unhurried catching-up, a celebration of what already was; and there was nothing in the world important enough to delay that celebration further. Death itself could be ringing the bell—he didn't have to answer.

They'd trundled off to Aaron's bedroom then. Their arms were wrapped around each other, faces close, pulse singing in their ears;

they would not have heard the dainty vandalism, if that's when it was done. And only now, the morning after, did it occur to Aaron to wonder if this pointless invasion was the work of the rude caller with the careful diction and the foreign cadences.

He went back to the kitchen. The woman who did the breakfast discreetly watched him fill a second coffee mug and move back toward his bedroom. Confirmed in her instincts that something large had happened in the old hotel, she dried her hands and went back to her bicycle with the bits of mirror on the fenders.

"Fred," said Piney, "ya know what I sometimes wonder about?"

It was late morning and they were wandering through the mangroves back behind the airport. Strung from one shrub to another, the tiny trampolines of spider webs bounced in a light breeze. Hot sun evaporated puddles, you could almost hear the gray water being sucked into the air like soda through a straw. Fred didn't answer.

Piney said, "Songs."

Fred said nothing, just stopped walking long enough to light a cigarette. The cigarette fit neatly in a notch in his walrus moustache, and around the notch nicotine had stained the hair like oiled oak.

Pineapple said, "The words and the tunes. The way they go together."

Without interest Fred said, "Yeah, Piney. That's why they call it a song."

"But ya think about it," said Piney, "it's a miracle. The tune's just a tune, the words are just words. Totally different things. A bird and a fish."

Fred smoked, kicked at porous rocks. "Fuck's a bird and a fish got to do with it?"

"Then someone puts the words and the tune together," Piney said, "and all of a sudden it's like they had to be together, like they were together from the beginning of time."

They walked. On their left, the airport runway showed now and then through gaps in the foliage; smears of rubber on the pavement testified to the violence of landing. Ahead and on their right, the ancient missile platforms loomed, fences rusted, concrete cracked. Fred said nothing.

Houndlike, Piney sang, "Blue-oo moon . . . You don't think that's amazing?"

Fred flicked his cigarette into a gray puddle. "Yeah, Piney. Real amazing."

Farther on, beyond the platforms, the scrubby pyramid of the archaic fallout shelter broke through the relentless pancake plane of Florida. A cloud blew across the sun and a shadow slithered up one side of the pyramid and down the other.

"And another thing," said Piney. "Ever notice how, even when you just whistle, you're still hearing the words?"

"I don't whistle."

"Hum then," Piney said. "Same thing hum—"

He broke off because a mildly uncanny sight had caught his attention. Uncanny sights were a feature of the mangroves, after all; the tangled choking greenery cried out for the peculiar. Ospreys landed in the mangroves with crushed terns in their talons; drunks fumbled through their knotted roots, groping after lost prostheses.

The present strangeness was more subtle: a fat man, furtive and well-dressed, carrying a shovel and pulling a little red wagon. His big pants were of expensive cloth that billowed into perfect pleats; his shoes were much too good to be covered as they were in limestone dust. The wagon's handle was too short for him, and its front wheels dangled pointlessly a few inches off the ground as the back tires labored over broken stones.

The mangroves were a neighborhood, and, as with any neighborhood, there were people who belonged and people who did not. This fat man who did not belong seemed to be approaching the earthen pyramid from the part of the wetland called Little Hamaca Park. He was on a collision course with Pineapple and Fred. He saw them and he slowed. He'd been carrying the shovel on his shoulder, as if it were a rifle, and he himself a deranged campaigner who'd lost track of where the war was. Now he dropped the shovel to his side, tried to hide it with his torso.

Pineapple, bold in his own neighborhood, walked on and reached out for the fat man's eyes. They slid away.

The stranger hesitated just a moment and then he turned his back. His shirt was glued with sweat against his spine. He walked off the way he'd come, the red wagon waddling after him like a duckling.

Fred said, with a soft and general defiance, "I don't whistle and I don't hum neither."

Piney said, "That guy. Whaddya think he's doin' back here?"

Uninterested, Fred said, "Stealing plants. Too cheap to buy 'em from the nursery."

"I don't think so," Piney said. "Stealing plants, ya don't put on good shoes."

"Burying a cat then. Who gives a fuck?"

"No cat in the wagon," Piney said.

"Buried already."

"Buried already, why'd he still be walking farther back?"

"Fuck you ask me my opinion then?"

"'Cause you're the expert digging holes," said Piney. "He was walking toward the shelter."

"Nothin' in the shelter but rat shit," said Fred.

"Useta be stuff in the shelter."

"Useta be stuff lotsa places. What's your point?"

"I don't know," admitted Piney. "But a guy with nice clothes with a shovel ... "

"My guys," Fred conceded, "we dig holes, we don't dress that nice."

"A wagon. It's a little off is all I'm saying."

"It's kind of strange," said Fred. "I grant you that."

FORTY-TWO

Tarzan Abramowitz was pacing, but the energy he burned with each deep flex of his thickly muscled knees was insufficient to work off the anger that was building in him every moment. He was being scolded.

Ivan Cherkassky, sitting at his desk in his dim and narrow office, was giving him a dressing-down. The criticism was calm, even polite, but the young thug resented it bitterly. In the old country he would have taken it better, would have felt he had to take it; but this was America, South Florida, and there was something in the air that defeated hierarchy and encouraged insubordination, that fostered a scrappy independence whose first premise was that you shouldn't have to take any shit from anybody, ever.

"Going in person," Ivan Cherkassky was saying. "This I did not want. Draws attention."

Abramowitz paced, stretched the wide suspenders that bit into the ropy sinews between his bare shoulders and his neck. His pacing was mostly turning, he was like a fish in a too-small tank.

There was a knock at the front door.

Cherkassky would not have been inclined to answer it, but Abramowitz heard in the knock an opportunity of escape. He said, "Is probably Gennady," and bounded into the hallway.

He sprinted down the corridor, lunged across the living room, undid the locks and yanked open the door. To his bafflement, he saw, framed by a brilliant rectangle of sunlight, two old men, perspiring and flushed, one of them wearing a lime-green pullover and holding a half-dead dog with cataracts.

For a moment no one spoke. Sam Katz, looking for he knew not what, tried to peek around the young man's hairy chest. Abramowitz shifted just slightly this way and that, guarding empty air. Then Bert said, "Hi. We live around the corner."

Abramowitz said, "So?"

Sam said, "Neighbors."

Abramowitz said nothing.

"We've met your father," Bert took a guess.

"My father's dead," the young man said.

"So's mine," said Sam. "I'm sorry."

Bert said, "The dog. I was wondering if the dog could have a little water."

Abramowitz was shifting foot to foot, his long arms bobbing from their sockets. "If only you live around corner—"

Bert held up the limp chihuahua. It sagged in his hand like an understuffed sausage. "Long way for a little dog like this. Little dog like this could drop dead 'tween here and there."

There was a brief standoff. Then Sam saw a waferish form slip around a corner from the hallway. "What is it, who's there?" Cherkassky said.

The young man turned. Sam saw an opportunity and leaned in through the doorway. "It's us. Sam Katz, remember?"

"Ah," Cherkassky said resignedly.

"Want water for dog," Abramowitz sourly explained.

"Dried out from the sun," said Bert. "Eyelids stuck. Nose all cracked."

Cherkassky looked at the ghostly pet. Then he said to Abramowitz, "Yes, of course, of course, you see this dog, bring bowl of water."

Tarzan, feeling scolded once again, clenched his fists and bounded off.

Sam and Bert stood, trying to look friendly, in the doorway that had lost its sentinel.

Ivan Cherkassky made a token attempt at a smile. His mouth corners twitched and there was a flick at the edges of his eyes. "Forgive me I cannot invite you in," he said. He pointed at the dog. "Allergic."

Making conversation, Bert said, "Same allergies in Russia?"

"You think we are that different?" said Cherkassky.

Tarzan Abramowitz came back from the kitchen. He carried a shallow bowl of water and he had to walk slowly so it wouldn't spill. Walking slowly stymied his athleticism, made him strangely awkward but gave him unaccustomed time to think. Tentatively, he stepped across the front door threshold, then bent to put the bowl down on the welcome mat. Straightening up, he said to Sam, "Did you say your name was Katz?"

"Katz. Sam Katz. And yours?"

Abramowitz stepped inside and closed the door.

Aaron leaned back against a stack of propped-up pillows and watched Suki brush her thick black hair. Her shoulder dimpled when she raised her arm. Her scalp moved ever so slightly under the tug of the brush. There was breathtaking privilege in being allowed to lie there, watching her. Love meant looking closely: being invited to, daring to. He watched her and felt a patient excitement that came full circle and melded with serenity. It was the primitive, solemn, and arousing peace of having taken a mate.

But having a mate gave a person a great deal more to lose, and Aaron was uneasy. "Suki," he said, "d'you remember last night, when we were sitting on the couch—?"

"The front desk bell?" she said. Their eyes locked in the mirror. She kept brushing her hair; with each stroke her eyebrows lifted just a tiny bit, then fell.

"There was a mess out in the office. And yesterday . . . somebody called a couple times. Asked for you. Hung up."

The brush dropped to her side. She turned around. "You didn't tell me."

"I didn't see the use," he said. "But now—there can't be secrets now."

She bit her lip, the upper one. Her eyelids came down to shade her unlikely blue eyes. "I have to leave," she said.

"No you don't."

"Sneak out of town, go far away."

"I want you here."

"So everybody's life gets turned upside down?"

"My life," Aaron said, "you just turned it right side up."

"No," she said. "It isn't fair."

"Fair?" he answered, and opened up his arms. "Come here, Suki."

She moved to him, lay down on the rumpled bed. Knees and ribs and tummies found facets and locks like puzzle pieces. Her face against his chest, she said, "If we weren't making love last night—"

"I would've answered the bell, and who knows what the hell would've happened."

She nuzzled his neck with her chin. "Making love," she said, "sometimes it really does stop the world."

He ran his hand through her thick black hair, undid the careful brushing. "Sometimes it really can."

FORTY-THREE

On Key Haven the door clicked shut, and Ivan Cherkassky sneezed. It was a clipped sneeze, abashed and joyless, stopping short of real release. He covered his scooped-out face with his hand, then reached for his handkerchief and fussily wiped his nose.

When the ritual was over, Tarzan Abramowitz said, "Katz."

"No," said Cherkassky testily. "The dog. Allergic."

"Katz," the shirtless man said again.

"Dog!" insisted the boss.

"The name," said Abramowitz, starting once again to pace, easing into it the way a sprinter loosens up. "Same name as reservation. Same name as at hotel."

"Ah," Cherkassky said. Cautiously, like a small plane at a busy airport, he cut across the path of his goon's accelerating step. He settled himself on the very edge of the living room sofa. "Perhaps is common name."

"Or perhaps they spy on us," said Abramowitz. "Dog so bad needs water three hundred meters from home?"

Cherkassky considered. His paranoia was not of the jumpy sort; he was not prey to sudden delusory panics. His anxieties, rather, were the result of rigorous constructs whose careful architecture made them all the more obsessing. He was building such a construct now.

His new neighbors—they'd been probing and intrusive from the start. Weirdly observant; gauchely open, even for Americans; intrigued that he was Russian. They showed up at the edge of his life and seemed, like germs, to be testing the membrane for a way inside. Why?

"If they spy on us," he reasoned, "is probably because they work with girl."

Abramowitz closed the circle. "And if they work with girl, then probably is same Katz from hotel."

Cherkassky pulled on his pitted face. "But hotel," he said. "Too public. Many people. I don't like it we go to hotel unless we know for sure."

Abramowitz was pacing hard now, fists swinging near his knees. He loved momentum, not details. He said, "But we will never know for sure unless—"

"The old Katz," Cherkassky interrupted. "This is how we will know for sure."

"But—" said Abramowitz.

"He wants to spy on us," Cherkassky said. "We'll let him."

"Let him?" The voice was squeezed and shrill.

"Let him," said Cherkassky. "Good and close we'll let him spy."

Lieutenant Gary Stubbs dunked his donut in his coffee then watched the coffee run back out of the shiny little chambers in the dough.

"Dave," he thought aloud in the direction of the young man behind the counter, "why would a guy who is not simple or obviously insane go into a park full of mangroves with a shovel and a wagon?"

Dunkin' Dave adjusted the angle of his paper hat, wiped his hands on his turned-down apron. "To bury something."

"Wagon's empty," said the cop.

"Well, then to dig something up," the donut man suggested.

"Wagon's empty when he comes out, too."

"Couldn't find it maybe."

"Find what?" asked the cop.

The man behind the counter shrugged. "Or maybe changed his mind."

"How come?"

"Saw you watching maybe."

"Me," said Stubbs, "I'm in the Little Hamaca parking lot. In the shade. Tailed him very carefully."

The donut man topped up the detective's coffee, poured himself a cup. "Comes back to what it was he went there for."

"Square one," said Stubbs. He took a bite of donut, washed it down with coffee. "Money? Guy's got much better places for stashing money. A body? Whose? And why not let it rot right where it is?"

"You got a weird job, man. Rotting bodies alla time."

"So what would he be digging up?" said Stubbs.

"You're sure he's not a nut?"

"I'm sure he's acting nervous."

"Lotta guys act nervous," said the donut man. "Too much caffeine. Too much sugar."

"This guy's nervous like the FBI is on the way."

"Is it?" asked the donut man. He smiled with his eyebrows. The FBI went through a lot of donuts.

"'Cause why?" said Stubbs. "'Cause some Russian's wandering around with a wagon and a shovel?"

"He's Russian?" echoed Dave.

"You didn't hear that part," said Stubbs.

"You got a weird job," said the donut man. Then he added, "Little Hamaca, you said it was?"

"Yeah."

"Russian. Be weird it had something to do with those old missiles and shit."

"Missiles?"

"From the sixties. Khrushchev. Cuba. Remember? . . . Kennedy dead a million years and Castro still hanging on. Amazing, huh?

Hey, the FBI comes down, you let me know. I'll bake some extra glazed."

Bert and Sam heated up some soup for lunch, and then they had a nap. But when they woke up Bert was restless.

Once again it came down to routine—the routine that for years had mollified his loneliness and had sufficed, no less well than most people's routines of work or play, as a proxy of actual purpose.

In the late afternoons, as the sun was slouching toward the Gulf, he walked his dog on Smathers Beach. He saw people there—the same locals season after season, arrayed against a background of tourists, who, in their sunburned and slightly desperate variety, also stayed essentially the same. He made chit-chat when the opportunity presented; when it did not, he murmured secretly to his chihuahua, and looked, as at a spouse's face, at the soothing variations in a scene viewed every day: the sun at one corner or another of a certain building as the months advanced; the tide line encroaching or receding according to whether the breeze was north or south.

Freshly awake now in the dead suburban silence of Key Haven, Bert yearned for that routine, and ascribed his yearning to his dog.

"Ah," he said, to the small blind creature that was curled up on the tile floor, "I bet you miss the beach. I know ya do. Tell ya what. I'll shave, I'll dress. We'll get in the car."

He invited Sam, of course. But Sam didn't want to go. He'd already launched into a project of his own.

He was fiddling with his yellow Walkman; transistors and transducers and tiny clips were laid out on a tile table. "Think I'll stay right here."

Bert was not without misgivings about leaving his housemate alone. "Come on," he urged. "A change a scene."

Sam shook his head so that light flashed through his Einstein hair. "My memory," he said, "everything's a change of scene. I'm fine here, Bert. Go have your walk."

Bert could think of nothing more to say that would not be wounding to Sam's dignity. So he found his car keys and he left.

Tarzan Abramowitz, keeping an eye on the intersection where the bridge crossed over the canal, saw him go, saw that there was only one person in the old beige car.

After a while, Sam Katz took a glass of seltzer and his reassembled Walkman and a Benny Goodman tape outside to the patio. The sun was getting low, it threw packets of glare that skipped like stones from crest to crest of the wavelets in the green canal; a rising tide brought the smell of iodine.

Sam watched the gray house across the way and worked to keep his thoughts right there, to concentrate so that he might be of help to Aaron. Aaron and the woman who worked side by side on the ground with him, and whom he seemed to like so much. He tried to keep his thoughts on the two of them, on their safety, but his thoughts kept trying, like eggs on a countertop, to roll away and smash.

He sipped his seltzer, he listened to music, and then he saw his scoop-faced neighbor come through the sliding door that led out from his kitchen.

The Russian, stiff-legged and pale, slowly walked beyond the shade of his awnings and continued down his swath of lawn toward the seawall. Sam watched him coming nearer and could not react; his attention had locked down like a cramping muscle, had grown entirely rigid. He simply stared as his neighbor approached, now squeezing forth a morbid smile that seemed to cause him pain.

"Mr. Katz," he said, across the width of the canal, "I was wondering you would like to come by for a glass of tea."

Sam saw lips move. He swept off his headphones and stuck his hearing aid back in. "What?"

Cherkassky repeated his offer.

For a moment Sam was too excited to answer. An invitation! A glass of tea! He would get inside, get to know these Russians. He would find things out, be of help to Aaron, and even Bert would be impressed.

"Yes," he said at last. "With pleasure."

Excited, puffed up with purpose, he rose. In a trance of new-found usefulness, he walked straight through the tiled house and out the door. It never occurred to him to leave a note where he was going.

FORTY-FOUR

When Bert got home the sun was down, and though there was still a multicolored gleaming in the sky, the day had lost the power to penetrate indoors, and the tiled house was dark. Bert called out, "Sam? ... *Sam* ... " But even before he'd heard the grimly answering silence, he knew that Sam was gone.

He turned on a lamp. It threw a meager and depressing pool of yellow, and he turned on another. He went from room to room, flipping every switch, and at some point he realized that the hand that held his dog was trembling. It was trembling not so much with fear as with shame. It had been his mission to look after Sam, to keep him out of trouble. He'd abdicated that responsibility in favor of a selfish preference of his own. Now Sam could be lost and wandering somewhere, could have blundered into something he'd never figure out, could be lying at the bottom of the Gulf. Bert had failed him, failed himself. What was left in the world when one old man couldn't look out for another?

He put his dog down on the floor. Dejected by contagion, the chihuahua dragged its paws across the mosaic pathway then curled up in a heap.

Bert went to look outside. The patio was lavender in the dusk. Half a glass of seltzer and Sam's cheery yellow Walkman were sitting on the table; there was something dreadful in the way they'd been left behind. Bert walked down the small lawn, felt his stomach knotting as he neared the still canal. He half expected to see a body there, face-down, bloating, white hair streaming out like weeds. But in the failing light he saw nothing in the water except a smudged reflection of the sky. Across the way, the gray house of the Russian was entirely dark and silent.

With burdened steps Bert walked up through the yard and back inside. The lamplight seemed grainy and sulfurous and horrid after the velvet outdoor glow. He paced; the dog tracked his pacing with its dry and scaly nose. He tried to think of some way to undo his dereliction, to redeem his falling-short. Search the streets? Blunder after him? Alone, his chance of finding Sam was slim to none, and he came to understand that he only compounded his fault with each moment that he stalled.

At length he did the thing he least wanted in the whole wide world to do. He went to the phone to call Aaron, and to tell him that, because of his own negligence, his father had gone AWOL.

"I'm sorry," said Bert, when Sam's son had arrived. "I'm sorry."

Aaron bit his lip. It was a habit of Suki's he was already picking up. He put his hand on the old man's arm. He wasn't quite sure if he did it to offer comfort, or forgiveness, or if it was a distant way of touching his own father. "No apologies," he said. "Let's just figure where he might've gone."

Bert sat down on the sofa. His dog splayed out across his lap and the dreary light from a rented bulb was washing over them. "He got really taken up, obsessed like, with the neighbor just across the way."

"Across the way?" said Aaron. "I thought that Markov—"

"Markov lives around the corner," Bert explained. "Much bigger house. Fancy. But Markov, we're not so sure he's the boss no more."

Aaron said, "I don't think I—"

"'S complicated," said Bert, and, wearily, he started standing up again. It took a while. When he was sure of his balance, he said, "Come on, I'll explain things as we go."

They went through the tiled doorway, Bert holding his chihuahua like the chihuahua was a loaf of bread. Outside, fronds hung limp and black. Crickets rasped; the sound rose to a crescendo, then abruptly stopped, precise as any orchestra. During the lull, Bert said, "The guy across the way, he could be the real boss maybe. Fits a certain pattern, like. Your old man, somehow he picked up on it."

They were walking toward the bridge that went over the canal. Aaron's legs were twitchy yet leaden, his steps awkward as they tried to adapt to Bert's resolved but plodding pace; and in some way this lack of flow, this trudging heaviness, connected with the stricken understanding that his father might be dead. Walking should be easy; suddenly it wasn't. Nothing was easy. With the loss of a father came a terrible exposure, a shocking grasp of one's nakedness, of one's secret but perennial unreadiness as a person in the world. Past forty, well-to-do, new lover of a lovely woman, Aaron suddenly felt green, unformed. He struggled to remember something, anything, that he knew with confidence of life. Nothing came to him. He said to Bert, "So what's the pattern?"

"Guy lays low," Bert said. "Normal house. Doesn't show off. Showin' off, luxury, that's for other people."

They walked. A plump moon topped the palms. Bert wheezed a little as he went and the dog's breath came in quick and labored snorts.

"Bein' the boss," the old mobster continued, "it's not about luxury. It's about responsibility."

They reached the small rainbow of a bridge that arced over the canal. Bert needed to rest a moment before they went across. "And he was kind to the dog," he said. "Gave him water."

Stripped of certainties, seeking to rebuild comprehension brick by brick, Aaron said, "The guy kills people."

Bert said calmly, "A boss will do what he has to do. Be a ruthless prick when necessary. Give a thirsty dog a drink a water. It's not about cruelty and it's not about kindness. It's about knowing. Knowing what you have to do and doing it no matter what."

At the crest of the bridge Aaron breathed deep of iodine and sunken weeds. On the next street over, the sickly glow of televisions played on shaded windows. They trudged toward Ivan Cherkassky's house. The blue Camaro was gone from the driveway. Windows were closed, curtains were drawn and there was no light at the edges. The place was as blank and silent as though it had been sealed up for a year.

Bert spoke quickly, before alarm could gain an even firmer purchase. "Let's try Markov's."

They turned. The moon heightened and raccoons came out to scavenge. Noses low, the animals scrabbled through thick foliage, and Aaron's head twisted toward every rattle of leaves and snapping of dry twigs, his eyes straining to find his father, even if broken and filthy and befuddled, crawling from a ditch.

They reached Markov's cul-de-sac.

The cul-de-sac was rimmed with mangroves. A ragged border of moonlight and shadow went down the middle of the pavement. They hugged the shaded edge and moved in closer.

Markov's house was all lit up. Lamplight spilled like cream out of the windows. Floodlights gave a surreal luminosity to the nighttime garden. Ground lights etched the canopies of trees, and bare bulbs shone harshly in the open garage that held a huge dark Lincoln, and next to it, absurdly, a small red wagon, a toy. There was no hint of sound or movement, just this extravagant and disturbing brightness, this arrogant refusal to let night be night, the revenge of a child afraid of the dark.

Bert and Aaron walked on, walked almost to the pillars that marked the driveway. Bert craned his scrawny neck to peer between them. Then he retreated to the shadows. He tried to keep his voice businesslike, unpanicked. He said, "The lights. One car. I don't know what to make of it."

Aaron heard himself say, "I'm going in."

Bert grabbed him by the arm, harder than he meant to. "I don't think that's a good idea."

Aaron peered off toward the garage. There was a door that led into the house. He swallowed. "I'm going in," he said again.

"What if they grabbed 'im?" said Bert the Shirt. "They grab you too, wha' does it accomplish?"

Aaron had no answer, nor was he persuaded.

"People like this," old Bert went on, "ya don't go up against 'em without ya got the force, the guns . . . Aaron, listen'a me. We go back home, we call the cops—"

"The cops?" Aaron whispered. "Sirens? Flashing lights? Cops sometimes protect a person right to death. Didn't you once say that, Bert?"

Bert could not deny it. He stood there in the shadows, moonlight arching over him like a wave about to break.

"I'm going in. I have to."

Bert tested Aaron's eyes a long moment then finally let go of his arm. There was affection and farewell in the reluctant ungrasping of his brittle fingers. Sadly the old mobster said, "Yeah, okay, ya do."

FORTY-FIVE

"I wish you would've called me sooner," said Lieutenant Gary Stubbs.

"And what difference would it've made?" said Suki.

She said it without rancor, but it stung because it was true. Whatever the official story was, whatever the official stance, there were still two dead Russians, no leads, and innocent people under threat. Stubbs's deeper involvement would not have changed a thing. Maybe the killings were linked, and maybe only grisly coincidence connected them. Maybe he was up against a mafia and maybe he was just plain stumped.

They were standing in the kitchen of the Mangrove Arms. Suki had called the cop just minutes after Aaron left. She didn't know if she was doing right—hadn't known for what seemed like forever if she was doing right. She only knew she couldn't sit there, passive, hidden away like some fairytale damsel, and relatively safe, while Sam was in trouble on her behalf.

"Still," Stubbs muttered, shaking his head so that his thick and pinkish neck chafed against his collar. "Two old men going off like that . . ."

"Look," said Suki, "it was a dumb idea, okay? They wanted to help. But in the meantime—"

"In the meantime one of them is missing."

"And it's my fault."

Stubbs was leaning back against a brushed steel counter, his meaty hands grabbing the cool edge of it. "Nothing's your fault," he said.

This was not a comfort and Suki didn't answer.

The lieutenant crossed his arms, stared off at the too-big coffee urn, the tall stacks of breakfast dishes that would always sadly outnumber the guests. Absently, or maybe to redeem himself, he said, "I've been keeping tabs on Markov."

"Oh?"

"Took him to ID the Russian woman. Lazslo's housekeeper. I think he got a little nervous."

"Morgues'll do that, I imagine."

"At first he sounded very hot to find his nephew's killer. Then I told him that the FBI might be on the way. He sort of lost his passion for justice when I told him that."

"Is it?" Suki said.

"Is what?"

"The FBI. You finally believe me? They're coming down?"

Stubbs looked away. "They're not coming down."

"Then—?"

"Just trying to shake something loose, is all," said Stubbs. "Just trying to scare up a mistake."

Suki bit her lip, ran a hand through her thick black hair. She looked at the floor a moment and when her eyes returned they were narrow and firm. "Okay," she said, "so let's do that."

"Do what?" said Stubbs.

"Pressure them. Scare up a mistake." She didn't seem to notice she'd started moving in a little circle, her sandals scuffing on the kitchen floor.

The cop said, "I'm not sure I—"

Suki said, "I've got an idea . . . What started this whole thing? . . . The paper. They were scared I was sniffing around their business for the paper."

"But that was before all this—"

"So let's put something in the paper now. FBI to investigate alle-gations. Coming to interview reporter in hiding."

"Bad idea," said Stubbs, though he said it without conviction. "Besides, your old boss doesn't have the nerve."

"He had guts once upon a time," said Suki. "I could talk him into it."

Stubbs was rubbing the bridge of his nose. He said, "It's a lousy time to get them mad. If they do have the old man, they'll connect him with this place, they'll know exactly where you are."

"Fine," said Suki. "Let them. They'll lose interest in Sam Katz. Look, I'm the one they want. That's why he's in trouble."

"We don't know for sure that he's in trouble," said the cop.

"I should be the bait."

Stubbs didn't like the trade-off: A young woman they definitely wanted dead, for a bewildered old man who might have only wan-dered to the beach, who might be contentedly sitting under a palm somewhere, talking to himself and throwing crumbs to gulls. He said, "But—"

"Lieutenant," Suki cut him off. "There's one more piece of infor-mation you should have. I'm in love with Aaron. You understand? His father gets hurt instead of me, I couldn't live with that . . . Now, could you please go round up Donald Egan for me?"

"My feet you need to tape?" said Sam. "What, I'm Jackie Robinson, I could run away so fast?"

"Shut up," said Tarzan Abramowitz, and kept winding shiny silver duct tape around Sam's skinny ankles and the spindly legs of the high stool where they had him sitting.

"Accordion player," Sam rambled. He was scared, though not as scared as he should have been, and in some outlandish way he was having fun. They hadn't really threatened him yet, just pushed him around a little, gave him a few little bruises maybe, and took away his will. He'd never gotten his glass of tea at his Russian neighbor's house. He'd barely settled in on the sofa when they bundled him out again, threw him in a car. Drove downtown, unpacked him like a shipment in an alley. Shoved him through some thick and blank back door. Now here he was, being taped to this high stool. If he rocked forward he'd keel over on his face like a stilt man. "Ventriloquist," he said.

"Fuck you say?" muttered Tarzan Abramowitz.

"What?" said Sam, and he reached up toward his ear. "*Oy*, I lost my hearing aid. This stool, it's like for a ventriloquist. Ed Sullivan, he had a stool like this. Ventriloquists. Accordion players. Dummies. Talking dummies."

"Shut up," said Abramowitz, and continued stretching out the tape.

"Almost the whole roll you're wasting," said Sam. He looked around. His taciturn Russian neighbor was sitting on a canvas cot, expressionless. A bare bulb hung from a wire. Stacks of cardboard boxes lined the room, necks and sleeves of T-shirts squeezed out like they were yelling for help. Music seemed to be playing far away, Sam mostly heard the thumping of the bass and now and then a disconnected twang.

The young man finished with his taping; Ivan Cherkassky rose and moved toward Sam.

"Mr. Katz," he said, "we are hoping very much to find someone. We think that you know where she is."

"What?" said Sam. He could sort of hear, he was mainly stalling.

The Russian moved in closer; Sam became fascinated by the bumps and craters of his lumpy face, it was like a close-up of the moon. "Suki Sperakis," said Cherkassky. "Where is she, Mr. Katz?"

Sam heard her name and his adventure stopped being any fun at all. He rocked on his stool. Suki Sperakis. She worked with Aaron in the garden. Side by side, knee to knee they planted things. Maybe they were gardening right now. No, Sam remembered. Now it was nighttime, and his legs were trussed up like a roasting chicken, and, no matter what, he was not supposed to mention Suki Sperakis.

Instead he looked toward Tarzan Abramowitz, bare-chested as always, whorls of damp hair escaping from his thick suspenders. Sam said to Cherkassky, "All these shirts, you couldn't give this boy a shirt?"

Cherkassky fell back a step, walked a little circle. Then, like a crow returning to a bit of carrion, he dove in once again. "You have relations here, Mr. Katz?"

"Relations?"

"Brothers? Nephews? Children maybe?"

Sam didn't like it that he mentioned children. That scared him. Aaron. He shouldn't make trouble for Aaron. He tried to shift on the stool. He couldn't really move. His tailbone poked down between his wizened haunches. It was starting to hurt. Then he remembered his cover. "Children?" he said. "No. Me and Bert . . . remember? Forty years already."

Abramowitz was doing laps among the leaning stacks of cardboard boxes. "You and Bert are *shpul na cacavyov*," he said.

"We are not," said Sam.

"What?" Cherkassky said.

Sam realized his mistake, backpedaled. Right back he said, "What?"

Cherkassky stepped away. He nibbled his thumbnail, rubbed his chin. Against the blasting music from the T-shirt shop on the far side of the double-locked door, he said, "That seat, Mr. Katz, it's going to get uncomfortable."

Sam, uncomfortable, squirmed a little. "What?"

"Tape his mouth," Cherkassky said, and went back to the cot on which Tarzan would be camping.

Abramowitz bounded over, ripped tape from the roll. Sam didn't close his lips in time. He tasted bitter glue and felt a puckering draw that pulled the moisture from his tongue.

FORTY-SIX

Aaron Katz longed for the cover of shadow as he scampered low toward the garage. But Gennady Markov's yard was lit up like a carnival, and the only shadow was the one that Aaron's leaning body threw. Gravel crunched beneath his feet and his heart rode up his gullet.

Inside the garage he paused, heard the hum of electricity and the torrent of blood in his ears. He looked around and nothing made sense. A red wagon. A damp shovel placed separately from the other gardening tools. In one corner, a motor scooter covered with a tarp. He walked over to the car. Its hood was still warm and Aaron had no idea what that meant.

He moved to the door that led into the house, put his ear against it. He heard nothing. Not his father's rising, falling, ending-with-a-question voice; not anything. He paused. He dried his palm against his pants. He tried the knob. It didn't turn. He gently pushed the door. It moved a fraction of an inch before the bolt collided with its frame.

Stymied, Aaron now had the misfortune of a little time to think. He had no weapon; he had no plan. He was armed with nothing more than caring. He could leave now. He'd tried the door, flirted with heroics. A retreat would not be shameful.

But once he'd thought about it, calculated it, Aaron could not retreat. He needed to find Sam or to persuade himself beyond a doubt that Sam wasn't there.

He left the garage but didn't head back down the driveway. Instead, he crouched low against the shrubbery and began to work his way around the house.

The thorns of bougainvillea scratched at his arms; his knees complained at their unnatural bend as he sneaked past the pretentious entryway. In the bushes on the far side, spider webs stuck to his face, their makers seeking refuge in his hair. He smelled salt and citrus, and now and then he dared to raise himself just high enough to peek through a brightly lit window.

He saw luxurious and empty rooms. The waxed mahogany of the silent feasting table. Leather armchairs with no one in them; a fireplace holding cool dead ash.

He skulked around a corner of the mansion and found the vacant master bedroom, saw corruption in the swollen mounds of pillows, a sensuous perverseness in the satin quilts defiant of the climate.

He moved on toward what appeared to be a guest wing, its dimmer rooms illumined from a central hallway, its single rank of windows stretching toward the Gulf. Spying through oleanders and buttonwoods, Aaron saw neat beds, uninhabited; reading lamps unread by. Nothing was rumpled; no one was there.

Skin itching, forehead dappled with sweat and bugs, he thought once more of giving up. Maybe his father had wandered back to the tiled house by now. Maybe this should all be left to the police. But he pressed ahead, not content until he'd counted every room; and then, at the very far end of the guest wing, visible in slices through the slats of a blind that was not quite snugly closed, he saw Gennady Markov, working in his lab, alone, his big face intent over an enamel tub.

Aaron froze, his breath arrested. Weirdly, his first reaction was one of deep nostalgia. A scientist at work. His father. The same concentration that made the tongue flick at the corners of the mouth. The same saving single-mindedness that held the world at bay. Good or evil, there was beauty in a scientist at work . . .

But what was Markov doing? Aaron wrestled with leaves and branches, leaned as near to the window as he dared. He saw canisters; electric coils; a fine gray gravel with a consistency like lentils. The gravel gleamed dully. It might have been some peculiar form of silver, some odd stuff to be transformed by a jeweler or a dentist. Then a dreadful thought occurred to Aaron: Plutonium? Was it possible? Suki had told him that Lazslo hinted at it. The source of the huge sums that needed laundering. Weapons for rogue nations. Bombs for lunatics. Being cooked up *here*?—in peaceable Key West, a few miles from the bars, from Duval Street, from the Mangrove Arms?

Aaron fell back, dizzy and suddenly exhausted. Through the slats, Markov's image blurred. Everything blurred. Aaron's search for Sam blurred against the enormity of nuclear material. His love for Suki blurred against the terror of what she had discovered. His sense of his own new life—small, quiet, accomplishment measured nail by nail—blurred against the sick size of the schemes that people found themselves embroiled in.

Puny and shaken under the stars, too rattled even to remember to stay in the shade of the shrubbery, Aaron turned at last and walked away.

Befuddled, driving all but blind, he made it back to the Mangrove Arms just as Gary Stubbs and Donald Egan were coming down the front porch steps.

It scared Aaron to see the cop there. His stomach burned. For the moment he forgot about weapons crossing borders and thought only of intimate losses. With effort he said, "Suki?"

"Suki's okay," said Stubbs. "She's fine. She called about your father."

Aaron said, "You know something?"

Stubbs shook his head.

"You'll help?"

Stubbs nodded.

Aaron glanced with vague recognition and no warmth at Egan.

The editor's cigar was glowing in the dark. In his fat soft hand he held some papers. "Tomorrow early," he said, waving them toward Aaron. "Special edition."

"Special edition what?"

"Talk to Suki," said the cop. "She's waiting for you."

The two visitors continued down the stairs.

Aaron said to their backs, "Wait. Markov."

Stubbs stopped walking, looked across his shoulder. "What about him?"

"He has a lab."

"A lab?"

"I saw him working."

Stubbs said, "So?"

"Lazslo used to talk about atomic stuff. Brag about it."

The cop and the editor shared a look. Egan said, "Jesus Christ, I should put that in the article."

Aaron blew. He hadn't had a fight since junior high and now he felt an impulse to shove the newspaperman down the last few stairs. "Fuck your article," he said. "These are people's lives. Who gives a shit about your article?"

Stubbs said calmly, "Can't go break into his house without a warrant. Couldn't get a warrant with what we have so far."

Aaron said, "What the hell's it take? Another person dead? My father? Suki? All of us?"

Stubbs said nothing, waited for Aaron to calm down.

Aaron didn't calm down. "And Markov's not the real boss anyway," he said. "The real boss lives around the corner. I think that's who my father's with."

"How you know all this?" said Stubbs.

"I know it . . . " Aaron said, and then he stopped. He stopped because the beginnings of tears—tears of worry, of frustration—were pressing like thumbs at the backs of his eyes. He choked them down like he was swallowing a rock. "I know it because I've been out there on the fucking streets, Lieutenant. Not waiting for a fucking warrant."

Stubbs grimaced and continued down the stairs. Egan followed.

Aaron went up into the office, where he took a slow deep breath and tried to remember how to recognize his world.

He looked around. He knew every potted palm and every promo propped up on its cardboard easel, but now it all looked strange to him, removed, as though his looming grief had built a warping membrane around him. Only vaguely he saw the slashed counter, the silver bell that needed buffing. In that moment it was someone else's hotel.

He went through the doorway behind the counter, took in the odd proportions of a commercial kitchen, the outsize pots and pans. Steel counters more like something from a hospital.

He moved on to the sitting room. In his exhaustion he noticed bizarre things: fringes on the bottom of upholstery, fringes at the ends of a rug.

Then he saw Suki. She was sitting on the sofa where they'd first held each other, at the soft edge of an arc of lamplight. Seeing her did not dispel the warping film but she moved somehow to Aaron's side of it.

"You okay?" she asked. She looked closely at him. His shoes were coated with dirt and his clothing was specked with sap and spider webs.

His lips moved but he couldn't speak. He stared at her. It was too dim to discern the color of her eyes, but their blue was absolutely present to him. Her shoulders were covered but he saw them.

She got up from the settee, didn't hug him with her arms, just stood against him, warm. She took him by the hand and led him to the room that had become their room. "He'll be okay," she said.

Aaron nodded, stared at her. Fear had jumbled time for them. As in some gaudy fantasy of traveling through bent and viscous space, the clock had sometimes raced like an exerted heart, and other times had stalled. The long wait to be lovers shrank down to a pendant and excruciating moment long ago. Their instant as a couple could be called forever, since the future might be snuffed out any second.

She led him to the bed that had become their bed. She began

undoing the buttons on his shirt. "I really think he'll be okay," she said again.

Aaron nodded, and he started to cry. Time was all mixed up; Suki was already burned deep into him, suddenly abiding as the world around them grew jittery and abrupt and blurred. Lovers for one day, he cried in her arms as easily as if they'd been together, helpmates, many years.

FORTY-SEVEN

Next morning, very early, too early for most people to be having conversations, Piney said, "Fred, ya know what I sometimes wonder about?"

The first yellow sun was starting to dry the nighttime dampness of the mangrove leaves. In the clearing by the hot dog, the flat cracked stones were beginning to get warm; lethargic lizards crawled up on them to bask. Fred, his eyes half-closed, was drinking coffee from a dented tin cup. He didn't answer.

Piney looked down at his rubbed-up hands, said, "Time."

"Oh Christ," said Fred. He lit a cigarette, squinted against the phosphorous that smarted in his eyes, and wondered if he'd go to work that day, if he'd bother with the seven-thirty shape-up. He glanced over at his shovel. It was leaning against the service window of the hot dog, next to Piney's PARKING sign. Tools of the trade.

"Think about it," Pineapple went on.

"Why?" said Fred, and picked tobacco off his tongue.

"Say there was no such thing as time," Piney said, undaunted in the sunshine that grew whiter every moment. "Does that mean nothing would happen or everything would happen all at once?"

Fred sucked his cigarette. "Who gives a rat's ass?"

"You in a bad mood, Fred?"

"'Bout like usual."

"I'm goin' downtown then," Piney said. "Take my sign, make a little money."

"'Bout time," Fred opined.

"Ya see?" said Piney.

"See what?"

"Time. Ya can't help but think about it."

Fred shook his head, looked off at an osprey circling over Cow Key Channel.

"At work, where I sit, there on the curb," said Piney, "I can lean back and look around the banyan tree, see Suki's balcony . . . Last couple days I haven't seen her though."

Fred gave a crude guffaw. "Course you haven't, Piney. Betcha anything she's shacked up with the rich guy, the owner, by now."

As blandly as he could, Piney said, "Think so?"

"Waya the world, friend," said Fred, and sucked deeply on his cigarette. "Rich guy gets the broad."

"Don't call her that," said Piney, and he looked away.

Fred chased his eyes to needle him. "You got a crush on her," he said. "Ain't this what I been sayin' all along?" He took a last drag on his smoke then doused it in a shrinking puddle, savoring the sizzle as the small fire was extinguished.

Donald Egan—his staff on indefinite leave, his publication schedule suspended due to vandalism—had worked through the night to write and lay out and print and fold a four-page special edition.

Not long after dawn, he bundled the papers with heavy plastic strapping, and horsed them into the trunk and the backseat of his car. The ink was still fresh; it smelled of acetone, you could almost see it seeping deeper into the newsprint.

Egan sucked a stogie as he drove the quiet morning streets of a town that stayed up late and slept late too. His pulse pounded with unaccustomed exertion as he carried the papers into empty grocery stores, guest houses that smelled achingly of coffee, laundromats with one lone dryer spinning.

He was bleary-eyed and unshaven and happier than he'd been for as long as he could remember. There was ink in the folds of his knuckles, and he'd written something that maybe could matter. He felt like a newspaperman again.

Not that most people got excited about his banner headline: "A Russian Mafia on Duval Street???"

Who cared? Not the tourists, as long as the sun was still hot, the beer cold and the music loud. And even the locals, glutted with malfeasance, weary of greed and scandal, mostly shrugged and snorted. More crooks; a next wave of carpetbaggers. What else was new?

In certain places, though, the *Frigate*'s special edition was very major news. One of those places was the T-shirt shop, at the back of which Sam Katz was being held.

The young man who opened the store at nine A.M. had found the papers leaning up against the door. He picked them up as he undid the double locks. He did not read English very well and he didn't care for reading anyway. He was about to throw the bundle in the trash when the headline caught his eye. "Russian Mafia" he could understand. The headline made him feel momentarily important and he could not suppress a stupid smile.

He went to the back of the store and knocked three times, then twice more after pausing, on the door that led to the stock room.

Tarzan Abramowitz opened up. He'd slept on the cot surrounded by leaning stacks of cardboard boxes, and he was standing in his underwear. Muscles twitched in his legs though his eyes were still narrow with sleep. Scratching his hairy stomach, he took the paper back to his cot and haltingly he read.

Sam Katz watched him read.

Sam's ankles were still taped to the high and backless stool. His spine had gone through several phases of pain, cramping, and fatigue, and by now he had caved into an S-shaped slump that hardly hurt at all. His sunken chest had compressed down onto his old man's little paunch; somewhere along the way he'd wet his pants. He'd known when he was doing it and he didn't care that much; squeamishness was a luxury that only the young and healthy could afford.

Through the night he'd dozed and awakened, dozed and awakened, feverish dreams resolving into no less feverish thoughts. At some point he understood that, no matter what he said or didn't say, his captors had to kill him. Obviously they did. He tried to get his mind around the idea of being killed. It seemed a crazy way to go. Old Jews, if they made it past the years when the driven ones dropped dead at their desks from heart attacks, died of cancer, diabetes. What kind of *mishegoss* was kidnapping and murder? Nothing in his life had pointed that way, not that it mattered.

If he could believe in an afterlife he would be quite content. He didn't ask for harp music, wings, nothing like that. He'd only like to be able to look down now and then and see how things were going for his son. Did things work out with Suki? The guest house—did he ever manage to turn it around? Sam wanted to keep track of those things. His own story was over. That was fine, fair enough. It had been an okay story. But it made him sad to leave Aaron's story in the middle.

He watched Tarzan Abramowitz read, wondered vaguely what he was reading.

The young man's lips moved as he read, and he seemed to gain momentum as he went, lips moving faster, thick fingers fumbling to turn the soggy page. After a time he slapped the paper down and climbed into his pants, clamped suspenders to the waistband. He moved toward Sam's stool, but only to make sure the tape was still secure around his ankles and across his mouth.

Then he left, the paper underneath his arm. Sam sat there, slumped and patient, removed already from the world, the bare light bulb shining yellow on his brittle tufts of sparse white hair.

FORTY-EIGHT

"You see?" hissed Ivan Cherkassky, pointing at the paper, slapping it. "You see?"

Gennady Markov didn't answer. He'd been roused out from under his satin quilts for this emergency, had barely taken time for coffee. He was still mulling over what he'd been told to read. He tried to settle deeper into Cherkassky's sofa, but the cushions lacked the squushy thickness of his own, and he found that he could not get comfortable. He squirmed.

Cherkassky was perched on the very edge of an austere and narrow chair. His lumpy face was blanched and taut, the lumps were shiny as boils. "Your nephew," he said disgustedly. "With his big mouth and his *schwantz* for a brain."

Tarzan Abramowitz was doing laps behind the sofa. Without breaking stride he snickered.

"His *schwantz*," Cherkassky hammered, "what it makes him tell that woman, it brings the FBI."

Markov winced by reflex at his colleague's words but then found to his surprise that they no longer hurt. He could say what he wanted about Lazslo; the nerve had died. Caring was finished, and what was left was stubbornness and spite and a pointless insistence on the last word.

"No, Ivan," he said, "what he tells that woman, this is not what brings the FBI. What brings the FBI is that you murdered him. His body, dead—this is why the FBI is coming here."

Cherkassky crossed his skinny legs. He did not take offense but he wanted to be logical, precise. "Here you are wrong," he pronounced. "The death of Lazslo—one death only. Burglary. Coincidence. Nothing here for FBI. Only for useless local cops. Two deaths, pattern. Your silly revenge, Gennady—this is what makes case for FBI."

Markov looked away. He squirmed, his fingers fretted between the cushions of the sofa. Then he smiled. It was the mean pathetic smile of an unhappy child who has succeeded in spoiling a game for everyone. He said nothing.

"The housekeeper," Cherkassky murmured disapprovingly. "This peasant cow Ludmila." He tisked. "Cowardly, Gennady. Idiotic."

There was a pause, then the fat man broke into a hoarse laugh that had tears in it, a keening giggle deranged enough to stop Tarzan Abramowitz from pacing. He rocked forward on the sofa, put fingers over his runny eyes. "When she goes into the water," he spluttered, gasping, "her legs, so far apart. Knees lifting up like she is ready to be fucked."

He laughed his baleful asylum laugh a moment longer then fell abruptly silent. Abramowitz resumed his pacing.

Cherkassky, immune to bedlam, calculated. The paper said the FBI was coming down. Coming down, it said. That meant not here yet. That meant maybe there was time. Time to silence people who could hurt them, time to hide the most incriminating things. But they would have to act quickly and they would have to work together. The thin man cleared his throat. "Gennady," he said soothingly, "whatever has happened—"

His old lieutenant cut him off. "Have we always hated each other, you think, Ivan? Or is it something new?"

Cherkassky let the question pass. It didn't matter. "Gennady, listen, what we have to do—"

"Because," the fat man interrupted once again, "I think maybe is not so unusual for friends to hate each other. Life throws them together, they have need of each other. They have dinner, tell stories, jokes, and hate each other for years and years."

"Gennady, please, what must be done—"

"Yes, yes. Is clear, is clear. What must be done, we have to kill this woman."

"And everyone who helps her," Abramowitz put in. "Old man Katz. Old man Katz's friend with worthless dog—"

"Who is Katz?" said Markov.

The other two ignored him.

"Local guest house," Cherkassky said. "Paper says that FBI comes to interview woman who is hidden away in local guest house."

Abramowitz pivoted, thrust a triumphant hairy finger in the air. "All along I'm saying this! I know this guest house. Owned by younger Katz. This thing, you wouldn't let me, I could have done this days before."

"We do it now," Cherkassky said. "All three together."

There was a brief silence marred only by the whisper of Abramowitz's relentless shoes against the carpet.

"And then?" said Markov. He said it tauntingly.

"And then the FBI has no one they can talk to."

Markov snorted. "You kid yourself, Ivan. Plenty people they can talk to. Busboys. Clerks. They will turn on us to save themselves. You know they will."

Cherkassky said nothing. Abramowitz stalled, plucked at his suspender as at a twisted bra strap.

"And the shops?" Markov went on, taking bleak delight in tracing out the contours of their doom. "There is time to hide the jewelry? The paintings—where we put them? The dollars? How you explain all this, Ivan?"

To Markov's disappointment, Cherkassky didn't rattle. He sighed patiently, leaned forward, spoke softly. "Gennady," he said, "you think I am a child? I have thought of these things of course."

Reassured, Abramowitz eased back into motion once again.

Cherkassky pulled his long and pitted face, and wondered vaguely why it was that the more he hated his life, the more desperately compelled he felt to preserve it. He inhaled deeply then went on. "And the solution is that of certain minor things—smuggling, washing money—of certain minor things, though it is sad, we will be guilty."

"Guilty?!" said Abramowitz, shocked and grievously offended.

"Guilty," said Cherkassky, with serenity. "These are things the underlings know of us, will tell. And on these things the authorities must win. Why? Because these are things the authorities do not care about. Smugglers. *Pfuh!* Deportation only. There are plenty other countries! Worst will happen, perhaps we have a short stay in a prison where we can buy ourselves some comfort."

Markov squirmed. So—Cherkassky had it thought out to the last lie and wriggle, was going to save them from the FBI. He should have been glad but he was desolate. Spite had carried him the insane way around to the side of justice. He said, "But—"

"The things they care about," Cherkassky implacably went on, "these things they will never find. The deaths? No witnesses to deaths. Our true business? Break down your lab, Gennady, the instant you get home. Equipment, throw it in the ocean, the tide carries it away. The pyramid—they will never know to look inside the pyramid."

Abramowitz smiled.

Markov rocked on the sofa. His thick lips flubbered as he sought for more objections to puncture his old friend's plan, tried to persuade himself that the skinny bastard would not win. He thought and his fingers fidgeted between the cushions of the sofa. They came up against something hard and cool, and he plucked it out.

It was a hearing aid. He held it in the air, stared at it a moment. Then he smiled snidely at Cherkassky. If he couldn't top his old comrade at tactics, he might at least annoy his vanity. He said, "Your ears are going bad, Ivan? Ashamed to wear your hearing aid?"

Cherkassky said nothing, just squinted at the small device.

"Must be the old man's," said Abramowitz. "He mutters something he lost it."

The muscular young man held his hand out and Markov passed the hearing aid to him. He crushed it in his fist. It made a high-pitched whistle then faded into silence like a dying bird.

Abramowitz cackled. "He doesn't need it anymore. Now I'll go to get his friend."

FORTY-NINE

A aron had dreamed of his father.

In the dream, Sam was dead and then he wasn't. Nonchalantly, he came back after what seemed to be a long, long absence. He was young when he came back. His hair was dark and wavy; his step had bounce in it, momentum, as a step must have when proceeding toward a future. It was wonderful to see him in the prime of life, but at some point Aaron knew the dream was fooling him. The man with the dark hair and the purpose in his stride was not his father but himself. His father's absence was the future he could not deflect himself from striding toward. So be it. Resignation made a secret progress in the damp dark of sleep, and lost ground again in the unyielding hopefulness of daytime.

He smelled salt air and coffee, realized that his cheek was pressed against Suki's shoulder, and jolted himself awake. His swimming eyes saw the wall of newsprint that was propped against her knees. He said, "What time is it? How long did I sleep?"

She kissed him on the forehead, said, "You were exhausted."

Impatient, he wrestled with the sheet. He had no idea what he needed to be ready for, yet he couldn't bear to be unready. "But—"

She stroked his hair. "There's nothing to be done right now," she said. "Have a little coffee."

He drank from her cup and she gestured toward the paper. "You know, he's really a good journalist."

Aaron grunted, got his eyes to focus. "But it's a made-up story."

Suki said, "Made-up stories change lives too."

For that Aaron had no answer. But he stopped fighting against the bedclothes, settled back against her shoulder.

"Cops'll be here soon," she said.

"Wish I had more faith in them." His knees and ankles twitched. There was more he should be doing and there was nothing to be done.

"That would be a comfort," Suki said. She said it blithely, but then her breathing changed. A hitch came into it, it was like a whimper but without the sound. "Aaron," she said, "whatever happens today—"

She broke off, swallowed, tried again to speak but couldn't.

Aaron came up on an elbow, looked down at her rare blue eyes, the joyful mouth with its disconcerting upper lip. Her face had shown him moxie and humor and passion and caring, and now for the first and only time, it let him see just how afraid she was.

Her face unmasked the fear in him as well. "Whatever happens," he echoed, and took her in his arms.

In the rented tile house, Bert the Shirt had already been awake for what felt like half a day.

He'd heard amorous doves cooing in the dark and woodpeckers probing the soft bark of dead and headless palms. He'd stood at a window to watch the sky lose its blackness and lift off from the horizon. He'd showered, put on a chartreuse shirt with a forest green monogram, and made his oatmeal, all the while wallowing in remorse.

He'd failed Sam, and Sam was suddenly his dearest friend, practically his brother. That's what happened in old age. The lusts and ambitions that made men separate fell away, and they regained the easy fraternity of childhood, when anyone could eat at anybody's table, join in anybody's game. And where it was the unquestioned role of the stronger to look out for the weaker. That was Bert's responsibility, to look out for doddering, slipping Sam, and he'd blown it.

An awful thought had occurred to him: Maybe that meant he wasn't the stronger anymore.

He'd finished his cereal and sat there at the tiled table. His blind chihuahua looked up at him and sniffed at the sand in the cuffs of his trousers. The forbidden notion that perhaps his strength was failing made him weak; he could barely muster the energy to walk the dog. They took a short walk only, and once back home, Bert moped.

He moped from the living room to the bedroom. He wandered to the kitchen and then outside through the sliding doors. Standing in hot sunshine on the patio, he looked out at the milky green canal, the mute gray house across the way.

Absently, he'd sat down at the patio table. Sam's sporty yellow Walkman was out there still; the sight of it was unspeakably depressing, like the favorite toy of a child who has died. Bert picked up his dog, scratched it behind the ears, and tried to ignore the thing.

Then he heard a whirring sound, and then a click. He couldn't place the noise, and by the time he looked around it had stopped.

It happened again: Click; whirr; click; whirr; click.

It was not a bird noise or an insect noise. It didn't seem to be coming from the kitchen behind him or the canal at the end of the lawn. He focused his ears, narrowed his eyes, and saw a tiny red indicator gleaming on Sam's Walkman. Then the light went out.

Click.

It was odd. It was spooky. With a not quite steady hand, Bert reached out and picked up the small machine. It started to whir and he almost threw it on the lawn. He looked through the little smoked plastic window and saw that tape was turning.

When the tape stopped, Bert put the Walkman down. He looked at the gray house across the way. The machine clicked on again.

Nah. Could it be? Sam with his tinkering, with his yearning to invent a useful gizmo—was it possible?

Bert sat there squinting, scratching his dog like the dog was his own chin. He sat there until a considerable time went by without the Walkman clicking on, then he went inside to listen to the tape.

He dropped onto the worn settee, hit rewind, and put the headphones on. He listened through the static and the squeaking of Cherkassky's sofa cushions, and his pulse began to race. Adrenaline surged, strength returned. He listened until he heard the part about killing everybody. Then, head spinning, he reached for the phone to call the Mangrove Arms.

He should have done it a minute sooner.

By the time he dialed, an electric blue Camaro was careening off the little bridge and toward his street. Engine popping, it pulled into the driveway just as the ring tone was beginning to rasp in Bert's hot ear.

The phone rang twice, three times. Bert heard a car door open and prayed for Aaron to pick up.

"Hello, Mangrove Arms."

The voice came just as the tile-rimmed door of the rented house imploded. It quaked on its hinges and Tarzan Abramowitz, his bare chest puffed with rage, came bounding through.

The chihuahua made one shrieky little bark.

"Aaron," Bert whispered, "Aaron, they're gonna—"

The Russian thug, suspenders stretched across his rippling neck, yanked the wire from the wall.

One hard pivot brought him to the sofa. He grabbed Bert by the front panels of his chartreuse shirt, jerked him to his feet. The Walkman skidded from the coffee table, came to rest against the tile pathway. Abramowitz paid no attention to it and didn't say a word, just bundled Bert toward the open doorway, the waiting car.

The old mafioso, down to a hundred twenty-seven pounds and on three different kinds of heart pills, tried feebly to resist. Mostly he just leaned backward like an ancient crooner, his empty hands grasping woefully toward receding space. "My dog," he sang out, "my dog."

Abramowitz ignored him, shoved him out into the sunshine.

Don Giovanni whined just for a moment, his whiskers probing in the roiled air. Then he pancaked down against the floor, and dragged himself over to the yellow Walkman, and covered it over with his meager bony chest.

FIFTY

When the phone rang at the Mangrove Arms, Aaron and Suki and four Key West cops had been standing in the kitchen, drinking coffee, talking strategy. Who stands where. Who covers who. When to wait and when to spring. Gary Stubbs was reasonably happy with the plan. It was him and Carol Lopez and two others who were less experienced. But it was four guns protecting two civilians, and the arithmetic struck him as okay.

Except that now Aaron was standing there with the phone receiver in his hand, his mouth half open, a glazed look in his eyes. Out of the blue, he announced, "I'm going to Key Haven."

Stubbs said, "What?!"

"Bert. That was Bert. He was trying to tell me something. Somebody yanked the phone, I think. I'm going."

Suki said, "But Aaron—"

"They have Bert," he reasoned, his face going red with quiet pleading, "that probably means they have my father. The two of them together. Don't you see?"

Stubbs saw. But the problem was the numbers. He said, "Listen, if we divvy up our forces—"

"So call more people," Suki said.

Stubbs's neck chafed against his collar as he turned. He gave a quick bleak smile or a wince. "You think we keep a SWAT team here? There are no more, okay?"

The phone started beeping in Aaron's hand, he finally remembered to hang it up. He pointed vaguely toward Key Haven, and with an immovable calm, he said, "Look, there's two old men in trouble up there, and they're not any less important than us. I'm going."

He turned his back. He was heading for the office door.

Stubbs blew air between his teeth, said, "You're staying. Two of us'll go."

Carol Lopez quickly counted troops, said, "But—"

Dryly, Stubbs told her, "If they're there, they can't be here. We'll be back as soon as we can."

And Stubbs left with another officer, their footsteps heavy on the front porch stairs. The ones left behind sipped their cooling coffee. The Mangrove Arms, as it almost always did, once again seemed emptier than it should have been.

Abramowitz shoved Bert into the backseat of the Camaro, quickly tied his skinny ankles in their sheaths of nylon socks, and drove the few short blocks toward Markov's house.

There, standing on the seawall, with Cherkassky monitoring his every move, the physicist was casting the last of his equipment to the tides. Beakers bobbed away like men-of-war, glinting in the sun; acid sizzled as it hit the ocean salts then became inconsequentially dilute in all that vastness. Pebbles of plutonium, far heavier than lead, defied the current and sank deep into the muck, becoming tiny heaters whose warmth would fascinate the fish and make the plankton glow.

When the job was done, Ivan Cherkassky pulled back his thin gray lips and said with satisfaction, "You see—like there never was a lab."

Markov said nothing, stared down at the water. Science was his secret edge and science now was finished. Underling and figurehead, nothing more. His humiliation was complete.

"Only we are small-time smugglers," said Cherkassky. "Like a thousand others. Hardly worth the time of FBI. Deported, Gennady. Where next you like to go?"

Markov didn't respond, and Cherkassky didn't care. Neither quite knew why he still bothered talking to the other.

The Camaro's tires crunched over Markov's driveway, and the two old comrades walked toward it.

The car's bright blue paint glittered in the sunlight. There was no foreboding in the sky, and this was somehow cruel. It should have been night, but it was day. It should have been stormy, but it was hot and calm, the cloudless sky imposed no mood. Silently, Markov and Cherkassky climbed into the car along with bound and stoic Bert the Shirt, and headed downtown to try to save themselves by murdering everyone who'd dared to know them.

At the corner of Whitehead and Rebecca, Pineapple sat on the curb in the moist shade of the banyan tree and thought things over.

He wished Fred wouldn't put sweet things so crudely. *Shacked up*. Made it sound rough when really it was tender. Aaron and Suki kissing; sharing a blanket; all that stuff. She'd liked him from the start; Piney had seen that right away. So he was happy that they were together. If they really were. He just hoped he'd get to see her now and then, visit for a while.

He sat there and he twirled his PARKING sign. Twirling it was something he did when he was preoccupied; the arrow faced all different ways, and people couldn't find his boss's parking lot. But there'd been a few distractions that day. Two unmarked cop cars had pulled up in front of Mangrove Arms. Four cops went in, three of them in uniform. A little while after, two came out again and drove away. Why all the coming and going? It was worrisome, and Piney closely watched the old hotel.

Inside, in the kitchen, Carol Lopez was worried too. But she was the seasoned one, the pro, and she couldn't let it show. She pushed her hat back and stole glances at the guy that Stubbs had paired her with. Rookie. He had pale pudgy fingers and the leather around the snap of his holster was perfectly uncrinkled, like the snap had never once been opened. She sipped more coffee and looked down at her watch. But the watch could only tell her what time it was, not when anything would happen.

Aaron and Suki were sitting at the unromantic table, holding hands. They didn't just hold palms, but interlaced each and every finger, and Carol Lopez looked at the twined-up digits as at a Chinese puzzle, trying to figure out which fingers belonged to whom. It dawned on her that once those hands were parted they might never be rejoined.

She put down her coffee cup, said, "I think it's time we went to our positions."

Music was blasting at the T-shirt shop.

Infernal bass shook the floor, screaming treble knifed through the racks of merchandise. Back in the stockroom, Sam Katz slumped and swayed on his hard stool, now and then humming scraps of tune that had nothing to do with the music that was playing. He did not hear the approach of a loud car in the alleyway that backed the row of stores.

Tarzan Abramowitz stopped the blue Camaro and opened up the stockroom door. A moment later, he half-shoved, half-carried Bert inside.

With his ankles tied the old man had to hop and shuffle. He hopped close to where Sam sat, mouth taped, wrists bound, pants stained. Their eyes met, Sam's soupy and facetious, Bert's vigilant and sly. A century and a half of life between them, and neither had any idea what to say or do.

Markov and Cherkassky wandered in. Cherkassky blinked around the ranks of cardboard boxes, the prodigious piles of shirts. Thinking aloud, he said, "Here they will search, find ikons, paintings, cash. These things we must let them find."

No one else was thinking of those things. Tarzan Abramowitz had reached into his pocket and produced a folding knife.

Unhurriedly, he opened it. The blade was long and slender, a filleting shape, with just a hint of an Arabian curve; it caught glare from the one bare hanging bulb and sprayed it back around the room. The music kept pounding, drum machines ruthless in their chattering.

The young man in suspenders clutched the handle of the knife and approached Sam Katz with the dispassion of a farmer moving toward a heifer or a suckling pig.

Bert, immobile, watched him for an instant, and there stampeded through his mind a lifetime's worth of playground bullies; he somehow found the archaic courage of the stronger kid trying to protect the weaker, and without deciding he hopped between the killer and his victim, making short and shallow leaps as though he was racing in a potato sack.

Abramowitz seemed amused by the absurd and gallant gesture. He snickered as, with one huge and hairy arm, he slammed Bert across the chest and shoved the old mobster aside. Bert went down like a toppled statue, his fleshless hips bouncing and scraping along the splintery floor. He groaned just once and then he lay there as the murderer turned his attention back to Sam. Bert found to his horror that he could not avert his eyes.

He watched as the assassin closed the distance to his prey. Saw the unpanicked sorrow in Sam's eyes as the killer grabbed him by the jaw. Almost gently, with a bizarre solicitousness, an art, like a barber preparing to trim behind an ear, Abramowitz turned Sam's head. Skin stretched across the neck, grew translucent above the blue and tired artery that carried blood to his flagging brain. Giving in to naked fear at last, Sam tried to cry out, his voice buzzed like a piteous kazoo behind the duct tape. Abramowitz changed the cant of his blade so that light flashed on the ceiling, shifted his stance like a hitter at the plate, and cocked his elbow high.

And Ivan Cherkassky, calmly and without hurry, said, "No. Wait."

Tarzan turned to look at him, still holding Sam's face, still wrenching the old man's jaw. Sam's eyes had lost the horizontal, they swam like the eyes of someone who was seasick.

"Blood on floor, no good," Cherkassky said. "Blood on floor ruins everything."

Tarzan was jumpy and unconsummated. His hand was sweaty around the knife. "Strangle 'em?" he suggested.

Cherkassky pulled his lumpy face, considered. Strangling was better. But then he shook his head. People thrashed, lost skin and hair while getting strangled. Skin and hair were bad things for the FBI to find. "We do the others first," he said. "Afterward we take these people somewhere else."

Abramowitz scowled, blew out a stale breath and, like a turned-down lover, reluctantly released Sam's face. It took a long time for Sam to straighten out his neck.

"This brave one," Cherkassky went on, pointing at the supine, panting Bert, "tape his hands, his mouth."

Bert rolled onto his side and protested that. He was a dead man; he felt he had a right to. There were things he wanted Sam to know. "Let us talk at least," he said. He gestured vaguely toward the thumping madhouse music. "No one's gonna hear."

Ivan Cherkassky, paranoid and brutal but not without respect for the obligations of a boss, pursed his lips and shrugged. He said to Tarzan, "Only do his hands."

He himself went up to Sam and pulled the silver adhesive off his face. It came away with a sound like ripping canvas and left a gray-white residue behind. He looked at Sam's cracked lips and withered gums, and shook his head. "Weak old men," he said. "Almost I am sorry."

FIFTY-ONE

O n Key Haven, Lieutenant Gary Stubbs unholstered his revolver as he slipped out of his unmarked car to approach the tiled house. Sweat prickled his neck; hot sun dried the sweat and left a paste of oily salt behind.

His partner covered him as he took low and furtive steps along the driveway, then flattened himself against the mosaic frame of the kicked-in door. His gun was propped against his breastbone, pointing at his chin. Hot tiles pressed against his back. He summoned nerve and stillness and listened hard.

He heard no breath or scuffling from inside, just a ticking sound, dry and faint and syncopated. It could have been a wind-up clock, a timer, just possibly, for a bomb. Waiting suddenly seemed a bad idea.

Stubbs braced his trigger hand and pivoted, facing full into the living room, and screaming "*Freeze!*"

His eye detected motion and he aimed his gun at a ghostly white chihuahua spinning in futile little pirouettes, its paws making tiny ticking tap-dance sounds against the tiled floor. Blind, the dog yet turned its milky eyes toward the barrel of the cop's revolver, its dry nose sniffing for a friend.

Stubbs plucked his wet shirt from his skin and looked around. The phone was pulled out of the wall. There were some magazines and a yellow Walkman on the floor right near the dog. Those were the only signs of a struggle.

He checked the bedrooms, the bathrooms, the closets. Nothing. He gave the dog a bowl of water and a scratch behind the ears, and left.

Next they drove to Markov's house.

The house was closed up tight. Stubbs parked in the shade of the porte cochere and went up to the front door. He listened, heard silence. He knocked and rang the bell, sang out, "Open up. Police." Even to himself, the challenge sounded thin.

There was no response and he decided to do some peeping. He stepped back around the shrubbery and soon found Aaron's footprints, still clearly etched in the moist soil of the beds. He retraced the other man's journey past the dining room, the master suite, down the long and narrow guest wing to where the lab was. He stopped where Aaron's steps had stalled and blurred and doubled back, and he peered intently through the slats of the not quite snug-fitting blinds.

He saw a small guest bedroom.

There was a Murphy bed, complete with fancy spread and flounce. A small nightstand held a reading lamp. There was even a book on the stand. There was no sign whatsoever of a lab.

Stubbs stood there for a moment. His shirt was soaked and sun was clawing at his neck. Suddenly it seemed like he had been away from Whitehead Street for far too long, and at the bottom of his stomach there formed a pulsing knot that had the weight and bitterness of a big mistake.

He ran across the lawn to his unmarked car and headed back to town.

The banyan tree had clustered trunks all squeezed together like organ pipes, and it threw a blanket of shade that covered a quarter acre. Once Pineapple had settled into that lake of shadow, he could keep the same position for hours at a time, only slightly shifting his butt against the curb so that his legs wouldn't fall asleep. He was sitting there, insignificant and loyal, when a blue Camaro came popping and growling down the street and parked outside the Mangrove Arms.

He watched. The driver got out without bothering to turn the motor off. He had big shoulders and narrow eyes and wore just suspenders, not a shirt. Then two older men stepped out. One of them was thin and brittle, a sick and sour pallor on his crescent face. The other was fat and sweaty. He was the man who'd brought the red wagon back into the mangroves, the man with the limestone dust on his expensive shoes.

The three of them hesitated just a moment by the car, then they headed toward the front porch steps. There was something in the stiff and sneaky way they walked that Piney didn't like. He waited for them to vanish through the picket gate, then, without bothering to stand, he slid his butt along the curb, closer to the entryway, and he watched and listened as he twirled his PARKING sign.

Bert the Shirt rolled over on the floor a couple times, until he collided with a heavy cardboard box that he could brace himself against. Straining so hard that he felt it in his bowels, he jerked and shimmied to something like a sitting position, and then he coughed and took a rest. When he had his breath back, he looked at Sam—the wild hair, the pinwheel eyes, the blotchy trousers. He said to him, "You look like hell."

Sam smiled at that. "And you look like a broken puppet. Like someone got your strings all twisted."

Hellish music hammered through from the shop, acid light streamed from the single naked bulb. Sam made a great effort to arch his back, pointed with his chin at the piles of T-shirts, the dusty floor. He went on, "What a way for it to end, huh, Bert?"

"It ends," said Bert, with just a suggestion of a shrug. "What's the difference how?"

Sam thought that over for a while. The music changed to some insane disco cha-cha.

Bert continued, "Somethin' that y'oughta know."

"Lotta things I oughta know."

"Your Walkman," said the Shirt. "It picked up a conversation."

There was a pause, then Sam Katz sat bolt upright on his stool, moved so briskly that the stool's feet chattered on the floor. He'd almost forgotten about the Walkman. All that fooling with the tape machine, the hearing aid, it seemed a long, long time ago. "It worked?" he said at last.

"Worked good enough," said Bert, "that anybody finds the tape, those bastards're goin' to the chair."

"It worked," said Sam, with wonder. "It worked. Ya see, I could still think up a gizmo."

Bert wriggled higher against the cardboard box. "How'd ya plant it, Sam?"

Sam started to answer, then stopped. He'd been smiling but now the smile went away and he fell back into his S-shaped slump. "Was supposed to help, though," he finally said. "Help Aaron and his ladyfriend. Who'd it help? Wha'did it accomplish?"

"Sam, hey, the gizmo worked," said Bert. "Ya can't ask more than that."

"Why not?"

Bert considered. He missed his dog, didn't seem to think as clearly without the small quivering creature in his lap. He wondered vaguely how long the dog could live after he himself was dead. He said at last, "'Cause sometimes ya do your very best and still it don't accomplish nothin'. That's just how it is."

Sam opined, "That stinks."

Bert squirmed like he was set to disagree. But he couldn't disagree. "Okay," he said. "It stinks."

They sat there a moment. The hideous music throbbed like a clot.

Bert couldn't disagree but he couldn't leave it right there either. "Stinks," he said again. "But still, ya gotta try."

Sam kept a pouty silence.

"Am I right, Sam?" Bert kept on. "Can ya tell me I'm wrong? I'm sayin' it stinks sometimes, but still, ya gotta try."

Sam just fixed him with his soupy eyes that turned down at the outside corners.

FIFTY-TWO

A aron Katz had been posted at the front desk like everything was
hunky-dory, as if it were a normal business day.

He sat among the potted palms and promotional brochures, shuffling papers, sorting keys, trying to keep his hands from trembling as
the three invaders came trundling up the stairs; trying not to glance
at Carol Lopez, who was crouched on a low stool below the level of
the counter, her revolver in her hand; trying not to be furious with
Gary Stubbs, who hadn't made it back in time.

The Russians came up single file, the shirtless Abramowitz leading. He moved thickly through the office door, took a couple steps
along the sisal rug. Almost shyly, Markov and Cherkassky slipped in
behind him and for a breathless moment no one spoke.

Aaron tried to swallow back the quaver in his voice. "May I help
you?"

The Russians stalled, took time to get their bearings. Narrowed
eyes flashed toward the doorway to the kitchen. "Please," said Markov,
"you have a room?" The *h* spent a long while in his throat.

Aaron, compelled by some grotesque logic, answered the question straight. "For three?"

Then the brief charade was over and Abramowitz had pulled the
gun from the back waistband of his pants. No one saw him draw it; it

was just there in his hairy hand. It was pointed at Aaron's chest. He said, "Where is she, Katz?"

A bubble of sweat broke at the nape of Aaron's neck and trickled down his back. "Who?"

"Who," Cherkassky mocked. "Lazslo's whore. Where?"

In the kitchen, Suki heard it all. In her mind she fled; in her heart she surged to Aaron's side, offering up herself to save him; in fact she didn't, couldn't, move at all. She looked at the new cop, her protector; his gun was shaking in his hand like he was mixing paint.

Aaron said, "I don't know what you're—"

"Tell us or you die," said Tarzan.

"Look—" said Aaron.

And Carol Lopez picked that instant to spring up behind the counter. Her revolver cocked and poised, her shoulders broke the counter's plane the way a leaping dolphin breaks the surface of the water, and she yelled out, "Drop it!"

Tarzan Abramowitz didn't drop it. He wheeled toward the motion and he fired. The shot cracked and whistled and Carol Lopez crumpled, a red stain wicking through torn threads at the front of her shirt.

Time stopped for an instant. In that silent and airless hiatus, Aaron Katz had somehow gotten to his feet. He'd reached out for the silver service bell atop the counter. Grabbing it, he'd slung his arm back, coiled every sinew in his gut, then rocked forward, hips and chest pulling through the average arm; mechanics and control, things learned from his father, standing in for strength. The bell sprang from his hand, turning like a satellite, ringing softly as it flew. It hit Tarzan Abramowitz in the triangle between his eyebrows and the bridge of his nose, wedged briefly in a soft seam of the skull. Sinus bones knifed inward at the impact, and the huge and hairy man was stunned.

He fell back half a step, his narrow eyes lost focus behind a wall of reflex tears; and the trembling rookie ventured into the doorway from the kitchen and shot him through the heart.

He would have been a hero if he kept on shooting but he didn't. Amazement at his own boldness made him indecisive. He watched the dead man fall, and by the time his furry back had hit the rug, Markov and Cherkassky had drawn out pistols of their own.

"Bravo," said an unshaken Cherkassky to the rookie. "Now throw the gun away."

The new cop blinked, counted weapons, blanched at the arithmetic, and did as he was told.

Cherkassky turned to Aaron. "Enough. Give us the girl or everybody dies."

Aaron looked down at his hands. He could faintly hear that Carol Lopez was still breathing. She was breathing through the hole in her shirt, and the wet sound of it made Aaron want to vomit. He looked up at Cherkassky. "Go fuck yourself."

Markov's flubbery lips were working, he licked them with a houndlike tongue. "Is only a woman. You cannot save her anyway."

"Where's my father?" Aaron said.

Cherkassky wagged his pistol. With his other hand he tugged his lumpy face. "Your father. Ah," he said. "Perhaps you like to trade? Your father for the whore."

The rookie trembled in the doorway. To get to Suki they would have to go through him, and he had no doubt that they would.

"Where is he?" Aaron said.

Markov smiled a salesman's smile. "Fifteen minutes you could see him, have reunion."

There was a pause. Carol Lopez gurgled softly from deep down in her punctured lung. Tarzan Abramowitz's right foot gave a slight but ghastly flick as some dead nerve finally shut down.

"A trade would be just fine."

It was Suki talking. She was standing barefoot at the bottom of the front porch steps. She'd slipped out the back door of the kitchen and come down the walkway with its ranks of new shrubs still waiting to be planted. No one saw her till she spoke. She could have kept on going—through the gate, onto the street, out of town, to the ends of the world. But she didn't. She stood there. Her voice was calm and her face serene.

The Russians wheeled cautiously at the words.

Aaron said, "Suki, please—"

She put a foot on the bottom stair and looked at him, her gaze slicing in between the Russians. Her hair was black and coarse, her eyes an unlikely violet. Her upper lip, disconcertingly, was lusher than the lower. She said, "Aaron, it's the only way. We should've seen that long ago."

"It's not the only way," cried Aaron, though he didn't see another.

To the Russians, Suki said, "I'm ready."

Markov and Cherkassky shared a glance. There still were witnesses to be disposed of.

Aaron, desperate, stalling, searching for a way to be by Suki's side, said, "Wait. You said a trade . . . "

A mocking twitch pulled at one end of Cherkassky's mouth. He quickly erased it. So trusting, these Americans. So stupid. A trade. Of course. A most convenient way to get all these insufferable and meddling people together to be killed.

Solemnly he said to Aaron, "We will bring you to your father, yes." With a gracious Old World sweep of his arm, he gestured for the man behind the counter to come join them.

"Aaron, don't," said Suki.

But Aaron's feet were moving. They didn't feel like his own feet and they didn't recognize the texture of the sisal rug, but they carried him around the counter and past the sprawling body of Abramowitz.

When he was close enough to grab, Markov seized his arm. And Cherkassky opened fire on the disarmed rookie, making, he believed, for two dead cops.

The Russians ushered Aaron through the office door and down the stairs. The sun was shining. Fronds were gently rustling. Suki waited patiently. Aaron could see the freckles on her neck, the rise of muscle in her shoulder. He wondered if the murderers would let them touch.

At the bottom stair he reached out for her hand. Their fingers twined, nobody dared to stop them. Ivan Cherkassky stepped across and put the muzzle of his gun against her ribs. Aaron felt it. He knew the flesh of her side where the gun was pressing in.

They walked slowly toward the picket gate. Foliage thinned and the noises of Key West intruded. A motorcycle revving somewhere; the bellow of a cruise ship's horn. They saw the blue Camaro at the curb.

Ivan Cherkassky said, "Very nicely, all together now, we get into the car."

In a clumsy cluster they moved across the sidewalk. There were people all around, heartbreakingly oblivious in silly hats and sunburns, licking ice cream, reading maps. No one, so it seemed, paid particular attention to the odd quartet, the couple being escorted to their deaths.

Ivan Cherkassky opened the passenger-side door, bundled Aaron, then Suki, into the backseat, and finally climbed in himself. Markov lumbered around the front of the car to get in behind the wheel. He did not notice a barefoot, ragged man sitting on the curb a little distance away, his beard scraggly and translucent, his face medieval, his mouth a mere dry slot.

Nor did he realize right away that the Camaro's engine was no longer running.

He put the car in drive. Nothing happened. For a moment he was utterly confused. He looked down at the ignition switch and found it vacant.

Cherkassky's pinched voice said to him, "Please, Gennady, why you wait?"

Markov's fat hand fumbled on the floor mat, underneath the seat. "Abramowitz," he muttered. "The key he took."

"Car was running," said Cherkassky.

A siren, faint at first, cut through among the sounds of moped horns and biplanes pulling banners through the sky.

"Big scientist," Cherkassky hissed. "Find a way to start the car!"

Markov sat there sweaty and helpless. "Is bad, Ivan," he said.

Aaron and Suki squeezed each other's fingers, their hips were pressed together on the seat. The siren grew louder, its whine began to fill the leafy tunnel of Whitehead Street.

"Fool!" Ivan Cherkassky said. Disgusted, persuaded to the end that only he could do things right, could ensure his own survival, he threw open the Camaro's door, stepped outside, and started walking round to start the car himself.

Piney watched him. Without the others clustered up against him, the skinny Russian could not hide the gun. Pineapple saw it and quick as a crab he scuttled across the warm stone of the curb. By the time the Russian was crossing the front fender, the ragged and devoted man was close enough. He swung his PARKING sign with all his might, and caught Cherkassky right behind the knees. The thin man buckled to the shape of a Z. His head clanged on the car's hood, then he slithered off the bright blue paint like egg.

Gennady Markov, baffled, fired blindly through the tinted windshield. Glass shattered; naked daylight, searing white, streamed in through the spiky gaps between the shards. Neither Cherkassky nor his assailant got up from the pavement.

The siren was growing ever louder. Bystanders, oblivious no longer, hunkered behind trees or bolted down side streets. Markov sat behind the wheel of the useless car and he started to whimper dryly. He was totally alone at last. There was no one to take responsibility for him, to prop him up, to tell him what to do. He listened to the siren. He wondered if his blind shot had killed his only comrade and his enemy.

He panicked. He opened his door and he began to run away down Whitehead Street. His shirt was soaked, his weirdly dainty shoes flopped and stretched under his weight. Fatly he ran, twisting his neck and brandishing his gun, using it to clear away a swath of the world wide enough for him to hide in.

Aaron rocked forward in his seat and took off after him. There was no time to think about what it was that called forth courage—

whether it was mere circumstance, or love; no time to wonder about the transformation that brought a father's son to readiness on his own. He just took off, running hard and low.

Markov looked back across his shoulder, saw him closing fast. Still lumbering and straining, huffing and off-balance, the Russian fired. Aaron flinched but kept on charging. The shot went wide and low, it raised a long welt in the asphalt.

Aaron sprinted, measured, and a heartbeat later he left his feet, dove headlong at the fat man's churning thighs, and clawed and dragged him to the pavement.

Air came out of Markov when he hit the ground. His elbow slammed down on the street; the impact sprung his fingers, and his pistol skidded off just beyond his reach. Moaning, he tried to slink and crawl to it, kicking out his legs like a giant wounded insect. Hand over hand, Aaron climbed up the man the way one scales the last vertiginous reaches of a peak, dug determined fingers deep into his flesh and held on for dear life, for several dear lives, till Gary Stubbs's tardy unmarked car screeched to a halt some three feet from where they lay.

FIFTY-THREE

Piney hated keys—those guilty emblems of things coveted and hoarded, things one would get in big trouble for messing with. He could not meet the lieutenant's eyes as he handed over the pilfered key to the electric blue Camaro. But the cop didn't scold him. He patted his shoulder. Then he turned his attention back to the two old Soviets who were spread-eagled across the hot hood of his unmarked Ford.

Cherkassky had a ripening bruise on his forehead; his manner was stoic and sullen. Markov was shaking; his pants were torn. He saw no virtue in enduring pain; in response to the discreet pressure of a thumb behind the ear, he quickly revealed where Sam and Bert were being held.

Stubbs radioed for a beat patrol to go there. The Duval Street cops met Aaron and Suki on the sidewalk, just in front of the same dim and recessed doorway where Aaron had first accosted Tarzan Abramowitz. Together they went in, and Suki took a quiet, chastened satisfaction in being there as the cheesy business was shut down.

Sam Katz, captive in the stockroom, did not immediately understand that he was being liberated.

He hardly noticed when the music in the T-shirt shop was suddenly turned off. Braced for death, he flinched and nearly toppled backward off his high stool as the locked door to his ugly chamber was kicked in. Seeing his son in the vacant frame, his first words were, "It isn't safe here, Aaron. Go away."

"It's okay, Pop. It's okay."

"What?"

"It's safe now," Aaron shouted. Shouting it brought it home to him, and the beginnings of tears burned the corners of his eyes.

"Really?" shouted Sam.

"Really."

Sam got a little happy then. "My gizmo worked. It worked."

"Your gizmo?" Aaron said.

Sam explained as Suki untaped his ankles. His legs and spine had forgotten how they fit together; for a while Aaron had to hold him up.

Bert, hostage for a shorter time, was in much better shape. He clambered to his feet as soon as he'd been untied; he had the presence to straighten the placket of his shirt. He didn't want to intrude on the family reunion, but he wanted very badly to go retrieve his dog.

So the four of them drove to Key Haven.

On the way there they were passed by the ambulance that carried Carol Lopez. The bullet that hit her had shattered a rib, missed her heart by an inch or so, and lodged in her right lung. She was conscious off and on, and she seemed to understand that the rookie cop, her partner for an hour, had been slain. His was the vague sad glory of the soldier killed in his very first foray, who went down with hardly a moment to savor what he'd done or to contemplate exactly why he'd done it. Carol Lopez, by contrast, an old campaigner, would soon rejoin the force. With a decoration on her shirt and a dented bullet carried in her pocket, she would be taken seriously at last.

In the crazy tiled house where Bert and Sam had posed as golden age lovers, the chihuahua was still curled around the yellow Walkman. Its blind eyes panned the room when people entered, then it dragged itself along the tiled floor. Its whiskers probed, its tail flicked, and, at the perfect instant, like one half of a long-established dance team, it arched its creaking back to accept its master's hand around its belly.

Sam reclaimed his souped-up Walkman, the proof of his abiding competence, with hardly less affection than Bert lavished on his dog. The cassette inside explained much that was otherwise obscure— the circumstances leading to the murder of Lazslo; the pathetic revenge attempted in the killing of Ludmila; Ivan Cherkassky's coolly premeditated plan to eliminate everyone who might testify as to his larger crimes, then to lie and bargain toward clemency.

But the full extent of the Russians' Key West empire could not be grasped until warrants were obtained to search the T-shirt shops. In various stockroom stashes, police found roughly fourteen million dollars in American cash. Paintings from Leningrad and lapis jewelry from the Caucasus. Tiger skins from Siberia; a Fabergé egg smuggled out of Moscow; sapphires that had once been worn by czars.

And even *then*, the real root source of all that wealth was not revealed until Pineapple had mustered his nerve and his composure, and asked Lieutenant Gary Stubbs to drive out to the hot dog and look at some things that he and Fred had dug up from the old fallout shelter in the mangroves.

Stubbs had never intended to call in the Feds, not if he could possibly avoid it, but when he saw the stacks of dusty, lead-lined tubes and boxes arrayed around the clearing, he admitted to himself at last that this was something that could not be handled locally. He called the FBI.

Within two hours the experts had descended. Men in what looked like spacesuits opened the metal containers and assayed the substances inside. Plutonium 239. Ninety-seven percent pure; weapons grade. Around seven hundred kilograms in all. Enough to build thirty bombs of the strength that leveled Hiroshima. Or to power three breeder reactors that would keep rogue nations supplied with fissionable goods for a millennium. It was by far the biggest stash of nuclear material ever known to have fallen into private hands.

Fred and Piney were treated with suspicion for a while. They were questioned for a long, long time, though they could tell their story in fifteen seconds: They had a friend in danger from Russians. They saw a fat man who maybe was a Russian in the mangroves with a red wagon and a shovel. He didn't belong there. They thought they should see what he was going to dig up.

The FBI concluded at last that Piney and Fred were not part of the conspiracy.

Huge military trucks arrived to take the plutonium away. It was hard to keep all this a secret, and someone—most likely Donald Egan—leaked the story to the national media.

By nightfall the TV crews had mustered, with their arc lights and satellite hookups and correspondents with sprayed hair, broadcasting live from the clearing near the hot dog and in front of the Mangrove Arms. The publisher of the *Island Frigate*, thrilled to be near the middle of a breaking story, spoke to everyone, told of how the phony article in his paper had forced the Russians' hand.

Suki Sperakis did a couple of interviews then retreated to her old hexagonal turret room, the site of her chaste, confused recuperation. But she and Aaron hid out there together now. With their arms around each other, they watched the bright lights play on the underside of the banyan leaves that tickled the railings of the widow's walk.

Then the lights were turned off, the media packed up and left, and things got relatively quiet.

But Key West, in certain ways, was changed. With the T-shirt shops instantly defunct, there would be a sudden glut of retail space on Duval Street, and rents would plummet accordingly. Local artisans could once again move in. There could be painters' co-ops and handmade sandals, tiny stores that would sell fedoras woven from palm fronds and brightly colored wooden fish. Much of what was offered would be pure kitsch—but authentic, local kitsch—and a hard-core local like Suki could take pleasure and vindication at the change.

Which didn't mean, however, that the new Duval Street would hold a place for her, or that surviving the Russians and bringing them down had solved the more mundane questions of what she would do for her living, how she would spend her time. She wouldn't go back to selling ads. She no longer fantasized about being a reporter; her brush with the media had cured her of that.

"So what *will* you do?" Aaron asked her some days later, as they sat in the unromantic kitchen, drinking coffee. Sam, fixed up with a brand new hearing aid, sipped tea.

"Oh, I don't know," said Suki, perhaps a little coyly. She looked up at the rack of outsize pots and pans, then through the doorway to the courtyard, with its shimmering pool and lounge chairs empty of guests. "Dreams are contagious," she said. "You once told me that, remember?"

Aaron looked at her unlikely eyes, then down into his cup.

"This place could really turn around," she said. "With all the work you've done, the free publicity . . . Will you let me be here with you, help?"

They were kissing when the silver service bell rang out from the front desk counter.

Sam Katz, very glad to see them kissing, started standing up to answer it.

"Sit, Pop," Suki said. She put her hands on his shoulders and went off to charm the guests.

Astronauts; football teams. Everyone invited went.

Still, some weeks later, when the weird case had been reviewed, and Fred and Pineapple were summoned to the White House, they hemmed and hawed about it.

"They're using us," said Fred.

"Using you for *what*?" asked Aaron.

"A coup for the homeless they're calling it," Fred said. "We're not homeless. We live in a hot dog."

"Ya go," Piney put in, "it's like saying y'approve, like everything is peachy."

"But Piney," Suki argued, "face it, you're a hero."

He could not quite squelch a smile that stretched his slot of a mouth. "Don't mean I approve," he argued back.

In the end, of course, they went. Aaron bought them shoes. Bert lent them shirts. Fred's was white-on-white, Piney's a navy blue silk; no one noticed that the monograms matched each other but not the wearers' names. Four men from the Secret Service came to pick them up, blinked behind their Ray•Bans at the fiberglass wiener squooshed down into its yellow roll.

Piney liked Washington more than he expected to. The Mall was nice and open. A lot of the buildings he recognized from postage stamps or dollar bills. The cherry blossoms were just getting ready to come out, and he liked it that people got excited. Key West was always in flower; no one bit their nails to see a bloom.

The White House itself he hated.

Big as it was, it was suffocating, as houses always were to him. Rugs to trip over, things that could break. Bullying hallways that pushed you one way or the other, walls that blocked the view. Ceilings that seemed to hover annoyingly like giant hat brims just above your eyes.

He couldn't wait to get out of there, and even while inside, his thoughts were other places, less confining places. He thought of mangroves, of green clouds out beyond the reef. He thought of airplanes etching lines between the stars, lizards basking on warming rocks as time passed and the sun got higher in the sky. And that started him speculating: Did lizards have a sense of time as a separate thing from cold and warm?

He was still trying to puzzle that one out as the line of people moved along and he found himself standing opposite the president of the United States.

The president's hand was hot from shaking so many others, but his eyes had a twinkle and his voice was mellow and sincere as he thanked Piney for his extraordinary service to the nation.

The words washed over Piney, whose mind had flown beyond the curtained windows to sample other things. "Mr. President," he said, "ya know what I sometimes wonder about? . . ."

Key West 1997